T·H·E

BOYFRIEND

SCHOOL

Doubleday

New York London Toronto Sydney Auckland

T·H·E

BOYFRIEND

SCHOOL

Sarah Bird

Published by Doubleday, a division of
Bantam Doubleday Dell Publishing Group, Inc.
666 Fifth Avenue, New York, New York 10103

Doubleday and the portrayal of an anchor
with a dolphin are trademarks of
Doubleday, a division of Bantam Doubleday Dell
Publishing Group, Inc.

Library of Congress Cataloging-in-Publication Data

Bird, Sarah.
    The boyfriend school / Sarah Bird.—1st ed.
        p.   cm.
    ISBN 0-385-24694-3
    I. Title.
    PS3552.I74B69   1989   88-26037
    813'.54—dc19   CIP

BOOK DESIGN BY CAROL MALCOLM

First Edition

BG

To "T" for Texas Thomas Zigal,
who said it shouldn't be burnt.

To Nemo Peavey,
who gives me more than I have Ernt.

To Annie Rooney,
in the saddle of her Detroit horse.

To Monsieur Le Bink,
why, naturally, of course.

And, for her instincts unerring,
to a Houston girl, Lucy Herring.

Thank y'all.

BOYFRIEND

SCHOOL

1

I pulled up in front of the *Austin Grackle* office, overshot the curb, and jumped the front wheel of my 1973 Delta 88 ever so slightly onto the sidewalk. Docking was never easy with the 88. I switched off the ignition and waited the long minutes it took for the engine to die. As the car convulsed, I steeled myself for the task at hand. Today, no question about it, I would collect at least a portion of the money Trout owed me for the seven assignments I'd shot.

The 88's seizures seemed to be lasting longer these days. I reeled off a wad from the roll of paper towels I kept in the car for her fifty-mile oil check-and-fill needs and sopped up what I could of the sweat sheeting my face. An Austin hot spell in May is neither the place nor the time to be lolling about in unmoving vehicles. As I sat and stewed with the car dieseling beneath me, I noticed that my nails were in worse shape than usual. Stained brown from photo fixer, they looked like a betel nut chewer's front teeth. The same brown freckled my entire wardrobe.

By the time the 88 shuddered out her death rattle it was

hot enough inside the car to manufacture pig iron. I scooped up a large gray envelope filled with my latest batch of prints, peeled the backs of my legs off the vinyl seat covers, and stepped out.

The *Grackle* office was located in what had once been a bathhouse. The front windows were still painted black to protect the confidentiality of the establishment's former clientele. It was afternoon-matinee-dark inside. Fans rattled and whirred, but all they accomplished was to speed up the time it took for the hot, damp air to reach me. I restricted myself to shallow breaths. The air smelled of mushrooms and any number of other more suspect fungi. The whole place had a squelchy, tropical feel to it that tended to bring athlete's foot to mind.

Once *Grackle* staffers had swept up the broken amyl nitrate vials, remodeling was pretty much completed. There was a tiny reception area mostly taken up by a floor-to-ceiling bank of shelves holding rows of empty wire baskets with numbered safety pins clipped to them. The former juice bar was now piled high with layout boards, unpaid bills, unsold back issues, and unpaid bills. The original bathhouse layout remained: a long dark hall with tiny cubicles branching off. Each cubicle had its own (nonfunctioning) hot tub. I made my way down the hall, catching glimpses of life at a shoestring biweekly.

A spindly guy, wearing pink socks, green espadrilles, baggy shorts, a Zippy the Pinhead T-shirt, and a gold spandex turban from which a shock of twisted bangs emerged, squatted in an empty cocoa-brown hot tub and drummed on an upturned trash can. Karen, a writer with thin lips and aspirations to higher things, crouched at his feet and attempted an interview. "Monty, uh, Monty, you said Call Key Operator will eat out of dumpsters before they turn into a jangly guitar band? Monty?" Apparently Monty was too far into his solo to answer.

Next door, Wayne, the latest in our revolving stable of ad

reps, was talking on the phone. A glossy corn plant stood hopefully in the middle of his hot tub. Wayne and his exuberant corn plant would be long gone before he realized there wasn't enough in the way of either light or commissions at the *Grackle* to keep a lichen going. For, Here at the Hall of Fame of Thankless Tasks, selling ads in Austin, Texas, during these, the Bust Years, was the gold-medal no-win winner.

Wayne was not wise yet. "Mr. Michael!" he brayed into the receiver. "Hey, big guy, it's Wayne, over here at the *Grack.*" He loosened his tie. "Mike, my man, did we do a job for you with that last ad or what? Mikey, May is the month for hair care. Listen, Big M, I definitely think it's time for the Mane Man to move up to a quarter page." I pushed on before Wayne could reduce Michael's name to an affectionate silence.

In the next cubicle Irma Quintana, pasteup artist par excellence, crouched over a drafting table trying not to drip sweat on the layout she was working on. Dennis Smeeks, *Grackle* art director, stood behind her.

"Irma, come on," Dennis whined. "I told you I wanted more of a free-form feel on this. I want the prints to appear as if they'd just *spilled* out of someone's hand. I want the feel that we're so excited about sharing these images we just *dropped* them all over the place in our excitement."

"But Dennis." Irma's smooth Aztec-princess features were impassive; her tone was calm, reasoned. Nothing about her betrayed the fact that she considered her boss to be a throbbing hemorrhoidal pain. "With the pictures all bunched up the way you want them, no one will be able to see them. They will be on top of each other."

"It's more a *sense* I want to communicate than actual, literal, visual information." Smeeks twisted his hands around each other to convey a sense of "sense." "Readers will get that information from the gestalt we create with the tumbling prints. With the confetti sprinkled over the page, with—"

"Confetti?" Irma interrupted, blinking rapidly.

"Confetti. Yes. I want this more . . . more a *party* than a layout." His twisted fingers exploded into shooting "party" fountains.

Irma Quintana, Master of Fine Arts degree holder and the only *Grackle* staffer to have previous experience with an actual publication, squinted against the pain stabbing through her frontal lobe. Dennis Smeeks's art training consisted of an extensive background in having a grandmother die and leave him enough money to be one of the rag's original investors.

I tried tiptoeing past without his spotting me, but Irma saw me and called out a greeting.

"Gretchen, there you are!" Smeeks said.

"Dennis! Hi!" I greeted Smeeks with the high-pitched effusiveness I reserve for people I've mentally murdered seconds before. He rushed over and threw a big hug on me to cover up the fact that he had, no doubt, just visualized a radio dropping into my bathwater.

"Coming to talk to me about an assignment?" he asked, just like he asked every time I came in. Since he was the nominal art editor, I probably should have reported to Dennis. Luckily, as a photographer who wrote her own cutlines, I could get away with reporting to Trout, the editor editor. There were other extenuating circumstances as well.

"Gee, of course I'd love to work with you, Dennis, but Trout and I already have some irons in the fire. 'Nother time, okay?"

"You're supposed to check with me first about any art."

I left Dennis kneading the spot where his gastritis was flaring up. I was pleased to see that he had not developed any personal grace; the *Grackle*'s continued existence in these the Bust Years, depended heavily upon his social ineptitude. We were the last in a long line of dominoes that had begun falling when oil hit $15 a barrel and bankers awoke from their long sleep, looked around, and realized that the high-tech miracle that was supposed to transform our little burg wasn't occurring quite on schedule. Land prices fell like meteorites, and the history of the capital of the Lone Star State ran aground at Chapter Eleven. One bankruptcy triggered the next, leaving most of our former advertisers turning to matchbook covers and sandwich boards. Oh, yes, without Grandmother Smeeks's legacy, we all would have been looking at alternate sources of employment, most requiring paper caps. Fortunately, thanks to the earlier-mentioned social ineptitude, Dennis kept funding the paper on a miserly scale. Even that would have dried up, however, if he'd had any other way at all of meeting women.

If Dennis was the *Grackle*'s pituitary, controlling her growth with infusions of his grandmother's money, Trout was her heart and soul. His office was at the end of the hall in what had once been the orgy room. My steely determination to collect softened for a second when I considered that I could be working for Dennis. At least Trout insisted that all my photos run front side out. Yes, Trout had made the *Grackle* what it was. Given that he could have named his publication after anything in the galaxy, I'd asked him once why he'd chosen to honor the trash bird that plagued Austin.

"Because it *is* a trash bird," he'd answered. "The grackle is a nuisance and a pest. It invades when towns metastasize into cities that can't support the more tender, rural native flocks. That croak," he rhapsodized. "I love the croak, Gretchen. That's us, jeering at Austin from the tops of the few remaining trees. From the penthouses of all those vacant office buildings. That's us, reminding this town that it turned itself into an overbuilt set for a movie that never got made."

It was as good an editorial policy as any.

Before I reached the orgy room, I had to remind myself

that, as good an editor as Trout was, he was an even better con man. Somehow, he'd managed to wriggle out of paying me for months. Well, not today. I stormed in, determined again to collect.

"Trout, I have to talk to you right—"

He held up his hand—he was on the phone—and kept on talking. Fast. "Hey, let him try to sue." There was a pause during which Trout rolled his eyes wildly at me, held the phone receiver out, and pointed at it with an expression of beleaguered incredulity. "Oh, is that so?" he sneered. "Well, the way *I* read the law, you can't libel garbage by saying that it stinks."

Trout's real name was Peter Overton Treadwell III. Whenever I tried to find out how he'd gotten his nickname, he always smirked and asked me what smelled like fish. I never wanted to pursue the answer. My own theory is that he was called Trout because he was just so damned slippery. But with Trout, who knows? He might have breathed through gills when he was younger. His chemically distended eyes bulged out even more as he listened to his caller. He tugged down on his Joe Ely bolo tie and unpopped the top snap of his forties Goodwill cowboy shirt, a threadbare tan number with maroon piping outlining the flamboyant yoke. A vein throbbed in his neck, and perspiration beaded his forehead beneath his rockabilly forelock.

Oops, I thought, I'd caught Trout at the top of one of his pharmaceutical arcs.

"Yeah, right." He snorted into the receiver. "Let me know where he finds this hidden fortune he's going to sue us for. And to save you some time, my trust fund is not attachable." He slammed the phone down. "Bloodsuckers. Jesus, every lug nut in the universe thinks his libel lawyer is Santa Claus. That it's Christmas Day if they get their fucking name in print. Gretchen, you're looking well."

Trout segued seamlessly from rage to smiling conviviality. Pinpoint mood management accounted for a great deal

of his success as an editor. "What'd you get on the rattlesnake roundup?" He ejected out of his swivel chair. In one
amphetamine-charged dive he lunged for the ten-by-twelve
gray envelope I held. I executed a timely half pirouette, re-
moving said envelope from Trout's grasp. He collapsed onto
the top of his desk, catapulting a bronze frog filled with
paper clips into the air. A silver rainbow spewed forth from
the creature's hinged mouth. Trout slumped back into his
chair.

I did not waver in my resolve; one waver and no rent
money. I was already so far behind that only the social hesi-
tancy of my shy landlord, Mr. Cleeb, had saved me from
eviction. I could not let Trout get the better of me today.
"The roundup pictures are great. Stupendous. Epoch-mak-
ing. Any editor who prints them will achieve immortality.
But you don't see them until I get paid for at least half of
the assignments you owe me for."

Trout lowered his head and chewed on his Dartmouth
class ring. "It's the trust fund, isn't it?" he asked, giving me
a doleful look as he continued sucking on the ring.

"No, of course not."

"Boy, once the word gets out about the trust fund the
chickens sure come home to roost. You know I can't touch a
cent until I'm thirty, don't you? I mean, you do know that.
You think I don't know what everybody says? That I'm late
because I'm cheap. That I'm hoarding a fortune."

"Trout, I've never heard a word about the trust fund from
anyone but you. All I want is to get paid what's owed me."

" 'All.' " Trout gave a friendly but overwhelmed little
snort. " 'All,' " he repeated wistfully, shaking his head at
the unfathomable enormity of my request. He sighed and
pulled out something I rarely saw, the checkbook. My heart
leaped. Visions of groceries, rent checks, quarts of oil
danced in my head. But somewhere between lift-off and
touchdown Trout's pen stalled, and with his schizophrenic
ability to jump the track he asked me, "Hey, Gretch, you're

a woman. Tell me, what's the most popular literary form in the world today?"

My eyes riveted on the faltering pen, I thought it best to humor him. "Well, Trout, let me see. I think *Newsweek* just ran a feature on that very subject. The romance novel, right?"

"Exactly right. Here, look what came in today." With his free hand, he shoved a press release across the desk to me. A red heart trailing wispy vines was emblazoned at the top. Below the heart was an announcement of the seventh annual Luvboree!, the yearly conclave of the Romance Novelists of America to be held in Dallas.

"So?" I slid the press release back to him.

"So why hasn't the *Grackle* done anything on romance writers?"

"I don't know. I buy *groceries* at the supermarket."

Trout's head did a loop-the-loop as he rolled his eyes around in exasperation. His check-signing hand dropped. "I love that. *No one* I talk to has ever read one of the frigging things, and they're selling, minimum, fifty million units a year. I want to know why. Don't you want to know why?"

I shrugged. I really didn't. My specialty was cultural phenomena: Rattlesnake buckaroos. Mud boggers. Skateboard punks. Low-riders. Pit bulls. Prosperity hucksters. I liked to work a tiny bit closer to the edge than romance novels.

"Listen, Gretch, because you've brought in some good work for me in the past, I'm going to give you this story."

"Could we talk first about paying me for the stories I've already done?"

"Are you telling me you don't want the chance to do *the complete story?*" Trout asked. Incredulity bulged his eyes. He breathed through his mouth. "I'm not talking here about just filling in the cartoons after the word balloons are written. No. Gretchen, I'm talking about the photos *being* the story. With a little text, of course. Basic stuff you can whip out to accompany your photos. Gretchen, if you'd care to answer, this is *Life* magazine calling."

Life magazine. Those two words have a strangely distorting effect on the thinking processes of cub photogs. Trout's soggy office faded away, and I was transported to an airstrip on a sun-blasted Pacific island. . . . I wear a garbardine jumpsuit with terrific shoulders. A B-47 revs up behind me. "Miss Bourke-White," the handsome pilot in the leather bomber jacket calls out, trying to capture my attention. "Oh, Miss Bourke-White?"

"Call me Maggie." A little electricity sizzles between us as he returns my jaunty grin.

"All right . . . Maggie. The navigator's getting nervous. He wants to get this bird up before Tojo starts nosing around."

" 'Nuff said," I assure him. I am known as a plucky gal who'd never get a flyboy in hot water. It is what has made me so popular in the Pacific Theater and helped me land all those *Life* covers. I grab up my selection of exquisite prewar Leicas and climb aboard as the ground crewman returns the handsome pilot's thumbs-up and begins spinning a propeller. . . .

"Here." Trout flipped something my way. I fumbled for it like a seal going after a piece of popcorn. It was a yellow pill. "You seem a little groggy." Trout popped one into his mouth. He held the pill on his tongue and asked around it, "So, what about the Luvboree?" He picked up a Pepsi can and shook it. Empty. Mountain Dew? Gone. Something sloshed at the bottom of a can of Dr Pepper, and he slugged that down.

I returned Trout's present. "Basically you don't want to pay a writer too, is that it?"

"Go ahead, play the cynic. What's the difference? What it comes down to is, for once, you'll be the one to decide the angle, how to treat the material." He held out the press kit with *Luvboree* written in large, swirling letters on the front.

I wanted the chance to do a story all on my own. To shape it, to develop it, to stamp it with my own philosophical impress. Even more than that, though, I wanted the chance to put a rent check in Mr. Cleeb's hand. I couldn't give in. I couldn't afford to. "About the assignments you already owe me for," I prompted.

"Gretchen, if you're upset about me not coming by last night, let's get that right out in the open. Just tell me you're angry. You know we promised each other from the beginning that we wouldn't muddy our professional waters with the dirty linen of our private involvement."

Have I neglected to mention that Trout and I were lovers? Considering how compartmentalized we kept our relationships, it's no wonder our *affaire de coeur* occasionally slipped my mind. For his part, Trout generally only acknowledged the private liaison when the professional one became inconvenient.

The problem, tedious as it is predictable, was fidelity. I'm sure there are women who never give the matter a second thought. I imagine them involved with morally upright, steadfast, dedicated guys with cowlicks. All Trout had was the cowlick. He'd taken care of morals and dedication by appointing himself Rock Music Critic.

After careful analysis, I've decided that the rock critic bears the same relationship to actual rock music that the manager of the high school football team does to actual football. Both dream of being heroes themselves but never quite make the team. Both live for the contact high of reflected glory. The difference, of course, is that the manager of the high school football team might grow out of adolescence. That, and, to my knowledge, Trout has never been depantsed.

Okay, the real, the tragic difference, is that musicians and those in the twilight world they inhabit are forced to take rock music critics seriously. Those inhabitants included a certain sort of woman who considers men with dyed-black pompadours, feather earrings, six-inch fingernails on their picking hands, and two appearances at the Club Ennui under their motorcycle-chain belts to be hotter than lava. Astonishingly, this notion extends far enough to actually include the rock music critic. In Austin, Texas, the premier representative of the species was Peter Overton Treadwell III, my alleged boyfriend.

Not that he slept with anyone other than me. In spite of looking like he'd spent the night on a bus station bench most of the time, he was very concerned about hygiene. Still, there was much playing around. Admittedly they sought him out. They waited to hijack the men in feather earrings in the alleys beside the clubs where Trout and the actual players went to smoke cigarettes and do the odd nondebilitating drug between sets. The hijackers broke down into two groups. The ones whose fashion daring extended to imaginative combinations of either black and white or white and black, topped by their choice of coal-black or bleached-white hair, usually just hung back looking bored and defiant and sexually depraved. The ones who risked actual colors, particularly pastels, came on more overtly with this New Wave Southern Belle routine that could induce dry heaves within minutes of the first "Y'all." They were always getting into distorted fashion-model poses with heads cocked at gamine angles and hands buried in their pockets. For the New Wave Southern Belle, life is one long photo opportunity.

Trout, Trout. In his own speedball kind of way, he was very sexy. And a heck of a rock critic. Since Trout took the kind of sleeping pills that replaced sleep with full-throttle wake, he had most nights free to prowl the clubs. What he didn't personally witness, his intelligence network caught. That, combined with a burned-out synapse where Feelings for Others usually resides and eighty-three synonyms for "stinks on ice," made him a natural in his field.

These were the same qualities that made him a less than

exquisite boyfriend. I had to forget him. I knew it in my brain. I knew it in my heart. The only dissenting vote was cast by my libido—usually around three in the morning when he would scratch at my bedroom window. He came to me then like a creature out of a dream, wild and exotic, charged with adrenaline and drenched in the naughty pheromones of women who wait for men in alleys.

The real problem was those nights when he *didn't* appear, when one of the alley crawlers snaked him away. Of course, since nothing had ever been officially declared between us, I had no grounds for complaint. Last night, the one he was asking me whether I was upset about, had been one of the ones when Trout *hadn't* scratched on my bedroom window. I saw a clear choice forming before me: I could either burst into heartbroken sobs or pretend to be a professional. The bathhouse didn't need the extra humidity.

"Trout, pay me what you owe me." My show of starch might actually have yielded some fiduciary results if a tiny voice hadn't piped up behind me.

"Mr. Treadwell, have you decided yet about the Luvboree piece?"

I turned around and faced Darci Hollister, pixie photographer. Darci got more mileage out of cuteness than Minnie Mouse. Photography, I've found, is one field where money can fill in a lot of blanks where talent ought to be. And Darci's daddy saw to it that his little girl would never want for macro lenses, slave units, and color analyzers. Normally, I wouldn't concern myself with someone cute as a bunny and about as brainy, with just enough native cunning to write large checks to camera stores and sleep with the art director. But I made an exception for Darci because of her habit of stealing assignments from me. Actually she—or rather her amour, Weasel Smeeks—nabbed them in midstream as they flowed down from Trout.

"Oh, Gretchen," she trilled. "I didn't see you sitting there."

"Hey, Darce," I greeted her, "looking great. The house must be keeping a good stock of ipecac syrup." Her sorority was notorious on campus for its binge-purge festivals, washing down cartons of Mint Milanos with ipecac syrup. We both laughed as if I'd been joking.

Darci Hollister even had a petite pixie laugh that tinkled like tiny silver bells. It fit her like her petitely perfect size three lilac walking shorts that showed off her perfectly tanned and muscled legs. Years of aerobics classes had left her with a body so pert and springy that she looked like she'd bounce if tossed from a five-story window. Well, maybe four. I was willing to run some tests.

"Darci," Trout burst out, "you're looking extremely well. Extremely . . ."—his eyes were like crab eyes on stalks bulging to survey Darci's five feet of midget aerobic perfection; even sitting down I felt like Paul Bunyan next to her— "fit. Gretchen and I were just talking about the Luvboree." Trout turned to me. "Darci is very interested in the romance phenomenon."

That was obvious enough to me from all the time she'd put into personal research on the subject. But this was not the moment to be peevish. Darci was poised, crouched down in her hightop size-two Avias, ready to pounce on another one of my assignments. Trout was still holding the press kit out to me.

The cozy tableau the three of us were locked into needed no caption. If I held out for the money Trout owed me, Darci would snatch up the *Life* story on the polyester penwomen. There was something sick about lunging for an assignment I probably wouldn't get paid for, but I did. I snapped the kit out of Trout's hand, figuring my only reward might be the precious moue that bloomed on Darci's face before she turned away and fled to Dennis.

"Sad fact of life number one," Trout enumerated for me. "There are a shitload of hungry photographers in Austin, Texas."

"Listen, Trout, Darci has to buy hunger by the bottle at the drugstore. I'm achieving the effect naturally, and it's not like this job is going to do much to remedy the situation. At least fork something over for my expenses."

"Expenses!" Trout howled, brushing his hand toward the press kit. "It's all in there. You're comped for everything."

I opened the folder and did indeed see tickets for workshops and banquets.

"What? You don't trust me?"

I closed the folder. "Just checking. So, I'm covered once I get there. I'm still going to have to pay for gas, film. . . ."

Trout looked at me like I was a government contractor billing him for coffeepots, but he finally pulled out his wallet. The twenty he handed over appeared to have been brutally fondled. I took it without saying a thing. My silence prompted him to excise another one. "Here, go get your nails wrapped or whatever it takes for you to blend in. Get accepted by your subjects like Diane Arbus did."

Diane Arbus. So he wanted a freak show. I could do that. I owned a wide-angle lens. "I know how to do my job."

"Good. Surprise and astound me. And don't forget the juicy quotes." Trout sank back into his chair, pretending I'd really skinned him. He jerked back again. "Hey, I've got a great idea. Why don't you write the whole thing all breathless and trembling, just like an actual romance heroine?"

I nodded as if I were seriously considering the idea.

"Or—no. No!" Trout waved his hands in front of his face, frantically erasing the previous idea. "Why don't you pretend that *you* want to be a romance writer and are trying to learn how to crank one out?" He beamed at me. I didn't have the heart to tell him how many times both his ideas had already been done.

"I'll think about it."

"Why not actually give it a shot? I mean, how hard can it be? Make some quick bucks."

"No, I prefer the slow ones I torture out of you."

"Hah! Hey, wanna slip on back to the darkroom?" Trout
wagged his eyebrows at me. I rolled my eyes in disgust as if
I were totally ignorant of the feel of the long, grooved developing sink cold against my back.

"Come on." Trout's normally screechy voice changed register, shifting down into a rumbling Barry White bass. "Let
me be yo' handyman, sweet thang. I'll grease yo' griddle. I'll
pick yo' peaches. I'll choin yo' butter. I'll oil yo'—"

"Trout! Were you at Antone's last night?" Trout's patho-
logical predilection for spouting blues lyrics flared up
acutely whenever it had been aggravated by a visit to the
"Home of the Blues."

"Oo-wee! You gots bad blood, mama, I believe you needs
a shot. I says, turn around, mama, let me see what else you
gots."

Whenever Trout applies the appellative "mama" to me, it
is time to leave.

Muttering, "I got a black-cat bone, got a mojo too. Got a
John the Conqueror root, I'm gonna mess witch you!" Trout
barely noticed my exit.

On my way out I caught sight of Darci in Dennis's office.
She was crushed against his chest, sniffling softly. He glared
at me and wrapped a protective arm around her. The smart
thing to do would have been simply to sell Darci the assignment. Of course, if I'd started doing the smart thing, the
very fabric from which my already frayed lifestyle was
woven would have commenced unraveling. I wasn't yet
prepared for that. I stepped out into the shriveling heat of a
summer that hadn't even begun yet.

2

Gravel crunched under my wheels as I pulled down the narrow driveway leading to my house, 4310 (Rear) Caliche Drive, nestled in pecan-tree-shrouded Hyde Park. A turn-of-the-century subdivision at the edge of town, the neighborhood had long become part of Austin's central heartland. Students occupied its mansions. Though many had been reclaimed and refurbished during the Boom Years, such activity was now stalled out. The neighborhood was dotted with brilliantly restored homes sporting much etched glass and For Sale signs with a bank's name on them.

My one-bedroom shack had never been part of any such real estate makeover. It is what real estate ads like to describe as a "mother-in-law's" addition. It might indeed have sufficed for a mother-in-law, provided she'd grown up in the Black Hole of Calcutta. Myself, I found the cheerless hovel a bit cramped. A bit hot in the summer and a bit cold in the winter, when I would lie in bed and blow smoke rings of frozen breath while, a few feet away, the space heater flared off dirigibles of gas. I found the wildlife—the squirrels that cavorted in the attic, the rat that tunneled in through the mushy boards under the shower and etched my soap with sharp gnaw marks, the weaving lines of sugar ants, the increasingly bold cockroaches—I found them all unamusing.

What *was* funny was that such a shabby rat hole should be annexed to the most fastidious of dwellings, 4310 proper, home of my landlord and his family, the DeWitt Cleebs. Mr. Cleeb's life was his lawn. Through endless hours of watering, mowing, fertilizing, edging, acidifying, dethatching, aerating, and pest annihilation, DeWitt had created a lawn so green, so thick, so lush you probably could have sewn something out of it. A pool-table cover, perhaps.

My theory was that Mr. Cleeb took his sovereignty where he could find it. He certainly wasn't able to exert much influence over his teenage daughter, Angeline. It was hard to figure out how Mr. Cleeb and his wife, a dour woman who left early each morning and returned home late from her job typing license forms at the Texas Department of Motor Vehicles, could have mustered up the genetic wherewithal to produce Angeline. Change-of-life child of their late marriage, Angeline was *una pistola.*

Pretty Angeline drooped around the house as pinch-faced as her mother until the moment when a carload of boys from McCallum Senior High School roared up, at which point she became as vivacious and giggly as a hebephrenic on nitrous oxide. Mr. Cleeb expressed his disapproval of the high school boys by glowering at them as he watered the corners of his lawn where his circular spray sprinklers didn't reach. If he took particular exception to one of his daughter's teams of pimply-faced suitors, he might go so far as to water their car. But that usually just resulted in Angeline's getting into the moistened vehicle and leaving.

Besides his lawn, DeWitt had one other passion in his life, his route. He drove a truck for Frito-Lay, an enormous yellow-and-brown truck that took up nearly the entire space on the road in front of his house. With pinpoint parking, however, he was able to get his truck in with just enough room for his wife's sapphire-blue Cougar. Occasionally Mrs. Cleeb would mess up her parking job and DeWitt would have to go in, get her keys, and reposition the Cougar himself.

Of course, if I hadn't been renting the back apartment, they could have parked in the driveway. They begrudged me the driveway, I could feel it. I felt it acutely as I pulled in that day after my misfired showdown with Trout. I was two months behind on the rent. As I slunk up the drive, Mrs. Cleeb stuck her head out the front door. As soon as she spotted me, she popped back into the house only to reappear a second later, her reluctant husband in tow.

I got out of the idling car, trying to think strategy. DeWitt, a stocky man in a V-neck undershirt who never missed a Saturday morning at the Hyde Park Barber Shop, shambled up to me, running his thumbs around the waistband of his dark brown Dickies work pants, his lips pressed together with embarrassed resolve.

"Mr. Cleeb," I called out with cheery respect, trying desperately to be the daughter I'm sure he wished he had. "Lawn looks great." The 88 did her Living Dead shudders and heaves behind me.

"Oh, thanks." His mouth lost its tight grip. "That Scott's Turf-Builder's doing good for me. I pretty much figured I was down on my iron some. But it greened up even better than I thought it would." We both turned and paid silent homage to the miracle of photosynthesis.

I sensed that DeWitt was coming out from under his rapture of the green and moving to the delicate subject at hand. He cleared his throat three times and folded his arms up under his armpits. He didn't like discussing money anymore than I enjoyed not having some to give him. If I'd been any kind of decent human being, I'd have put him out of his misery and offered to move and let him keep my damage deposit. But I had no place to go. I could already imagine the blood draining out of Trout's face if I were to appear on his doorstep holding a suitcase. It made him nervous when I forgot my panties at the foot of his bed. I had no choice but desperate improvisation.

"Hey, Mr. Cleeb, I was over at Tom Thumb Grocery real, real early the other day, and you'll never guess what I saw."

"A pyramid floor display of Brawny paper towels?"

"Well, yes, that, but the Gordo's Chips man was there unloading."

Mr. Cleeb pivoted warily to face me. "Gordo's, hm-m-m." From past conversations, I knew that DeWitt harbored dark suspicions about this rival in the chip game.

"I couldn't believe it." I popped my eyes a little for effect, then waited.

"What?" Cleeb prompted.

"Well, he moved a whole rack of your Cheetos Cheese Curls and part of one of the Nacho Cheese Doritos and put his Arriba Corn Crunchies in front of them."

"Dog it!" DeWitt muttered, more in sadness than in anger. "Those independents. I know they're fighting for survival but, shoot, rear-racking me like that?" He gave me such a look of crushed idealism that I wanted to tell him it was all a lie. There *was* honor among chip men. But I didn't and Mr. Cleeb walked away, shaking his head in bewildered disappointment. I broke for my front door before the missus had a chance to remind her husband of his mission. Mr. Cleeb had a sweet cowboy shyness about breaching the sanctuary of my home, so once I made it inside I was safe.

♥   ♥

Just after dawn the next morning, the sound of crunching gravel woke me. One of Angeline's suitors, no doubt. I reached up and bent back one of the slats of the aluminum blinds and peeked outside. Sure enough, a motorcycle rider in acid-washed denim was pulling away just as Mr. Cleeb strolled down the front walk in his brown uniform with the yellow bow tie, ready to start his route. He watched the cyclist careen down his gravel drive and looked to the back of the house, where the screen to Angeline's bedroom window lay discarded atop the bed of impatiens he'd put in last week. Mr. Cleeb shook his head and swung heavily into his truck.

"Whuzzat?" Trout muttered, his voice muffled by a pillow.

I slid back down under the covers. "Nothing."

"C'mere." He rolled over and pulled me toward him, pressing the Peter Overton Treadwell III love rod against my thigh. He snuggled up against my neck, where he nibbled and smacked until he had all the right neurons firing and I was snuggling back. At the precise instant when every cell in my body went on Full Red Alert and was tingling in anticipation of something truly delicious occurring, the slurping noises in the vicinity of my ear abruptly turned to snores and Trout rolled onto his back gargling air, felled by a coma that would have made Karen Quinlan look like a light sleeper.

There was no chance of slumber now with all my molecules doing jumping jacks and limbering up for the Big Fun. I propped myself up on an elbow and stared down at Trout. His skin was pale as any pre-Raphaelite beauty's. Tiny blue veins showed in his twitching eyelids. I leaned over and kissed him on the lips. In his sleep, Trout snorted pleasantly and smiled. No question about it, he liked being kissed. I cuddled up to him and pulled his arms around me. The posture had all the warmth of being trapped under a fallen log, but I lay that way until the clock radio alarm clicked on half an hour later. I punched it just as the early morning weather came on with the sparkling news that temperatures would be over 100 again, with humidity in the same swamp. Reflecting on how delightful a four-hour drive to Dallas was going to be in a car where air conditioning meant opening all the windows and gripping a Big Gulp with extra ice between my thighs, I hauled myself out of bed.

In the shower, I noticed how exquisite my skin was. Had Trout? I'd spent the previous evening hours from nine to midnight giving myself Day One of the Home Spa Weekend as outlined in *Glamour* magazine. First, I'd wet down, then abraded myself with kosher salt in a stocking moistened with almond oil. This was followed by an hour of steam. Then I replaced the kosher salt with bay leaves sopped with peppermint oil and continued exfoliating. By the time I stepped out of the bathroom three hours later, my body was ready to be served on a lace doily. Had Trout noticed its scrumptiousness in the two minutes before he passed out? Hard to say.

After the shower, I plugged my dusty box of hot rollers into the outlet on the bathroom light. I hadn't warmed my locks since an ill-fated interview for a state position when I'd been asked to rate these three qualities: attendance, job knowledge, and attitude. I tried to be clever and said the most important quality was a knowledgeable attitude about attendance. I didn't get the job, but I still believed an actual hairdo could be an asset in certain circumstances.

Next, I dumped all the makeup I owned into a zippered bag to apply at the stoplights which is where my maquillage artistry seems to reach its height. Back in my room, I leafed through my wardrobe. I was woefully low on ruffles and things pink, but I did have a blue-striped shirtwaist dress left over from my work wardrobe. I slipped it on and packed a few other artifacts collected from that brief and disastrous period of gainful employment—bras, hose, a half-slip—then spent considerably more time on my photo equipment.

I decided to take only one camera body, since I wanted to blend in. I left the 28-millimeter medium wide-angle lens on the body and tossed in a 100-millimeter for portraits and medium-long shots. Instead of an all-purpose 50-millimeter

normal lens, I took along a rarely used extra-wide-angle
fish-eye. If Trout wanted goon shots, I'd oblige. I dug out
my flash unit, a couple of extra battery packs, the pistol
grip, and the bounce flash attachment. As an afterthought, I
threw in my small range finder. It had great optics but
looked like a 110 party camera, which tended to intimidate
subjects less than a full-sized 35-millimeter. I hefted the bag
onto my shoulder and was creeping out of the room when I
was stopped by "T'm'car."

Take my car, I translated from the original grunt. At first I
thought Trout was talking in his sleep, but his furrowed
brow showed that he was concentrating very hard on trying
to wake up.

"T'm'car," he repeated. "Yours bad." He strained to form
distinct words. Without opening his eyes, he flopped an arm
out of bed and felt for his pants. He dug his keys out of his
pocket and tossed them at my feet. I picked them up and
went to sit beside him on the bed. He'd opted for a modified
rockabilly look last night with a fountain of black curls that
spilled down onto his forehead. I attempted to brush the
curls back tenderly, but Trout had bronzed them in mousse
and they weren't going anywhere. I settled for a gentle kiss
on his cheek.

"Trout, that's very sweet, but your car is missing a door."

"Uh." He settled back onto the pillow and I stood up.

I wanted nothing in the world at that moment more than
to take off every stitch I had on and lie back down and feel
Trout's skin against mine. But I didn't. I hitched up my
camera bag and headed out to the Delta 88. I stopped to
pick up the screen squashing Mr. Cleeb's impatiens, then
headed up the trail to Dallas.

3

"The *Austin Grackle,* right?" the hotel desk clerk asked, flipping through her reservation cards a second time.

"Try Peter Overton Treadwell, then. Maybe my editor made the reservation under his name."

Microscopic lines of irritation pressed around the clerk's mouth. She was a perfect representative of all Ludgow's Savoyard Inn strove to be: elegant, welcoming to the rich, intimidating to the poor. Not unlike Dallas itself. I let my camera bag sag onto the floor, where it sunk half a foot into the carpet. She ran a long plum-colored fingernail up and down her guest list.

Behind me was a space city straight out of "The Jetsons," with clear-glass pneumatic people tubes lifting off at various launch pads around the lobby to soar a couple of dozen floors up. I stared at dizzying rings of rooms whirling up over my head until I lost them in some low-lying cloud cover. At the front of the hotel, a bank of doors whooshed open to admit a stream of middle-aged women in flouncy dresses. Flounces. My first clue. I attempted to track their progress visually across the lobby but lost them in the mangrove thicket over in the Rain Forest Atrium.

"I'm not finding anything under either Grackle or Treadwell," the desk clerk informed me.

I dug through the side pocket of my camera bag and retrieved the press kit Trout had given me. I plucked out the press badge. I hadn't wanted to flash credentials, to throw my weight around, but the woman was leaving me no choice. I slapped the badge on the desk. "There should be a complimentary room for me. I'm with the press."

"Complimentary rooms for the press?" The notion amused her, and she repeated it as if I'd suggested free luxury suites for the Hod Carriers Local. "I'm afraid there's been a mistake." She pushed the badge back to me. "This badge merely entitles you to entrance to the"—she cleared her throat, glanced around, and finished in a lowered voice —"Luvboree."

I returned her thin smile and and retook the offending badge. Trout had conned me again. "What does a single room cost?" I asked. "A very simple single room. No frills."

The clerk, trained not to display loathing, was politely frosty. "Just a moment, please, I'll check for you." She tapped awhile on a terminal, squinting at the tiny screen on the desk as she scoured her inventory. Her eyes still on the screen, she said, "We have one Thriftiway Single over in the Conquistador Atrium." She pointed toward a far-distant chamber where a gigantic stone carving of the Aztec serpent god Quetzalcoatl hung. "I can let you have it at a special commercial discount of ninety-nine ninety-five a night or one eighty-nine for both nights of the convention."

"Sounds good." I nodded, reaching into my purse almost as if I might find something other than a few dollars and change. "Oh, darn. I left my wallet in the car. Be right back." In a mild panic, I backed away from the desk, grabbing my camera bag and suitcase. "Right back," I mouthed, tacking erratically over toward the Rain Forest. A crabby parrot croaked at me as I slipped into the foliage. I was oblivious to the waterfall that cascaded into the stream burbling at my feet as I considered my few paltry options.

Jumping right back into the 88, barreling on home to Austin, and not stopping until the hood ornament was embedded in some tender portion of Trout's anatomy was the plan that appealed most strongly to me. The only obstacle was the valet parking attendant I'd encountered on the way in. He'd smirked openly at the 88. If I went back out this soon, he'd know he was right, that I *hadn't* belonged.

A scrawny howler monkey slid down the mangrove tree I hid behind and stared at me with big blank amber eyes. His BB pupils skittered around nervously. When I didn't get the message that this was *his* mangrove, he pulled back his tiny monkey lips to reveal Doberman incisors. I edged quickly away from the little guy and found a clump of bougainvillea to hide in. Two women hurtled past. One was large, with the face and build of an overgrown Pekinese dog—wet bulging eyes, squashed-in piglet nose, no neck to speak of. Her companion, a much smaller woman, was trotting furiously to keep pace with her friend. They stopped in front of a display of poster-sized romance novel covers.

"Good heavens," Peke-a-woman sputtered, "if I could get a cover like *that* I could put my *grocery lists* between it and have a best-seller."

The cover in question was significantly different from any I'd ever glimpsed on the racks at the supermarket. The hero's head, instead of hovering tantalizingly in the vicinity of the heroine's hydroponic bosom as it usually did, was hovering much farther south. Much farther. In fact, it was almost hidden in a froth of petticoats. With the addition of a speculum and stirrups the cover might have passed for a re-creation of a pelvic exam in period dress. Judging from the heroine's expression, however—she appeared to have just taken one between the eyes from a tranquilizer gun—it was clear that things distinctly nonmedical were happening.

"Now, why can't I get a cover like that?" Peke-a-woman stopped in front of another lushly colored cover. This one featured a busty blond heroine swooning in the arms of a razor-cut, blow-dried crusader. Kind of a Ken-and-Barbie-Go-on-a-Crusade motif.

"Because you're not Viveca Lamoureaux?" her friend offered, timidly mentioning the author's name. It was swirled in gold-foil letters larger than the title, *Love's Fevered Fiefdom.*

"Well, I've heard that even Viveca Lamoureaux is not really Viveca Lamoureaux. She's a man, an Oxford don, who's ashamed of writing romances."

Beneath the blowup was a review from *Publishers Weekly.*

"Oh, get this." The larger woman quoted from the review. " 'Lamoureaux has once again demonstrated her singular ability to transcend the genre with this unusually literate look at the Albigensian crusades. Skip over the mandatory heavy breathing and what you have left is simply a jewel of a novel within a setting of impeccable scholarship.'

" 'Unusually literate.' " Peke sniffed. "Unusually boring is what they mean. Skip the heavy breathing and you can skip nine tenths of your readers. Right?"

"Oh, yes. Right."

I pushed a few fronds aside, stepped out of the tropical interlude, and trailed the two women to the Shiva Atrium. Beneath the fierce gaze of a four-armed god dancing on one leg, the couple joined what appeared to be a Tootsie look-alike contest. Hundreds of women wearing oversized glasses with sidepieces that swooped down at the temples to connect with the bottom of the lenses were gathered in front of a long row of folding tables. A sign over the tables read LUVBOREE REGISTRATION.

Peke-a-woman and her friend headed off for a table with the sign PUBLISHED AUTHORS overhead. Harassed convention hostesses handed them packets of material and blue badges. The vast bulk of the crowd was huddled beneath the ASPIR-

ING WRITERS sign, waiting to check in and collect the plain vanilla badges that identified them as Aspirants. The Aspirants were, for the most part, wearing typing-pool chic, ensembles in cunning synthetics made to look like silk. The Published Authors favored the same style except that their outfits were real silk that only looked like polyester.

I saw no surprises and no prospect of any. If I left at that very moment and drove straight through with only a short stop in Waco for bathroom, pork rinds, and a diet Sunkist, I could potentially be back in Austin before Trout got out of bed. I was hiking my camera bag onto my shoulder, ready to hit the road, when a new entourage swept in.

Peke-a-woman glanced up from pinning her badge onto her linen-look suit and shrieked loudly as she caught sight of the contingent. One of the new arrivals shrieked back, and the two women hurtled across the lobby and collided in a long-lost-sister embrace. Other reunions were accompanied by more shrieking. Up in the high branches of the mangroves, the howler monkeys and macaws picked up the alarm until the cries reverberated around all twenty-five floors. I hadn't heard so much squealing since the winners of pep squad tryouts had been posted back at Woodrow Wilson Junior High.

Against my will I started framing up those hugging figures in eight by ten. There is nothing quite as photogenic as high histrionics. With the fish-eye in place I could capture the true fun-house flavor of the event. With any luck, I could bang off a few rolls right here in the registration line and be on my way back to Austin inside of an hour with no further need of a Thriftiway Single. I was reaching for my camera when a gravelly voice behind me advised, "Oh, get those two ninnies over there, they're fixing to start blubbering all over each other."

I turned around to find a woman in her early fifties at my elbow. She had a craggy Lillian Hellman face full of wrinkles of the type that only a couple of decades of cigarettes and coffee can lay in. She put a True cigarette to her lips and followed it up and down with a match while it bounced between her lips as she asked, "Can you believe the hissy fits they're pitching?" Then she laughed. It was a laugh that came from the belly and whipped around unmentionable amounts of phlegm on its way through her lungs. I searched for a name tag on her navy blue jacket. There was none.

"Juanita Lusader," she supplied, sticking out her hand. Only when it was out did she notice the smoldering match. She flicked it into a nearby planter and we shook. "Who are you shooting for?"

I didn't need a press badge perched in the hatband of a crumpled fedora to tell me she was a reporter. Civilians always asked who I was taking—or, in Texas, "making"— pictures for. I answered her question and reluctantly told her my full name, Gretchen Griner. I know it's supposed to be a symptom of a poor self-image to hate your name, but I genuinely believe an exception can be made when that name sounds like brakes grinding.

"What's your angle, Gretch?" She squinted one eye against the plume of smoke snaking up from her cigarette. "Housewives Making Millions? Novels by the Numbers? Or is it a think piece? Pastel Porn?"

A sense of professional camaraderie made me less uncomfortable to be playing the journalist's most characteristic role: an out-of-place alien poking around like a gawker at a five-car pileup. "I'm not actually going to write a full-blown story," I confessed. "I'm mostly just doing a photo essay."

"Best kind of story there is," Juanita countered. "We had a saying over at the *Austin American Statesman*. 'A picture's worth a thousand words, and that's still about nine hundred and ninety-nine more than most readers want.'" Juanita aimed the True at me. "Photos are where it's at, believe you me. A picture and a cutline, that's about all the readers can handle."

"You're from Austin? I'm from Austin." The sense of camaraderie between us grew exponentially.

"Outside of Austin. Leander."

"Well, you're probably right about photos and a cutline." She nodded at me—"I guarandamtee I'm right"—and sucked on the True.

Buoyed up by this moment of Fourth Estate and hometown bonhomie, I glanced around at the flounced *Hausfrauen* and muttered, "Quite the little confab," with as much jaded cynicism and condescending disdain as I could muster. It was an air I knew writers to be fond of. "Have you ever been to one of these . . . these Luvboree things before?" I rolled my eyes at the ridiculous name so she would have no doubt that we were both on the same side of the bars in this zoo.

"Um, not that many."

"I know what you mean." I snorted. "I don't exactly intend to make them a lifelong habit either." Relief at finding someone who neither squealed nor wore flounces made me garrulously expansive. "It's kind of pathetic, isn't it? All these frumpy housewives in polyester either writing or reading about raven-tressed sex goddesses. You kind of have to feel sorry for them in a way." I drew in a pitying breath. "So, what's your beat at the *Statesman?*" I gave "beat" an insider's casual fillip.

"It was police when I was there, but I've moved on." Juanita had the cigarette planted in the middle of her mouth and was speaking out of the corners. "My beat now is l'amour. As Johni Lewis I write contemporaries and family sagas for Secret Moments' line of Surrender Romances. And as Lunita St. John I do historicals for Parchment's Scabards and Lace series."

A sick feeling rolled up from the pit of my stomach, and the din in the lobby was replaced by the deafening echo of my own hasty words: Frumpy housewives . . . frumpy housewives . . . frumpy housewives. Kind of pathetic

. . . kind of pathetic . . . kind of pathetic. "You're a . . . ?"

"For crying in a bucket, girl, you look like you just ate a bug. Am I a what? A child molester? A horse thief? A Republican? No. Come on, spit it out, we're all consenting adults here. I'm a romance writer. You can say it. Romance . . . writer. No one'll wash your mouth out with soap or tell your pastor they saw you talking to one."

"It's not that. It's just that . . . forget it. I'm sorry. I didn't mean you."

"Don't shovel me that bullcorn, Gretch, 'course you did. I'm maybe a little different from most of these gals here, but I'm not a whole 'nother species entirely."

I stared at her, trying to imagine Lillian Hellman in pink. "You mean you write those books about quivering virgin governesses trapped in creaky mansions?"

"Jeezo-beezo, darlin', you're about fifteen years out of date. You're talking about Gothics. Gothics are the buggy whips of the industry. The single solitary place they still survive is in the minds of you bumfuzzled media types."

"Oh."

" 'Oh,' " she repeated, holding her elbow in one hand as she pressed the True to her lips and stared at me, evaluating. "You know what chaps my behind? You're probably proud of your ignorance. You're an I've-Never-Actually-Read-One, aren't you?"

"Pardon me?"

"I get it all the time. There's a certain type, when I tell them what I do, first they say, 'Fascinating'; then they say, 'Of course, I've never actually read one.' Have you? Read one?"

"Well—uh, no."

"Good night, nurse! Never read one. That means you come in, find the battiest broad you can because she fits all your stereotypes, snap a few pictures, grab a few dingbat quotes, then hit the trail like a cow pattie. You look a little green. Did I smack the nail on the head?"

"No, not at all. I intended to—you know—sit back, get an overview first, read a couple—read *several* romances. You know, just lay in a good solid groundwork before I started."

Juanita cocked an eyebrow at me that said she'd been lied to by professionals and I shouldn't quit my day job yet. "Well, great. But just to be on the safe side, why don't you holster your weapon for right now? Let me show you around. Then, if you still think we're all a buncha bonbon-gobbling cretins, go ahead and photograph us that way. Sound fair?"

I agreed that it did, and Juanita suggested I put the cameras in my room for a while. My room.

"Uh, actually, there's been a mix-up with the reservations and they gave my room away and there're no more available, so I guess I'll just have to be going." That settled it. My mild interest and excitement about doing a story on my own was dissipating in the presence of snooty hostelers, shrieking matrons, and the prospect of having to read an actual romance novel. I shouldered my camera bag.

"Aw, come on, G.G." She gently removed the bag and hitched it onto her own shoulder. "I've been around that block a few times myself. Riding on the rims, huh?" When she winked at me, a nation of wrinkles squirmed around. "You don't have to answer that. If you're anything like I was, you'd never admit you were on your uppers even if it meant sleeping in the train station and having a Payday for breakfast. Hoo boy, those were the days." She smiled and shook her head, her eyes filming with a nostalgic haze. "Crazy? We were all nuts back then. Well, grab your grip, honey, you're bunking with Juanita Lusader."

Juanita's room was on the twenty-fifth floor. Actually, she confessed to me as we got on the elevator, it wasn't even her room. She was staying in the illustrious Viveca Lamoureaux's suite. Just to get onto the twenty-fifth floor required a special key card that Juanita jammed into a slot in the elevator control board. When the elevator doors opened, an elegant man seated behind a desk greeted Juanita.

"Miss Lamoureaux's editor has been calling all morning. You wouldn't know how to get in touch with her, would you?" he asked, clearly perturbed by his inability to locate Miss Lamoureaux herself.

"I'll keep an eye peeled for her, Wendell," Juanita answered.

"Well, if you should see her, also report to her that KDAL-TV and the *Morning News* would both like interviews."

"Good luck!" Juanita snorted, fingering a floral arrangement on Wendell's desk. It was of a modern design with strange, swan-necked lilies, feathers, and scary exotic blooms that looked as if they could trap and digest small animals. "You know how Viv is about publicity."

"The arrangement is for Miss Lamoureaux." He pointed to the flowers as he leafed through the stack of messages in front of him. "So are those." He indicated a stack of manuscripts a foot high.

"She's such an easy mark," Juanita said as she gathered up the messy pile. "All these Aspirants know it, too. They track her down at these shindigs, look hopeful and forlorn, tell her they want to write just like her, then dump their writing exercises on her and expect she'll pull some magic strings. I tell you, someone comes up all worshipful and tells me they want to write just like me, I tell them I'm sorry as can be but that position is filled. *I* already write like me. I guess she's just a lot nicer than I am. Kind of compulsively helpful."

"The rest of these can wait until Miss Lamoureaux appears." Wendell looked up from the stack of messages, duty done, pressed his palms together, and asked, "What can I fix you to drink? Weller's and water?" He was already up, but-

toning his jacket as he moved to the bar in an alcove behind
the desk.

"You talked me into it, Wendell. What'll you have,
Gretch? Wendell's buying."

"Gosh. Is it even lunchtime yet?"

"Wendell," Juanita directed, "run some Weller's around
the blender with a tuna fish sandwich for our friend here."

Wendell bowed his head into his hand as if the burden of
his chortling mirth were almost more than he could bear.
When his shoulders stopped shaking, he poured two bour-
bons and droppered in a couple of ccs of water.

Juanita tested hers. "Just right, Wendell. Just right." She
handed me mine. "Let's go check out the Holy Trinity
suite."

The suite was opulent and triplicated: three phones, three
televisions, three priceless bronzes, three enormous fruit
baskets. Juanita sighed. "Two more johns and they'd have
achieved perfect symmetry in here."

"My God!" I said. "Romance writing must be awfully
lucrative."

"It's been good to Viv, all right. She got in early and
carved out the intelligentsia market. Now, me and Lunita
and Johni are just poking along. No, if old Secret Moments
was putting us up, we'd all be over at the No-Tell Mo-tel.
But Viv said, as long as her publisher was springing for this
deal, I might as well help her fill up some of the empty
space."

"Why do you call her by her pen name?"

"Just a habit. She asks me to do that when we're at deals
like this. Publicity-shy." Juanita sank into the pewter
leather sofa and kicked off her heels. I dumped my luggage
in a heap and joined her. At that moment—with road whirl-
ies still buzzing in my head and the prospect of, once again,
sticking a camera into the faces of dozens of strangers loom-
ing before me—at that moment I would have been entirely

content to sip bourbon forever on Miss Lamoureaux's cushy couch. But Juanita brought me back to business.

"Did you see that survey in *Psychology Today* where they found out that women who read romances make love twice as often as nonreaders?"

"Twice?"

"Reason enough to read."

"So it's not all vicarious thrills."

"Oh, they're getting their jollies out there." Juanita's eyes sparkled and she laughed her phlegm-rattling laugh. "Okay, now." She snuffed out her cigarette and put her glass down to indicate that this was serious. "We've got to get you educated." She picked up a list of conference events. "Great, there're four workshops starting in"—she flipped the list over to glance at her watch—"fifteen minutes." She read aloud from the list. " 'Author/Editor: A Love/Hate Relationship?' "

"Boy, I could *teach* at least half of that one."

"I know just what you mean. Okay," she continued. "Number two, 'Whither the Occult-Fantasy-Adventure-Intrigue-Sci-Fi-Regency Romance?' No, you need something more basic. Here we are: 'Put *All* Your Senses into Sensuality.' " She glanced at her watch. "Perfect. You've got fifteen minutes to make it." She shooed me out the door. "I'll be in the lobby waiting for a full report."

I thought fifteen minutes would give me plenty of time to find the Zirconium Room. But I hadn't reckoned on the geography of Château Jetson. I was certain I was on the trail when I passed the Amethyst, Opal, and (eureka!) Zircon rooms. But they dead-ended at the Chrysoberyl Room. I asked a man puzzling over a hotel map if he knew where the Zirconium Room was. He didn't. He was trying to find the Specialty Fibers meeting taking place at that very moment in the Amber Room. After careful study of the map, we discovered we were in the Semiprecious Gems Wing and he wanted to be in the Organic Gems Wing and my meeting was way over in Industrial Elements.

I had to stop for light sustenance a couple of times along the way, but when I passed the Potash and Graphite rooms I knew I'd made it to the Industrial Elements Wing at last and headed on confidently. Sure enough, just beyond the Bauxite Room, I found Zirconium. And only half an hour late.

The sign by the door assured me that this was indeed the sensuality workshop and that the mid-thirtyish speaker at the podium was Andrea Bronstein, a top editor with Cameo Romances. The bio on the handout said she'd graduated from Sarah Lawrence with a "concentration" in the classics. From the look of Andrea's cream-colored raw silk suit and rope of pearls long enough to lasso a buffalo, it appeared she'd managed to break her "concentration" long enough to notice that Homer would never put the round, shiny ones around her neck. She was already concluding her presentation when I scrunched down and slipped in.

". . . but not least, is the sense of smell." Andrea stopped her index finger half a foot from her (surgically?) pert nose and pointed in its general direction to indicate from whence hailed this sense of smell. "Cameo readers want to walk with our heroines into that English garden redolent with the scent of lavender. They want to writhe upon those Porthault sheets smelling of Ivory soap flakes and sunshine. They want to fold into their embrace a man tangy with the intriguing scent of cedar wood shavings and his own indefinable masculine essence."

The grandmotherly woman next to me scribbled *Use smells!!!* in her notebook, then raised her hand. Andrea pointed a Mandarin-princess fingernail at her and the woman stood up, tugging at her dress. The floral-printed synthetic remained plastered by static electricity along the backs of her legs and up into her crack. "I was wondering, Miss Bronstein," she said, in a thin voice that went reedy when she raised the volume. "Do you want your writers to use the senses differently in your contemporary as opposed to your historical lines?" She sat back down.

"Differently?" the speaker echoed. "As far as I know we still smell, taste, hear, see, and touch the same way our ancestors did." The crowd chuckled like a bunch of salesmen trying to make points with the boss. The woman next to me reddened with embarrassment, and I fought the urge to garrote Andrea with her string of pearls for the cheap shot.

"I was only kidding," Andrea went on. "I understand what you mean and am grateful to you for bringing the point up because, yes, there are differences."

Okay, Andrea could live.

"We live in a more explicit time. I doubt that we experience life with any greater degree of sensuality, but we're certainly more open in describing sensory input. You can see this difference beautifully illustrated by comparing, say, Tyrena Gallant's historical, *The Tender, the Tormented,* with Gamine MacPherson's latest, in which the heroine saves the family's timbering business, *Pulp and Pearls.*"

"What line are they with?"

Andrea lost her regal bearing for a second and gaped peevishly at whoever had asked the question. Then she regained her composure. "Gamine MacPherson and Tyrena Gallant are two of Cameo's most popular authors."

Throughout the room heads bent down as the titles were duly noted. Tyrena, Gamine, and Cameo scored a few hundred new readers that day.

The woman next to me muttered loudly, "They're two of my favorites. Cameo's the only one I still buy the whole line of every month." Murmurs of assent rippled through the crowd. Andrea smiled, touched by their brand loyalty.

A woman with a head of hair that looked like a furry black Cossack hat stuck her pen in the air. Andrea stabbed a dagger nail her way. The woman stuck her chin up and asked in a clench-jawed William Buckley accent, "Tell me,

Andrea, what are the current pet peeves, the bête noires, if you will, among editors."

"Pet peeves," Andrea repeated. "Well, for one, I think I'll scream if I read 'vicelike grip'—v-i-c-e—or 'to the manner—m-a-n-n-e-r—born' one more time."

The group tittered at such faux pas. The woman next to me, still chuckling, wrote *Manor, not Manner!*

"And, I'm sorry," Andrea continued, "but my eyes are too precious to destroy on dot matrix manuscript. Get a decent printer or don't submit to me."

Lady Buckley hoisted her pen again and elaborated. "Yes, yes, but syntax and dot *ma*-trices aside, are there any, let us say, occu-*pa*tions, settings, and so on that are disfavored?"

"All right. For one thing, people, the Wine Country and Thoroughbred racing have been done to death. I can't speak to historicals, but in contemporaries we're up to here"—she stabbed at a point between her pearl necklace and earrings —"with tough, savvy lady lawyers and paleobotanists. And people, people, people!" Andrea rested her hands on the podium, her head lowered as though bowed down by a great weight. "Try to tone down the mugging. I see much too much eyebrow arching, shoulder shrugging, mouth pouting. Don't forget, you're writing a romance novel, not doing mime theater."

I chuckled and started taking notes. These quotes would make great cutlines.

"Are the rumors true that—" the next question started off. It was lost in knowing laughter.

"That Cameo will be launching a new line this fall?" Andrea finished for her, then paused. As the pause lengthened, the crowd grew quiet. "The rumors are . . ."—she stopped to toy with her pearls, prolonging the suspense—"true!" The crowd erupted into excited chatter. "And it's going to be called Languor!"

The jubilation perplexed me. I leaned over to ask the woman next to me why everyone was going *boing-boing.*

"A new line!" she repeated.

"Right, a new line," I prompted.

She looked at me as if she were wondering if English were my first language, then explained patiently, "Well, you want to be in on the ground floor. Since the heyday of romance is over, how else can we get in?" She squinted at me suspiciously, then became quite animated. "Are you published already? I know you. You're what's-her-name, Lavoris—no, *Tre*voris D'Argent."

"Me? No. I'm not anyone."

"Oh." Her face fell. "No one who's anyone ever comes to these things anymore. They used to in the heyday. All the authors used to come. Now it's just us writers."

"Writers but not authors?" I questioned.

"You know, unpublished. Aspiring. Whatever they call it. Oh, shush." She flapped her hand at me. "She's going to give the guidelines."

I turned my attention back to the podium, where Andrea had pulled out a sheet of paper with GUIDELINES handwritten at the top in giant letters and was waiting for the furor to die down before she spoke again. A hush fell over the Zirconium Room.

Andrea stared into the crowd for a dramatically sufficient moment. Then she very carefully balled up the sheet of paper and dropped it into the wastebasket. "Those are the guidelines," she announced. "For anyone who didn't get the message, we're tossing out the tipsheets on this one. Languor is going to be the first out-of-category category line. We want fresh voices, fresh insights, fresh characters, fresh stories."

I wondered if Andrea might have considered a career in produce management at one time.

"The line will be a mainstream romance in a series format. A medium-length book with big elements. Languor will give the reader more of everything, but mostly more of what she wants: more sensuality, more story, more glamour, more romance. Languor will also"—Andrea paused and raised a cautionary finger—"give the reader *less* of what she *doesn't* want. Less clichéd dialogue. Less needless bickering. Less superficiality." She ricocheted a piercing stare around the room. "I don't ever want to see a manuscript submitted to Languor wherein the plot consists entirely of the heroine changing her clothes and bathing. Basic hygiene does not a riveting romance make."

The woman next to me squirmed like a sinner exposed, jotted down the note *Fewer baths,* and stuck her hand into the air again. Andrea called on her after a few others on the far side of the room had whispered questions I couldn't hear. Amid the crackle of static electricity, the woman slid off her chair and stood. "So what you're saying," she encapsulated, "is that you don't want the typical john-ray type book."

"Right," Andrea confirmed.

She opened her notebook and wrote *No genre stuff.*

"Languor wants drama." Andrea clenched her fist and hammered "drama" home. "We want larger-than-life emotions powerfully felt and powerfully portrayed by powerfully strong characters."

I visualized *La Traviata* being sung by weight lifters.

Lady Buckley raised her hand again. "Not to *press* the point, Andrea, but could you be a bit more specific about Languor's parameters, if you catch my meaning?"

"Numbers." Andrea sighed. "You always want numbers. All right. I'll be looking for a hundred and twenty thousand words, which will make this a big four ninety-five book. We plan an initial press run of two hundred and fifty thousand. Royalties will start off at seven percent, escalating to eight at a hundred thou and nine at two hundred. Advances will be commensurate with previous experience."

Some distant reflex that took comfort in writing large numbers that I didn't understand made me jot down the figures Andrea was firing out, but my attention had drifted. I was eager to get back behind a camera. I'd already visualized a whole new motif, a boldly different way of seeing romance writers and fans that was sure to surprise Trout: as the wildcatters of the writing world.

I turned in my seat to behold the sea of rapt faces behind me, every one of them transfixed by talk of subsidiary rights, payouts, and multiple-book deals. With just the barest of cosmetic adjustments—a Marcel wave here, a Cupid's-bow lip there, some shadows under the chubby cheeks to simulate gauntness—I could imagine those same faces listening just as intently to an emcee explaining dance marathon rules during the darkest heart of the Great Depression. My shutter finger was itching. I crouched down and slipped out.

4

I made my way downstairs and out of the Industrial Elements Wing, through the Painters of the French Impressionism atelier, around the hotel planetarium, and in between a dozen boutiques selling ceramic masks of Pierrot and five-dollar jars of jalapeño jelly. The sound of the cascading waterfall and howler monkeys led me to the lobby.

The Luvboree had burst into full flower. A thousand or so fevered conventioneers milled about, all engaged in high-volume chatter and clipping along like they'd just been paged for a Code Blue. Everyone was clutching a special Luvboree conference notebook printed with the trademark heart trailing twining tendrils.

"Hey, Gretchen!" Juanita hailed me from across the lobby, where she was seated with two other women on a couch and chairs clustered around a coffee table littered with glasses. On the floor beside her were two large aluminum Halliburton cases. In the vast enormity of the lobby, the three women looked like dolls sitting on dollhouse furniture. As I approached, however, the smell of True cigarettes and the sound of Juanita's mucoid laugh dispelled the dollhouse image.

"Well, what did you learn?" Juanita picked up her drink, scooted over, and patted the empty space on the couch beside her. I sat down.

" 'Basic hygiene does not a riveting romance make,' " I quoted.

One of the women chortled appreciatively. In her early thirties, she had giant eyes and long, long dark eyelashes behind her swoopy-templed Tootsie glasses. Combined with thin lips, short, fuzzy hair recovering from a bad permanent, a receding chin, and a hyper-alert perkiness of manner, she ended up looking like an amused ostrich. It occurred to me that a fuzzy stuffed toy in her likeness could be a real money-maker. Then I remembered Big Bird. Too late again.

"Andrea Bronstein, right?" With a quick twitch of her head, she identified the source of the quote. "Truer words. Contemporaries." She sniffed. "A person could get water-logged just reading them."

"Gretchen," Juanita said, "meet another Austin gal, Lizzie Potts."

Lizzie scooted forward in her chair to extend her hand to me and accidentally knocked her purse off its perch at her side. Out tumbled a dozen or so of the hotel's complimentary bottles of shampoo, conditioner, lotion, foaming bath mousse, and mouthwash, along with a selection of their French-milled hand and bath soaps, three felt shoe bags, five tiny sewing kits, two transparent shower caps, a melted mass of what had once probably been the chocolate mints placed on turned-down beds. The handshake was forgotten.

Lizzie chuckled and bent down to gather up her loot. "My little girl will almost forgive me for leaving if I bring home enough tiny vials and brightly colored packets." I had never heard a voice like Lizzie's before. Her tones and inflections trilled up and down scales I was unacquainted with. I

couldn't quite place the accent but I think it was Elf. Upper
middle class. I looked for Lizzie's name tag to see if she was
a Published or an Aspiring, but she wasn't wearing one. An
aspirant, I figured, probably groupieing Juanita in hopes of
getting her manuscript to this Viveca Lamoureaux person.

Juanita introduced the other woman, Cari Lindell. After
Juanita's introduction, Cari did something with her mouth
that was meant to simulate a smile. The exact expression,
however, was lost beneath a layer of makeup of a thickness
not seen since *Planet of the Apes.* Smears of iridescent high-
lighter, mud-colored contourer, apricot blush, navy mascara, khaki shadow, and amethyst gloss had been troweled
onto the ivory canvas of her face. I guessed her age to be
somewhere in the late thirties, but only a carbon dating of
her bronzing gel would ever tell the true tale. Her blue
badge identified her as an Author and listed her aliases:
Splendora Lattiane and Topaz LaTour. I peered at Cari, trying to see if she had any of the exotic dancer about her that
might explain the crotch-drop resonance of those pen
names. Cari spoke even as I observed her.

"What publication are you with, Gretchen?" she asked
warmly, her eyes twinkling with the astral blue radiance of
tinted contact lenses. The twinkling ended abruptly when I
failed to name any large-circulation national magazine.

I turned to Juanita and asked her what the Halliburton
cases were for. She popped one open and I saw the familiar
waxy face of a Resusci-Annie dummy. "My assistant for a
little sensuality workshop I put on."

"Oh," I said, not really comprehending.

"Hey," Juanita announced, latching Resusci-Annie back
up, "Gretch is going to be doing a photo essay on all us
chickens." "What do you think so far?" she asked me.
"Buncha nuts, huh?"

"I think I can get some good images."

Juanita held up her glass in a toast. "Start with me." The
vertical crags in Juanita's face split up and went horizontal

as she threw her arms open, sloshing bourbon on the couch, and beamed at me. "I'll give you a quote for the cutline that'll make an oil rigger blush. Editors love that kind of contrast."

Lizzie the Friendly Ostrich chuckled madly. "Hey, hey, hey, Juanita, you're not just fueling around, are you?"

A punster, I thought. Oh, whee. Except that Lizzie's childlike delight in her wordplay made it impossible for me to react in total keeping with my strongly held belief that puns are not the lowest form of humor, they are no form of humor at all. I laughed along with Juanita and ended up glad I wasn't sitting there prissy-mouthed like Cari. It had been too long since I'd laughed with women.

Juanita was 100 percent right: Trout would wet himself if I turned in Lillian Hellman writing romance novels and talking salty. "Okay, you're on." I jumped up, ready now to get to work. "Just let me run up and grab my equipment."

Juanita laughed. "That's exactly what my third husband used to say when he went to the little boy's room."

"From what you've told me of Carl's endowments"—Lizzie's large eyes twinkled mischievously, and she held her mouth in a suppressed titter that rendered it even more birdlike—"he must have been speaking metaphorically."

"Y'all," Cari whined, stopping me in my tracks, "we need to be getting ready for the Love's Leading Ladies Gala." Tiny lines of vexation fissured the latex sheen on her forehead. "My editor's probably already there. I have to go."

Juanita turned to me to explain. "Cari's got a multiple-book deal cooking."

"Jua-*ni*-ta." Cari stamped her little foot. "Why don't you just tell the whole world?"

After Cari's departure, I turned to Juanita. "What's this gala?"

"A fancy dress ball," Lizzie answered. "All the authors are going costumed as their favorite or most famous heroine. It's really a shame you can't come."

"Why? I have tickets for all the events. They're in the press kit."

"Not *this* ticket," Lizzie informed me. "It's off limits, *verboten, prohibido* to the press. This is strictly members only. Just published authors. Not even writers can come."

Forbidden. That was all I needed to know. "I'll just take off my press badge. How'll anyone ever know?"

"Well, for one, you won't be wearing a costume," Juanita pointed out.

"Oh, Juanita, come on," I pleaded.

"Kid, if it were up to me, you'd be in like Flynn. It's not my say-so."

I have a tendency to deflate quickly, and I wanted, suddenly, to go home again.

"You know, I'm not half bad at costume improvisation," Lizzie said. "Bowels of God, after all those years as Maîtresse de Raiment for the Society for Creative Anachronism, I ought to be. Spinning abbesses from paint-and-body-shop receptionists. Minstrels from tile salesmen. Lairds and ladies from computer programmers. Hah! Transforming a photographer into a romance heroine will be child's play."

Juanita hunched forward and sized me up. "I don't know."

"Bah! Don't be a naysayer. This isn't to be the Madrigal Ball. All we have to do is create the barest semblance of a costume. You do have two tickets, don't you?"

"By jingo, you're right, Lizzie. Gretch can use Johni Lewis's ticket."

"By the Holy Face!" Lizzie trilled, her little ostrich mind happily diverted by this problem. "Mark what I say: given the variables, there's always a solution. Let's go up and see what we can organize."

Fortunately, Trout had accustomed me to people breaking off into alternative communication modes. Given clues like minstrels and lairds and ladies, I figured Lizzie's must be some medieval offshoot. Given her eagerness to help me, I found it charming. I didn't understand *why* she was so eager, but I didn't resist. Journalists take more than their fair share of favors in life.

Back in the Holy Trinity suite, Juanita and Lizzie picked over my clothes.

"Not much here," Juanita noticed. "I hate to be a Gloomy Gus, but Johni Lewis's most popular heroine is Daphne St. Regis Devine from the Tolliver Saga."

"The flapper?" Lizzie asked.

"You got it." Juanita turned away, defeated.

My heart sank. With my wad of shirtwaists and dirndl skirts, I just might have been able to pull off—oh, a stenographer, maybe, but a flapper? Undaunted, little Lizzie rummaged through my clothes.

"You kids have fun." Juanita took a vanity kit and her costume wrapped in a dry cleaner's bag into the bathroom.

"Foh!" Lizzie muttered. "If it were only a matter of a simple *bliaut* or an abbess's habit, *those* I could easily fashion from a bed sheet. But, soul of a virgin, a flapper!" She pawed through my suitcase. Suddenly, her big peepers lit up. "Christ's wounds!" She whisked out from the pile the midi-length apricot half-slip I'd bought at St. Vincent de Paul's back when they were still on Sixth Street and all the transvestites bought their clothes there. "Finery made to fit the task at hand," she announced. I was dubious in the extreme.

Much to my surprise, however, the slip, hiked up under my armpits, made a very respectable chemise once Lizzie belted it at the hips with a drapery cord. Then she set about creating a headdress out of a scarf and some feathers from Viveca Lamoureaux's flower arrangement.

"Are you sure you should be doing that?" I asked as she kneecapped a couple of the scary lilies. I could just imagine the exalted Viveca Lamoureaux popping in to find a couple of strangers in her room demolishing her floral tributes. Lizzie didn't answer. As a matter of fact, she barely seemed to notice I was there anymore as she stitched together a head-dress using one of the complimentary sewing kits she pulled from her overstuffed purse. Her absorption in my transformation was eerie. I couldn't remember ever seeing anyone quite so single-minded.

"God's teeth!" she cursed when she pricked her finger. She pressed out a tiny bubble of blood, sucked it away, then went immediately back to stitching the lilies into place. A few minutes later, she was finished and stood on tiptoe to fit her creation onto my head, leaving a thumbprint of blood on my temple as she did. The headdress had a distinctly twenties feel to it with the feathers rearing up from my forehead. The effect got even better after Lizzie plastered my hair down into a sleek Pola Negri do with a single curl curving over my forehead.

Her kindly, single-minded attention made me feel like Walt Disney's Cinderella when the mice and birds and other wee creatures all got together to whip up a ball gown for their giant human buddy.

"Beads, beads, beads," she muttered, searching through drawers that held only hotel stationery. She stopped her search at the pile of Aspirants' manuscripts Juanita had collected from Wendell for the still-absent Viveca Lamoureaux. "Ah-hah! I do love a problem with strictly controlled parameters." She was practically chortling as she pulled the paper clips off dozens of bundles of paper, looped the clips together, and in no time had a string several yards long that she connected around my neck, adding a knot at about waist level.

I was starting to look pretty darned flapperish, even before Lizzie did the makeup. She stood close to me, breathing into my face as she applied pale foundation, eye pencil, Vaseline on my upper lids, and a tiny geisha mouth drawn on with vampire-dark lipstick over my own rubbery mouth. I jumped up, looked in the mirror, and a vamp of the silent screen stared back. Lizzie was a genius.

Juanita emerged from the bathroom dressed as an eighteenth-century bar wench, her Pat Nixon frosted hairdo only slightly incongruous beneath the milkmaid's cap. "Well, twenty-three, skidoo and oh, you kid," she cheered, making Charleston circles with her palms. "You do Daphne proud." My costume was a success.

Lizzie looked at her black-plastic-strapped digital watch. "God's teeth, look at the hour! Be off with you!"

"Are you sure you don't mind?" I asked. I now felt like one of the wicked stepsisters, leaving Lizzie behind after she'd effected such a magical metamorphosis even if she was still just an aspirant. I told her as much.

"Oh, well . . . it was fun." She shrugged, briefly rejoining us in this century. "Enjoy the barley mead!" she called after us as we left.

"She gets that way when she's happy," Juanita confided as we waited for the elevator. "Me, I like a person with a colorful way of speaking. Seems to get to other people, though. That and some of her other little peculiarities."

"Peculiarities?" I thought of my pill-popping, trust-fund, blues-boy boyfriend, of everyone else at the *Grackle.* I thought of the subjects of my photography. "Peculiarities are a way of life for me."

The hotel ballroom was thronged with historical authors dressed as Southern belles in hoop skirts, squaws in buckskin, Scottish princesses in tartan, governesses with parasols, bar girls in seamed stockings, settlers' wives in sunbonnets, and duchesses in bustles. And damned near every one of them in those Tootsie glasses.

Among the contemporary authors were an anthropologist in a djellaba, a dressage champion in jodhpurs, a caterer in a white apron and toque, a rodeo contractor in a Stetson and jeans, a cross-country skiing instructor in knickers, and a primatologist in khaki shorts. These were some sturdy heroines.

I slipped in easily. A fevered gaiety spiked the chatter in

the room up to controlled-substance levels. But none of
these women had ever been closer than a *Newsweek* cover
story to any mood-altering chemicals. No, it was the sheer,
glamorous thrill of being part of this particular elite that
had everyone so highed-up. It was also being furloughed
from solitary confinement with a word processor. But most
of all, it was money. My wildcatters were all together here
doing exploratory drilling in the richest field of editors currently assembled anywhere in the world.

Off in a far corner of the room I spotted Cari, dressed as a
French hooker in beret, seamed stockings, and striped
T-shirt, buttonholing a neurasthenic-looking woman lost in
a jacket with shoulders that John Wayne couldn't have filled
out. The dark circles behind the woman's red plastic-framed
glasses spoke of too many late nights with too many eye-
straining dot matrix manuscripts. Obviously an editor.
Probably the one Cari was priming for the multiple-book
contract. Cari wrapped the woman in an enthusiastic embrace that knocked the editor's glasses off, then scrambled
to retrieve the red plastic specs. She almost succeeded in
replacing them on the woman's face, but the editor grabbed
her glasses and backed away from the chummy assault. Her
shadowed eyes searched the crowd over Cari's shoulder until she found a familiar face and waved frantically. Ges-
turing to her acquaintance, the editor smiled thinly and left
Cari. So much for the multiple-book deal.

"Here, take this." Juanita shoved a Bloody Mary into my
hand.

"Juanita," I protested, "I haven't eaten anything all day."

"Stir with your finger," she said, poking the drink's stalk
of celery between my teeth. "C'mon, it's a convention;
nothing counts." Juanita hoisted her drink and we clinked
plastic cups. "Let's mingle."

Juanita's idea of mingling turned out to be cutting a zig-
zag pattern back to the bar for refills. Many refills. She convinced me that the drinks were watered, and I lost track at

eight. With the distance I gained from a wee buzz, the whole affair came to resemble a square dance with costumed writers do-si-do-ing from one suited editor to the next with a mechanized frenzy.

"Why aren't you out there jollying up the editors?" I asked Juanita from our position on the sidelines. It wasn't until I spoke that I became aware of how long it had been since I'd done so and how many empty glasses with sprigs of celery leaves in them sat in front of me.

"You mean, why aren't I pimping for Johni and Lunita? Praise the Lord, they don't need the business."

"Now, which one is which?" My memory was starting to blur.

"Lunita writes historicals and Johni does the family sagas and the contemporaries. Which is to say that Lunita sets the five whoopie scenes in Old Vienna or the court of Mary Stewart or in Comanche country and Johni does them in Cape Cod hideaways or along the Formula One race circuit or up in a danged hot-air balloon!"

In a distant corner of my mind I was thinking that these were great quotes and I should be writing them down. I should be shooting Juanita strapped into her milkmaid vest, showing her cigarette-stained teeth in that great horselaugh. I should be snapping surreptitious pix, probably with my range finder, of Cari crumpling beneath her beret when she came up with a dry hole on the multiple-book deal. I thought all those things but didn't feel particularly motivated to do much about any of them.

I got up to weave my way back to the celery stand. I brushed past a hatchet-faced woman in calico settler's-wife regalia who looked like a transvestite Comanche. Behind her was a Lady Guinevere complete with high, pointed dunce cap, wimple, diaphanous gown, and trailing veils. I must have gawked a bit too openly because she stopped and smiled at me. In my state of detached inebriation, her goofy smile turned her into a cartoon fairy godmother.

Fairy Godmother spoke. "God's body, woman, what ails ye? Have ye partaken too freely of the grape?"

"Lizzie?" I wasn't entirely sure until she gave a quick ostrich twitch of her head. She whipped her glasses out of the folds of her gown, put them on, and Fairy Godmother vanished. "Lizzie, that is you! You snuck in too! I can't believe it. That's you! I didn't recognize you at all until you spoke." I glanced around and moved closer to her. I didn't want to tip anyone off that there was yet another crasher in their midst.

Lizzie gave me a Fairy Godmother smile, delighted at my confusion. "Well, not to put too fine a point on it, this isn't really *me.* I'm Fredegunde, Queen of all the Franks." There was a majestic lift to her voice, and a regal presence surged through her as she announced her true identity. "Of course, my hennie is anachronistic." She touched the dunce cap. "I should be wearing just a plain linen headrail, but then everyone would think I was a nun."

I stared at her headgear. In my concentration I lost track of balance and listed perilously.

Lizzie grabbed my arm before the slight list turned into a full header onto the ballroom floor.

Juanita appeared out of nowhere and grabbed my other arm. "Hell's bells, Gretch, you're three sheets to the wind. Appears your dance card has been punched for this night."

"I'll take her up to the room," Lizzie volunteered.

It felt as if we crossed continents and galaxies and marched through several different eras in the near future before Lizzie finally steered me onto a bed. I collapsed. A far-off tugging turned out to be Lizzie taking my shoes off.

I tried to thank her, but she just laughed and turned to leave. Suddenly, one clear thought surfaced in the rocky sea of my mind. "Hey, what's the illustrious Viveca Lamoureaux going to do when she finds me passed out in her suite?"

"I wouldn't concern myself overly much on that score," Lizzie advised me.

"Well, yeah, but I worry about what kind of impression I make on literary legends."

"Alack, the hour has passed for that worry." I didn't like the way her Fairy Godmother smile was scrunching into mischievous elf-type configurations.

"You're her, aren't you?" I said.

The last thing I remember, before sliding into darkness, was Lizzie pausing at the door to nod. Her veils bobbed about her. With the hallway light streaming in behind her, she looked again like a fairy godmother. Suddenly the names of Sleeping Beauty's fairy godmothers popped into my head: Flora, Fauna, and . . . what was the third one's name? I started to ask Lizzie what the third one's name was, but all that came out was *"Wha'—wha'!"* Lizzie smiled and, even as my brain labored to retrieve that third name, the flickering light of consciousness blinked out.

5

Many hours later, I awoke with a breeder-reactor headache. Juanita was in the next room snoring. In addition to feeling greasy, clammy, morally unfit, and spiritually anguished, I noted that I was monumentally hungry. Since I didn't want to wake my roomie, there wasn't much I could do about any of the above except hunger. I dressed, located the room card, and tiptoed out, carrying my shoes and purse. I peeked down into the lobby below and sighed with relief. It was deserted. I could search through Château Jetson in relative privacy for an all-night eatery.

I hadn't counted, however, on the vigilance of our concierge. At that moment I would have paid a lot *not* to have the privilege of a fastidiously elegant man monitoring my comings and goings. "Care for a nightcap?" he asked in a jaunty Fred Astaire way.

I declined and turned to punch the elevator button. It was only then, staring into the polished steel doors, that I beheld the wraith that was Gretchen Griner. My eyes were puffy and ringed in smeared mascara. My face was sallow and

creased. Where my hair didn't cling in greasy strands to my
scalp, it stood off my head in terrifying horned cowlicks.
Not only was my bra strap showing, so was most of my bra
where the front buttons of my dreary shirtwaist had
popped open. I hunched over and hastily buttoned up. I
punched the elevator button again. Two weeks later it
hummed to a stop in front of me, giving Wendell and me
ample time to practice our tightest, prissiest smiles.

As soon as the doors shut, I spit on my finger and
scrubbed away at the mascara skids under my eyes, then
tried to fluff and flatten my hair to a roughly uniform depth.
Only after I'd rubbed my furry teeth with my sleeve and
recalibrated my bra straps did I notice that the other glass
elevator riding beside me was packed with Japanese busi-
nessmen watching me perform my impromptu toilette. I
punched every button on the panel and managed to escape
two floors later. I located the stairwell and hiked the remaining fourteen floors down to the lobby.

Finally, off in the Carousel atrium, I found the Three-
Ring kiosk still open. A bored-looking black woman put
down the Stephen King novel she was reading and heaved
herself upright as I approached. The digital clock radio she
had turned to an easy-listening station said 3:16. I scanned
the right side of the menu board and put a hand to my chest
to still the fibrillations triggered by the $1.50 cup of coffee. I
scanned so long that the black woman sat back down again.

I peeked swiftly into my malnourished wallet and
counted six ones. I had enough gas to get home and tickets
for meals the next day; I could sacrifice the six. The cheapest thing on the menu was the Bearded Lady, a bagel with
cream cheese and jelly, for $5.95. I ordered it. And a glass of
water. I put them both on a tray and slid them down the
cafeteria tracks. The woman padded along beside me on the
other side of display cases holding cottage cheese and pear
salads, Saran-wrapped sandwiches, and cans of V-8 juice
sunk into a bank of ice.

"That'll be six twenty-four." The black woman held out her hand.

Tax. Damn. My stomach growled. I'd already picked off a corner of my bagel and eaten it. It had been, quite possibly, the most delicious morsel I'd ever consumed. I handed over the six dollars, bitterly regretting the extra gallon of gas I'd pumped into the 88 in Waco and cursing Trout for luring me into this humiliation. With the woman's palm still outstretched in front of me, I searched through my wallet again, pretending that I might find something there. "Heh, heh. Looks like I left all my *plastic* up in my room."

It was clear from her expression that she saw immediately that the only "plastic" I owned might be a suspended Montgomery Ward's blue card.

"Uh, could I *owe* you the twenty-four cents? Until tomorrow?"

The woman closed her hand around the bills and stuffed them under a clip holding down ones in the cash register. "We'll let it slide." Without looking at me, she went back to her stool and her novel.

I moved as far from the cashier as I could and parked my bagel. Next to me was a wooden cutout painted to look like a cage on wheels stuffed with clowns. Orange hair. Red bulb noses. Whiteface. Ruffled collars. Polka-dotted clown suits. Big shoes. All grinning garish circus grins. I turned my chair to them and fell upon my bagel, inhaling it before my hunger even had a chance to notice. My stomach growled for the next seven courses to start. I was scraping cream cheese and grape jelly dabs off my plate when a voice behind me trilled, "The flapper!"

Lizzie, sitting three tables away beneath a cutout of a seal balancing a ball on its nose, grinned at me from under her sheepdog perm. Uneasy recollections formed in my abused brain, something having to do with a fairy godmother and the true identity of Viveca Lamoureaux. I waved feebly.

Eight ninety-five of smoked turkey breast on an onion

roll—the Lion Tamer, what I'd *really* wanted—appeared on my table. "Might I join you?" She dumped a canvas bag laden with books down and sat. "God's feet, I thought I would be the only insomniac abroad at this hour. Back home, I usually just go to my study and work. Are you chronic or intermittent insomnia?"

I forced myself to pry my eyes from her hands, which were distributing lettuce leaves and tomatoes over the top of the turkey, and answered, "Neither. I just got up from my little before-dinner nap."

Lizzie pressed her sandwich together, held it up, and inspected it from all sides before taking it by surprise with a big bite off the right side. She grinned at me as she chewed as if we'd pulled off the attack together.

"So you're a big dog in the romance world?" I said as she eyed the sandwich, planning strategy.

"Would that be the equivalent of being a general in the Italian army?" she asked frostily.

"Oh, no, no, I didn't mean it that way at all." I apologized hastily. The cardinal rule in journalism is: Maintain rapport with the subject. Unless you're Mike Wallace. "No, I'm impressed."

Lizzie put down the sandwich, now maimed with craters where her thumbs had dug in, and flicked a puff of hair out of her eyes. "Forgive my haste to take offense. I suppose I became overly sensitive to condescension while I was at the university. Oh, mystery novels, particularly if they were English, were fine. Spy novels: quite acceptable. Science fiction: none of *them* were cause for gossip in the faculty lounge. But woe betide the unsuspecting innocent who defiled the temple of learning with a romance novel. By the Bread, Jeff Hawkins even taught an idiotic course on the detective novel! For graduate credit!" She barked out a short laugh and raised her mug. "Here's to Viveca Lamoureaux. If she did nothing else, she forced me from the musty halls of academe."

I chugged a gulp of water. Lizzie banged her mug down heavily, still troubled, and stared off, apparently thinking bitter thoughts about Jeff Hawkins and detective fiction. After a moment, she glanced down and stared curiously at her sandwich. "I don't want this." She pushed the plate toward me. "Take it."

I pushed it back. "No, go ahead, eat your sandwich. I just finished a bagel."

"A bagel? That's not enough for a whelp." She slid it back. "Go on. Eat."

"No, I'm stuffed." Back it went. "But thanks."

She noticed the way my eyes were oscillating as I stared at the sandwich and shoved it back at me decisively. "God's teeth, but you're a plaguey wench. Take the cursed victuals and be done with it!" Black Death and flying buttresses cracked through Lizzie's voice.

"Thanks," I mumbled and became one with her sandwich. A brief vision of Scarlett O'Hara grubbing for roots and swearing she'd never go hungry again blipped through my mind. Unlike Scarlett, I swore I'd begin looking into solvency just as soon as I'd dealt with hunger and continued inhaling the thumb-cratered sandwich. It was quite good.

"Is it coincidental," Lizzie asked, apparently of the seal balancing the ball on the end of its nose, "that the most denigrated literary form on earth is one created and enjoyed nearly exclusively by women?"

I had not counted on the Luvboree being a hotbed of feminism. I'm certain I would have commented insightfully had my mouth not been full. As it was, I barely managed a thoughtful nod.

"And don't you think it odder still that the most virulent, least-informed critics of romance fiction are frequently feminists?"

"They are?"

"By the Face, they are. I'll never forget the way Harriet Nestor flayed me at an Honors Department brunch. She excoriated me for supporting a patriarchal system by fostering unrealistic expectations in impressionable female readers. She charged that I was leading readers to expect that a sort of *deus ex machina* handsome prince would descend into their lives and turn them into utopias of love." Lizzie was still obviously bitter. "You know what I told her?"

I swallowed. "What?"

"I asked her if she'd ever read a Superman comic. Harriet the Harridan sniffed in her supercilious way and admitted she had, once, for a paper on male empowerment myths. At that point, *I* sniffed, asked her if she'd ever tried to catch a bullet with her teeth, and walked away."

Imagining dizzy Lizzie at a faculty brunch proselytizing for romance fiction made me chuckle. It was a mistake.

Lizzie's big ostrich eyes flashed. "The assumption that romance readers are utter cretins who can't distinguish between fact and fantasy is the ultimate condescension."

"Isn't it just," I agreed, with a turncoat's fervor, since she'd just nailed my own operating assumption. "I hope you don't think I was being condescending. I'm just surprised you're not swamped with fans and spending all your time in high-level confabs with editors and publicity people. Doing signings. Stuff like that."

Lizzie sighed. "There was some talk of that. At first. Fortunately, I look about as much like Viveca Lamoureaux as the Venerable Bede. Oh, they're quite happy for me to remain Lizzie Potts and for Viveca Lamoureaux to stay shrouded in mystery. And for both of us to continue to do the same thing we've been doing." Lizzie sighed again and returned to staring at the ball on the seal's nose.

"And you don't want to continue?" It was a canny guess.

"My editor is just so closed-minded. She insists that readers aren't ready for what I truly want to write about."

"Your editor thinks readers are too delicate?" I suggested.

"That's it, too delicate. Too mentally inert to break that last taboo."

After gyno exams on the front cover, I wondered what taboo was left to break. Incest? Bestiality? Sex with household appliances? "I didn't realize there were any frontiers left to explore in the romance novel."

"Oh, merely the biggest one of all." Lizzie sniffed. "The one their small minds can't accept."

Whoa. "Biggest one of all?" What was that? Necrophilia? Bigger?

"Why can't they understand that readers are ready?" she wailed. "They *want* the Merovingians. I mean, don't you think that Fredegunde would make just the most wonderful heroine? In a suitably romanticized form, of course."

"Fredegunde? Your character tonight?"

"Yes, the Frankish queen. Mistress to King Chilperic the First of Neustria and *murderer* of his wife, Galswinthia. Can't you just see a grand romance set against the sweep of the fifty-year war between Neustria and Austrasia? Of course, halfway through, in 584, Fredegunde had Chilperic done in so she could rule as regent through her son Clotaire. I'd have to smooth all that over, but can't you just see it? The *early* Middle Ages. The grand *barbarian* sweep of it all." Lizzie was transported. She was with Fredegunde and Chilperic back in Neustria. Abruptly the dreamy look left her face and she was recalled to the present. "Why do editors think history started at the tenth century?"

I shrugged.

"I mean, for God's sake. Editors like American history." She looked around, then leaned close. "I *loathe* American history." Her eyes grew even larger behind the thick lenses of her glasses with the audacity of her confession. "There's simply no grandeur. No majesty. No intrigue. No interfamily squabbles that plunge tribal baronies into war for decades.

"Southern belles. Farmers. Whalers. Tobacco traders. Prairie housewives snatched by Indians. Yuck. Where's the grandeur there? The majesty?" Lizzie wondered. "Where are women manipulating history with their ova?"

I could not tell her where these things were happening.

"You'd think after forty-eight books, my editors would trust me a bit."

"You've written *forty-eight* books?"

"Of course, some of them are sweets." Lizzie reached over and grabbed one of her French fries. I pushed the plate back toward her. "Sweets only run a hundred and eighty-nine pages, and not a bedding on any one of them." She squirted ketchup the length of the fry and popped it into her mouth.

I guess I still looked blank.

"All right, then, for your erudition"—Lizzie dipped into her book bag and slapped a slim paperback entitled *Finders, Keepers* by Tracy O'Rourke on the table—"this is a sweet." A border of lilac encircled a blond couple clasping hands. Possibly in heaven. "And this is one of the longer ones." She plunked down a thicker volume. Its cover featured more recumbency. A Western couple in boots and jeans lounged amid some saguaro cacti. It looked as if the hero were either whispering sweet nothings or checking his beloved's ear for blackheads. It was by Johni Lewis.

"Hey, one of Juanita's!"

She handed me another, much fatter book. This one was by Viveca Lamoureaux.

"This is what's called a mid-list."

"All right! Embossing." I ran my fingers over the swirling, gold-stamped letters of the title, *Love's Fevered Fiefdom.* I looked at the familiar Ken-and-Barbie-Go-on-a-Crusade cover, then turned it over to read the jacket copy on the back.

Daughter of a Frankish prince, lovely Herleva bolts from the prison of an arranged marriage into the camp of her family's hereditary enemy, Ethelred of Vaudreuil. There she hides her raven-tressed beauty in the guise of a boy and her sorrow in her work as Ethelred's squire.

What she cannot disguise is the impossible love that flames within her for the wild warrior, Ethelred. A force of nature, prey to no man's law, Ethelred is as untamable as the land he loves. Bold in war and even bolder in wenching, Ethelred has never tasted defeat until he tries to conquer the Frankish spitfire, Herleva!

"Praise the saints for the romance novel," Lizzie exalted. "They've allowed me to spend my life doing what I love most."

"And what would that be?"

"Breeding and reading." Little Lizzie let out a laugh that was a cross between a whoop and a squeak. "That's how Mitchell puts it. And it's true. Researching and raising babies are my two obsessions. Do you have any? Children?"

"What?" I looked up. "Oh, no." I wanted to read more about this Frankish spitfire, but Lizzie was eagerly waiting for me to put the question. "How many do you have?"

"Just one. Annabelle."

My eyes drifted back to the jacket copy and I read aloud. " 'Bold in war and even bolder in wenching. . . . Ethelred. A force of nature.' Do you draw your heroes from real life?"

"Oh, romance heroes." Lizzie dismissed them with a whisk of her hand. "Who would get involved with someone like Ethelred?"

"Yeah, I have a hard time featuring old Eth at a PTA meeting."

"I jest not." Oh, good, we were back in the Middle Ages, the early years. "I swore that I would nary spouse with a man who would not be a boon father for my children. What about you? Have you met the father of your children yet?" She crouched forward avidly. We were now into the Girl Talk portion of the interview.

Trout as a dad? I was fully aware that he would not make a fit father for a lichen. Lizzie sat across from me, her head cocked, radiating an oddball aura that for some reason made me think of the child genius who cracked under the weight of his massive intelligence and ended up a trolley car conductor. It had been a long time since I'd known anyone who'd gone out and, even in Lizzie's cockeyed way, done all the normal things like marrying a decent guy and spawning. I couldn't bring myself to admit to her that my pilot light ignited for a mousse-plated pillhead who was not quite as faithful as your average Chihuahua dog.

"Actually, with the men I meet, the subject doesn't come up much."

"Oh, I'm sorry," was her annoying response. Talk about condescension. And then her mouth dropped open and her eyebrows shot up in the kind of expression that goes so well with light bulbs over the head. She stared at me. Hard. After a couple of seconds I touched my nose to make certain that nothing untoward was happening there. She kept staring, her ostrich eyes strafing every pore on my face. I glanced around the deserted coffee shop. Yes, it was definitely me she was staring at.

"I have the perfect man for you," she finally announced, in a way that called to mind the salesman who sold me the Delta 88.

"You do?"

Her face glowed. I tried to imagine the sort of pun-cracking, born-to-be-a-dad man Lizzie would consider perfect. Sweater vests and Hush Puppies came to mind. "Indeed I do. Oh, Gretchen, this is too perfect."

"Well, who? Who is he?" Curiosity. An occupational hazard.

"My brother! Gus!"

"Oh, you have a brother?" I struggled to maintain rapport. In the course of our conversation, I'd seen a glorious sidebar to my photo essay taking shape, a Q and A with Lizzie featuring her intriguing revisionist view of the romance. I didn't want that to slip away.

"Yes! Gus, Gustav. Mother was mad for Mahler. Gus Kubiak by name, and a more sterling character you'll never meet." She dug into her purse and pulled out a battered datebook. "When should I organize a rendezvous?" She flipped it open and waited, her pen poised over the coming week.

"You mean a date?"

"Something of the sort."

"Uh, actually, Lizzie, I'm already sort of involved with someone." "Involved" was far too solid a description of what was transpiring between Trout and myself, but it was convenient at the moment. Lizzie sensed my ambivalence.

"You are?"

"Well, sort of. Off and on."

"Perfect. You can simply go out with Gus on an off night. I'll have him call and find out when would be convenient."

I figured it would be easier putting her brother off than it would be derailing Lizzie. With any luck, my interview would be done by the time he called anyway. I reveled in the thought of a double fee. Not to mention an entire new arena, actual writing, opening to me. "Sure, have him give me a call."

Lizzie took down my phone number, then slapped her datebook shut. "Did you want to read those?" She gestured toward the small, medium, and large-sized romances on the table. "To have actually read a few romances will put you way ahead of ninety-nine percent of the people who write about us."

"Oh, gosh." I stalled. "I'd love to, but I wouldn't want to wake up Juanita."

She pushed Mama Bear, Papa Bear, and Baby Bear Romance toward me. "Have no care on that score. I quartered with Juanita last year in New Orleans, and by the Rood of Christ, that woman could have slept through Dagobert's siege of the Black Castle. Including the drawing and quartering of Prince Arnulf the Stammerer." Lizzie pressed a knuckle against her lips to stifle her mad mirth.

"Oh, well. In that case. Thanks." I took the books.

"Who knows? There might be all sorts of romantic surprises awaiting you." She beamed her fairy godmother smile at me, and I realized she meant her brother. I smiled back and reflected on the romantic surprises my life usually yielded and how they so often seemed to involve massive doses of penicillin.

Lizzie patted away a tiny yawn. "By God and His Mother, I think I might actually be able to sleep a little now." She stood up, hoisted the canvas bag onto her shoulder, and, without further farewell, left. Or took her leave, as she would have put it.

Nearly out of the dining area, she stopped and turned back to me. From that distance, she looked more like an ostrich chick than an ostrich. "Do you know how you could *really* distinguish yourself?" she shouted to me.

The black woman put down her novel and stared at the small frizzy-haired woman yelling in the middle of Ludgow's Savoyard Inn.

Lizzie answered her own question. "When you write about us, don't use the word 'formulaic.' It's never been done before."

I reflected on how rare it is in life that you run across a true original.

6

"Is that the look or is that the look?" Juanita whooped to Lizzie and Cari as I stumbled in to breakfast behind her.

Juanita had found me that morning just finishing up *Love's Fevered Fiefdom.* I'd returned to the room and tried unsuccessfully to get back to sleep. Given a choice between watching a retrospective of Robby Benson's film career on late-night cable or cracking into the romances, the romances had edged out Robby. But only just barely.

Baby Bear left me unimpressed. Plot conflicts that could have been resolved by a couple of love-crossed gnats, characters thinner than the soles on a pair of Taiwanese shoes, and, worse, as Lizzie had warned, no juicy stuff. Mama Bear was Juanita's cowboy story. There were still too many agate-flecked eyes glittering dangerously and trembling chins thrusting up in brave defiance, but it was an improvement. During Papa Bear, Lizzie's historical, however, a subtle enchantment stole over me.

I galloped along for lengthy stretches entranced by Lizzie's story of the delectable Herleva dueling with the ruthless, sexy Ethelred, before I would thud up against her luminous violet eyes sparkling mischievously or his large hand covering her much smaller one protectively.

It was during the long galloping stretches, when I became hopelessly caught up in the story, that I crossed over the border that had always separated me from romance novels. Once there, I didn't find the terrain as alien as I'd always thought I would. In point of secret fact, I had inhabited it myself—in my dreams. Dreams of a man among men and a rake among women falling at my exquisitely sculpted, shell-pink feet in a lathered heap of adoration. Hey, I *could* dig it. So it was, while reading my own politically incorrect dreams, that the first nubkin of the germ of the kernel of a thought occurred to me: I could do this. I could write one of these.

I hinted as much to Juanita that morning after she woke up with a loud snort as if gentle Morpheus had drop-kicked her over the goalposts of morning. Lizzie was already up and gone. Juanita steadied herself by sitting up, lighting a True, and doing some inhalation therapy. My comment didn't sink in until we were on the elevator riding down to breakfast, at which time Juanita cackled maniacally and welcomed me to the club.

"What club?" I asked, but Juanita was already dragging me into the El Dorado room, where the Luvboree breakfast was being held. Lizzie flagged us down, motioning to the seats she'd saved. Cari, buffed to a high gloss, was beside her. Juanita presented me triumphantly. "Is that the look or is that the look?" she asked, funneling their attention through her outstretched palm to my face.

"The look! Yea, verily!" Lizzie cried.

"What look?" I asked, sinking into one of the empty seats and lowering my voice in the vain hope that they might follow suit. Amused conventioneers were already beginning to stare.

"The look that says, 'I could do this,' " Lizzie exploded.
" 'I could get paid to do this.' "

"You mean, write romances?" I backpedaled furiously.
"Me? No chance." I denied all. "What do I know about a
man's calloused hands spanning the gossamer expanse of
my waist?"

"What do any of us know?" asked Juanita, tugging her
baggy blouse printed with hibiscuses and smiling black men
in straw hats down over her Weller's kettledrum tummy.
Cari sniffed, mildly aggrieved until Juanita deferred to her
willowy figure. "Except Cari, of course." Mollified, Cari
dipped a spoon into her grapefruit compote.

"Should I arrange a meeting for you with my editor?"
Lizzie asked, already rising up out of her chair.

I stopped her with a hand on her forearm; her maternal
instincts were swift and well-developed indeed. "Hey, I'm
here to *report* on all of you, not *become* one of you."

Juanita snorted. "That's just what I said six years ago
when I covered the first Luvboree."

"That's how you got started?" I asked.

"Participatory journalism at its finest." Juanita shoveled
up a forkful of rubbery scrambled eggs, touched her tongue
to them, made a face, and put her fork down.

"Well"—I glanced from side to side—"the thought did
cross my mind that I might possibly—I mean, it's conceiv-
able, I could *think* about *considering* doing one."

"I knew it, I knew it!" Juanita crowed. "Slide on over,
Janet Dailey, your throne is being challenged."

"I'm only *thinking* about the possibility of attempting a
romance," I equivocated. "But not a sweet one."

Lizzie shook her head. "Oh, no. Try for mid-length, at
least. You can't even get warmed up in less than three hundred pages. Do you want to meet my editor? There she is."
Lizzie pointed to a woman with large nostrils whose vulcan-
ized eggs were cooling in front of her as she turned to talk
with a crowd of writers pressing in. I didn't care to be the

thirtieth person thrust in her face while her first cup of coffee that morning cooled in front of her.

"Thanks a million, Lizzie." I slid my chair out. "But I have really got to start working." It was true. I hadn't snapped photog one yet. I stood. "I'll catch up with y'all later and immortalize you. How about it?"

"Sure," Juanita agreed. "As long as you've got something that can filter out three bad marriages and every date I've had in the past five years."

"All in my bag of tricks," I promised. As I was leaving, I spotted Andrea Bronstein. Since I'd already snagged some good quotes from her lecture, I figured I might as well start with her. The group around Andrea melted away when they caught sight of my press badge, and before I knew it I was mumbling my request to her.

"Let's go," she answered, dropping her napkin onto her plate. I followed her out, trying to figure out how I should photograph her; I hadn't expected such swift compliance. It took a second before the obvious setup for capturing my wildcatter motif occurred to me.

"Andrea, could you wait up?" She halted. "I just had an idea. How about shooting you back there at the table with all those writers jockeying to talk to you?"

She paused and glanced back, giving me a second to study her. Her long black hair was pulled back into a French twist. Today's suit was ivory linen with jade beads. She turned back to me with one word, "No," and continued toward the door. Then she halted to offer additional explanation. "Fluorescent lights make me look as if my hemoglobin count is low. We'll use the gazebo. We can get some nice diffuse light there." She forged ahead, and I scrambled after her.

The gazebo was set up beside the jogging track, which wound through acres of grass so perfect I thought I'd suggest it to Mr. Cleeb for a possible pilgrimage. Andrea stepped into the little octagonal building and studied the morning light, making it throw shadows with her hand and framing up various backgrounds. Finally she settled herself into a pensive, moody pose, told me where to stand, licked her lips, and looked off to glory.

What I saw through the viewfinder was to photojournalism what Leni Riefenstahl was to documentary filmmaking. Still, I clicked the shutter a few times and figured I'd catch her later when she wasn't doing John Barrymore imitations. But Andrea started making minute shifts in her pose, tilting her head slightly, staring directly into the camera. It dawned on me that Andrea was "working with me." After each modification, she froze, holding the new pose like a *Vogue* model until I dutifully clicked off another frame. I hoped no one was watching.

She had her chin lowered and was staring up and into the camera when she asked, "Do you write?"

She knew I'd crossed the line. She intuited my craven impulse. "You mean romances?"

"No, Vedic love chants. Of course I mean romances." She gave me her left profile and froze.

I clicked. "No. Why?"

"Nothing, I'm just looking for new writers to launch Cameo's latest line is all. Not necessarily romance writers. Not even necessarily writers. I need fresh voices, fresh talent, fresh approaches. I want people who can write for all those women who are proud that they've never read a romance. Know anyone familiar with that market?" She quirked an ironic eyebrow and held it. I clicked. I'd been introduced to quirking eyebrows last night, since that's what Ethelred did with his all through *Love's Fevered Fiefdom.*

"Uh, I might."

I had only a fraction of a second to be cynical about Andrea's motives before a blinding field of white blocked out my vision. I pulled my eye from the camera. Andrea's business card covered the front of the lens.

"Here." She handed me the card. "If you think of someone, let me know." She bent her wilted lily of a wrist to look at her watch. "Ee-oo, I'm already late for my 'Torrid but Tasteful' workshop." She jumped up and was almost out of the starting blocks before she stopped, turned back to me, and tapped me on the shoulder with a sheaf of papers she held rolled up in her hand. "The field of photojournalism presents limitless romantic possibilities." She sprinted away.

I watched her for a minute striding across the Platonic ideal of grass, the sun of a new day at her back. She'd seen something in me. My eye for detail? My visual storytelling ability? Talents that good editors can simply intuit. Talents that Trout had conspicuously failed to remark or reward. Or had she simply seen a way to soften up a reporter?

I tucked Andrea's card into the pocket of my skirt. Before I could fantasize any further, I reminded myself that I was there to do a job, dammit, and do it I would. Margaret Bourke-White would have expected nothing less. For the rest of the day I put aside photojournalism's romantic possibilities and bore down on the technical realities.

I pretended I was an anthropologist documenting the discovery of a heretofore unknown cult that consisted mainly of middle-aged white women who lived in suburbs and wore swoopy-templed glasses. These women were the dream spinners. Though widely mocked by the tribe at large, they were handsomely paid and many wished to learn their secrets of dream-spinning.

With Margaret Mead looking over my shoulder, I bounce-lighted, flash-filled, stopped down, opened up, and motor-drove my way through a dozen rolls of film. Photographically, the day was magic. Concept and execution pulled together like a couple of old sled dogs. I scurried around catching expressions of hope, greed, rapture, and dyspepsia on the faces of would-be writers cramming into workshops and dancing around editors like trained poodles.

Of course I spotlighted my new trio of friends, Juanita, Lizzie, and Cari. I caught Juanita in a number of straight-shooter poses, squinting at the camera with cigarette smoke twining around her. I even saw the cutline jump into print in my mind as soon as she uttered it. "The feminists and that whole outfit accuse us of making our readers substitute vicarious thrills for real life. Well, I'll tell you what, there was a time when it got to where I'd look over at my second husband, Wilmer, and he'd be there with hair coming out of his ears and blackheads on the back of his neck, and I'd *grab* for my romances. Vicarious was as close as I cared to come to any of *those* thrills."

Cari was good at portraying what Lizzie called the true-believer romance writer. I got any number of tight-assed portraits of her squirming around behind her makeup, trying to look warm and sincere, twinkling her eyes at the camera, and staring deep into the lens. Mostly she came off looking like her contacts were bothering her.

She delivered her piece on romance writing with an aggrieved air. "You know, the critics are always so down on us for writing popular modern fiction for a mass market. What they fail to realize is that today's popular fiction is tomorrow's literature, what they're going to be teaching in college. Don't they know that Shakespeare and Dickens were the popular writers of *their* day? They wrote for money. They wrote for the mass market just like us."

I snapped Cari, her forehead wrinkled with vexation as she explained how she was today's Shakespeare. She insisted on my taking several shots of her with her latest, *Love's Brazen Ecstasy*, pressed against her cheek. The bard himself couldn't have looked saucier. I couldn't wait to help my grandchildren with homework from their Topaz LaTour seminars.

Lizzie was like photographing a light bulb. From any angle, she glowed with a daffy incandescence. She tugged at her frizzy ends while she came up with delicious answers to my questions.

"The idea that romance is the female equivalent of male

porn is silly. You know what romances are? They're the female equivalent of the NLF."

"Pardon me?"

"You know, the football federation. Since we don't have a television set, I haven't experienced this personally, but again and again I hear from my readers that their husbands spend all their free time watching football on television. Now the question is, why?"

"Why do men watch so much football?" I hazarded a guess, "Alien mind control?"

"No. To vicariously experience a potency they've either lost or never known. Sports are the essential drama in Everyman's life. His one moment of personal power comes on the playing field. Or, if it doesn't, he dreams of it. Dreams of being the quarterback and making the tackle that wins the game and, by extension, the fair maidens.

"The fair maidens, meanwhile, also dream their dream of power. They dream of love. Their moment comes during those few brief years when nature brings them into full breeding allure. For the first time, they have the power to turn a boy's fancy.

"God's teeth, modern life is queer, isn't it?" she asked. "He's off watching some football tournament dreaming of being seventeen again and she has her nose buried in a romance, chasing the same illusion. It all comes down to this, Gretchen: we all want to be the center of the universe. We all want to be gods."

I snapped Lizzie laughing like a demented chipmunk peeking out from under her ruffle of caramel hair. It didn't seem that *she* wanted to be a god, but you never knew.

Once I'd shot up all my film, I couldn't see that there was much reason to hang around for the rest of the 'Ree. Juanita loaned me twenty dollars to make it home.

Lizzie promised she would have a reunion dinner for us Luvboree vets. She wanted me to meet her husband, Mitchell, and the baby, Annabelle, and who knew who else would be there. In the meantime, she'd have her brother get in touch with me. I nodded vigorously and told her to be sure and do that.

Cari asked if she could screen the photos I took of her. I was flipping my hand at the three of them in a cross between a wave good-bye and an imitation of a porpoise's death throes when Lizzie rushed up and threw a full-body hug on me, clutching me about the midsection, her frizz of hair beneath my breasts. Juanita dropped her white vinyl purse and came over to join in the sisterly embrace. It was quite cozy until Cari shrilled out "Group hug!" and, clapping her tiny fists together, pressed into the dog pile.

Juanita cleared her throat. "Uh—yes, well. . . ." She backed away. Lizzie gave me a peck on the cheek and went with her. Cari, her eyes squeezed shut in group hug bliss, remained tightly affixed to my side. After I succeeded in peeling her loose, I left.

Outside, the valet parking guy, the frat rat type who'd shown such disrespect yesterday, recognized me instantly.

"The Eighty-eight?" he said, loudly enough for his buddy, another parking valet, to get in on the yucks.

I bestowed a pinched smile and my keys on him.

"Right away, ma'am. We don't get many *1973 Delta Eighty-eights,*" he said with elaborate enthusiasm, sauntering away.

The scene would have been sufficiently embarrassing without an audience. But too late I noticed Andrea Bronstein on the other end of the entryway. She raised the ivory flag of her palm to me in a wan wave. One of her star authors, a local Dallasite, stood next to her. A periwinkle Mercedes glided to a stop in front of them. The author went to the driver's side and took the keys the valet respectfully offered to her. He stood back and swept the door open for her, then squeezed it shut behind her with a loving gentleness.

The smell of burning rubber and the squeal of worn brake

drums being brutally stomped upon brought me to attention.

"Here. Catch." My keys clattered into a heap at my feet. "Doggone." The valet beef-kabob snapped his fingers. "They musta slipped."

I straightened up from retrieving my keys and held out the twenty Juanita had loaned me. "Well, doggone, Bubba" —I got into the 88—"I guess your tip is just gonna have to 'slip' back into my pocket then." I revved up the 88, planning to leave the smirking frat boys in a satisfyingly choking cloud of hydrocarbons. She responded with a roar I hadn't heard in years. They say cars don't have feelings. I slid my foot off the brake and braced for the jolt when we peeled out. Instead we crow-hopped forward two, maybe three lurching feet.

The Neanderthal had put the emergency brake on. A shift in wind direction blew the 88's cloud of exhaust into my open window. I fumbled through the noxious fog for the brake. When at last I found and released it, the 88 was spent. It was all she could do to creep away, not even fast enough to escape the jeering laughter that followed our departure.

By the time we'd shuddered out of the Savoyard's grounds and onto the freeway, the periwinkle Mercedes was almost out of sight. As it effortlessly crested a rise, I caught a glimpse of the customized license plate. Spelled out in large letters was the reason why this middle-aged woman with Tootsie glasses and frosted hair was driving a Mercedes.

I read it and wept: CAMEO.

7

Back at 4310 Rear, Mr. Cleeb was mowing the road. This was the final step in a complex ritual I had witnessed many times. First, DeWitt would mow the grass in a crosshatch pattern, cutting every blade first one way, then coming back to get it in a perpendicular direction. Then he would run the mower over the sidewalk to blow any grass he hadn't caught either back onto his cut lawn or into the street. To finish up, he'd get out onto the asphalt and mow back and forth until he'd chased every speck of severed foliage into the gutter.

This particular day he left a clump of grass approximately five and a half feet long unmowed. I'm certain this omission galled him mightily, but since his daughter, Angeline, was occupying it with a beach towel and her bikini-clad self, he had little choice. She appeared to be working on tanning her palms and the soles of her feet that day, for she spritzed them with a plant mister, then assumed a dead-dog posture with the pale areas aimed at the sun. When I drove up, DeWitt turned sadly to his front door. Sure enough, Mrs. Cleeb was there making whisking motions with her hand, shooing her husband in my direction. His shoulders, broad from decades of yardwork and chip delivery, slumped resignedly and he cut off the mower.

I grabbed my camera bag and attempted to scuttle into the house with my back toward him. He must have put on an unexpected burst of speed because he reached me before I made the door and tapped me on my shoulder.

"Why, Mr. Cleeb, hi! How are you? Hot for May, isn't it? I don't remember it being this hot last year. Still, it's better than it was up in Dallas. Or maybe it just seemed hotter there with all those high rises and all that asphalt reflecting the heat right back at you. Not that Austin doesn't have her share. Of high rises *and* asphalt, I mean." I was blathering. Being a deadbeat is a desperate and undignified business.

Mr. Cleeb looked down at his Red Wing work shoes. I knew that if Mrs. Cleeb hadn't been waiting, I could have worked out some sort of deferred payment plan. But with her exerting God knew what pressures, I didn't think it wise to even bring up the subject of the r-e-n-t. I cast about frantically for a topic of consuming interest to DeWitt Cleeb.

"Uh, you know"—he continued staring at his shoes—"it *is* the twentieth of the month and—"

"Is it that late already? You know, we're just not getting the rain we should have this time of year. This heat keeps on, we'll be on water rationing before you know it."

For the past few years Austin, bursting with newcomers drawn by the quality of life they promptly destroyed, had been like a ficus suffering transplant shock. Its roots, even soaking wet, couldn't support the rampant growth on top. A city located on a river and nestled between several lakes, Austin had water but couldn't treat it fast enough for all the summer swelterers who wanted to drink, bathe, wash cars, and water lawns. You could still *drink* all the water you wanted to in Austin during the summer and you could also *bathe* whenever the fancy struck you, but lawn watering was restricted. The prospect of his tiny green babies parched and dying ignited a fire in the otherwise phlegmatic DeWitt Cleeb.

He jerked his head up. "No!"

"It's possible."

"They wouldn't. You know what this whole rationing deal is? Just a great big squeeze play the city's throwing on us to get those bond packages passed. That's all in the world it is. A squeeze play. There's water. You cain't *tell* me there ain't water."

DeWitt was just starting to get really wound up about collusion between city hall and the big developers who had literally wrung the city dry, when my phone rang. I scampered away with apologies about having to cut our discussion short and promises to get back to him on this issue. He nodded and looked down at his shoes for a while before leaving. My grace period was running out.

I dived for the phone, it had to be Trout.

"Gretchen Griner?"

My spirits sagged like cheap panty hose. No one can say an ugly name uglier than a collection agency operative. Over the past few lean months, I'd gotten good at spotting the type as my creditors had escalated from politely inquiring letters to ominous phone calls about the adverse effect my delinquency was going to have on my "credit rating." Particularly tenacious was Montgomery Ward. Their mistake had been to send me a blue charge card. Blue for the probationary creditor. They'd been hounding me for months about some sheets I'd charged, horrible cheap sheets that pilled immediately so it felt like I was sleeping on gravel. There were a few other purchases as well, but nothing to justify the shocking finance charges that multiplied like pill bugs under a wet board.

I answered the usurer in his own language, "No. There's no Gretchen Griner currently residing at this residence."

The house seemed preternaturally quiet after I hung up,

as if it hadn't been inhabited for weeks. A jangly energy prickled through me. I wondered where and with whom Trout was. I picked up the book I'd been reading, *Part of a Crowd: Loving the Womanizer.* I read several chapters. They asked why I chose men who damaged my self-esteem. I asked them where my terrific alternatives were.

I went into the kitchen to compile the culinary delight that was my chief form of sustenance: cheese toast. As I waited for the cheese to melt in the broiler I read a chapter entitled "Fighting Fire with Fire." It was an admitted break from the up-with-people, I-am-the-driver-of-my-own-bus tone of the rest of the book. Fluffed up with psychobabble, it basically advised the roaming man's mate to stir up some action of her own. The author warned that this sauce-for-the-goose type of thinking was a symptom of a dangerously diseased relationship. As this pretty much summed up the state of my relationship with Trout, the strategy held a particular appeal. I saw clearly that I needed to begin building a fan club of my own. *Tout de suite.*

I was so engrossed that, at first, I didn't hear the soft knocking at my screen door. When I did, I froze. This was it. Ward's had discovered I had no credit rating to adversely affect and was moving in for strong-arm tactics. I plastered myself against the Sheetrock partition that screened the kitchen from the living room and peeked carefully around the corner.

At first glance, it appeared that Tweetie Pie had dropped down on my front doorstep. Closer inspection, however, revealed not a big-headed canary but a guy with wispy blond hair, a puffy moon face, glasses, and sloping shoulders. It was hard to really make out anything more through the screen door, caked in decades of dust and decaying insect parts as it was. But I sensed more than actually saw a certain tentativeness, a jerkiness of manner that I wouldn't have associated with collection agency leg-breakers. The

Wisp tapped again and put his face up to the screen, shielding it with his hands so he could see in.

"Hello. Anyone home?"

He knew I was there. Car out front. Door open. I'm sure they are trained to notice things like that.

I tried to remember if it was illegal for creditors to show up in person. They did it all the time in Dickens, but surely there were laws now. Laws to protect hapless deadbeats like me whose only real sin was not being a better collector myself. I needed help. I needed expert legal advice.

I dropped to my knees and scuttled to the trash can. I rummaged through many empty Cup O's Styrofoam containers in search of the name of the guy who did the "Ask an Attorney" column. Maybe he would take an emergency phone call on shady collection practices if I promised to write it up for later use in the column. I was trying to scrape desiccated Cup O' Noodle noodles off the column when I heard the latch rattling. The Wisp was coming in!

He tapped more forcefully. "Hello. You in there?"

His voice was soft, undistinguished. Probably also part of the training. Play nice guy until they open the door, then, *wham!*

My heart hammered in my throat.

Still on my hands and knees, I peered around the corner at the Wisp. Definitely from Ward's. He had on clothes like those I'd seen in the Assistant Manager at Wendy's collection. His glasses were an out-of-date aviator style.

"Yoo-hoo. Oh, yoo-hoo!"

The "yoo-hoo" calmed me. I doubted that someone who said "yoo-hoo" would break legs. If I didn't face him now he'd only be back. Persistence was surely at the heart of the collections racket. I had to end this awful game of cat and mouse right here and now. I got to my feet and stepped out from behind the Sheetrock partition to make my stand.

"Okay, look, I know you have a job to do. Fine. And I know you hear stories all day long and meet some pretty scummy people, but I just want to say that those sheets pilled up almost from the instant I put them on the bed. I should have returned them, is what I should have done. And now I owe more than the damned things cost just in finance charges. What's your cut on this going to be?" Somehow the charge from my cringing guilt got turned around and I'd talked myself into a pretty fair self-righteous outrage. I advanced to deal with this hireling of the avaricious. "You want to see them? Do you? Huh, do you?"

I didn't let him give whatever calm, reasonable response he'd been trained to give irate customers speaking out against shoddy merchandise. I rushed into my bedroom and ripped the top sheet off my bed. Actually, it was already off the bed, I grabbed it up from the floor. The moment I touched its pebbled surface, my anger truly flared. I rushed back to the front door.

"Here, here's your piece-of-shit sheet. Take it!" I unlatched the screen door and stuffed the double flat Savannah pattern out through the crack. It wafted down onto the concrete porch, and I slammed the screen door shut again.

"Uh—"

"You want the whole set? Fine. No problem. I'd rather sleep on the gravel driveway out there." I went back and ripped off the fitted bottom and both pillowcases and stuffed them out too. "Okay? Happy? We'll just call it even and I won't even press charges for harassment to collect an unfair consumer debt as my attorney boyfriend who has a thriving practice in consumer law has advised me to do."

"Uh, I think there's been a misunderstanding." The hatchling had a nice voice, low and soft. Obviously trained to be disarming.

"You said it," I snarled. All you really had to do to stand up to the merchandising monolith was speak out.

"I'm Lizzie's brother?" The way he goosed his neck out and dipped his head back and forth like an ostrich trying to draw a bead on you made his next questioning statement unnecessary. "Lizzie Potts?"

I was so relieved that he wasn't a corporate button man that I threw open the screen door. He smiled. His smile changed everything about him and made him appealing, in a goofy sort of way. Like a big ugly baby. He really did look like a monstrous newborn, with his big moon-shaped Ferdinand Marcos head, his downy hair, his eyelids puffing into Eskimo folds behind his aviator-style glasses.

"You're Lizzie's brother," I said with sudden warmth. It had just occurred to me that the first member of my fan club had dropped onto my doorstep. Even though I didn't actually want to recruit him, I knew if I were ever to battle Trout on his own turf, I would have to be alert to every opportunity.

"Oh. Well. Yeah. I know we don't look too much alike. Now. Not that we ever do." He shrugged and jerked and grimaced. "I . . . uh . . . I tried to call before I came over, but Lizzie must have gotten the number mixed up. They said there was no Gretchen Griner there. Anyway, Lizzie told me that you'd be expecting my call, so I thought, you know, I'd better come over and explain."

"Well, I'm mighty glad y'all did." I experimented with the slightest hint of magnolia in my accent. Why did I do it? Why did I lean toward him in a display of interest? How did I know he wanted me to do these things? No doubt the last was a matter of pheromones, of the unknowable wisdom of glands. As for the magnolias and the leaning, they sprang from a little vision that popped into my head. I imagined Trout crouched behind the pyracantha bushes that ran the length of the driveway, watching me speak with this male visitor and seething with unsuspected jealousy. Of course, in real life Trout was about as jealous as the average mollusk. Still, the vision cheered me up.

I draped myself against the doorframe so that salient parts of my anatomy jutted out in a sultry *Tobacco Road* fashion. Much cheering up was effected when this attitude caused my gentleman caller to gulp audibly, his Adam's apple yo-yoing in a spindly neck. "Great T-shirt."

I looked down at my chest and held the T-shirt out to read the message: "Life Is Uncertain, Eat Dessert First."

"You could say that sums up my own personal philosophy."

"It does?" I prompted. "Why?" In my formative years I'd learned from *Seventeen* magazine that "why" and "how" questions are best for drawing boys out, getting them to talk about themselves. I sometimes wanted to cauterize whatever lobe of my brain that tip resided in.

"Uh, well, I just kind of realized that life is like a hard disk drive. It's not a question of *if,* it's a question of *when* it will crash. And since it can crash at any time, taking all your data with it, you'd better enter ye rosebuds while ye may. Hah!"

That sharp bark of a laugh must run in Lizzie's family, probably cultivated to signal to the denser inhabitants of the planet they were forced to dwell with that a communication of a humorous nature had just been transmitted. He waited expectantly with his sparse to nonexistent eyebrows arched hopefully above dark brown eyes. Imagining Trout lurking in the pyracanthas, I threw back my head and laughed a golden, throaty laugh. The brother beamed.

"So, Lizzie's brother." I moved up to intermediate flirting, dropping my eyes and cocking my head to the side. "What do you call yourself?" I hadn't really paid any attention when Lizzie told me his name.

"Well—hah!—*I* call myself brilliant and bedazzling, but most everyone else just calls me Gus." He oscillated with delight at his riposte, vibrating in my doorway, and I did my Lauren Bacall laugh again. "Gus Kubiak."

On cue, I stuck out my hand, palm down in the papal kiss-my-ring position. I watched Gus cup it as if he were taking a dragonfly skeleton.

When he unloosed my hand and I looked back up he was twitching one finger and his overripe head from side to side. It took me a few unsettled seconds to realize that he was keeping time with the tinny tune clinking out from the ice-cream truck toiling up the block. He looked off into the treetops and spoke the song. "There once lived an Indian maid. A shy little prairie maid. Who loved a warrior bold." The lenses of his glasses flashed silver as they caught the sun.

I knew the song too and joined in speaking it. "This shy little maid of old. And brave and gay he rode one day to battle far away. And now the dah dah dah. Something something." The words bubbled out of me, pulling a dim memory of sitting on a cool linoleum floor on a hot summer day at camp learning that song. " 'Little Red Wing'!" I laughed, not believing I'd retrieved the title. The ice-cream truck had been clanging past for a month without triggering the tiniest flicker of recognition, and suddenly there it was. I kept smiling until I noticed the Wisp grinning and staring at my teeth with a strangely fond gaze.

"You must be like me. I always hear that stuff," he said. "Muzak in elevators, background music in restaurants. It's white noise to most people, but I hear it. I guess you do too. The actual songs. I couldn't believe it, the other day I was on hold and they played 'Jumpin' Jack Flash.' In Muzak! It's distracting."

"I bet." I was still trying to remember the end of "Little Red Wing." What happened to the warrior brave and gay?

" 'Little Red Wing,' " he mused, as if we'd been discussing the old gang back at Woodrow Wilson Junior High. "Hey, listen," he piped up, sticking a finger into the air to denote sudden inspiration. "I've got an idea. Since life *is* uncertain, could I buy you an ice-cream? I noticed a B-R just up the block."

An ice-cream? *A* B-R? Flirting practice on my doorstep was one thing, but to consciously appear in public with the

Wisp was quite another. It would only encourage him. "I'd love to, Gus, but I'm right in the middle of . . ." Of what? The smell of what I initially took to be barbecuing provided an olefactory hint. "Of cooking dinner for friends. I'm entertaining." This part of the fantasy exercise was especially enjoyable, as the only "entertaining" I'd ever done in the hovel consisted of squirt cheese on crackers.

"Oh, sure." The Wisp backed away, stepping down off the porch. "You're entertaining. Sure, I—" With a swiftness that made me think "psychotic break," Gus's expression changed from dejection to frenzy and he bolted back up the steps, pushed me aside, and burst into my house.

"What the fuck do you think you're—" My inquiry into his motives ended abruptly when I turned around and saw black smoke billowing out of my kitchen. I ran screaming into the house after him. My oven had become a smelting furnace. I threw on both water faucets and shoved my teapot under the rushing flow.

"No water! It's a grease fire! Do you have an extinguisher?"

"No!"

"Baking soda?"

"Baking soda toothpaste!" I offered.

He left. Abandoned now, I stood rooted to the spot. I was still trying to figure out how to avoid phosgene gas poisoning when Gus rushed back in carrying the pilled-up sheets I'd left on the porch. He wadded them up, yanked the broiler open with the toe of his shoe and beat out the flames from my blackened cheese toast and surrounding tar pits of old grease.

"I guess your dinner party's ruined." He held up a scorched sheet with the charcoal square of my still-smoking dinner adhered to it.

After saving me from immolation, what else could I do but go have an ice-cream with him?

As we walked into the ice-cream school with pink and

orange desks lined up facing the tubs of flavors to be learned that month, I made the awful discovery: the Wisp wore Hush Puppies. Charcoal gray. In this case accentuated with stripes of actual charcoal across the toe where he'd kicked open my flaming broiler. Trout would never in a million years be jealous of anyone wearing Hush Puppies. Fortunately, since the designer ice-cream shops had opened where you could have your choice of accessories battered into a scoop of ice cream, Baskin-Robbins was usually deserted. Certainly no one with any aspirations to trendhood frequented it.

As we stood studying the flavors, I hazarded a quick sidelong glance. The Wisp's puffy head was as raw and shiny as the new skin under a scab. It showed up purplish in patches under the fluorescent lights. The rest of his body, from his spindly neck, sloping shoulders, and concave chest on down, was desperately out of proportion with his overinflated head. I stepped away, leaving him at the ice creams as I slid over to the sherbets.

"Hey, they've got Died and Gone to Heaven Mocha Almond Fudge Ripple," he announced. "You've got to try it. It could 'mocha' believer out of Madalyn Murray O'Hair. Hah!" He grinned at me.

I stepped a bit farther away and asked for one scoop of plain vanilla.

When we sat down, both of us facing forward, I divided my attention between a paranoid scrutiny of the door and our feet: a pair of pink huaraches with a set of slightly pigeon-toed charcoal Hush Puppies trying to close in on them.

As I slurped and stared at the door, he asked me softly spoken questions about myself: what I did, where I did it.

"That's where I recognize your name." He pointed two scoops of Died and Gone to Heaven at me. "The *Grackle*. I read the *Grackle* every week."

"It only comes out every other week."

"You're right, it does. Good publication. Do you like your work? Photography?"

"I like not having to go into an office. Yeah, sometimes I like it a lot. When the assignments are interesting."

"Do you think you'll stay in photography for a long time? I mean, is it a life's calling?"

"A life's calling? I don't know."

This was a change for me. Trout and I were always talking, but what we always talked about was Trout. Or the *Grackle*. Usually Trout as he related *to* the *Grackle*. I take the measure of his self-absorption from the time when I rushed, panic-stricken, into his office, closed the door, and told him I'd found a lump in my armpit. He looked at me, glad I'd brought the subject up, and said, "Yeah, I've got this thing right here." At which point, he rooted through his hair, waved me over, and put my fingertip on his own lump. It turned out to be a sebaceous cyst. Mine turned out to be an ingrown hair.

Trout's was not the first one-way conversational path I'd traveled. I didn't want to contemplate the number of times I'd returned home from dates and the guy would have been hard pressed to come up with my last name. First, in some cases.

So it was kind of nice to have the spotlight flit briefly across my existence. Also unnerving. I wasn't used to filling so much dead air time. I told the Wisp that, yes, I did have some reservations about my career field, but he kept pressing me for details. I shrugged off his inquiries. I honestly didn't know what I wanted to be doing. About halfway through my cone, his third degree started making me feel mildly claustrophobic. Also, I couldn't be sure, but I sensed pulses of light blinking out from the Hush Puppies. Every time the door opened, I jumped, certain that it was Trout.

"Do you think it's just the money or are you unhappy with the whole field?" he was asking when the door opened. It wasn't Trout, but it might just as well have been.

It was Chuy, the keyboard player in Trout's current favorite group, the Ton Ton Macoutes. He weighed about 300 pounds and considered ice cream to be proof of a loving god. He was probably only stopping off here to gather sustenance for the trip onward to a designer ice-cream shop.

I hunched over quickly so he couldn't see my face. I could already hear Chuy telling Trout that he'd seen me at Baskin-Robbins with "this geeky dude in funny chews."

"What's wrong?" The Wisp doubled over too so that he could snake around and look up into my hidden face. I grabbed my elbows, my arms guarding my stomach. "I'd better go." I tried to sound ashen-faced and trembly with some vaguely gynecological complaint. The Wisp helped me to my feet, then held the door for me.

Back at 4310 Rear, he helped me onto the couch, a formerly white piece of furniture that I'd gotten at a garage sale which now resembled an especially unfastidious polar bear.

"Nice place," he said glancing around at my rat hole. I clutched my sides, and he gestured beseechingly with his hands as if playing an accordion. "Can I get you anything?"

I waved a feeble negative.

"I guess I should just mosey on, huh? I know Lizzie used to like to be alone at these, you know, times." I nodded and he backed out toward the door, still playing the accordion. "Hope you get to feeling better real quick."

I nodded, pretending to be too racked with pain to speak.

The last thing he said was, "Don't let anything cramp your style. Hah!"

8

Later that evening, tired of pretending I wasn't waiting for Trout to call, I headed over to the *Grackle* office. I dug through Trout's desk until I found the key to the darkroom. We had an unofficial agreement: he could cheat me and I could steal darkroom time from him. It didn't really work for either of us.

I forgot all about Trout once I was in the darkroom. Running negatives has a soothing effect on me. It's like cooking with a recipe you know by heart. The lack of variables calms me. Particularly calming is rocking the stainless steel canisters, sloshing the developing solution over the negatives. Over time I've worked out my own special motion, back and forth with wrist swoops. I'm convinced it brings in those luminous blacks photogs crave, without any untoward grain problems. On the other hand, it could be an anal-compulsive flourish contributing nothing other than a marked wrist flexibility.

I peeked at the negs before I dumped them into the foaming column of the film washer. I couldn't really tell much until I got a loop on them. Still, I felt the little clutch I get when I gaze upon a perfectly exposed negative. That clutch is nearly as accurate as a spectrophotometer. I stared at the tiny squares for a few minutes, squinting at Lizzie and Juanita, their faces gray, their grins a ghoulish black.

It was late by the time I finished. I left the negatives hanging up to dry and went home. As soon as I was back outside the antsiness I'd been staving off jumped right back on me. I tried to think of this edgy, wound-up feeling as a bargain, one that Trout, for instance, spent a lot of money to achieve. I couldn't understand why anyone would seek out this sensation. It just made me want to press my palms together in rigid isometrics and shriek loudly. Instead I cruised over to El Azteca for Tex-Mex, my preferred comfort food and one guaranteed to add needed ballast.

A couple of carne asada tacos, some refritos, and a pineapple sherbet later, I felt a bit more grounded. Probably not enough to face Club Ennui. But then again, very little that is legal can prepare anyone for Club Ennui. I hold *Interview* magazine responsible for its existence. It introduced impressionable young Texans to the concept of jadedness and left them with the idea that such a state is to be desired. Here kids who grew up in homes with sprinkler systems came to slouch about looking anemic while wearing sleeveless black turtlenecks. Sunday was always a big night at the Ennui because the Ton Ton Macoutes played.

Since the tacos had pretty much exhausted my capital, it was fortunate that I pulled up just as the Macoutes were trailing out for a break. Trout was sure to be birddogging them, so I wouldn't have to pay the cover.

It was easy for me to spot him in the maroon silk bathrobe with the gold paisley lining that I'd found at St. Vincent's swirling over his pants. A white cravat wound around his throat made him look like a doomed aristocrat. A pair of pointy-toed patent leather shoes made him look like a doomed toupee stylist. But on the whole he came off moderately swoony. A gaggle of the dreaded pastel belles

was forming about his person. The 88's trademark death
rattle caught Trout's attention before they could descend.

"Pretty woman," he sang, sauntering over. He threw in a
Roy Orbison gargle growl to punctuate the greeting, then
swept me into a theatrical embrace. A muted sigh went up
from the belles as Trout pressed his lips against mine. They
might not have been quite so vaporous if they could have
heard Trout whisper in my ear, "Whew, you smell like Enchilada Day at the school cafeteria," before he returned me
to my full and upright position.

"Oh, sorry. El Azteca."

"I guess." His eyes roamed toward the gaggle as he slunk
down, leaning against the 88.

"Have you talked to Smeeks yet about the music
awards?" I referred to the Lone Star Music Awards, a plum
assignment I had requested. "Trout?" I prodded, attempting
to recapture his attention, which had snagged on a bottle
blonde sporting the Glasgow waif look, which combined a
knitted tam and much hair falling forward into her eyes
with a pair of shoes that in years gone by were mostly associated with a failure to vaccinate for polio.

"Um, haven't quite got around to it." The waif sauntered
back inside and Trout made actual eye contact with me.
"Come here, baby," he growled at me. "I'm a crawling king
snake, baby, and I rule my den. If you got anything I want,
I'm gonna crawl right in." With that he slithered on over
and coiled about me. Blues Boy Treadwell was channeling
again.

"You ever seed peaches growin' on a sweet 'tater vine?"
In these moods he was much given to the gumbo-fed
double entendre accompanied by throaty chuckles. He
pulled me to him so that I might enjoy the feel of his nether
parts being ground soulfully into me.

Something about Trout's blues persona brought the English governess out in me. "No," I replied. "I don't believe I

have ever seen actual peaches growing on a sweet potato vine."

He chuckled meaningfully, as if my peaches had clamored for his sweet potato vine. "Ooh, dog me, mama! You can't get her when you want her; you got to catch her when you can! Low-*down* woman!"

"Hm-m-m, indeed."

Humid, unhealthy air exhaled from Club Ennui, carrying with it clumps of wobbly girls in mini-skirts followed by skinny guys with an inadequate grasp of the fundamentals of dental hygiene. A sudden pulse of music throbbed, three chords of the soaring variety. Trout straightened up.

"Oo-wee, gots to work now, shoogah. Turn on yo' love light, the midnight crawler be slidin' by. Mmmm-mmmm! Hitch me to your buggy, mama, drive me like a mule."

"What an enticing invitation," I said primly. "I guess this means you're coming by later?"

"Mmmm-mmm-mm. The King Bee gonna buzz roun' yo' hive, honey. Good God!" With that, Trout gave me a sleepy-eyed look meant to be sensually devastating and shuffled off, back into the fray. In spite of the fact that he came off looking more like a mental patient who'd doubled up on his Thorazine, I wanted him to come over. I stayed up late waiting, but he never showed.

The next day I was well into Day Two of the Home Spa Weekend when the phone rang. As Day Two involved soaking one's hands in a mix of warm olive oil and crushed rosemary leaves, I had to knock the phone off the hook with my nose, then lie down on the floor next to it to speak.

"Gretchen? Hi, it's me, Gus Kubiak. Remember? You feeling any better?"

Just in time I remembered my "female trouble" and told him that symptoms had subsided. As he spoke, I straightened up, lifted my hands from the oil, and let them drain. All the while Gus's tiny voice peeped on. By the time I'd toweled off my hands and picked up the receiver again, Gus was asking, "Well? Gretchen, are you there?" I thought of his soft voice coming out of his big, soft-looking head. "Can you make it?"

"Oh, excuse me, a plane just went over, I didn't hear what you said."

"Um, Lionel Ritchie's playing Saturday at the Erwin Center. Interested?"

Lionel Ritchie? How do I loath thee? Let me count the ways. "Oh, gosh, my parents'll be in town then."

"Hey, bring 'em along, I'll get extra tickets. Ritchie's for the whole family."

For a second I hesitated, almost taken in by his exuberance. Then I imagined Trout seeing me enter a Lionel Ritchie concert. Escorted by Tweetie Pie.

"Oh, thanks, but they're Church of Christ."

"No suggestive lyrics, I've checked him out."

"Naw, I don't think so."

"Let's just scratch Ritchie then and all go out to eat. Threadgill's or the County Line. Parents love those places."

It was a cozy image: me, my parents, and Gus Kubiak all gathered around a checkered tablecloth stacked high with platters of ribs and brisket. Cole slaw and pinto beans. My parents would adore Gus Kubiak, my mother in particular. One look at the Hush Puppies and my mom would be calling caterers. Great, so let *her* date him.

I stretched out of the chair and rapped loudly on the wooden floor. "Oh, shoot, there's someone at the door. I better go."

"Yeah, okay, 'nother time."

♥   ♥

The birds were chirping the next morning by the time I finally admitted that, once again, Trout wasn't going to show up. I wanted desperately not to care. The last woman to carry off waiting for a man in a stylish manner was Penelope, and at least she'd had something to keep her hands occupied. I'd had to make do with warm olive oil with rosemary leaves crushed into it. My palms were soft as bread dough and no one had appreciated the fact.

If it hadn't been for those perfectly exposed negatives waiting for me, I might never had gotten out of bed that morning. I was in the bathroom, still dripping from a shower and pulling on my tattered terry-cloth robe, when I heard a knock at the door. Trout. I dropped the robe and wrapped a towel about the size of a washcloth around myself instead. After pinching my cheeks, I quickly spritzed myself with perfume. Too late I noticed it had gone bad and I now smelled like DDT. I stepped out, flung the door open, and there was Lizzie.

I crouched over, trying to minimize the number of exposed acres of flesh. "Lizzie. Hi. Come on in. Just got out of the shower."

She touched the scrap of terry cloth I clutched. "We had those exact same kind of towels when we were first married. Practically water repellent, right?"

"Be with you in one second." I backed into the bathroom and grabbed my nightgown.

Back in the living room, Lizzie had her fuzzy head cocked to the side and was reading the titles on my bookshelf. She finished perusing my Jacqueline Susann collection, looked up, and sniffed. "Gretchen, are you cooking something?"

"I think I did a little toast a couple of days ago."

"Hm-m-m. For a moment I thought I smelled Mitchell's Poulet Provençal." She sniffed audibly. "Yes, olive oil and rosemary and an undertone of something else." I didn't mention the DDT.

I came out dressed in shorts and a camp shirt.

"I'm glad I didn't wake you up. Usually when I visit people this early they're asleep. But then I remembered you're an insomniac like me."

"Under normal circumstances, I *would* be asleep at . . ."—

I turned Lizzie's wrist so that I could read the face of her digital watch—"six thirty-eight."

"So why are you up?" Lizzie plunked herself down in the spindly-legged fifties chair I'd gotten from Goodwill.

I sagged onto the couch. Knowing what time it was made me tired. "I was up all night waiting for someone."

"You mean, someone male?"

I nodded an admission.

"Gretch, you deserve someone nice."

"Don't we all. That's why romance novels are so popular. They're the only way left to spend an evening with a decent guy."

"Now that's not true. The world is teeming with fine men."

"Teeming? Uh, Lizzie, I think you've been out of action too long. There's a lot of algae in today's candidate pool."

"What about Gus Kubiak?" Her eyes twinkled. I was coming to fear twinkling. "He's pretty dreamy."

I didn't know what to say. If she considered a hatchling in Hush Puppies to be dreamy, we were clearly working from irreconcilably different frames of reference. "He seems like a very sweet guy."

"Uh-*huh.*" Her watch beeped. "Oops, I'd better be running along. Mitchell will be feeding Annabelle quenelles for breakfast if I'm not there to intervene." She paused at the door and did an unconvincing imitation of sudden inspiration. "Gretchen! I have it! How about coming by for dinner tonight?"

"Gosh, I'd really love to, but I'm going to have to be in the lab till late tonight. Maybe some other time. I'd love to meet Mitchell and—"

"You mentioned something about a Q and A?" She meant the interview I'd asked her for. "What better place to conduct it than in my home? Beard the lion in her den, so to speak." Lizzie's expression of eager indomitability froze my usually prolific excuse-making apparatus. Besides, I was getting tired of my usual Cup-a-Soup with cheese toast.

"Sure. Yeah. That'd be great."

Lizzie was delighted. She gave me directions, told me to appear around seven, hopped into her forest-green Volvo station wagon, and drove off. I knew without being told that Brother Wisp was sure to be in attendance.

I went back to bed, put a pillow over my head to muffle the psychopathic squawks of the crazed grackles outside my window, and slept for a few hours.

♥   ♥

"Gretchen!" Irma sang out from her cell as I passed her door at the *Grackle* late that morning. "How was that romance thing?"

I couldn't clear my head. Her voice seemed to come from a long way off. I felt like an invalid on her first day out of bed. The light was too bright and everyone too energetic. "Good, actually. Kind of surprising."

Irma nodded, and the thin gold rings looping up along the side of her right ear tinkled. As she started to tell me about her weekend, a conversation behind me caught my attention.

"Oh, Trout's an okay guy really. It's just that his work has no context."

"And no wit. I mean, I really like him personally too. A bit self-destructive, but aren't we all? But you're right. The time is passed when you could write about music in Austin as if it were occurring in a vacuum."

I recognized the voices of two *Grackle* stringers, Jeremy Mapes and Larry Esler, frustrated critics. Like sharks, every *Grackle* columnist had a school of remoras nibbling at him. The *Grackle* columnists in turn sniped at *River City* writers, Austin's uptown monthly publication. The writers there talked about what a pathetic travesty *Texas Monthly* had become. No doubt writers there slagged Tom Wolfe, and so on right up the writing chain. I was certain some writer some-where was confiding that, in his opinion, Moses could have benefited from heavier editing on the tablets.

"There you are." Trout careened down the hall. He swept me away with him as he hurtled past and deposited me in his office. He had definitely replaced the Mississippi mud in his veins for something considerably speedier. I wanted to ask him where he had been last night but chose instead to pretend I hadn't noticed his failure to appear. I wondered if he'd gone to Glasgow. "Luvboree, Luvboree, Luvboree. Where's the stuff?"

"I left the negatives drying. I was just getting ready to go in and print."

Trout jumped up out of his chair. "Well, let's not malin-ger." He shooed me away with his hands. "Scoot, scoot, scoot."

Before I scot, I caught a glimpse of an envelope with my name on it. Actually, my name had been crossed out and Darci Hollister's written in. The return address was the Lone Star Music Awards. I grabbed for it. "Why does this have Darci's name on it?"

"Look, this is not my idea. I am only part owner of this rag. I know everyone hears Trout Treadwell and they go 'Media Baron,' but I don't run this show. Dennis has veto power."

"And Dennis wants Darci for the awards."

"In the strongest way possible."

"And you didn't mention that you'd already promised the awards to me?"

"Look, kid, you've got my vote, but I can't override Smeeks. He's an original investor."

I was stunned by Trout's, by Smeeks's, ingratitude. The one assignment I'd ever asked for. After all I'd done for them.

"Thanks, Trout, thanks a lot. Give me the key to the darkroom." Trout knew I was too furious for his usual arguments and attempts to deduct an hourly rate from what he owed me.

I stamped off to my sanctuary. Nothing and no one could touch me once I was inside my dark womb. I reached the door that I'd fixed up myself with light baffles around the frame. I turned the knob and threw on the light. In my haste it took me a few seconds to notice Darci and Dennis frozen there in the sudden burst of illumination in a posture reminiscent of the historical pelvic exam.

"Oh, gosh." I gulped. As I turned to flee, I noticed something more urgent than embarrassment. "Darci! You're on my negatives!" And indeed, her tiny but taut body was strewn in wild abandon across my drying negs.

Darci stood, attempting to disentangle herself from the strips of film curling about her like kelp on a mermaid. As they dressed, I checked for damage from bodily fluids, then shut and locked the door behind them.

Only a set of truly great negs could have helped me out of the slough of raging despair I'd fallen into, and luckily I had them. I slid the first one into the carrier, gave it a blast of canned air to chase away dust, and popped it into the enlarger. The shadow image cast by the enlarger light fell across the easel.

I focused the light until the flounces on the dresses of two hugging writers were crisp, turned off the enlarger, slipped a sheet of paper onto the easel, and exposed it. All the ambient chatter came back to me as I slid the exposed piece of paper into the developer bath, then rocked it like a baby. It was always at that point, when the image first began to appear, that my subjects started talking to me. These rectangles of gray called up a Greek chorus of ghostly echoes in my mind.

"Oh, Nancy," I heard a writer shriek again, "I loved your last Moonstruck. I cried. Lord, I cried. Ed told me if I didn't quit I'd curl the wallpaper."

"Your characters in *Passion's Avalanche* were your best ever,

Eve. I mean to tell you, I was ready to run away with that Forrest."

Even the onlookers in the photo's background behind the huggers found voices with which to whisper to me in the darkroom.

"That's Aubergine O'Donohue."

"Passion Storm? I love that book."

"Her *Angel's Rhapsody* is even better. That's the one where the hero, Fletcher, goes off on a whaling expedition and his wife, Rue, gets told that he died off the Cape of Good Hope, so she remarries—"

"Ooh, I hope she's working on another one."

"Me too. Have you heard back yet about your proposal for *Destiny?"*

"The big thanks-but-no-thanks."

"No! Those fools. Editors keep talking about breaking out of the cliché formulas. Then, when you actually send them something a bit different—"

"Really. You read articles all the time about men who are just physically too well endowed. It's a genuine problem when—"

"And the thing is, you treated it so tastefully. You should send it to Chandelier, you really should."

"That's an idea."

The voices, girlish, animated, crowded in. They carried the pitch and cadences of other voices I hadn't heard for a long time. My seventh-grade friend Betsy's voice excited about our science fair project, three spindly bean plants grown under different-color light bulbs. Claudette's as she told me to quit jerking my eyelid or she'd put the mascara wand into my eye and I'd never get to find out what I looked like with visible lashes. Donna announcing the name of the design empire we were founding together. Donchen Fashions, or, okay, if I was going to be *that* way about it, Gretchna Fashions. The women at the Luvboree reminded me of that earlier time, a time before sisterhood became earnest, self-conscious. Before it stopped being just a lot of fun.

I heard Juanita's phlegmy crackle again when I slid her portrait into the developer. Lizzie's giggle tittered in my head when she peered up at me through the foaming ripples of the print washer. Even Cari's laughter seemed less artificial as I trotted her augmented features through the trays.

During the hundreds of hours I've spent in darkrooms, I've streamlined my technique so there's no wasted time or motion. Normally, I expose batches of prints, then soup them en masse. With the Luvboree, however, I found myself lingering over each print, reluctant to dry them and hand them over to Trout. I wasn't so sure anymore about the words I wanted to accompany the pictures. I was losing my motif. The more I stared at the women's faces, the less they looked like wildcatters or anything else I'd assumed they would be. They especially did not look like Arbus freaks. They looked like my friends.

Trout pounded on the door, startling me out of my reverie. "Gretchen! You fall in?"

"What! I'm working."

"Irma needs the Luvboree prints. We gotta start laying them out if they're gonna run next ish."

I panicked. I was no longer sure I wanted to surrender the photos of my friends to Trout.

"Gretchen, you okay?"

"Be right there." What had I been thinking of? I'd shot these photos to be printed. That was what I did, take pictures for publication. Half an hour later I handed the Luvboree women, still hot from the print dryer, over to Trout. He dug into them greedily.

"You nailed it, babe. Congratulations." Before I had a chance to do any basking, Trout continued. "You really caught it, didn't you?" He plucked out Lizzie's happy chipmunk face. "The empty lives. The yearning for Hollywood dreams they can never have. The cooption of ambition into soap opera fantasies."

"Trout, you're kidding. That's Lizzie. She reads medieval Provençal. She—"

"These are just too outré." Ignoring me, Trout started culling out prints. They alarmed me. He was zeroing in on the few freak shots I'd taken when I'd first gotten to the convention, before Juanita and Lizzie had educated me.

"Trout, wait, can't you see beyond the stereotypes? These are real human beings populating the pink ghetto. They support each other like no other writers I've ever known. They're bright, they're resourceful. What right do we have to condescend to them because they dare to keep the dream alive that a woman can find a man who will love her?" My defense of the flounced *Frauen* surprised me more than it did Trout.

He paused and looked up at me. "You know, Gretchen, I think you've really got something to say here. I think you've got a life-affirming message about the precious thing these women are doing. And I think you should probably try publishing it in *Guideposts.*" He pulled out a shot of Lizzie looking especially avian and fuzzy next to the gyno exam cover. "Oh, Arbusesque!"

I was reaching out to rip the print from Trout's hand when Dennis barged in, cutting in front of me. He walked around and jerked open the top drawer of Trout's desk.

"Hey, thanks, guy," Trout snarled as the drawer caught him in the stomach. "A couple inches lower and you'd have ended the Treadwell line."

"Sorry." Dennis dug out the ledger-sized company checkbook. Balancing it on his knee, he filled one out and ripped it from the book. The sound of money on the loose lured Darci in. Dennis handed her the check.

"Smeeks," Trout wailed, but his partner, paramour in tow, kept on walking. Trout sighed and scooted back in his swivel chair to replace the checkbook. As I watched it sliding back into the drawer, panic overtook my urgent need to correct Trout's misconceptions about the Luvboree ladies.

"Uh, let's not be too hasty," I trilled, dunning Trout in the cutest way imaginable.

In spite of cute, Trout slammed the drawer shut. "Sorry. There's no way this month."

"No way?" I didn't understand. First the Music Awards were snatched away from me, now this. "No way to pay me?" A sense of unreality clouded my vision when Trout nodded affirmatively. "Darci just got money. Why can't I have money?"

"Exactly *because* Darci just got money. That check cleaned out operating capital until the middle of next month. This has been the tightest time yet. Everything hit at once. All I get all day is writers snarling at me. It's been extremely stressful. The worst of it is, none of them believes me. That's what really hurts. I can feel my colon twitching right now. Even as we speak. . . ."

Trout went on, but something was happening to me. Maybe hearing the same words so often had rendered them mildly hypnotic. Maybe I decided I couldn't stand by and let him turn Lizzie, Juanita, and the Luvboree into a sideshow. I don't know. Whatever it was, instead of listening to Trout's heartrending tale of publishing penury, numbers began parading through my mind. Luscious, seductive, bewitching numbers.

I vaguely noticed that the veins in Trout's neck were swelling and that his blathering had a cocaine compulsiveness to it. I noticed, but didn't particularly care. Didn't care that my editor and erstwhile boyfriend had already that day probably snorted up several times what he owed me. My attention was riveted by the numbers whispering through my brain. Those numbers were $4.95 cover price times 7 percent times 250,000. I scratched the numbers Andrea had divulged onto Trout's blotter and started multiplying.

"Seventy-eight thousand, seven hundred and fifty dollars?" I could barely believe the figure even as I muttered it aloud. "God, even if it's only half, a tenth, of that!"

"Gretchen." Trout was unnerved by hearing someone other than himself carrying on incoherent monologues. "Gretchen. You okay?"

I was too busy juggling decimal points to answer.

"Look, I can let you have twenty . . . twenty-five dollars right from the emergency reserve."

"Hay-*soos!* Even one tenth is still—what? Almost eight thousand. I could *do* things with eight thousand."

"Okay, fifty. But don't tell anyone else that you got anything. It'll start a run. Promise?"

Trout, a pen poised over the open checkbook, had to ask "Promise?" a couple more times before I could free up enough synapses to agree. He made out the check and I distractedly stuffed it into my pocket, then gathered up the prints scattered across Trout's desk.

"Gretchen, wake up. What are you doing?"

"Oh, I'm taking these. Our vision of the Luvboree women is in direct conflict." It's not often in life that the right thing is also the financially expedient one. I enjoyed the novelty.

Trout was puzzled. "Taking them? No, Gretchen, you just sold them to me. Leave the prints here. Go home. Lie down. Is this some premenstrual thing?"

I continued gathering up the prints. I was still uncertain about exactly how I felt re the romance novel, but I was sure of one thing: "This is no freak show."

As I left the office, Trout was still calling my name, in what, for him, would pass for a concerned tone. But he was becoming harder to hear all the time. My mind was racing after a receding image: a customized license plate on the back of a periwinkle Mercedes, the letters spelling out CAMEO.

9

I went directly from Trout's office to the library. My branch librarian and I had built up a cordial, if distant, relationship over the years. She'd monitored my progress through John Updike and V. S. Naipaul, Joyce Carol Oates and John Barth, nourishing writers whom I checked out in the same way I bought vegetables, then let them wither untouched. For my part, I'd kept up with how often the librarian had lipstick on her teeth. It was hard going since she didn't smile much. I couldn't bring myself to ask her where they kept the Cameo Romances.

Instead, I wandered around the small library for half an hour, searching first the card catalog, then the shelves. Finally, in a hidden alcove, shielded from the view of innocent schoolchildren writing reports on marsupials, I found a carousel of heavily embossed and foiled paperbacks. I plucked out every book that looked like a box of drugstore chocolates, for that was Cameo's motif, heavy on the red foil hearts.

At the precise moment that I approached the checkout counter, a tall middle-aged woman with a Dutch-boy hair-

counter, a tall middle-aged woman with a Dutch-boy hair-cut, half-moon glasses, and an air of the podium about her headed for it. A good candidate for president of the local NOW chapter, I decided. Arguments about romance novels being housewives' porn and all pornography being violence against women flashed through my mind. I clasped the Cameos to my breast, hiding the covers, and scurried back to the hardcover fiction shelves, where I grabbed a few worthy selections to use as camouflage.

When I returned, the NOW president was waiting with noticeable peeve at the counter while the librarian waved hurry-up gestures at her balky computer terminal.

"I'll take you over here." The librarian scooted her rolling stool over to another terminal while the first terminal worked on whatever task it was performing for the NOW president. Probably a hit list of romance borrowers.

"Uh . . . ," I stammered. I stepped up and held out my stack of books. The ringers were on top.

"Gee, I hope this one's as good as her last," I commented loudly in the direction of the NOW president as the librarian ran her computer wand across Doris Lessing's latest. "Just couldn't resist an old friend," I chuckled when she hefted *The Second Sex* off my stack.

I didn't expect the librarian to invite me to her Great Books discussion group when she hit the first Cameo, but I didn't expect her to stop dead either—to perch the glasses hanging on a chain around her neck on her nose and peer down at *Love's Reckless Bounty*. But that's just what she did. Then she held the book up so that the president could see the candy-box cover. The straining breasts. The priapic, predatory male. The stunned, languishing heroine. The president, a look of morbid fascination on her intelligent face, leaned in for a closer look.

"For my niece. Angeline. Angeline Cleeb," I explained.

Half a menstrual cycle later, the librarian spoke. "I didn't know Serena Lyndell had switched to Cameo."

"Oh, Betty," the president said, "I told you that last August when she had the lead title."

"That's right, that's right. I keep getting her mixed up with Lynda Serynda."

"Well, just remember this." The president stepped past me and held out a book from her pile. Its cover featured a rugged cowboy flicking the head off a rattler with a bull whip while a settler woman, her blouse torn from her heaving bosom, cowered behind him. "Lynda Serynda writes for Vinegaroon as Wade Gamble."

"Okay." The librarian plucked a pencil from the bundle of her wiry hair and made a note. "Lynda Serynda is Wade Gamble, and Serena Lyndell writes for Cameo. Got it." She reached for my next selection. It wasn't a Cameo. I'd found one of Lizzie's books *Destiny's Desire,* "a tale of a noble lady's passion for a Tatar prince set against the sweep of the 12th-century Mongol invasion of Europe."

"Oh, I love her!" The woman in the half-moon glasses swooned. I'd stopped thinking of her as a feminist queenpin. "Not only can she really tell a story, she's the only one of the historical gals who gets her facts straight." She looked at me and said apologetically, "I guess I'm a stickler, but that's what thirty years of teaching history will do to you."

A nice clubby feeling had sprung up between all us johnray readers, which made me remark casually, "Yeah, Lizzie is a real demon on accuracy."

"You call her Lizzie! Hardly anyone knows her real name. I heard from a friend of a friend of the hygienist that cleans her teeth that she lives right here in Austin."

"She does," I affirmed.

"You *know* Viveca Lamoureaux?" She reacted as if I'd claimed acquaintanceship with the Queen Mother. "What's she like? You know, in person."

Like an ostrich with a Fulbright? "She's really nice. Really smart."

"Well, tell her hello from a fan."

"From two fans," the librarian added, stamping due dates in the rest of the romances.

"I will," I promised, gathering up the pile of books the librarian slid my way, my library card on top of the stack. "We're having dinner together tonight." I waved a gracious good-bye at the door.

♥   ♥

The Bel-Air station wagon was outside 4310 Rear when I got home and my bedroom screen was off the window, which could only mean that Trout had come calling. My heart leaped. I told it to calm down and stop leaping for individuals of a clearly deficient moral character who failed to show up for assignations. I managed to stay pissed off for about five seconds, and then the leaping started up again with a slam-dunk fervor I couldn't control. Still, I talked myself into a state of moderate dudgeon and would have given Trout the verbal lashing I hadn't been able to give him at the office, except that I found him curled up like Goldilocks asleep on my bed.

He opened his eyes, smiled, and informed me, "Mama, tell yo' little dog yo' big dog's home."

"Trout," I had to remind him, "you're the one with the kennel."

He gave me his bluesman chuckle. Besides Antone's and various chemical additives, the other mood alterer that could effect this transformation was lust. "Rock me, baby," he suggested. "Rock me like my back ain't got no bone." For the moment, he seemed to have forgotten my abduction of the Luvboree women. He moved over and held up the covers for me. Of course he was naked. Of course I joined him.

We "rocked" and snoozed until twilight, when Trout left. Twilight in songs is hazy violet; in reality it can frequently be scummy gray. As I lay in bed oozing a puddle of bodily fluids and diaphragm jelly, my whole life started to seem like one gigantic wet spot. I was working into a deeply satisfying melancholy when I remembered Lizzie's dinner party.

I have to admit that, on a list containing: clean the baseboards, weep while reading five-year-old love letters, or go to dinner at home of happily married couple, dinner would have come in a distant third that particular night. Still, I'd given my word. And since honoring commitments is the only thing that separates me from the Trouts of the world, the ants from the grasshoppers, the drudges from those who have fun, I peeled myself off the sheets and headed for the shower.

♥   ♥

Lizzie's house in affluent Northwest Hills was a lot like Lizzie herself, cheerfully chaotic. An old power lawn mower lay disassembled on newspapers on the living room floor. "Mitchell is modifying it," Lizzie explained as we hopscotched through the wreckage to the kitchen. "He's been experimenting for years with methane. He wants to design a mower that kills its own fuel. Great idea, huh?"

I had to admit that I'd never heard of anything quite like it.

Every inch of counter space in the kitchen was occupied by dirty dishes, bottles of brown sauces with Chinese writing on them, cleavers the size of axes, and leathery bits of withered fruits, roots, and fungi. The air was peppery with the smell of various chiles of a lethal minuteness sizzling in hot sesame seed oil.

The husband, Mitchell, stood at the stove, a wok balanced over a flaming burner, whisking rondelles of garlic around in the popping sesame seed oil. He was a chunky fellow with meaty calves who looked as if he'd be fierce in a pickup basketball game, making up in spirit what he lacked in height. He didn't turn around when we entered, merely put his hand behind his back and snapped his fingers. Lizzie fluttered frantically over the debris before settling on a bowl of snow peas cut on the diagonal. She put the bowl into Mitchell's hand. He brought it around, inspected the contents, rejected them, reached his hand behind him, and snapped again. Lizzie fluttered and came up this time with a bowl of ginger slices. Mitchell accepted the offering and dumped them into the hot oil. Their spicy orchidlike odor filled the air.

"Mitchell, Gretchen is here!"

"Hel-lo, Gret-chen!" Mitchell called heartily into the wok. "Nice to meet you!"

"When Mitchell does one of his productions, I just act as scullery help," Lizzie explained proudly. She had bits of carrot peelings stuck in her hair, and her glasses were speckled with oil spatters. As Mitchell stuck his hand out and started snapping again, Lizzie's two-year-old Annabelle toddled in on spastic baby steps. Her chubby face was streaked with black grease from the lawn-mower bolt she gripped in her hand.

Lizzie handed bowls of chopped vegetables to Mitchell with one hand and grabbed for a paper towel with the other. "No, no, Piglet, we don't put Daddy's lawn-mower parts in our mouth." She slipped her fingers into her daughter's mouth to retrieve the bolt. "What has Mommy told you about putting mineral oil compounds in our mouth? They dissolve our oil-soluble vitamins, which means vitamin deficiency and disease." To me, she added, "I like to acquaint her with the consequences of her actions."

"You like to have her in a state of permanent paranoid anxiety," Mitchell corrected. Lizzie held up a clawed hand and menaced his back with it until her daughter caught her attention.

"Guh," Annabelle said. Lizzie immediately dropped to her knees in front of the little girl.

"Good? Did you say 'good'?" Lizzie pronounced the word slowly.

"Guh," Annabelle repeated.

"She's not verbalizing yet." Mitchell looked over his shoulder to explain to me. "She's twenty-six months old and has yet to say one complete word."

"She does so." Lizzie contradicted her husband, who'd turned back to his popping oil.

"Forgive me. *One* word: 'un-kow.' Not mama. Not papa. Un-kow."

"Can I help it," Lizzie asked, "if she likes Gus?"

"Did I suggest that you'd programmed your daughter to speak only that one name and none other?" Mitchell asked, his voice rising with the question. "I'm not worried." He looked fondly down at his daughter. "When Piglet makes up her mind to speak, she'll speak. She doesn't have to be at the far right of every bell curve, does she? Does my little Piglet?"

"See?" Lizzie implored. "Bell curves. That's why she won't speak. You're oppressing her with all these Superbaby expectations."

"Superbaby? She's over two years old and she *grunts*. We should have named her *Clara*belle."

"Mitchell Ramsey Potts!" Lizzie picked up a cleaver and brandished it at her husband. "You are putting me in a mood to stick you like a pig with no more ado!"

Mitchell glanced over his shoulder at his wife slicing the air behind his kidneys and shrugged. "Hey, I wouldn't have talked either if my mother had terrified me about every possible disastrous thing that could befall me if—"

The doorbell rang. I offered instantaneously to answer it.

"Why, Gretch, you wretch!" Juanita whooped. She fell upon me, and I was engulfed me in the scent of True cigarettes and Adorn hair spray. A man in tan Sansabelts with a white Ban-Lon golf shirt tucked into them grinned and stuck a bear paw of a hand out to me. "Gretchen meet my escort, Garnell Foy. Garnell, this is Gretchen Griner, girl photographer."

Garnell looked to be in his mid-fifties. "Pleasure," he said, smiling and dipping his head at me. He took a seat in the living room. I joined him while Juanita went in to say hello to Lizzie. I asked Garnell if he worked outside or if he came by his sun-kissed complexion on the golf course.

"Little of both." He laughed, showing large teeth. "I'm Garnell Foy of Foy's Patio and Porch. Big operation out there on 290. Fifty acres of all-weather furniture. You know," he prompted, "we've got the golf carts with the striped surreys."

"Oh, yeah, right, right, I know the place," I lied. "Out on 290. Big operation."

Annabelle toddled over to him.

"That'd be the one." Garnell told me how PVC had pretty much revolutionized the business, rendering your wrought iron obsolete. He noticed too late that Annabelle had brought him a present. The bolt, slobbered with black grease and baby drool, sat on his knee. A dark puddle widened on his tan Sansabelts. As he handed the bolt back to Annabelle, Lizzie came in from the kitchen.

"Mitchell has asked me to announce that the first course is served." She gestured to the dining room, where Mitchell, his arms lost in kitchen mitts up to his elbows, entered bearing a steaming tureen.

"The Thai people call this soup Than Vo Chi, or Maiden's Treasure," Mitchell informed us after we'd sat down to doll-sized bowls of an almost clear liquid with a few sprigs of what appeared to be St. Augustine grass floating in it.

"Very tasty," Juanita commented. "Very light."

"You got the coriander undertone just right this time, darling," Lizzie said.

"Yes. I think the coriander-to-ginger ratio I'd been working with was skewed."

Annabelle, in a high chair next to Lizzie, slapped a chubby fist into her bowl of Maiden's Treasure. Lizzie took off her glasses and scraped away the grass clippings.

"Next is Cho Minh Haiya." Mitchell nodded to Lizzie, who bounded out to the kitchen.

"No preconceptions," Mitchell warned as Lizzie placed a platter of some clear, gelatinous substance on the table.

Biting into one of the pellucid bits was like chewing tears: a slight saltiness, then nothing. I looked over at Juanita and Garnell. Juanita was gamely chewing through her portion while Garnell poked at the springy mass. An unsettling suspicion began to form. It was the gritty crunch of sand between my teeth, however, that clinched it. "This isn't jellyfish, is it?"

"It is indeed. Good palate," Mitchell congratulated me. "You know what's missing?" he asked.

Real food? I wondered.

"Music." He jumped up and popped a cassette in. George Winston's aural water torture filled the room. Mitchell listened a moment, adjusted the treble and bass and a few dozen other levels, then turned George up until his relentless piano plunking sounded like paratroopers landing on the roof.

I really didn't think many more ways remained to dampen my appetite, but Lizzie had a "surprise" for me. She jerked up when a tapping at the door was dimly heard over the booming threnody. She and Juanita exchanged delighted glances; then they both looked at me before Lizzie scampered off to answer the door. I didn't have to hear Lizzie trill out, "Why, Gus-Busters! What a surprise!" to guess what the conspiracy was all about.

Gus Kubiak entered. He wore a navy blue knitted tie with a short-sleeve shirt. Sort of the Regional-Science-Fair-winner look.

"Un-kow!" Annabelle screamed from her high chair, holding her chubby arms up to the Wisp.

"Un-kow." Mitchell shook his head in mock exasperation as he joined Lizzie and Gus at the door. "Hey, dude!" Mitchell captured Gus's hand for a shake. "What died on your chest? Or is that a—? No! Not a tie? Last time I saw you in a tie was at our wedding. Isn't that right, Lizzie? As a matter of fact, there's some icing from the cake right there." Still gripping Gus's hand, Mitchell pointed with his left index finger to the tie. When Gus looked down, Mitchell pulled up his finger and bopped Gus's nose. "Gotcha!" Mitchell crowed.

Gus grinned sickly and looked to Lizzie, who looked to me. I looked to Annabelle, trying to pretend that Gus's tie had nothing to do with me. Lizzie shot her husband a warning look and jerked her head over to me.

Mitchell remained oblivious and brayed, "A tie, whuddya make cravat. Get it? Whuddya make *of that? Cravat?* A tie? Hah!"

I began to suspect that I had fallen into the clutches of some Goon International whose members, known to each other by their trademark bark of laughter, *Hah!,* came together to tell each other execrable puns and secure group discounts on the purchase of Hush Puppies.

Gus Kubiak followed Lizzie in. As he passed Annabelle, he bent down and blew a raspberry into her neck. She squealed with delight.

In the hubbub, Gus greeted me shyly, "Hi. You excited about your parents?"

I tried to make sense of this inquiry. It wasn't that I was *un*excited about my parents, though I did lack a certain passion on the subject. Just slightly before it was too late I remembered my alibi. "Oh. Yeah. You mean, them coming to visit. Oh, very excited."

Lizzie seated him next to me and slid a plate of jellyfish in front of him. Everyone stared at us until Lizzie launched into a spirited disquisition on her latest topic. "You won't believe what I found in the PLC today. The complete correspondence of Bishop Gregory of Tours writing about the marriage of Clovis in 496 to the Burgundian princess Clothilde!"

Throughout Lizzie's discourse on Bishop Gregory's reaction to the garish display of Christian pomp and pagan militarism, Garnell studied Gus. For his part, Gus was poking gelatinous blobs of jellyfish around on his plate, attempting to convey the impression that he was actually eating. "Boy howdy, you got one heck of a burn there," Garnell said.

"Actually, I haven't been out in the sun for months," Gus answered.

"Tanning boutique," Garnell decided. "I knew a feller oncet, fell asleep in one of them things. He shed his whole danged face like it was a snake's skin. I thought they rigged them up now so you couldn't scorch yourself."

"I suppose they do," Gus answered mildly, fussing with the napkin in his lap.

Lizzie, upset, looked over at Gus, then caught my eye and shot me an expression I couldn't translate. "Gus, did you finish it today?" she asked, her voice too loud in the sudden silence.

"Uh, not quite," Gus answered. "But I came up with a real neat algorhythm for determining bound water of formation based on neutron density curve and the gamma ray trace."

"Using Archie's equation?" Mitchell asked.

"No. I kind of played around with something of my own, and it actually worked."

"Gus's working on a well-logging program for the Kuwaiti government," Lizzie explained. She leaned in close to me and whispered, "Can you believe it? Something better than Archie's?"

"So, what? You going to retire now?" Mitchell teased. He looked at me and waggled a finger at Gus Kubiak. "This guy, this guy, King of Code. No one's faster, and I should know; I was the fastest until he came along." He turned to Gus. "Hey, dude, you ready yet to get out and fling a little friz?" Back to me. "Has he told you"—finger pointing to

Gus—"that we almost went to the world freestyle finals six years ago?"

"Well, not quite 'almost.'" Gus could have saved his modesty. I had no idea what Mitchell was talking about.

"Hey! I bungled the leg trap. I admit it," Mitchell announced bellicosely.

"I fumbled my share of maneuvers." Gus's tone was conciliatory. "The reverse stork?"

"Let's bring 'em back!" Mitchell announced. "Let's show these disc punks that the grand old men of Frisbee have still got the moves. Whuddya say?"

I assumed that this lively conversation had gone from computers to Frisbees. As Mitchell tried to talk Gus into "gitting the act back on the road," I slithered the jellyfish around on my plate. At one end of the table, talk about leg traps and reverse storks whizzed back and forth; at the other Garnell and Juanita started arguing under their breaths about whether Garnell could call himself a true Democrat. In between, Lizzie helped Annabelle spoon in her pureed apricots and talked about translation traps that had her wondering whether Clovis had brought 3,000 barbarian warriors to the wedding with him or 3,000 salted cod to offer as tribute.

Prickles along my spine made me turn to the picture window at my back. I could feel Trout watching me, his ankles deep in dwarf holly. But all I saw reflected back was a suburban dinner party with terrifying food, excruciating music, and incomprehensible conversation about Archie's equation and *leges barbarorum*. My life seemed to freeze in that reflection as if it would be stuck there forever in the suburbs of weirdo hell. The vision was too threatening. Suddenly the St. Augustine soup and marinated tears started to work on my knotted stomach.

"Excuse me." I bolted for the bathroom. It was blessedly quiet inside the small room. There was a window. I stared at it and thought about escape.

A few minutes later, Lizzie tapped on the door. "Gretchen, you okay in there?"

"Yeah, sure. Fine." I felt better the instant I no longer had to look at either a plate of flayed jellyfish or Gus's swollen face. I unlocked the door. Juanita hovered in the hall behind her. They both squeezed in.

"Was this an ill-starred notion?" Lizzie wondered.

I shrugged. It was nice to have someone care about my emotional well-being.

"I'll tell you one thing," Juanita said, flipping on the vent fan as she fired up a True. "That boy is nuts about you. I can see it in his eyes when he looks at you. He wants to make a pillow out of the leftover hair from your brush." She meant Gus.

"Oh, don't tell her that," Lizzie chided. "Women only want men they can't have unless the woman is quite extraordinary."

Lizzie was clearly giving me the opportunity to prove what an extraordinary individual I was now by grabbing for the brass ring that was her brother.

"I don't know, Liz-zardo," Juanita said. "You might just be a tad biased on the subject of your baby brother."

"Of course I'm biased. What with being several years older than Gus, and with Mother being gone so much to work on her anthrolinguistic description of the Kurdish language, and Father . . . well, Father is a physicist. Need I say more? He was always a bit baffled by people, and small people such as his children completely mystified him. So there was nothing for it but that I raise little Gus." She looked down at me. "You know how it is in academic families."

I nodded politely, although I had about as much knowledge of the way it was in academic families as Lizzie would of how to keep a bowling score, which was one pastime my family preferred to anthrolinguistics.

"Still, if I might offer an admittedly biased plug." Lizzie's eyes did their little twinkling thing. "Gus is wonderful. He adores Annabelle. Children in general. And"—more twinkling—"he is going to make buckets of loot on his program for the Kuwaitis."

"Listen, Lizzie," I said gently. "If I could program my emotions, I have no doubt that the smartest thing I could do would be to fall in love with a guy who likes kids and is going to make buckets of money. But I can't. The chemistry just is not there."

"Chemistry." Lizzie snorted.

"Chemistry." Juanita snorted. "Look where it got me." I didn't want to contemplate the prospect of chemistry between Garnell Foy and any friend of mine.

"And look where it's getting you," Lizzie put in. "Lonely nights of waiting while this Truitt person prowls the town."

"Trout. His name is Trout."

"Whatever, he's wrong for you," Lizzie declared with a surprising urgency. "He's wrong for any woman who's not trying to reprise Edith Piaf."

Juanita nodded her head into her wrinkled neck in agreement.

I sat on the lid of the commode and absorbed this judgment on my life. I stabbed a fingernail into the green-striated soap on the sink. This had not been the most terrific of days, and I wasn't in the most receptive of moods for a total personality critique. Ergo, I lashed out. "At least Trout doesn't look like someone tried to dry him in the microwave."

Lizzie and Juanita gasped. The air molecules that had been zipping around the crowded bathroom screeched to a dead halt. Everything froze. I noticed how assaultively crisp the smell of the mottled green soap was.

"I promised Gus I wouldn't mention this," Lizzie started off softly. Too softly. "But I'm going to. Gus was very sick for a long time. Acute myelogenous leukemia. He lost his hair, and his skin peeled off during chemotherapy. Then, when that didn't halt the disease, a bone marrow transplant was required. I was the donor. Unfortunately, he developed graft versus host disease. That nearly killed him. He survived and is now taking prednisone, a steroid. As you know, steroids suppress the immune system. Basically they lower body surveillance. That screws up the electrolyte balance, makes you retain salt and swell up, which is what has given Gus the characteristic Cushingoid features. But his platelet count is right where it should be." She beamed.

"God, leukemia." I felt sick again.

"It's okay, you didn't know. Besides, there have been some positive by-products. It made Gus realize he'd spent too many years chained to a computer terminal. He was looking for something to merit the return of his life, and he found it when he met you."

"Give me a break, Lizzie," I moaned. "All I did was have an ice-cream cone with the guy. I can't pay my rent. My editor cheats me. As my boyfriend he cheats *on* me. A midget is stealing all my assignments. Rats chew my soap. My wardrobe is freckled. All my magazines smell better than I do. Believe me, I'm not someone to merit the return of anyone's life."

"It was love at first sight," Lizzie continued undaunted. "He loved the way you sang 'Little Red Wing' with him."

"We *talked* a few verses. Neither one of us could remember the end. Every girl who went to camp learned 'Little Red Wing.' "

"I know. That's where I learned it and taught it to him. Who can explain these things? Perhaps you reminded him of Mother. Perhaps his electrolytes were out of whack that day. Perhaps he was simply ready and you were there. Who can explain love at first sight?"

"Look I'm really, really flattered that he liked me. I don't know if I believe in love at first sight. Okay, so maybe it can happen. Fine. But it didn't happen to me. I'm sorry if it happened to Gus, but I can't be responsible for his happiness. As you all've pointed out, I haven't been doing too great a job with mine."

"That's precisely why you and Gus would be so perfect together."

"Lizzie, I—"

Someone pounded on the door. "We're losing BTUs out here!" Mitchell bellowed.

"Oh, he's served the Loo Kao Win." Lizzie headed for the door. When I didn't move, she turned back to me. "Come on, it's Mitchell's special, pork liver in fermented black beans."

Lizzie left and Juanita stayed behind. "I'm sorry now I collaborated on this shindig. But, you know, Lizzie can be more convincing than a rock in a sock when she puts her mind to it. Downright compelling is what she is. She *is* right about one thing: adoration's nothing to sneer at."

When I didn't respond, Juanita put a comforting hand on my shoulder. "Ah, Gretch, I know exactly how you feel. I felt the same way when Ardell Pegram fixed me up with Edward Duchamps. Nicest boy in five counties, but the smell of his Vitalis hair oil turned me pea green. Life would be just so boring if we always did what was good for us, wouldn't it? 'Course, that Edward Duchamps did end up a millionaire. Still, if you can't stand the way they smell, it's just not worth sniffing around. Come on, let's go push some pig liver around our plates."

I told her I'd be right there, and she left me alone. I took a few deep breaths and stepped out into the dark hall. A light with Mickey Mouse as the sorcerer's apprentice painted on the shade was on in a toy-cluttered bedroom. As I walked down the hall to the living room, I could barely make out Gus's and Lizzie's voices; the George Winston pounding almost covered up the sound of the conversation. I would have veered off back into the dining room if I hadn't heard my name.

"A 'few minor mishaps'? How can you say that? This

whole evening has been a howling *nightmare* for Gretchen."
Gus's voice was different with Lizzie. The hesitant reediness
was gone.

"That's putting it a bit drastically. Romances that run
smooth from page one never last."

"Lizzie, you're talking about romance *novels.* I'm speaking
of real life here. Mine, to be exact."

"As am I."

"Lizzie, you have even less experience than I do in real-
life romance. You *married* your first date."

"Ah, the gods smiled. In your case, we will have to work
with them a bit more. All right, I'll admit it, we might have
gotten off to a rocky start, but I think a spark has been
ignited here tonight. A spark that, with a little judicious
fanning, will grow into an all-consuming, all-forgetting,
mutual *blaze* of passion."

"*You* have been reading too much Viveca Lamoureaux,
Liz-bo."

"No, no, trust me, I know my business."

"Okay, but quit meddling in mine, all right? I mean, you
told me Gretchen knew I was coming. She didn't know, and
she wasn't happy when I showed up."

"Possibly caught the tiniest bit off-guard, Gus-Busters."

"Lizzie, just butt out, okay? I'm your brother, not your
retarded son."

"All right, if you feel that way about it." Lizzie's tone
turned icy, then melted into a weepy blubber just as suddenly. "It's just that I want you *attached.* You know. Here. It
was hard, Gus. We were so scared for so long. I couldn't
have . . . I just want you to be happy so you'll be around
for a real long time."

"Aw, Liz-bo, I will be. Hey, the Human Night Light, no
one's going to snuff him out. Hah!"

"Hah!" Lizzie answered. "Come on, the Loo Kao Win's
going to be all gone."

Perplexed, I retreated back to the bathroom. This Gus I'd

heard speaking to his sister was funny, warm, and real. He was someone I wanted to get to know. I decided to hide out in the bathroom a bit longer, then reemerge and find out a little bit more about who might be the real Gus Kubiak.

When I came out again, they were gathered around the table. I stood in the shadowy hallway and watched. All I could see of Gus were wispy fluffs of downy blond hair— the new hair he was growing for his new life with me. They and his Science Fair tie oppressed me terribly. He might indeed be a stellar person with his sister, but what good would that do *me* if he turned into a squeeb in my presence?

I was pulled into a downward spiral of self-recrimination by the burden of hope this nice man had misplaced in me. Guilt tugged me even lower when I thought of how he'd battled those diseased platelets to live and how I couldn't even overcome George Winston and pig liver to sit down next to him. But I couldn't. I just could not.

At the table Garnell put his hands in his ears and waggled them at Baby Annabelle, who'd been happily blowing apricot puree bubbles. She stopped and stared, looking for Lizzie for reassurance, but her mother was in the kitchen. Annabelle's chin quivered. She tried a wobbly smile, but the next instant, as Garnell kept waggling at her, Annabelle dissolved into wailing, gasping, gulping tears. Gus jumped out of his seat and rescued the baby, pressing her small puree-smeared body to his chest.

That was it. They were right. My mother was right. I was sick. I had no idea what was truly important in life. I ducked out, the sound of maniac piano plunkings and terrified toddlers ringing in my ears. I felt like a total shit in sneaking out. The only thing that could have made me feel worse would have been to stay.

10

Brooke twisted her lips, still bruised by the ardent expertise of his plundered kiss, into a mocking sneer. "Do you always greet the chief executive officers of large international conglomerates threatening to take over your company in a merger buy-out with such familiarity?"

"Only when I've dreamed for fifteen years of the sweetness of their lips."

The deep bass rumbling of his voice plucked chords buried deep within Brooke Sinclair, chords that she had fought for years to silence completely. Still, every molecule of her being resonated to the vibrations they set off. "My God, no," she whispered, paling. "It can't be."

"Did it only take a beard to wipe my memory away?"

Brooke cursed herself for not taking the time to read the name on the door she'd burst into. She didn't need to now, for that marauding name was permanently emblazoned upon her heart, where the rakishly smiling man behind the desk had carved it fifteen long, empty years ago: Chase Peters. But Brooke was no longer the moonstruck teenager who'd given her heart and virginity away a decade and a half ago. She'd learned the hard lessons the hard way in a hard man's world. The first lesson had been: hide weakness. Never again would Chase Peters or any man get the better of her. Not in business and never in love. She'd learned too well.

The cornflower-blue softness of her eyes iced over, freezing up with an Arctic hardness that no amorous invader from her past would ever pene-

trate. "Actually, Mr. Peters, I don't think the beard was necessary to keep you from my memory. Shall we begin negotiations?"

The pirate grin chilled on Chase's male lips, lips that were full with an almost cruel sensuality. He raked her with a shrewdly appraising gaze and husked, "I thought we already had."

"In that case," Brooke shot back, her gaze as cutting as his, betraying none of the tempest boiling within her, "you have started at a disadvantage, Mister Peters."

"You idiot!" I hurled *Joint Venture* across my room, where it joined the half-dozen other Cameos I'd launched in disgust. How could someone forget their first love just because he grew a beard? Okay, fifteen years later, maybe it was possible. But, jeez, if she'd been glowing for this Chase for fifteen years she should do something about it. "Jump on his bones, you nitwit," I coached Brooke. Rip away the fantasy. Discover that the attraction doesn't hold beyond the back seat of a Ford Falcon.

End the book on page three?

Okay, I could see the need for a few plot contrivances to keep the principals apart for 280 pages, but I could also understand why Andrea was interested in "freshness." Six Cameos, and I felt as if I were looking down an endless hall of mirrors. In them were reflected an infinity of pert heroines luscious as honeysuckle but convinced that they're really stinkweeds. They may be investment bankers or cross-country truckers, but they are still the most toothsome morselettes around and the masterful Chad or Dru, Linc or Trey, gets like King Kong on Spanish fly whenever her pertness is near.

Then there were the conflicts the Cameo authors used to keep the young breeders from fulfilling their titanic impulses shortly after page one. I'd noted repeating motifs there as well. She's a forest ranger, he rapes the land. She's an archaeologist, he rapes the dig site. She's a shepherdess . . .

Basically, there had to be a situation that kept them in

close but hostile contact. Not hostile enough, though, that the mandatory *action amoureuse* couldn't be worked in with touches that trailed paths of liquid fire and kisses that stirred whirling vortexes of desire and opened chasms of aching need.

But what bothered me most was that all the heroes seemed like someone's father. Their idea of a big laugh was to threaten to turn the heroine over their knee and paddle her adorable fanny. A million yucks. Then, if the authors were trying to go really contempo, they'd pour their Mr. Wonderful into a pair of skintight jeans (so handy for displaying the full extent of his "male arousal"). The stink of Brut aftershave wafted over these clucks stronger than at a Rotary Club Prayer Breakfast.

I perceived an aching chasm where today's rumpled hero needed to be. A slapdash guy who's kind of sexy as an afterthought. Never overtly. Insidiously, letting you do all the work but keeping you stoked with that lopsided little smile and smoky voice.

Before I knew it, this updated hero was gestating, demanding to be given life, saddling me with unsought responsibilities: I had to come up with a name, occupation, philosophy of life, romantic interest, and shoe size for my rumpled hero. After much reflection I had it, ten and a half. Bigger than my feet but not monstrously so. Okay, my hero was shod. The other needs remained. I lay in bed and stared at the ceiling fan. The blades trailed streamers of cobwebbed dust as they made their languid circles. Outside my window a pair of blue jays hectored a mangy tortoiseshell Manx cat creeping across the gravel driveway.

Manx, I thought. Not only was it a manly-*sounding* name, it actually contained the word man in it. A good subliminal cue. I'd noted how popular Celtic last names were and attempted to think Hibernian: Manx. . . . Manx Donnelly. It had a breezy, offhand quality to it. Manx took shape quickly around his name. Dark, tousled curls that were probably the tiniest bit musty from neglect. A few acne scars, because no one you'd ever want to get naked with had a painless, unblemished adolescence. The nose had to be odd, perhaps a tad bulby, once broken, a bit hooked. But great eyes. My hero would get the heroine's eyes, laughing, dancing, warm, merry. Color was immaterial, but they had to be alive with intelligence, humor, and an endless capacity for dreaming up sexual innovations.

Now I had to find employment for him, a life's work. Music critic? It did have a certain tawdry charm, but I gleefully eliminated it anyway. Just put an enormous *X* over the entire field and labeled it and all its practitioners "Unsuitable." The arbitrary power of authorship was beginning to appeal to me. Formula One race car driver? I liked the life-and-death edge on that one, and the locales would be great for exotic dalliances. But the thought of researching pistons and gear ratios sent me into a coma. Formula One was out. This was wonderful. If I didn't want to, I didn't have to do it. I ran through a broad list of occupations: pastry chef, mergers and acquisitions man, gem trader, dermatologist. After much dithering, Manx spoke up and told me he wanted to be a screenwriter like everyone else. The difference was, I had it in my power to let Manx *be* anything he wanted, and if screenwriter it was, screenwriter it would be.

A real plus in the profession's favor was that research would be minimal. Anyone with a subscription to *Newsweek* knew that screenwriters made swimming pools full of money simply for providing an excuse for teenage boys to sit next to teenage girls in dark movie theaters. Screenwriters "took" meetings and "did" lunch. I was certain that Cameo readers would thrill to these bits of insider info.

What of the heroine? Pert was out. Darci Hollister was pert. An author can't work with a major character whom she wants to squash like the bug she's cute as. Defiantly upthrust chins were out. An unruly cap of golden curls, ixnay. Pixieish smiles of merriment, *verboten.* A gossamer lack of interest in food, you're kidding.

No, my heroine would fly in the face of all these clichés. My romance would star a size-ten-shoe gal who called out for pizza a lot. I wanted to call her Helga, but I knew that would be pushing the limits too far. The only name farther beyond the romantic pale was Gretchen. I had to strike a blow for all us unfortunates burdened with names out of the Half Sizes department. I settled on Hattie. Hattie Beauclair. There are far too many Whitneys in romance fiction and not nearly enough Hatties. Hattie began to take shape in my mind, although it was a very stolid shape indeed. Hattie dreamed of training as a licensed vocational nurse. I saw that the line between bedpans and ingenues would be a tricky one to tread. I made Hattie take off her support hose. We needed someone with a bit more dash.

Hattie, she let me know, was the type who didn't want to fuss with her hair. A braid down the back would be fine with her. She'd worn her hair like that for so many years she was a bit thin on top from the years of continual stress on the follicles. I compromised and gave her a utilitarian Dutch-boy cut. She wanted a hair color the shade of compost or asbestos shingling, but I'd always harbored a secret desire for the kind of white-blond Appalachian hair Cameo authors described as "corn silk." Hattie refused. She didn't hold with such fripperies, and when could her LVN training begin, if that wasn't asking too much?

LVN training was out, I decreed. The best I could do would be to make her a photographer. Why not a photojournalist? I suggested.

Because, Hattie sneered, being a photojournalist was only marginally more glamorous than emptying bedpans and didn't pay as well. I asked Hattie to keep that our little secret. According to Andrea Bronstein, photojournalism was an occupation rife with romantic possibilities.

Yeah, Hattie sniped, like maybe Manx is a rattlesnake

handler and in the course of a photo essay he is called upon to cut X's in my hand and suck venom? Very romantic, she sneered. Or perhaps Manx is the dashing editor of the glamorous publication I shoot for.

Hattie's derisive commentary was getting out of hand. I knew that if I didn't take her in hand I would never get anywhere. I adopted an Hitchcockian perspective and took to viewing my characters as cattle. I herded her into line and insisted on corn-silk-blond hair. It jazzed up her entire outlook, and she completely forgot about LVN training.

Now she wanted to be a fashion model. I reminded her sternly that we had voted against the stereotypical butterfly bone structure, that she was a substantial size-ten-shoe gal who'd never met an enchilada she didn't like.

Once I laid down the law, Hattie stopped talking back and I applied myself to the essential problem of getting my principals into contact close enough to snipe but not succumb. All right, I dictated, Hattie would work for some sleazy rag where her boss was a chemically distorted con man who sends her out to shoot Manx's movie, being filmed on location.

When Manx meets minx, he wants to share a toothbrush with her so bad every sinewy cord in his body aches. Hattie is not left unaffected by this initial encounter either, though she hides her vaulting attraction behind a line of snappy banter. Still, they're both hotter than Austin in August. In fact, I command, it *is* August in Austin. With that decision my characters come to the life I've chosen for them. They're both clad in thin, sweat-drenched cotton that clings to their mutually magnificent bodies. I'm happy to discover that Manx's whippet leanness hides a nicely corrugated stomach and buns springy as old licorice. And, woo-woo, our corn-silk Hattie is built too, for that matter. This is a couple equipped for good times.

Hattie meets Manx and cannot deny the power of his fiercely frisky pheromones. Since it *is* August in Austin and a little carnal knowledge could hardly defray anyone's personal daintiness, Hattie, in a most uncharacteristic moment, succumbs on page three. They commence to stripping off right there in his trailer, where he is staying while he finishes up work on a rewrite. Since Manx is supposed to leave the next day, Hattie believes theirs will be a once-in-a-lifetime encounter, an interlude so brief that it won't "really count," sort of like calories consumed while standing in front of the refrigerator. But the director—let's call him Marion Dodge Caponata—demands that Manx stay to provide an endless variety of alternatives to the original script.

This alone is enough to thoroughly chap Manx's independent ass, particularly since he has a play opening on Broadway next week. Even more nettlesome, though, is his discovery that Hattie, the sweet-hipped vixen who is like unto a fire in his blood, works for the odious tabloid *Celebrity*. He is convinced that the moment of intimacy which seared his soul was but a canny career move for her.

There it was: I'd found my Pushmepullyou, the incredible forces that would drive my couple together, then blast them apart. I sighed with satisfaction. They would be driven into contact by their work, each of them frenzied by the memory of their transcendental coupling. Yet suspicion and misunderstanding would be the bundling board keeping them apart. Oh, not entirely. Naturally they would be overpowered again by biological imperatives. Four more times, if my Cameo quota count was accurate. But their souls would not twine together until the last few pages, when the purity of their motives would shine forth like the sun on a new day.

I saw my yeasty young couple panting to get at one another and thought immediately of temptation, guilt, mortal sin, and the fires of hell, all the things that had once elevated sex into a grand pageant fraught with consequence. A title came to me: "Gain the Earth." With springy buns and corn-silk hair, someone was sure to lose their soul.

I got out of bed and dragged the Sears portable manual

my parents had given me when I graduated from high school out of the closet. I hadn't cracked its hinges since I typed a paper on "The Role of *Weltschmerz* in *Atala and René*" in my junior year of college.

My fingers were poised over the keys when I started wondering if I had the right kind of paper. I was halfway out the door to search for novel-writing paper when I stopped myself. In a moment of blinding clarity I saw the two ways I would ever do this. The first, the way most natural for me, would be to go to the stationery store, then decide I needed expert advice. I'd spend the next week reading back issues of *Writer's Digest.* I wouldn't find the definitive word on paper selection. I'd inch along an intricate network of friends and friends of friends or acquaintances and finally call an actual novelist, who would then tell me that she didn't know exactly what kind of paper she used. Whatever was cheapest.

Then I would buy a ream and sit down again. This time it would occur to me that I'd never actually taken a writing course in my entire life and didn't have the first clue how to set out. A couple of semesters later I'd try again.

Or there was the second way, the way in which I actually wrote something.

I started to type the title, but after five years in the closet the ribbon had dried out. Years of my life began to slide away from under me like a sandbar at the change of the tide. I either started right then or I would be doomed. Tucked at the back of my desk drawer was a wadded-up sheet of carbon paper. I smoothed it out, put it over a sheet of notebook paper, then fed them both in. The letters formed in carbon on the paper, and I spelled out "Gain the Earth." I had started.

I filled in a bare sketch of Hattie's background. I wanted to pit her with Manx as soon as possible. My fingers were stiff and rusty on the keys until she sashayed into the trailer and poleaxed Manx with instant lust. Boy, I'd give the romance reader more bang for her buck than she'd ever had before. She wouldn't have to dither around with first kisses and a hundred pages of teasing. My young breeders were going to get right to it.

I was pretty certain I'd stumbled onto something new and exciting here, sex right up front. I had Hattie and Manx slapping tummies together as quickly as they could shed their sweat-soaked gauze. At last, romance readers would have a writer bold enough to give them what they wanted without all the coyness and delays. I felt so bold, in fact, that I dispensed with romance jargon. I could not imagine that my New Wave of readers would be anything but grateful to see the "throbbing evidence of his male desire" replaced by boner. So I tossed out the flowery euphemisms and got right down to cases: they had at it.

It was nearly dawn before I took my fevered fingers from the keys and went to bed. An emphysematic puff of cool air wheezed in my window. Summer was settling in early. Already it was taking most of the night to cool the city down. The scent of honeysuckle, growing in a wild, collapsed heap along the chain-link fence, crept in on the breeze. I fell asleep breathing it in and dreamed of Hattie and Manx. They had their gauzy clothes on again, though they had metamorphosed into starched-and-pressed dazzling-white Victorian garden-party outfits. They were taking a train trip through the redwood forest and stopped to have a picnic on a white cloth atop a high hill.

I moved in for a close-up of the mistily bucolic scene and found that *I* was Hattie and Manx was a baby lying on the white cloth. He was someone else's baby, but one I was very fond of. The baby put his toes in my mouth, and a cool breeze dried our sweaty cotton clothes.

11

"You cannot have your main characters making whoopie in the first chapter," Juanita declared categorically. She slapped the pages down on the rickety wooden café table we sat around.

I'd bounced out of bed the morning—okay, early afternoon—after finishing the first chapter of "Gain the Earth" and had rushed it over to Lizzie, begging her to read it and then pass it on to Juanita. Lizzie was still miffed that I'd skipped out on her dinner party, but she was excited that I'd started a book already and promised to read it. The very next day, Juanita called, and I met her and Lizzie with Annabelle in tow at Kerbey Lane Café.

I am compelled to go to Kerbey Lane with alarming frequency to consume their gingerbread pancakes. That day, however, I allowed my gee cakes to grow cold as I listened to Juanita's critique.

"Why?" I wanted to know.

"You . . . it's . . . I" Juanita sputtered. She looked to Lizzie, who had been remarkably silent. Lizzie gave Annabelle, sitting in her booster seat, several packets of crackers, which she proceeded to consume, seeming particularly to enjoy the cellophane.

"Okay, I've got it," Juanita proclaimed. "The heart of the problem. You write like a man."

"You mean," I said, "because I didn't flowery the love-making all up. Women read those things for romance. I gave them an extra helping."

"Hoo, boy." Juanita fidgeted with the True she couldn't light since we were sitting in No Smoking. "You are about to make me mad, sister. 'Those things'? Boy howdy, talk about your condescension." She pointed the True at me. "Let me give you lesson numero uno. You can't write and condescend at the same time. That's one. Two is, you didn't give readers an extra helping of 'romance,' you gave them a quick screw, pardon my French." Juanita looked around, her face glowing red beneath the Revlon Moondrops. Then she stuck the cigarette into her mouth and fired it up, defying me or anyone around her to do anything about it.

Lizzie, oblivious to the slurry of mulched crackers and shredded cellophane her daughter was creating, swabbed up some syrup with a forkful of pancake and popped it into her mouth. We all chewed or smoked in silence for a few seconds, until Lizzie cleared her throat and spoke. "Gretchen, you've unwittingly stumbled upon one of the crucial issues underpinning romantic fiction: the mechanistic versus the ethereal paradigm of love. Readers face a surfeit of the mechanistic in their lives. What they seek is the ethereal."

I looked to Juanita for clarification.

"They want the sizzle, not the steak," she growled. "They want the flowers, not the"—she lowered her voice and spelled—"F-U-C-K." She glanced around to see if any of the other diners had overheard. A young couple, both wearing expensive, gaudily colored Benetton play clothes, pursed their lips and glared pointedly at her cigarette.

"I don't know," I murmured. "I guess I was just trying to do something, you know, different. Fresh."

"Ah-*hah!*" Lizzie dropped her fork. For the first time since the doomed dinner party, she sounded like her old self again. "You scamp you, you were planning to 'transcend the genre,' weren't you?" She made it sound like the tritest and most predictable of aspirations.

"What's wrong with that? You do it. *Publishers Weekly* says so."

She flashed one of her sealed-lip leprechaun smiles. "I most certainly did *not* do any genre-transcending my first time out," she informed me. "I observed every classic convention of historical romantic fiction at that time: the dark brooding hero, the innocent ingenue of a heroine; the half-witted misunderstandings. You think I didn't strain against the conventions those first dozen or so books? Of course I did! I still do. But you have to remember the fundamental impulses the genre springs from. Readers do not want to go ripping off on some cross-country literary gymkhana where the author bounds away on wild, uncharted tangents."

"They don't?"

"Of course they don't. They want a safe, comforting plod down a reassuringly familiar path. Now *maybe* if they'd gone riding with you before and you'd led them to a happy ending several times, they'd accept your flouting the conventions. But face it, Gretchen, you're an unknown."

"But readers have *got* to be tired of those conventions." I feebly defended my brainchild. "I think my book would do well in the marketplace."

"Shoot." Juanita cut in. "Let's get down to brass tacks here, Gretch. Your book is never going to get anywhere near the marketplace. Readers are never going to get a chance to find out if they like your experimental fiction because it'll never get published in the first place. You won't make it out of the starting gate because your first reader is going to be a romance editor, and she's going to throw it out because it ain't romance! Are you following me here? You've got to put peaches in the peach can. Not tomatoes. Not okra. And not heavy groping."

Juanita gave her little diatribe a moment to settle in before continuing.

"On the positive side, I loved Manx. Dated a fellow once could've been his brother. Tell Hattie to keep an eye peeled. She thinks she's discovered her very own diamond in the rough? Tell old Hattie she's got another think coming. Every woman Manx meets thinks the same thing. And Manx is the type'll meet bunches. Imperfection." She aimed her True at me. "That's their secret weapon, believe you me."

"Would you mind putting that out?" The male half of the Benetton couple stood over our table, pointing to Juanita's cigarette. "This is supposed to be No Smoking, you know."

I was glad for the interruption. Juanita's critique had mildly devastated me.

Juanita reared back to take in this person in pastel shorts and round, horn-rimmed glasses. "Well, *excu-u-use* me for living. This is sup*po*sed to be a free country. Sheesh." Juanita stubbed out her cigarette. "Nicotine Nazi," she hissed as the guy sat down.

I gathered up my pages off the table. "Okay, so much for romance writing."

Juanita mirrored my glum expression. "Oh, now don't go getting down at the mouth."

"No, no, don't," Lizzie said. "Your characters are believable, you can write dialogue, and you've invented a most intriguing conflict."

"Really? It sounded like you both hated it. You trashed it pretty good."

"No. Perhaps our criticism was a bit pointed, but only because Juanita and I both believe you're capable of so much more."

"All you've got to do," Juanita put in, "is drop the *Pent-*

house stuff, cut out the condescension, and you've got it made in the shade."

"You really think so?"

"Absolutely," Lizzie said. "Now, you just need to finish up three chapters and an outline of the rest and ship it off. You probably won't get a contract, but Andrea will tell you whether she's interested."

They both fed me tips from the pros. Put in lots of dialogue; it fills pages faster. Don't skimp on foreplay; provide acres, tundras, galaxies of foreplay. Don't let your main characters use drugs or even appear overly familiar with alcohol. And never, never use the words boner, dick, pussy, shit, puke, or pus. "Actual body parts and functions are big no-nos," Juanita summarized.

I was rapidly changing my mind about the whole enterprise. I couldn't follow this format, actually write about "the pulsing evidence of his male arousal." Maybe Lizzie and Juanita could absorb and regurgitate a fantasy formula of pert heroines and happy-ever-after endings, but I was too much of a realist to be an accessory to such delusions.

"And now for the fun part." Lizzie's oversized eyes gleamed with yet another delicious secret. "Your pen name."

"My pen name?" I had forgotten that authorship would entitle me to adopt another name, a name of my own choosing. A name as frothy and euphonic as Gretchen Griner was croupy and harsh.

Lizzie had more suggestions. "You could come up with something that would put you up on the stands right next to—oh, let's see, who's big in contemporaries? Janet Dailey?"

"Yeah," Juanita broke in. "How about Jeanette Daley?" They both chortled, tickled by the notion of such an affront to one of romance's reigning queens.

I paid little attention as they batted about candidates: Chelsea Dalton. Cheyenne Dale. Geneva Dailtwistle. For I knew, as I'd always known, that should a merciful God ever allow me the chance to rename myself one criterion would prevail: how the name sounded. I'd always dreamed of responding to a name that was a sweet whisper upon the wind. I listened to an inner chorus chime downy pseudonyms: Solange Shaughnessy. Melanie San Domaine. Lorelei Beaumatin. Lorelei Beaumatin. I liked that name. It was a name you could fall asleep uttering. Lizzie had hit me in a weak spot.

Why should Hattie be a pawn to hormonal impetuosity? I began to wonder. Why shouldn't my heroine profit from my mistakes? Hormonal impetuosity tended so often to accomplish nothing more than make a girl privy to anatomical irregularities she would be better off knowing nothing of. So why not, after a couple of melting moments when surrender seems inevitable, simply put the smelling salts under Hattie's nose? Still punch-drunk with lust, she'll snort a few times, come to her senses, and leave Manx turmoiled in his trailer. So there had been one night that turned out to be a disastrous mistake? Instead of blood tests and recriminations, all I had to do was tear up a few pages, and Hattie starts with a clean slate. Romantic fiction had much to recommend it.

Lorelei Beaumatin. The tiny silver bells of the name were chiming in my mind when I recalled my major objection to the romance novel. "I can't write one according to the formula," I protested feebly. "I'd feel so guilty about raising false expectations in readers. I mean, romance heroes are just too perfect. They're always in command. Handsome. Educated at Oxford. A slashing wit. Virile. And, of course, secretly crazed about the heroine. No, I just can't perpetuate that kind of myth."

"So you think we should be presenting more realistic heroes? Average-looking fellows with a couple of years of junior college?" Lizzie asked.

"All I know is that if you met a romance hero at a bar"—I

spoke now of Chase Peters—"he'd be one of those colossal jerks who spend the entire evening telling you so much about himself that you could ghostwrite his memoirs and he wouldn't even get your name right." This was the voice of experience.

"And that's not what you're interested in?"

"Of course not!" I felt it my duty to educate Lizzie. She had been spared the Single Years and knew not of their treachery. "If you're a halfway intelligent woman, you leave the handsome-rogue fantasy behind in high school."

"And what is it you think women should look for?"

I shrugged. It was clear enough from my own personal life that I hadn't thought the matter through. "Integrity." As soon as I said it, I knew that such was indeed the precise quality *I* should be screening applicants for.

Lizzie beamed at me. "Oh, Gretchen, I knew you had substance. I mean, at this point Gus may not be the stuff schoolgirl crushes are made of, but he'll always have integrity to burn. I'm certain that—"

"Gus?" I felt like a witness who'd been boxed into a corner by a crafty cross-examining lawyer. "Lizzie, I was speaking in the abstract. Not about any realistic—"

"It's not at all unrealistic. I think I can safely say that you have a very good chance with Gus."

I saw clearly that Lizzie was out of touch on the subject of her brother and the best thing to do would be to not excite her any further. "Oh, well. That's nice."

"So can I tell Gus you're free this Saturday?"

"Free?" I asked, astonished. "You don't mean, like, for a date?"

"Something of the sort. Dinner. Dancing. Skeet shooting at sunset." Lizzie tittered. "Name your pleasure. Gus is extremely flexible. Flexibility and integrity, his watchwords."

I looked to Juanita for help. She dropped her eyes.

"Lizzie," I said. "I really appreciate what you're doing, and if I had a little brother who was in the market, I'd probably be out scouting prospects for him too. But I am just not interested. I'm sorry. It's my fault."

Lizzie's lips tightened dangerously. "I'll bet you would have been interested if he'd had a sardonic sneer and thick spiky eyelashes."

"He doesn't have eyelashes of *any* kind." Too late, I remembered the chemotherapy. "Oh, God, Lizzie, I'm so sorry. I forgot. I'm really sorry."

"That's all right. Normally his eyelashes are quite thick."

"It's not looks, Lizzie, honestly. When you meet someone and they're the one, you just know. Looks don't really have that much to do with it."

Lizzie lunged forward. "Hah! Hah! And double hah! You would have fallen for Gus like a ton of bricks if he'd been devastatingly handsome and treated you despicably!"

"Lizzie." Juanita put a restraining hand on Lizzie's arm. "Ease off, babe."

Lizzie let out a long hissing sigh and sagged back into her seat. "I don't know. Maybe I'm overreacting out of guilt. I've been thinking about this ever since reading your first chapter, Gretchen. It bothers me inordinately that we all grow up with the same benighted fantasy of the ideal man we're supposed to love."

I thought I'd done a pretty fair job of beating the romance hero stereotype, but, wanting to smooth things over with Lizzie, I agreed. "Boy, that's the truth. We're all set up for some impossible combination of the mind of William Buckley, the looks of Mel Gibson, the cash flow of Malcolm Forbes, and the sex drive of Java Man."

"That's it exactly." Lizzie pushed her glasses back up her nose. "And I'm contributing to this horrible, destructive myth. My heroes are rakes and rogues. I tell myself it's only fantasy, that readers can make that distinction. Then I meet you"—she meant me—"an intelligent woman—"

"Oh, well—" I began to demur modestly, but Lizzie cut me off.

"—and you're just as deluded as any two-sweets-a-day romance addict."

"Hey, thanks."

"Good God, Gertie," Juanita protested. "Men and women were making fools out of themselves centuries before Harlequin came along."

"Oh, I know. I haven't totally formulated any kind of coherent thesis yet. It's just that watching Gretchen turn down someone who would be perfect for her because, in spite of her protests to the contrary, her head is all clotted with the kind of fantasies I'm spending my life purveying has been upsetting for me."

"Clotted with fantasies?" I echoed.

"Not just you," Lizzie said.

"I guess not," Juanita added. "I mean, *someone's* out there keeping Paco Rabanne in business."

Lizzie ignored my protests and Juanita's kidding. She heaved a few more deep sighs and looked off out the window. I'd known from her first words that Lizzie was a genuine eccentric, the kind who worked at being normal but would never make it. Now she was showing signs of being seriously disconnected. A silence followed that was just starting to get awkward when Juanita, attempting to lighten the atmosphere, asked, "You know how we could solve this whole problem?"

I waited for Lizzie to answer. When she didn't, I filled in. "Hermaphrodite breeding colonies?"

"By starting, as a service to all of womankind, the Potts-Griner-Lusader Boyfriend School. Why, with our accumulated wisdom, we could turn any low-down dog into a fit companion for a woman within a few short weeks."

"Start with Trout."

"Okay. We'll offer a couple different levels. Basic level, we'll train those hounds to remember phone numbers, birthdays, and ring size. As we move along, we'll tackle more advanced subjects like not bringing up old girlfriends or the size of our derrieres."

"How about postgraduate work in controlling compulsive TV remote control roulette," I suggested. Lizzie still hadn't emerged from her fugue state, so I prodded her. "Any additions you'd like to make to the curriculum?"

She smiled weakly. "No. I think it's women who need to be trained. There's an ample supply of material. Women just need to learn how to recognize the good ones."

Before I could spring to my own defense again, Lizzie noticed that her daughter was quietly opening and consuming packets of sugar. A dozen empties littered the floor.

"Piglet, darling, no." Lizzie took number thirteen from Annabelle's chubby grasp. "We don't want to eat excessive amounts of white sugar, sweetie, because excess blood glucose leads to increased protein and fat catabolism, a condition that can cause premature vascular degeneration and atherosclerosis. Now, we don't want that, do we?"

Annabelle lunged for the one remaining packet. Lizzie wrestled her out of the booster seat. "She's getting a little restless. We'd better be moving on."

After Lizzie and Annabelle left, Juanita turned to me. "Gal's got a heart of gold, but sometimes she acts like she learned her social graces by correspondence course."

"Ah, well, I wouldn't know what to do with a socially graceful friend anyway."

"She'll snap out of it. Hey, get on home and pound those keys, girl. I want to see ten pages, minimum, by the end of this week." We left money for the ticket and exited. On the way out, Juanita torched up a True the instant we crossed over into the Smoking section, inhaled deeply and sent a big fat smoke ring wobbling over to the Benetton couple's table.

12

The day after my lunch with Lizzie and Juanita, I axed the steamy opening scene in Manx's trailer and substituted a pounding pulse instead. Hattie is, naturally, mightily galled by her immediate attraction to the high-handed, broad-shouldered screenwriter. Particularly when he makes it painfully obvious that he considers her a king-sized nuisance. Hattie will be the last to know that it's all just a smoke screen, that Manx lost his heart to her the minute he set eyes on the golden cap of her corn-silk hair. He's been hurt before, though, a tartlet who pushed back her cuticles every night and used him to advance her career. So he's wary. Doubly so since Hattie works for *Celebrity* magazine. His head tells him to run, but his heart keeps saying she's the only one.

After a long day of rewriting, I slid into sleep that night devising new ways for Manx to be tortured by the taunting vision that is Hattie. I dreamed I was Hattie. That *I* was fatally alluring. Odd characters from my past popped into my dreams.

I hadn't thought about Ray Gutierrez in years. He'd been

my very first bad boy and probably the one who established what became a disturbing trend. He sat in front of me in geometry, a class ruled by Mr. Peppel. Canny teens that we were, we all knew that Peppel was "schizzed out," though it would take years of exposure to Freud and Dr. Ruth to be able to attach names like "Napoleon complex" and "sado-masochist" to the little man's assemblage of psychic quirks.

Peppel had his desk mounted on a dais that elevated it into a control tower, where he perched and monitored the inmates of his classes. Occasionally he would descend and pass among us as we labored over the theorems and axioms that he had made into an impenetrable puzzle with his impenetrable teaching style. During these in-country missions, he liked to pause for a bit behind three different guys, all of them tough, surly, and built like *Blue Boy* centerfolds. He'd stop and watch these students labor over the problems he muddied so badly. Then he worked in a little neck massage that was supposed to be avuncular and encouraging. On the rare occasions when he deigned to attend class, Ray Gutierrez was one of the massagees.

The other guys submitted to the massages with much eye-rolling and head-ducking. But when Peppel laid his hands on Ray I could feel every ion in the room pick up a negative charge. The delicious, suffocating thrill of suppressed conflict electrified us. Little savages that we were, we felt the charge grow each time Peppel dug his tiny, impeccably manicured hands into Ray's young bull neck. We could smell the tamped-down violence sharp as sulfur on the air. The tension built into a barricade around Ray. Peppel broke through once too often.

That last time the atmosphere in the room was as spiked as an EKG chart. I watched Peppel approach, pause, and reach his tiny hands down toward the tensed lumps of muscle humped up on either side of Ray's neck. At first I didn't hear what Ray said. Neither did Peppel.

"Did you say something, Señor Gutierrez?" Peppel's

elbows flapped up with each word as he kneaded Ray's neck. "Perhaps you'd like to repeat what you said for the whole class."

Ray jerked away from the prodding hands, then took about ten seconds to plan out the rest of his life. For the first time I heard the big electric clock over the blackboard grind out each of those seconds. "Yeah," Ray finally answered, his voice as flat as if he were telling what the axis of x plus y would be. "You put your cocksucking hands on me ever again and I'll break 'em off at the elbows." Then Ray picked up his books, stood, shook his head laughing at himself, put the books back down, smashed Peppel in the face, and walked out of school forever.

"Oh, big man, big man," Peppel hissed with frantic excitement, touching his nose to see if it was broken. "Biiig man."

Peppel and I shared something in that moment: the thrill of the bad boy. I was the one, however, who ended up dating Ray when he got out of Juvie Hall. Though I tried with every fiber of my middle-class being to be truly tough, Ray knew I couldn't keep up the pace. One night he called me up to tell me we weren't going out that night because he had to get married the next day and his primo Trini was having some bullshit bachelor's party for him. And maybe we shouldn't see each other for a while. At least until after the baby came.

In my romance dream that night, Ray came back to tell me he'd never stopped loving me. As did Jeff Eckart, collector of Silver Surfer comics and solitary drug abuser. Dal Davies, moody Lord Byron lookalike, also appeared to pledge his love. So did Arnie Kwalwasser, moderately distorted heir to a tuna canning fortune. They all appeared to express deepest regrets for ditching me. They mourned the loss of my love and cursed their stupidity. Of course, they were just dreams. But dreams that tied up a lot of loose ends anyway.

♥   ♥

On June seventh, a week after the lunch at Kerbey Lane, Lizzie stopped by at seven in the evening. I answered the door and she handed me a Corning Ware casserole dish, white with blue flowers scrolling over the sides. Inside was something that looked like most of the dinners my mother ever made. I could smell the Campbell's cream of mushroom. Noodles and canned onion rings were also involved. Steam from the still-warm dish condensed on the clear glass lid. It was a wonderful peace offering.

"Here. I hope leftovers don't offend you."

"Are you kidding?" I took the casserole and stepped aside to let Lizzie in. "Any food not prefaced by the words Cup-a is a big step up for me." In spite of the fact that I still wouldn't relinquish my Luvboree pictures, Trout had been leaking me some of what he owed me. Tens and twenties. Not nearly enough to get me out of Beatrice foods and clear my bill with the Cleebs.

"How's the book coming?" Lizzie looked around until she spotted my typewriter, then beelined over and picked up the pages sitting beside it. "You mind?" she asked, already reading.

"Uh, sure. No. Go ahead." I shrugged.

"Go on and eat that and I'll read." Without looking up, she waved in the direction of the casserole.

I had trouble concentrating on the food as I studied her face for clues to her reactions. Finally she whacked the manuscript down and looked up at me.

"Major improvement." Her digital watch with the black plastic strap beeped. She jumped up and grabbed the almost empty casserole dish out from under my fork. "Oops, time for Mitchell to leave for his T'ai Chi class. I've got to take over Annabelle." As she banged out the front door, she yelled over her shoulder, "See you tomorrow."

And that was that. No mention of Gus Kubiak or the lunch at Kerbey Lane.

The next evening Lizzie came over with Annabelle and thrust another half of a casserole into my hands.

"I can't take this." Perhaps because my protest was so heavily muffled by the chicken lumps I was picking off the top and stuffing into my mouth, Lizzie was easily able to turn it aside. She shoved it back into my hand, and I followed her inside. "It's just leftovers. All you're doing is saving me from having to wait a couple of weeks to throw it out when it goes all green and fuzzy. Consider it a favor. It's a far cry from one of Mitchell's gourmet productions, but it will support life."

We settled onto the couch, me forking in chicken à la king, Annabelle getting down to run around, and Lizzie reading. Her fuzzy hair fell into her eyes as she hunched over the scene I'd written last night. Hattie and Manx are in a Mexican restaurant secluded in the mountains, breathing in the spicy scent of piñon logs burning in the round-bellied adobe fireplace. They listen to the distant serenade of a mariachi singer, and Manx translates the tale of a love so powerful, yet so forbidden, it fractured the singer into heartbroken blood-red rose petals that rained forever on his beloved.

Lizzie clasped the pages to her chest. "La Chanson du Solange." She exhaled the name on a tremulous breath.

"Come again?"

"You *did* steal this from the exquisite 'Chanson du Solange,' didn't you? I didn't know you were familiar with chivalric songs of the fourteenth century. Very crafty. Steal from the best. Well, not steal, really—'adapt.' The story of how rose petals came to be red works perfectly as a popular ballad. What inspired you?"

"Uh, actually I made it up. You're sure it's not too . . . schmaltzy?"

"Schmaltz? 'La Chanson du Solange?' I hardly think so."

"So it works?"

"Oh, wonderfully. Wonderfully." Annabelle grabbed her mother's legs and proudly offered Lizzie a BB-sized pill-bug corpse. Lizzie plucked the bug out of Annabelle's hand, put it to her mouth, and made nibbling motions. "Ooh, yum-yum." Annabelle gurgled a happy laugh and trotted away to find more treats. Lizzie turned back to me.

"That sense of overripe melancholia is what readers look for. We all know how the dream of perfect union flits forever out of reach. How much better to have the proof of a perfect love rain down on you in clean, fragrant rose petals? . . . Not very tasty, is it?" Lizzie asked her daughter, who had just sampled a June bug. Annabelle looked helplessly up at her mother, her tongue, sprinkled with crispy wings and scratchy legs, sticking out slackly.

"Spit it out," Lizzie said. "That's a dead arthropod. Their exoskeleton and opaque wings are hard and chitinous. They could get caught in your throat if you swallow them and cause you to choke." Persuaded to the wisdom of her mother's suggestion, Annabelle redeposited the insect on my floor and scurried away. "I can't wait to get back to 'Betrayal of Passion' now." Lizzie referred to her own work in progress. "No, Annabelle!" she shouted at her daughter, trying to sound stern. "Take that out of your mouth!"

The little girl looked up from her position on the floor, where she was happily gumming the hose to the gas space heater.

Lizzie tried to look mean as her young one continued sucking on the gas coil. "If you breathe gas, it will tie up all your available hemoglobin so that there is none left for oxygen transfer; then your lips and nail beds will turn cherry red and you'll die of carbon monoxide poisoning."

Annabelle cut her big brown eyes over to me for confirmation of her mother's lecture on blood gas chemistry. "That's right, Piglet, cherry red."

Annabelle stopped drooling on the tubing and moved over to a wall lamp.

Lizzie jumped up. "I'd better go before she discovers the electrical outlets." She scooped her child up and headed for the door while Annabelle tried to poke pill bugs into her mouth. Lizzie held the screen door open long enough to let in a few dozen assorted insects and to perform that twinkling activity about the eyes; then she left.

13

Once this Meals on Wheels deal got going, I almost never had to leave the house. Lizzie showed up nearly every evening with something homey and rib-sticking half filling the Corning Ware casserole: beanie weenies, Frito pie, hamburger Stroganoff, or a poultry dish involving pineapple chunks that she called Chicken Don Ho.

I was glad to be able to hide out, as DeWitt Cleeb now spent every moment when he wasn't sleeping or riding his route waiting out in his front yard. I knew he was laying for me because the missus would come home, they'd confer, and much pointing at my front door would follow. Usually this most covert of couples just hissed in low voices at each other until DeWitt clamped his jaw into a hard line, turned his back on her, and returned to snipping whatever he'd been snipping.

One day near the end of June, however, DeWitt was using some gas-powered entrenching machine to dig out the perimeter of his lawn. Every time he finished a section, he went back and poured grass-killer into the little moat, then filled it up with Dursban granules. It was his own little line of death. The machine was roaring away when Mrs. Cleeb came upon the scene, so they both had to raise their voices to the point where I could actually hear them.

"Don't even tell me. You still haven't done it, have you?" Mrs. Cleeb demanded the instant she got out of her Cougar. DeWitt kept right on furrowing. "I am fed to the teeth with this whole deal." The finality of Mrs. Cleeb's words scared me.

"What's keeping *you* from going over there yourself?" DeWitt demanded.

My heart stopped. This woman was an employee of the Texas Department of Public Safety. She trained daily on license seekers. She delighted in telling people who'd stood for half a day in her line that they'd have to go stand the rest of the day in someone else's line and, furthermore, she wasn't paid to listen to *any*one talk that kind of trash. Tossing me out on the street would be a paid vacation for her.

"I wasn't the one got the bright idea to rent out Little House," she snapped back. *"I* wasn't the one went and put the ad in the newspaper—the *student* newspaper because it was *cheaper. I* woulda been perfectly happy to use Little House for the purpose for which it was intended. 'Mother-in-law addition' is what it is. Be cheaper to get Mother out of that home and just—"

Guh-r-r-r-a-a-a-w-w-w! DeWitt tried to entrench the sidewalk, and that pretty much ended the conversation. But I knew I was living on borrowed time. I rushed back to the typewriter to continue my desperate race with eviction.

♥   ♥

Three weeks later, I stood up and looked around. A Panzer division of June bugs was battering itself senseless against my front door screen. A couple of the bronze-toned beetles were thudding against the window. Hairy legs skritched on the pane as the downed bombers tried futilely to climb the glass.

It was done, the first three chapters and an outline. I'd finished as much as Lizzie had told me I needed to start off with. I gathered up my nascent manuscript and stowed it in the freezer. I'd heard that the freezer was the last thing to burn in case of fire.

My house seemed unfamiliar, as if I'd been gone for the past three weeks. Suddenly it contained my life again. I wondered why Trout hadn't called, until I saw the phone cord snaking across the hardwood floor and remembered that I'd unplugged it a couple of weeks back after some jerk from the Fraternal Order of something had insisted I "help him out" by buying a couple of hundred lawn and garden bags. He wouldn't believe that the only gardening I did involved periodic mold harvests in the refrigerator.

I also wondered briefly about Gus Kubiak. I'd fully expected him to launch a prolonged attack just because that's what happened only when I didn't want it to. It was a letdown to think of how easily he'd given up. He probably fell in love with someone else at first sight immediately after jellyfish night.

Oh, well. I called Trout. He was happy to hear from me but completely unaware that weeks had passed since this event had last taken place. He promised he'd come by that night after the clubs shut down. I was mad that I hadn't told him not to bother and sure I'd never get to sleep that night waiting for him. But I drifted off as soon as I started plotting out how producer Shel Goldstein would demand that Manx stay around past the first three chapters. And how *Celebrity* magazine would insist that Hattie produce a photo feature on triple-threat novelist/screenwriter/playwright Manx Donnelly.

In my dream, Ray Gutierrez and I were at the train station in Nuevo Laredo working out our differences when a swarm of June bugs invaded. I was batting them away frantically, knowing that Ray would leave again without me if I couldn't get rid of them. I was depressed when I woke up and found Trout scratching on my screen . . .

"Mama, if you don' want my peaches, why'd you shake mah tree?" In his inimitable way, Trout had noticed my detachment after we'd been intimately engaged for about ten minutes.

I raised my knees up to my armpits and swiveled until the Delta Dartmouth man groaned and lost coherence. I slipped back into my dream and it was Ray inside of me. I'd always wanted to make love to him, the first bad boy to steal my heart, and now I was.

The next morning I achieved another first: I was the first to willingly abandon a bed occupied by Trout Overton. I was that anxious to get my proposal into the mail. Trout stumbled into the kitchen, just as I was extracting my manuscript from the freezer. I put it back in and slammed the door shut. Though Trout misses a lot, he's a bloodhound for dirty secrets.

"Whatcha got there?" He flapped a wave in the direction of the freezer.

"A couple of years of permafrost."

Trout wasn't to be put off so easily. He opened the freezer and pulled out my frosty masterpiece. Mist swirling around his head, he read the title page. " 'Gain the Earth?' by Lorelei Beaumatin. Lorelei Beaumatin?" I grabbed for my manuscript, but Trout pivoted away from my grasp.

"Trout, give that to me. I did not say you could read that. Trout! Trout, please!" It had been a long time since I'd begged for something with such cringing desperation. To Trout it was a game. He cackled maniacally and repeated, "Lorelei Beaumatin?" Some malignant instinct guided him unerringly to the steamiest passage in those first three chapters. Holding the pages high over his head, safe from my clawing grasp, he read:

"Hattie watched, mesmerized by the savage pounding of

the vein pulsing in Manx's neck. And he watched her. She
felt as if he were absorbing every particle of her being
through his dark eyes. 'What do you want from me?' The
question was pulled from her.''

"Heh-heh." I could laugh at my own drivel. At the way
Trout had fluttered his voice when reading Hattie's line. I
was a good sport. "Okay, we've had our little joke," I said
with deadly calm. "Give it back." I put every ounce of au-
thority I could muster into those three words because I
knew what was coming and would have given anything to
stop Trout's voice. It didn't work. Trout read on.

" 'I want to know you,' Manx breathed. His voice trembled with the need he was restraining. 'I want to know the
look in your eyes the first time we kiss. I want to know the
feel of you when we make love. I want to know the sounds
you make when my love has satisfied you.' "

"Gretchen Griner," Trout looked at me, his eyes glittering
with malicious glee, "we need to try out some of these
sounds of satisfaction."

"Forget it. I already know your sounds of satisfaction.
Snoring. Give me the manuscript." I made another grab.
Trout danced away.

"No, this is spicy stuff. You wrote this? What is it, a letter
to *Penthouse?*"

"Give that to me."

"Gretchen, you're writing a romance novel. That's it! A
romance novel. Oh, Lorelei, you vixen you."

"Trout . . . give . . . me . . . the . . . manuscript." I
spaced the words out, giving each one equal heavy weight.
But Trout started again. I could not stand for him to read
one more word.

" 'Manx's feverish litany was like a wizard's chant. It
brought her further and further under the influence of his
magic until she too—' Jeee-yaaah!" Trout screamed, and the
pages fluttered down on the kitchen floor. He grabbed his
foot. The instep was mottled with a waffle pattern from

where I'd pounded it with my cast-iron meat-tenderizer mallet.

"The fuck you do that for?"

"I told you to stop reading."

"Christ almighty, you crippled me." He had his foot up on my kitchen counter.

"I asked you several times."

"Hey, well, pardon me, I don't speak Hammer." Trout limped out of the kitchen. He dressed quickly. I was down on the kitchen floor gathering up my pages when he stopped at the front door to inform me, "You are not a lot of fun anymore, Gretchen."

I let him go. I had to get to the post office.

♥   ♥

For the next couple of weeks after I sent my proposal off, I did nothing but work on the rest of the manuscript. I felt the Cleebs circling my house like sharks waiting for the castaway in the lifeboat to lose her grip on the rudder. Finally, I had no choice but to go to Trout.

"What can I tell you, Lorelei?" Trout asked me when I confronted him in his office. "The printer is holding the paper hostage until we pay him part of what we owe. I've been calling every advertiser on our list, dunning them for what *they* owe us. Hey, you're part of the new Austin, babe, where there's always a place to park, always a table, and always a bill that will never be collected."

He meant his bill to me. I sank into the crippled swivel chair on the other side of Trout's desk. I couldn't go on dodging the Cleebs and letting Lizzie sustain my parasitic life. Trout clearly read desperation in my face.

"Look, there's one possible way I can get some money to you." Trout held up a finger. It jittered wildly. Nerves. "Irma quit. We need someone to do simple layouts and darkroom work."

"I'm not a pasteup artist. Darkroom is no problem, but

I—" I stopped myself. "This is ludicrous. I'm applying for a job where I'll get paid money I've already earned? Trout, there are lamprey eels with sturdier moral fiber than you've got."

"Lorelei, I have no choice. You know that if I had the money I'd be showering you with Krugerrands at this very moment."

"Stop calling me Lorelei," I requested dispiritedly.

"I'm sorry, Miss Beaumatin, but there ain't no dough. We set a tiny sum aside for someone to do simple pasteup—nothing fancy, the kind we've all done with those jars of white paste and turkeys made by tracing around our little hands—and darkroom processing. I could advance you something right now." He handed over a couple of his moist twenties.

I should have snatched them and left, but we were both up against the wall. "I'll do the darkroom stuff but no hand turkeys." I demanded enough extra to save Mr. Cleeb's marriage, stuffed the bills into my pocket, and headed for the darkroom. "You'll do extra time in Purgatory for this," I promised Trout.

Secretly, though, I was not entirely displeased with this new arrangement. We were coming up on August 1, the absolute, final deadline in Austin, Texas, for securing access to AC. Since I couldn't afford to while away the rest of the brutal summer months in polar-chilled movie theaters and the frosty netherworld of the shopping mall, gainful employment was actually my only other option. Distasteful as it might be, during August in Austin one really had no other choice. One had to be out of one's un-air-conditioned dwelling between the hours of twelve noon until approximately eight in the evening, when the varnish on the furniture stopped bubbling.

The familiar vinegar smell of stop bath greeted me as I stepped into the darkroom and flipped on the light. The closet of a room looked like something out of the New York subway system. Every inch of the walls was covered in manic scrawls. Through the pictures of knives dripping blood and hands shooting the bird, I made out scribbled testimonials to the fact that Trout Overton was a pimp, prick, exploiter of women, cheat, *pendejo, chingadera,* and a fish-faced rat fuck. I liked the way Irma said good-bye.

There was a basket marked ASAP in one corner next to the enlarger. It was filled with rolls of film. They were all marked either URGENT!, URGENT!!, or URGENT!!! I lined up the largest film canisters I could find, the ones that hold eight rolls and look like stainless steel fireplace logs. All the equipment was in perfect shape. Irma was a professional. She hadn't taken her wrath out on the tools of the trade. I mixed up a couple of gallons of solution, developer, stop bath, and fixer, set everything up, and switched off the light.

I'd gone through these motions so many times that my mind fled the instant my hands were engaged. As my fingers threaded the Tri-X film onto the spools, I flew off to be with Hattie and Manx on location.

Hattie is ready to leave the set, still ripped asunder by her pulsating attraction to Manx and her hardheaded refusal to admit as much to the gallingly arrogant screenwriter, when her boss at *Celebrity* calls. In a flash of inspiration the boss's name came to me: Lampré Underton.

"Hattie," I planned on having the scurrilous Underton say, in his trademark whine, "you can't leave, babe. We just lost a big spread for the next issue and only you can fill it. We need a full layout on Manx Donnelly, screenwriter, novelist, playwright, actor."

"No can do, Lam," I'd have Hattie bark back. She knew Lampré for the bloodsucker he was and gave him no quarter. "I'm slated to shoot the Betty Ford Rehabilitation Center Alumnae Banquet next week for *Life.*"

"Whatever they're paying you, I'll double it!"

"Sorry, Lam, when Hattie Beauclaire gives her word, it's a done deal."

"I didn't want to have to do this, Hattie," Underton would whine, "but we won't have an issue without your photos. So unless you cancel the *Life* gig and shoot Manx Donnelly for us, I'll print the whole story about your wastrel father, Smiling Jack Beauclaire, and how he dissipated the once-massive Beauclaire potted meat fortune."

"You wouldn't," Hattie would grit through clenched teeth —or clench through gritted teeth. But she knows Lampré Underton most certainly would. No matter what the cost, she must protect her lovable roué of a father, Smiling Jack Beauclaire. But that's the *only* way a boss could ever get the best of Hattie Beauclaire, gal photographer.

♥   ♥

As the weeks went by, I became increasingly involved in this alternate reality I'd created, wherein gal photogs were anything more than a sticky booger to be shaken off an editor's finger. From simply liking my daily fixes of fiction, I went swiftly to needing them like a drug. They helped me to ignore Trout's surly sleaziness, the void that was my social life since I'd tenderized his foot. The fixer freckles on my wardrobe were starting to meet in one enormous brown stain that made all my clothes look as if I washed them in Folger's instant. I hadn't done a Home Spa Weekend since Trout walked out. My nails were not just stained anymore but had commenced peeling off.

Through it all there was Hattie. Hattie had nails that could turn letters on television. And Hattie. Hattie would have Manx. And Hattie would have love.

♥   ♥

I didn't see much daylight for most of August. After working in the darkroom until nine or so in the evening, I came home and wrote until three, then dropped into bed. I rolled out around noon each day, just as the heat reached a level that woke me up stunned and stuporous.

I got up exhausted, thinking that this is the way pregnancy must feel, as if the characters I was creating were sucking away all my energy. I had to sit and drink several glasses of iced tea made with three rounded teaspoons of powder in every glass before I could start moving around. Since I'd started paying off my rent debt to the Cleebs, I'd taken to sipping my instant tea on the front porch. I suppose I could have taken the time to brew some strong tea every morning, putting several fat bags into a small pot the way my mother did, then pouring the liquor over tall glasses of ice with a slice of lemon or sprig of mint on the rim. But I didn't. I actually came to like the foam on the top of instant tea and the bitter brown patches that clung to the ice cubes. It fit in with my new life, where I spent so much time mixing water and powders.

It was the end of August. I was sitting on the front porch trying to get functional with a megatumbler of brisk, refreshing caffeine foam when the phone rang. I answered and tried to sound as if I'd been up for hours.

"Gretchen Griner. Am I speaking with *the* Gretchen Griner?"

I admitted as much, my fogged mind trying to suss out what the caller was selling. All that registered was Fast-talking Flake. The Flake continued.

"What an honor. And I do not say that lightly. Gretchen, my dear. I am Pinkie Levinson of Triton Productions. Perhaps you've heard of us?"

"Uh-h-h—"

"You're probably most familiar with our mini-series work. *Conway Twitty: a Man, a Song?* Or *Bitter Harvest,* our three-parter about a family citrus empire?"

"Mm-m-m." I hadn't had enough tea yet to deal with this.

"We've heard exciting things about your latest project,

Gretchen. 'Gain the Earth' has Triton written all over it. I love the larger-than-life sweep, I love the behind-the-scenes intrigue, I love the insider's up-close look. . . ."

He loved the hyphen.

"It's got to be a Trident picture."

"How did you happen to see my proposal?" The first wave of caffeine shock troops had reached my brain.

"How? How's not important. Let's talk deal. Let's talk a deal I guarantee you aren't going to beat anywhere in this town, and that includes them out-of-state operations shipping in low-grade cast iron from Taiwan."

"Garnell, I knew it was you all along."

"Did not!" Juanita shouted on the extension. Both of them were honking and snorting. "Pinkie, you were going great until you deviated from the script."

"Thought I'd improvise there a little," Garnell explained. "Selling's selling."

"You should have stuck to what I wrote out for you."

"You two sound awful jolly for so early in the day." It eventually came out that they were making Margarita Pies to take to a potluck and had started sampling the product. I told them it had been a barrel of monkeys, and they rang off.

I slumped back out to the front porch and thought about asking Mr. Cleeb to install air conditioning, just a window unit in my bedroom. I had lost my faith that summer would ever end. Then Mrs. Cleeb drove up. She and Mr. Cleeb came home every day for lunch. She had to pull in and back out several times to execute the precision parking job required to wedge the Cougar in between their property line and the chip truck. She got out and glowered at the Delta 88. No AC. It was pretty clear that even though I was nibbling away at my rent debt, if I caused any further aggravation, "Mother" would have a new home.

The ice-cream truck came by. "There once lived an Indian maid, a shy little prairie maid." I sang as much as I could remember, trying to recall what had happened to the warrior bold who "brave and gay had rode one day to battle far away." And, for that matter, what had happened to Gus Kubiak? Had I been too hasty? He *did* have a sweet smile. And he *had* wanted to take me to expensive concerts. I shook my head, thinking of how he was going to be the first member of the fan club I would use to turn the tables on Trout. Now I had no one except Manx.

I went inside and tried to figure out how I could drill some holes in my window frames and fit nails into them so I could raise the windows enough to let in puffs of tropically hot air but not high enough that scary guys could crawl in. I was becoming security-conscious. I'd learned from Trout how ridiculously easy it was to break into my house. I found a sixteen-penny nail in the shed and hammered it with a rock into the window frame. I figured I'd pull it out, then have a big hole to slip my smaller security nail into. I hadn't figured on the fragility of the window frame. With the first rock pound it split. One of the panes in the six-paned window fell out and shattered at my feet. That would not help security.

Even as I was trying to figure out how to dance away from the glass shards, someone knocked on the door. I peeked out the window. It was Mrs. Cleeb. I dropped my rock hammer and tiptoed onto it, then over to the door.

"Mrs. Cleeb!" I edged out onto the porch with her, so that I could close the door behind me and she wouldn't see what had become of her window. I'd never had the opportunity to examine Mrs. Cleeb at close range. She had an upswept hairdo that crescendoed into two air scoops on either side of her head. Her eyeliner left a smudged crescent on the blue eyeshadow on her upper lid. She wore a navy blue pants suit with a short-sleeved jacket and a polka-dotted blouse.

"I'm not going to beat round the bush," were the first words to leak out from her tightly seamed lips. "You're still two months in arrears, and we're going to have to have that money."

I sagged onto the wrought-iron banister. It was a relief to have it over. "I know. I'm ashamed of myself. I should have just cleared out. But I sent in a book proposal a while back and I was hoping—dreaming—that I could sell it and settle up."

I guess she'd expected more resistance. Some wily debit-column tricks. I had none. Though not one of her major muscle groups so much as twitched, her eyes flicked nervously from side to side as if checking on the squirrels watching overhead. Finally, she said, "A book?"

"Yeah. A romance novel. 'Gain the Earth.' I just sent it in."

"To who?"

"A publisher called Cameo. You wouldn't have heard of them unless you read romances."

"For what line? Scintillations? Candelabra? Orchids and Leather?"

"You're a reader?"

Mrs. Cleeb nodded modestly as if I'd just mentioned her Pulitzer. "Well, I guess I am. I had to have DeWitt put up shelves in the utility room, all the rest of our walls are already covered. So, which line are you writing for?"

"A new line they're launching. Languor."

"So the rumors are true." Mrs. Cleeb's eyes glittered. "I sure hope you're not going to write one of them far-out ones. I'm getting sick of them. I swear, I'm not buying Gamine MacPherson again. Half the time, her heroines have either a chain saw or a cattle prod in their hands. Now, I'm all for liberation, but she carries it a little too far."

I jumped up. Hope stirred in my veins again. "Oh, I know just what you mean! She really stretches it. No, my heroine is a . . . a secretary. Well, actually, more an administrative assistant."

Mrs. Cleeb thought about that for a moment. "Hm-m-m.

It's been a long time since I've read one that had a secretary for a heroine. Have you read Violet Wispfeld's *Private Secretary?*"

"Oh, yeah, that's the one where what's-her-name—"

"Callie. Where Callie is hired by the reclusive tycoon to come work on his personal island in the Caribbean. I thought I was the only one remembered that one. It came out fifteen years ago. Oh, if you're writing an A.A., you got to have read *Sweetheart Deal.*"

"I don't think I—"

"You just wait right there. I'm pretty sure it's in the 600s in with the Candelabras. I'll be right back."

Mrs. Cleeb came back half an hour later with a stack of romance novels all featuring secretarial sirens. Without words being spoken, she became my patron. She clearly believed so deeply that the rest of the world was waiting with her for the return of the secretary romance that she was willing to spot me a few months' shelter.

Mrs. Cleeb's misplaced trust spurred me on. I dove into "Gain the Earth," determined it would sell. That Mrs. Cleeb would have her money. When the book came out, I'd tell her my obtuse editor made me change my heroine's occupation to something boring like movie starlet.

Over the next couple of weeks, the few old friends I still had called to ask if I was in love, heartbroken, agoraphobic, or what. I told them all I'd developed an eczemalike skin disease that was triggered by exposure to the sun. That I was having to take massive doses of cortisone and it had blown my head up like Tweetie Pie and I would get back in touch when I'd recovered. It was better than admitting I was writing a romance novel. Lizzie and Juanita were the only ones I could really talk to anymore.

By that time, I was thoroughly grooved into my hermit's routine. After I stumbled out of my soggy bed around noon, my eyes still stinging from developing chemicals and late nights, I'd pour down enough instant tea to crank myself

up, then stagger in to the *Grackle.* I made for the cool darkroom that had become my domain like an albino cave rep-
tile running from light. I purposely tried to avoid completely waking up for the first few hours. In that cozy state,
the darkroom became an isolation tank. I floated through
my mechanical chores, my mind still on the latest complica-
tions in Hattie and Manx's romance. It was like going to a
movie that would run as long as I chose to keep it playing.

About the only thing that could bring me around to the
point where I was aware of spending my days in a black
silence was printing Darci Hollister's stuff. Most other pho-
tographs now registered only as patches of light and dark.
Occasionally they irritated me when the patches weren't
uniform and I'd have to dodge and burn, holding the light
away from areas where the negative was thin and giving
extra time to those sections that were overexposed. I hardly
noticed the actual content of the images. Not the tubby sax
player in a beret making his Dalmatian play his instrument.
Not the beautifully ravaged face of a weeping neighborhood activist. Not the grandiloquent hand gestures of a
touring novelist. Even the photo essays—self-portraits of a
photographer's trip to an avant garde haircutter, a low-rider
show, mythical Austin musicians and their favorite hats,
mythical Austin musicians and their favorite bolo ties, a
night on Sixth Street, mythical Austin musicians and their
favorite pinkie rings—failed to stir me. But Darci's pictures
always brought me around.

In spite of owning the best spot meter her father's money
could buy, she never managed to nail a single exposure. Her
negs were invariably so dense with silver particles I had to
shine a klieg light through them to get an image, or else
they were tracings so ghostly that the barest flicker of light
left what appeared to be renderings of unlit mineshaft in-
teriors. She also had a singular way with the people picture.
When she covered Jerzy Kosinski, she came back without
one piercing glance. When Refrigerator Perry appeared at an

arthritis benefit, she photographed him next to an earthmover so that he looked petite. Her essay on the plight of the undocumented worker captured an optimistic, upbeat Heriberto Alvarez showing off a new pair of Tony Lamas.

Still, by default, the pixie photographer became the Grackle's star shooter. Other, newer names, associated with competent, well-composed, even imaginative images, came and went swiftly. Only Darci could afford to stay.

♥   ♥

On the last day of September, I spent several hours printing some Darci classics: grinning men in tuxedos shaking hands over an award and a busy person talking on the phone. By the time I hit her speaker at the podium with outstretched index finger, I was tempted to burst back into the sunlight and pick up my camera again just to show her how it was done. But Manx and Hattie proved more compelling. Once my blood pressure came back down to slumber level, Darci again seemed like an amateurish cartoon marring the seamless flow of my sublime movie.

As usual, it was dark outside by the time I emerged. I left a stack of the prints I'd done on Trout's desk and took the real product of my dark hours home with me.

I got home that night and gobbled down the macaroni and cheese Lizzie brought by. As soon as she left, I set to work. Tonight I was going to write my first sex scene. Manx was driving Hattie home from their cozy dinner in front of the abode fireplace. I had them there, in his pickup truck (he'd fallen in love with the area while writing the novel and bought a spread up in the mountains). During dinner, Hattie had shared with Manx the searing pain of her unpopularity in high school, and Manx had hinted at some hidden tragedy of his own. The time for the first kiss was upon them.

Setting the stage was a breeze. The night was a deep and fathomless black except where pinpricks of crystalline star-

light pierced the sky. The soft glow from the truck's dash-
board lights faintly outlined Manx's features. Hattie was
free to study them in the darkness. He scared her with his
honesty, his intensity. She'd never had any trouble keeping
the men in her life in a back corner, but Manx Donnelly
was not a man to be so tidily arranged. He was a wild,
sprawling force neither she nor any other woman would
ever control. And that scared her, almost as much as it tan-
talized her. Guided by an instinct that told her there would
be just one Manx Donnelly in her life, Hattie slid a few
fractions of an inch closer to him.

And there I stalled out. I tried again. Hattie slid closer and
. . . and . . . Manx jumped her bones. No. I needed the
galaxies of foreplay Lizzie had told me readers crave. I
needed the gauzy pink fantasies. I needed a moment tender,
sublime, and hot as road tar in August. I needed to copy
from someone else.

I leafed through my pile of Cameos, checking on how
other authors handled this pivotal moment. Most of them, I
found, lavished a minimum of five pages on the initial oscu-
lation, during which mouths claimed, possessed, mastered,
enslaved, captured, welcomed, repelled, surrendered to, and
exalted in. These were kisses that stirred whirling vortexes
of desire and opened chasms of aching need. I cribbed many
of these boilerplate bits trying to jump-start the motor of
passion, but I couldn't pencil in so much as a pucker on
Hattie's plumply luscious lips.

It was very late when I finally gave up.

14

That night I dreamed that Trout and Hattie met at a party. It was one of those brilliant, brittle affairs where everyone slouches beneath the weight of a drink, looking too rich and too thin and batting bon mots at one another. The kind of affair where I would come off like Minnie Pearl, had I been invited in the first place. Then, even as I was watching this glittering soiree from the Little Match Girl spot at the front window, I became Hattie.

In a crystal-clear dream revelation, I realized that I could indeed be Hattie: defiant, pouting, mercurial, and always a great manicure. I could, in short, be the woman who would finally tether a bad boy's wandering heart. Trout, who had, in my dream, magically inculcated all of Manx's finest qualities, leaned in to kiss me. Too late I noticed that he was neither Trout nor Manx and that I was French-kissing Gus Kubiak. Suddenly his head went all pulpy and I was being slurped by an enormous tomato in rut. Odder still, it was not half bad. I made myself wake up.

It was the first day of October in Austin, Texas, and summer had not budged one degree. Four and a half twenty-two-ounce tumblers of tea were barely enough that morning to bring me out of the infrared lobotomy performed by the hundred-degree-plus heat. I wasn't cheered in the least to know that I was participating in a heat wave that was breaking hundred-year-old records. A shower helped. Until I turned off the water.

I patted dry the patches of heat rash on my neck and brushed my hair up into a ponytail. My hair wasn't quite long enough to be swept up, and damp tendrils flopped around my face. Tendrils. I whisked them back. I would never have used that word B.C.—Before Cameo. If I wasn't careful, I'd start noticing the lissome way my waist nipped in before flaring gently into the womanly curves of my hips.

I delayed dressing as long as I could. That day even shorts and a T-shirt seemed *de trop.* I leafed through my closet in search of less constricting garments. The only item I owned with no discernible waistline was a summer dress made of white gauzy cotton I'd had to buy last year when a yeast infection demanded increased air circulation. I slipped it on.

Unaccustomed puffs of air billowed up between my legs. No stern fabrics tugged at me as I walked. It was a weightless, unconstrained feel that required me to do something I rarely did. I went to the bathroom and rooted through the cabinet, filled with tubes of lipstick that turned pizza-grease orange on my lips and a sample size of Estée Lauder Renu-triv cream that had hardened into a gamey-smelling puck. Way at the back, I found what I was looking for. It might possibly have been the last *tin* of Cashmere Bouquet bath powder ever manufactured. I'd used roughly two sprinkles from it each year since my tenth birthday, when Aunt Nina had presented it to me along with a set of lace-trimmed hankies. I held the elasticized front of the dress away from my chest and shook in several fragrant puffs. The fine white powder avalanched over my nipples, down my stomach, thighs, slid off my knees and landed in twin plumes, outlining my feet on the pink and gray linoleum.

Aunt Nina's Cashmere Bouquet in the tin must have special dainty-making properties, for that day nothing could wilt me. I developed, then printed, an entire photo feature, "Austin Musicians and Their Breakfast Nooks," with ease. Even the mad iconoclastic chanteuse wearing black lace demi-gloves and a black velvet strapless while she munched on a bagel with cream cheese and Pickapeppa Sauce seated on a commode did not daunt me, even though printing contrasts like black velvet and gleaming porcelain is a bitch.

Even the grab shot of Trout nuzzling an anemic beauty did not throw me. I admit, I may have dodged in what appeared to be a spectral bolt of light shooting through both their heads like an atomic arrow; still, the print didn't dent my daintiness. Besides, my mind was on Hattie's big event.

She had succumbed, or would as soon as I got around to filling in the details. The conventions of the genre now demanded a contretemps to keep the loving couple apart. "Plot contrivance," I whispered to myself as I watched Trout and the iron-deficient lovely twirling around in the wash water. Once they were clean, I was through for the day. Still thinking plot contrivance, I dumped out the developer bath, now exhausted to a weak instant-tea color, and washed trays, careful not to slop any of the solutions on the parts of my dress not covered by my black plastic apron. I stacked the trays in the sink to let them drain, whipped off my plastic apron, turned off the light and the exhaust fan, and stepped out.

As always, the office was deserted by the time I crept out of my burrow. That was fine with me. It was a strain trying to keep up with Trout's snappy banter when my mind had been seized by the urgent necessities of the romance I was tending. The building seemed darker than usual. The dark of my darkroom seemed cozy and protective, but the greater dark outside gave me the creeps. I could fill up the little lab with my presence, but once I stepped out, I bumped into a whole platoon of other presences that lingered on in the former bathhouse. I hurried down the long, dark hall, no longer thrilled about the light, unencumbered feel of the dress, of air wafting up to my butt. I felt exposed and vulnerable.

The reception area with its blackened windows, was no better than the hall. Seams of light from the street cracked around the door. I made for them and banged my shin against the wooden corner of a chair with my first eager step. A loop coiled around my ankle with the next step, and a chrome pole lamp crashed to the floor.

By the time I reached the door, fumbled with the lock, and made it outside, I was as jumpy as ten toy poodles. The Delta 88 was parked down the empty street. My unprotected crotch prickled each time I passed a shadow. I raced for the 88, jumped in, and locked her up tight. I hadn't been so wide awake since mid-February. Nothing like a charge of adrenaline to get you cranking.

I didn't see another car until I hit Lavaca. The street deadended against the outskirts of the university. I took a right on MLK. Only the nighthawks—or were they bats?—were still working the Capitol. They darted through the misty light that blazed around the grim-eyed Goddess of Liberty perched on the building's domed top. I headed north on Red River, past Memorial Stadium, past the LBJ Library. The stolid, square massiveness of LBJ's vault, its travertine siding shimmering in the moonlight, reassured me. I rolled down my window, then, driving with my left hand on the right side of the steering wheel, I stretched across to open the other window to get a little cross-ventilation going.

With a highway breeze hitting me in the face, I relaxed enough to laugh at myself for being so twitchy and took in my first real deep breath since leaving the lab. The air was moist and heavy with the scent of green things going tropical in the autumn heat. A surge of high spirits capered

through me. I thought about turning around and heading
back to the Ennui to dance with dangerous characters and
possibly, Lord forgive me, flirt with Trout again.

A frolicking sense of being fully alive after months of
dormancy kicked through me. It felt like Halloween night,
and I wanted something fun and wild and unimaginable to
happen. I sat through two lights trying to think of how to
help that something happen. Everything I came up with,
however, including the Ennui, seemed too predictable. My
life had too much predictability.

A single headlight, a motorcycle's, approached slowly behind me, so I had to pull out, still racking my brain for
fabulous fun places to go and people to be with. I suddenly
regretted having let nearly all my friendships lapse. I knew I
couldn't root Lizzie out of bed to prowl the town, and I
surely wasn't sturdy enough for Juanita's brand of good
times. Oh, well, my cut-loose spree would have to be a Big
Wheel ice-cream sandwich from 7-Eleven. A red and green
hut beckoned up on my left.

Resigned to fun from the frozen foods section, I slowed
down to turn in. Suddenly the single headlight I'd noticed
earlier filled the 88 like a floodlight. Dazzled, I saw that this
idiot biker was coming up on me like a locomotive. I was
already turning left when I realized he was going to pass me
on that side. I wrenched the 88, not a vehicle known for
cunning shifts in direction, to the right. My heart trip-ham-
mered again for the second time that evening. I leaned out
the window to yell frightened, mad insults. But as the biker
drew abreast of me, my mouth stopped working.

I don't pretend to understand what it is exactly that flips
the switches in the more primitive regions of my brain. All I
know is that my heart lurched in recognition before my
brain could process the image flying past the window. For a
fraction of a second the rider looked over at me. Wind
pushed into my mouth, and I breathed in the frantic, speed-
ing molecules. A streetlight overhead Dopplered across his

face. Blasting down the road at sixty mph, riding the center line, he continued to stare at me. All that registered was leather jacket and beard stubble. Whips of hair stung my eyes. Then, in one frozen fraction of a second, he slowly tipped his head up and jutted his jaw at the road ahead in an invitation to me to follow him. With a large hand, he twisted the throttle and the bike gunned forward.

The interior of the 88 seemed airless and static when I put my head back in. I couldn't find breath enough to think. The red taillight glowed in front of me. It was too blatant, too dangerous. Even on my private Halloween night, I wasn't going to trail after some midnight biker. I pivoted my foot off the accelerator. It hovered a second, then slid onto the brake pedal.

Bars of silver-white from the streetlights striped his back as he moved ahead of me. The red light slid over a hill and into darkness, but that look in his eyes stayed with me: hungry and way too used to demand feedings.

I had no doubt that this guy had little trouble making new friends: women, riding alone late at night, who followed where the upthrust jaw pointed; waitresses, nurses, IRS shift workers, women with too much routine in their lives and not enough excitement. Women like me.

I crested the rise where I'd lost this Lothario of the Lonesome Highway, half expecting him to be waiting on the other side. I imagined him, slouched against his bike, knowing I was hot on his trail. I looked forward to blowing by him and watching his swollen self-confidence detumesce in my rearview. But not even a flicker of the ruby taillight gleamed in the distance. He was gone. I slumped back against the seat. Hound that he was, he'd probably already cut over to Burnet Road to cruise the night shift getting off at Denny's.

I sighed and made my usual turn at 41st.

I'd stop at the 7-Eleven on Duval for my Big Wheel.

The turn at 41st was a special detour I took every night

just to look at the Shackleford mansion. I loved the old place's spooky elegance at any time, but only after dark could I fully appreciate the arthritic creepiness of the dozens of century-old live oaks gnarled up all over the mansion's park-sized grounds. That night, though, I made the turn automatically. Of course, I wouldn't actually have gone anywhere with that hound of a biker, but this one night, my early Halloween, I wanted a bit more of a chance to flirt with the possibility. Sure that he was long gone, I began to seriously regret my prissy caution. I could at least have talked to him through the window. With my door locked. And the motor running.

The *blap!* of water being hurled onto my windshield brought me around. As often as I drove by the place, I never remembered that the mansion's inhabitants were secret sprinklerers who crept out at night under cover of darkness to drench their greenery in water that, because of the record heat and accompanying drought, was still rationed. The fat drops slung by their supercharged sprinkler system blasted in through the open window on the passenger's side. These cheat waterers were profligate. They drenched not only their block of rolling lawn and giant bonsai live oaks but most of the street as well. Water was flung and ran off the soaked lawn to pool in one large pond that covered a valley half a block long where the road dipped in front of their estate. I stretched across the seat, smelling the mildew growing there from past waterings, and rolled up the window.

When I straightened back up, my windshield was a wavy sheet of water. A streak of red smeared across it. A motorcycle taillight. I jerked back to attention. It was him. He was there, right in front of me, meandering through the mechanical downpour. Eek! He would think I had followed him after all.

I groped for the windshield wipers. They screeched on and cleared a strip two inches wide at the top of their arc, the only place where the bowed arms actually made contact with glass. I watched him through the sheets of water. Before I had time to slow down and let him disappear again, the smeared red slash of his taillight dipped as he followed the sloping road down. Tall plumes of water flew out on either side of the bike when he hit the pond collected in the dip in the road. The streaked taillight abruptly shot over like the hour hand of a clock flashing from twelve to two.

My foot flew to the brake pedal as the distressed slash that was the taillight careened crazily back and forth. I stuck my head out the window, and water slapped me in the face. I squinted through it. The man was fighting the motorcycle, trying to wrestle it back under him, but the rear tire continued spinning out on the wet pavement, levering the big machine down. I knew the instant he went into the final slide that he would never pull out of it. I slammed on the brakes. Wings of water spumed up, covering the 88's windows.

Silver sparks sprayed over the gleaming asphalt as the handlebar grated across the road. The bike spun away to the left; the rider was flung to the right. His body pirouetted over the slick pavement, slamming to rest in the gutter.

I jumped out of the car and landed ankle-deep in the pond that had caused the accident. My foot crunched against the sandbar that had formed there. It was their fault: the cheaters in the mansion. My thoughts scrambled around. I clung to the number 911 and ordered myself not to be sick. From a distance all I could make out was the white strip of his T-shirt beneath his jacket, his hands pale at the ends of outflung arms. I told myself that I was good in an emergency. Not the kind to shriek and faint. I rammed a fist into my mouth to stifle a shriek and made myself walk forward.

He'd landed in a patch of moonlight unshaded by the live oaks that darkened most of the mansion's grounds. I always imagined I'd have an immediate gut knowledge of death.

No instinct screamed when I looked at the sprawling body, but he sure seemed dead. His head was pillowed on the sidewalk, while the rest of him slumped into the gutter. Runoff water eddied around him. I dreaded the thought of touching him. I admitted the truth: I am hopeless in an emergency. I glanced around. Surely someone must have heard. The water squanderers should come to check on their bayou, if nothing else. But no lights went on in the big mansion and no one came out. I was the only one in the world who could help. I had to *get* good in an emergency. Fast.

I squatted down in the gutter, bent close to him, and went weak with relief when I heard the calm, uncluttered sound of his breathing. He *was* alive. I knew I shouldn't attempt to move the victim. But what else? Water swirled around my knees, soaking my dress. Look in his eyes, that was it. Look in his eyes and see if they were rolled back in his head. After I knew whether they were rolled back or not, I could run screaming to the mansion's front door, yelling for an ambulance. I steadied my hand on his cheek, my palm against a stubble that felt comfortingly alive. I was just about to thumb up an eyelid when the jet sweep of a sprinkler sprayed across us.

The blast caught him right in the nostrils and he inhaled a snootful. Snorting and gasping, he came alive. He reared up. Water trickled down his face, running from his nose, his hair. He opened his eyes. They were Bunsen-burner blue. He stared blankly, blinked three times. His head wobbled as he brought me into focus; then he spoke.

"Crikey! What the bloody hell happened?" His accent was some British derivative. Australian?

"You've had an accident. You're probably in shock. Do not attempt to move. I'll go call an ambulance." I was impressed by my imitation of a calm in-control person. I started to stand and an iron bar wrapped around my wrist. It was his hand. He pulled me back to my knees.

"Don't . . . call . . . anyone." His voice was harsh and urgent. My heart battered around. I thought of all the enchanting individuals one can encounter on America's highways and byways. Henry Lee Lucas, for example, sprang to mind. Then the grip slackened, and he slumped back against the curb. "I'm sorry. That crack to the nana must have bent me a bit. But you really mustn't call anyone." His hand, still on my wrist, tightened a bit. This time, though, it didn't scare me. It was more of a clutching than a trapping gesture. "Promise?"

"Yeah. Okay."

He took his hand away. I didn't know what to do. Was he psychotic? Deranged? Should I take control of the situation? Maybe there was internal hemorrhaging? What on earth was a "nana"? He didn't look like he was losing blood. He sparkled wetly in the moonlight. Droplets of water glistened on his dark hair and in his thick eyelashes. While I was trying to make up my mind whether to bolt or to elevate his legs, the sprinkler swept over us again. He rolled away from the spray and tried to stand. With a choked grunt, he crumpled back to his hands.

His breathing was ragged and harsh, a fair indication that he was in pain. He crouched there for a minute like a sick dog. My hands floated out to him of their own volition, wanting to do something useful and not knowing how. He shook his head to clear the pain and looked over at me. The moon was in my face. "Come on, then"—he reached an arm out to me—"give us a hand."

I fit myself under his armpit. There was, of course, the smell of leather, of sweat sharp with shock and pain, but under all that was a vaguely cedarish fragrance. His chest rose and fell, pressing against me as he drew in several deep, steadying inhalations. He stood with his weight on his left leg. I felt the machinery of his body work against mine, the muscles and tendons of his hip, thigh, pulling him upright. It was like dancing with a crippled bear. I reached one of my

arms around his waist and with the other one grabbed the
wrist he dangled over my shoulder. It was slick with blood
and gritty with the pebbles scraped into his skin. He tried to
walk.

"*Jee*-sus," he exhaled, the instant his right toe contacted
the wet earth. His arm tightened around my shoulder as he
struggled to regain his balance on his unhurt leg. I hugged
him tighter and felt pain shudder through his body. "My
ankle," he gasped. "Puckerooed, I reckon."

We stood there, both of us sodden, him crouched over in
pain, bleeding, who-knows-what fractured or hemorrhaging, his motorcycle crumpled, mosquitoes finding their way
to us in droves. Then, for the final indignity, the damned
sprinkler twitched through another arc and smacked us
both in the face.

"Ah-h-h, now that's refreshing." He beamed down at me,
grinning as a bucket or so of water dripped off his face. We
got slapped half a dozen more times before we could hobble
out of the sprinkler's reach.

He sagged onto the first patch of dry earth we came to
and lay there panting, on his back, his eyes closed in concentration as if he were adding large numbers in his head
instead of trying to get ahead of the pain in his leg. Gradually, his breathing steadied and he lifted himself up on his
elbows, opened his eyes and studied me. I was crouched
warily down beside him, still ready at any second to run for
an ambulance. Or the police.

"You're giving me a lot more credit than I deserve if you
think I'm going to attack you."

I didn't answer.

"I'm sorry about your frock."

I looked to where he was staring. Blood from his hand
had seeped onto the white gauze, marking the shoulder
with a dark stain that the sprinkler water spread down over
my breast.

"Is it ruined?" He reached up and touched the lowest border of the mark. His hand lingered there.

I tried to form some snappy reply, but the entire snappy division of my brain seemed to have called in sick. "Hey, no great loss." I shrank back from his hand and he let it fall. He propped himself up on his elbows and straightened his right leg out in front of him, his head jerking back in pain as he set the broken ankle on the ground.

"Okay, that's it." I hopped up from my knees to my feet. "I'm going to go now to call an ambulance."

His hand manacled my wrist before his eyes were open again. This time he held me. "No ambulance. No authorities."

That word "authorities." It was a Henry Lee kind of word.

He snorted a laugh and loosened the grip on my wrist. But he didn't let me go. "I'd be in a plurry picnic if you was to sic some official drongoes on me. I'm up a gum tree as it is with the green card people, if you take my meaning."

This Alice in Wonderland outburst momentarily boggled my fear. The only part of it that meant much to me was green card. I put that together with the accent and came up with: "You're an illegal alien." I sank back onto the grass. He let go of my wrist.

" 'Illegal'? That's a bit harsh, eh? Just overstayed my visa a bit. A year or so."

His words trailed off, as did his gaze. Only when it came to rest well below my clavicles did I become aware that sprinkler-soaked gauze is nearly transparent. And that my nipples, always hams for attention from the right audience, were going all out in the pert'n' perky department. I had not given my permission for this performance.

Without lifting his eyes, he spoke one word that again scattered my concentration. "Kiwi."

I forgot my stagestruck nipples. Were random references

to fruit or shoe polish a sign of shock? Should his feet be elevated?

"You *were* trying to place the accent, weren't you?" He stopped addressing my aureoles and looked up at me. "It's New Zealand with a bit of Scottish boarding school thrown in and six months in the states to blodger it up right and proper. I sound almost Yank now, don't I?"

He sounded about as Yank as Margaret Thatcher, though his choppy accent was far from crisply British. It was an oddly unplaceable hodgepodge that did sound jauntily Australian, with the occasional vowel either dropped or transformed so that "accent" became "ik-sent" and "Texas," "Tik-sus." I'd never heard a New Zealand accent before. From an unseen control, the sprinklers were shut off. Without the mechanical tick and hiss, the night fell deeply silent. The scent of the illicitly lush grass rose out of the damp earth.

A trickle of water ran down his forehead into his eyelashes and hung there in a drop. Suddenly the smell of the grass was suffocating. I tried to come up with some casual, solicitous remark. He looked over at me and my mind emptied.

"Well, I should be all right now." He pushed himself up, lurching onto his good leg. Once upright, he reached over his head into the twisted arms of the live oak above us. A dead limb came loose in his hand. Using it like a cane, he leaned his weight on it.

"Can I pay you for your . . . ?" He gestured in the direction of my dress.

"It's a rag, forget it."

"Well, thank you. I'd better be going. Someone might call after all." His accent made the statement sound babyish, turning "call" and "all" to "caw" and "aw."

I was still trying to think of something to say when he half hobbled, half hopped away toward his bike. It took me a second to realize that he was actually leaving. This stranger in the night was not only *not* going to dismember me, he wasn't even going to ask for my phone number. "Uh, wait up a sec." I followed him down to his motorcycle. It had spun across the road, landing in a drain culvert on the edge of a junior high school playground. "What are you planning to do?"

"Get her out."

"You can't."

Even as I spoke, he stepped off the road onto the gravel along the side. The improvised cane couldn't find a solid surface and slid away. Unbalanced, he landed on his right foot. An animal grunt went out from him and I lunged forward to catch his wobbling weight. He slumped against me with a dead heaviness. For a few seconds it was all I could do to stay upright. He hung onto me, on the verge of passing out. Gradually he took back some of his weight. I realized that the shock of the accident had disoriented him and that someone lucid would have to take control.

"You're not riding that motorcycle anywhere tonight. I'll drive you wherever you need to go."

He made a small noise of acquiescence at the back of his throat; then we staggered together over to the 88. I slid into the driver's side after I'd loaded him aboard.

"My bike," he half groaned.

I looked over at the machine lying in the culvert.

"Can't leave it."

"Can't leave it?" I echoed. "Got to leave it. Can't move it. Too heavy." I was speaking his language, pain.

His head sagged wearily onto his chest and he started to open the door. I grabbed him.

"No, okay. Look, we'll hide the bike." I jumped out of the car. The parched sycamores and elms in the playground had been losing leaves since August. I transferred the pile that had drifted into the culvert to the bike and humped them over it until it was completely hidden. My passenger wasn't ecstatic about the camouflage job, but at least he didn't try to leave.

When I asked for directions to wherever he lived, he insisted that it was too far for me to drive and that I could just drop him at the nearest "kiosk" and he'd "ring" for a taxi. The nearest phone turned out to be at my house.

Once there, I offered to at least wash the road grit out of his hand. He looked at his pulped hand and agreed casually that it might not be a bad idea to get some of the asphalt out.

His engineer boots were starkly black, covering the Cashmere Bouquet tracks my feet had left earlier on the pink and gray linoleum of the bathroom. He held his hand under the faucet, and tarry gravel washed into my sink in the pink puddle of his blood. It made me woozy to scrub at the gash on his palm, but if I didn't get them out the pebbles would heal up into him. Guaranteed infection.

In spite of knowing this had to be done, I got woozy when his breath whistled in between his gritted teeth as I tipped hydrogen peroxide over the whole mess. I had to stop and put the brown plastic bottle down. He picked it up and dumped the solution on his hand himself, making his palm turn fuzzy white everywhere it was cut. His good hand shook as he put the open bottle onto the sloppy oval of soap at the edge of the sink. He didn't notice when it slid onto the floor. The solution fuzzed around his feet and over the powder tracks.

I knelt down to grab the bottle. When I looked up his face had gone a pale fluorescent green beneath his road tan and his eyes were wobbling. I slapped a gauze pad over his shredded palm, then helped him to my couch.

"I'll just have a bit of a rest," he muttered. "Then I'll ring for a cab." Those were the last words he spoke before passing out.

I hadn't dealt with a comatose person since my high school buddy, Joy Houtenbreiker, discovered the soda-pop drinkability of Ripple. As we were attending the Latin League convention at the time, I merely had to haul Joy (fortunately a size five petite) back to our motel room and tuck her into the sheets she already wore. My current situation wasn't quite that simple. There could be injuries to the head even more severe than those inflicted by Ripple. I put my hand on his chest and jiggled him lightly. No response. I jiggled a bit more forcefully. He tensed up, shouted, "Stone the crows! That's a ripper!" and slumped back down, breathing heavily. I decided he wasn't a vegetable yet and should probably rest for an hour or so. If he wasn't coherent by then, I would definitely call an ambulance.

I thought about draping a blanket over him, but we were both dripping sweat in the dead air of my house. Instead I unbuttoned his shirt a bit and patted his vest pockets. His jeans pockets held only a penknife, which I removed and slipped into my own pocket so he wouldn't inadvertently stab himself. Other than that and a wad of bills, mostly tens and twenties, he carried nothing else. No identification whatsoever.

His booted feet were still courteously planted on the floor. I remembered RICE—Rest, Ice, Compression, Elevation —for sprains and lifted his right foot. He growled but didn't come to as I propped his injured foot on a mound of cushions. The heel of his boot made a long muddy smear on the bedraggled polar-bear-hide of my couch. I tossed a towel over the lamp above his head to dim the light and stuffed a pillow under his head. That was the extent of my nursely ministrations.

When they were over, I had to deal with him as a human rather than as the injured lump on my couch. His presence, even unconscious, was all around me. I felt it noticing my shabby furniture and reading the titles of my books: *Love's Reckless Bounty, Thinner Thighs in Thirty Days, How to Flirt Like a Chi O.* Especially ashamed of the last title, I gathered up all my dirty secrets, dumped them into the laundry hamper, and replaced them with books that showed better: *Gödel, Escher, and Bach, Humboldt's Gift, Typee,* and a few other selections whose pages had never been exposed to the light of day.

I hid the TV in my closet and replaced it with the chess set abandoned three years ago by an old boyfriend who'd tried unsuccessfully to teach me the game. I was putting the Bruce Springsteen albums at the back of the pile and bringing Gato Barbieri to the front when I stopped myself. This was crazy. I was pretending to be some hip Fulbright scholar for a comatose biker?

I turned around to have another look at this specimen and caught a glimpse of him that made my heart stop. Towel-filtered light shone on his face. His mouth hung open the tiniest bit and his eyelids twitched. I never would have studied his face, moved close to him again, if he'd been awake. But in sleep I was free to watch him and wonder about the universes behind those twitching lids. *And* to fully appreciate the dark lashes out front.

Why, I asked myself, unable to quit staring, is it always the bad boys with their air of danger and unattainability that cause the cardiac arrhythmia? It's probably all snarled up in some prehistoric genetic code that made the biggest maniac with the atlatl the hottest number among the berry gatherers. I noted the pattern of his beard, the way it was scalloped out under his cheeks, how it climbed up over his lips.

What truly captivated me, though, was his mouth. I tiptoed over to have a better look. Sure enough, it was just the sort I liked best: a lived-in mouth, a mouth that had been around. The kind that engulfed new tastes, strange textures. It welcomed strangers and appreciated old friends. This mouth was not overly fastidious. Kissing it would be like wearing someone else's shoes. I could never fall in love with a finicky mouth, and this one wasn't. It had pecked girls when he was young and suckled women now that he wasn't quite that young. I wanted this mouth.

I leaned in closer to him, then stopped myself. I spread my hand across his chest and shook him one more time. His lids fluttered, his brows furrowed in annoyance, and he growled muffled protests, but his eyes didn't open. He would never know. I bent over him. My mouth hovered against his for a few seconds, breathing his breath and inhaling his cedary smell. His chest rose and fell beneath me. I licked my lips and pressed them lightly against his. It wasn't really even a kiss. It was more like finding my place in case artificial respiration should become necessary. Except that something crazily erratic suddenly happened with my pulse and I was now dying to feel his hair against my palms.

I pulled back. This was sick. The word "necrophiliac" jumped out at me and I stood abruptly, glancing around, checking to make sure the Cleebs weren't peering out of their back window. I scurried into my room, slammed the door shut, grabbed the first book I found, and started to read.

The honeyed touch of his lips sent delicious charges of electric warmth spiraling through her to the secret innerness of her melting core. . . .

I tossed the Cameo aside, feeling even more perverted. Still in my soggy clothes, I pulled the covers up and switched off the light. Sleep was impossible. My mind came vividly, untiringly awake, replaying every word he'd uttered since the first "Crikey!" and every glimpse I'd had of him since he'd blown by me in the light of the 7-Eleven.

I *thought* sleep was impossible until I awoke sometime before dawn when the screen door slammed shut. By the time I freed myself from the sheets twisted around my legs and ran into the living room, the cab was already backing into the street and pulling away. I looked over at the couch, unable to believe that he wouldn't be there. All that was left of him was a mud smear on the polar bear's coat.

I raced into the bathroom. A note, in lipstick or eyebrow pencil perhaps, would surely be scrawled on the mirror. The only thing I found there was a woman bewildered by disappointment.

He was really gone. Departed. Vanished. It was only then that I realized I didn't even know his name.

15

Later that morning I stood at the doorway with my third glass of iced tea and studied the cracks fracturing the dry earth around the hovel. Mr. Cleeb was out in his yard watering by hand. Because of rationing, you were only allowed to have your sprinklers on for a few hours every week, but you could water by hand all you liked. So that is what Mr. Cleeb was spending his one week of vacation doing.

I consciously tried to concentrate on the world around me.

The rainbows refracted in the silver spray hypnotized me. The instant I stopped paying close attention to immediate reality, I became a zombie mind slave to the stranger who'd left me nothing but a boot mark on my couch and a lot of unspecified yearnings.

The phone rang. It was him! I practiced saying "Hello." After a few tries, I stopped sounding like I'd just sniffed up a tank or two of helium. I forced my voice into an earthy register and answered, holding my breath for that "Crikey" accent. Instead, a cartoonishly nasal Brooklyn-accented

voice said, "Cameo calling, hold please for Andrea Bronstein."

I could see Juanita on the other end of the line with a
clothespin stuck on her nose, holding her hand over the
receiver so I wouldn't hear Garnell chortling. She picked a
bad time for one of her little phone frolics. Disappointed, I
sank into the chair.

"Gretchen, good morning. I'm sorry to be so long in getting back to you on the proposal."

I was impressed. Juanita must have studied Andrea; the
imitation was pretty fair. Still, she was overplaying wildly,
biting off her consonants too much in an overdrawn ap-
proximation of Andrea's lockjawed accent. "No problem,
Andy." I figured I'd let Juanita know early that I was wise.

"Uh, yes, well . . . I passed the proposal for 'Gain the
Earth' around and it's gotten several enthusiastic reads. Of
course, we can't go to contract with an unknown. But we
were tossing around figures, and thirty-five was mentioned."

"Thirty-five *thousand* dollars!" I whooped. "Well, it's a little less than I'd expected, still thirty-five thousand dollars *is*
a moderately mentionable sum. Aw, what the hay? Boozers
can't be chiggers, right, Ange?"

I was sure that Garnell would come on the line now, guf-
fawing at the punch line to a terrible joke he liked to tell
about an alcoholic insect. Instead, there was puzzled silence;
then, "Pardon me?"

Every molecule of my being winced. A sick feeling
pressed me, squirming, into the chair.

"Am I speaking with Gretchen Griner?" Andrea was not
amused.

"Oh, y'all want *Gretchen?*" I hid behind a clownish Texan
accent, held the receiver away, and yelled, "Gretchen!
Phone!" I carefully laid the receiver down on the chair, tiptoed away, and yelled, "Thanks, Tina. Be right there." Then
I trod heavily back across the floor. I hoped Andrea would

think I had a roommate, possibly a slightly retarded roommate employed at a sheltered workshop, who delighted in prankish patter with my callers. I hoped Andrea would admire me for taking in such an unpredictable individual.

"Hello, Gretchen Griner speaking."

Andrea repeated her news in a suspicious voice. She didn't quite believe in the puckish Tina. My squeal of surprise came out about as spontaneous as a Japanese tea ceremony.

Embarrassment interfered with my concentration. Consequently, when Andrea said, "So thirty-five is acceptable?" I agreed eagerly. I would have agreed if she'd been talking about thirty-five wolverines.

"Wonderful. When you submit the finished manuscript we'll go to contract. In the meantime, I have a few minor changes to suggest. First off, your heroine's name, Hattie. Margaux has so much more panache, don't you think?"

"Well, yeah, sure. But Hattie's not a Margaux," I squeaked. "She's a Hattie. A real person with a real person's name."

"All right, let's compromise. Cassie."

"Cassie?"

"Short for Cassandra. Cassie is too feisty, too independent, too much today's woman to put up with such a formal lump of a name like Cassandra."

"Hattie likes her name. It was her grandmother's."

"Exactly the problem. Readers don't want to think about their grandmothers when their heroines are experiencing shuddering fulfillment. Market research shows that quite clearly. Readers indicate strong preferences for smart-mouthed tomboy heroines with names ending in -ie or -y who worry that their slim-hipped figures aren't womanly enough for the hero."

"Hattie's not slim-hipped. She's the tiniest bit broad in the beam. She wears size ten shoes. She has *real* imperfections, not imaginary ones like hips that are too skinny." I added hopefully, "Her name *does* end in I-E."

"No, I see Cassie as the type who forgets to eat. What you've created, Gretchen, is a heroine who buzzes with life and energy. The pounds just can't find a restful spot to stay on her boyish frame."

"How about Maggie?" I tried.

"That's awfully close to Cassie. If she can be Maggie, why can't she be Cassie?"

I didn't say anything. Andrea knew what she wanted, and if she couldn't get it from me, there were thousands of other "writers" who dreamed of becoming "authors."

"Oh, and one other thing: no ethnic types."

"I didn't use any, did I?"

"The producer, Goldstein: make him a WASP."

"Sure."

"And Gretchen, are we committed to Lorelei Beaumatin?"

"Well, I don't know. I like the way it sounds."

"Mm-m-m. You are aware that Cameo already has a Lorraine Beauville? How about a hoydenish, contemporary appeal? Penny McCall?"

"Penny McCall." I hated it. "That's good. Penny McCall. I'll think it over."

"Yes, do. Oh, and one last thing."

"Yes?"

"There was no love scene in your proposal. We'll be paying particularly close attention to how you handle them."

I gulped. She heard me.

"You aren't having a problem with the love scenes, are you, Gretchen?"

I thought of the failed first kiss; she'd zeroed right in on my problem. "No. Oh, heck no. They're the icing on the cake for me. The Tootsie Roll in the Pop. The warm, moist center flowing with honeyed syrup in the middle of a—" I tried to think of something with a warm, moist center flowing with honeyed syrup so I could show Andrea just how

tuned into the sensuous I was. I didn't think Chewels gum
was quite right.

"Well, I hope so. As you know, in the murder mystery we
must have the murder, and in the romance novel—"

"Gotta have that romance," I chimed in.

"Absolutely."

"I'll bear down on them," I promised.

The first thought I had after I hung up was, I can't wait to
tell the nameless stranger. I wanted him to know that I
could write a successful book proposal. But for a romance?
No, I'd wait until we knew each other better. I then had to
remind myself that this individual I was planning to expose
myself to in subtly nuanced stages had clomped out of my
life without so much as a *hasta luego*. I put him out of my
mind. I had more important things to worry about. Now, I
had to get the steamy stuff right.

♥   ♥

"I quit." Given my job history, those are the two most
satisfying words I can imagine speaking. Uttering them to
Trout was a special joy.

"You can't quit," he informed me.

I told him that, indeed, I could and I would.

"Wow, I can't believe you'd do this. After I went way out
on a limb lining this job up for you because you were hurting for cash. Then you turn around and quit." He shook his
head in sad bafflement at my perfidy. "It's not like I expect
any of you to stand watch by my grave or anything, but,
Jesus, a little human decency? You're probably going to step
up, go shoot for *River City*. That's it, isn't it?"

"No, that's not it."

But Trout wasn't listening. "I don't know why I'm surprised. A woman who would come after me with a hammer."

"It was a meat tenderizer, and you gave me ample provo-
cation."

"I should expect this by now. I cultivate new talent. Give you guys a start. A home. Then you all leave. No thanks. No gratitude. Not that I expect that anymore. But you, Gretchen, I thought you were different."

"Different? How? I don't need to eat?"

"Gibes. Mock me. You all do. I know it. Use me in your ruthless drive to the top, then laugh at me." Trout reveled in his King Lear impersonation, hamming it up with his head in his hands and big gusty sighs of despair. As theatrical as it all was, he still managed to make me feel like a sniveling ingrate turncoat. In that weakened state, I revealed to Trout that I was quitting not to shoot for anyone else but to finish writing the romance novel I had hammered from his grasp.

" 'Gain the Earth?' " Trout lifted his head from his hands. "Lorelei Beaumatin lives?" His dull, lifeless eyes regained their malevolent gleam. "Someone is going to pay you to write that?" His sagging countenance snapped back into its usual lines of sneering contempt. *"To write a romance novel!"*

Trout's braying hyena laugh followed me down the hall and out of the *Grackle.* I swore the next time I laid eyes on Trout Treadwell would be when I deigned to allow him an interview at the National Book Awards. Or possibly when I returned to Austin for the filming of the mini-series to be based on "Gain the Earth."

Back at 4310 Rear, I called Juanita to give her the good news about the book and the better news about quitting my job. "I figure, if I'm writing full-time, I can zip through the rest of the manuscript. Then I'll be getting a big fat check from Cameo real soon."

Juanita laughed and gave me the bad news. "Soon? 'Soon' is a measure of time that does not exist in the publishing world. I bet my editor once that I could write a *book* in less time than it'd take Secret Moments to cut a *check.* Now, I'm not saying they're slow, larcenous, and using my money for their float, but I was typing "finis" a month before I ever

filled out a deposit slip. Besides which, you don't even have
a finished manuscript."

"Well, yeah, but, working full-time I should be able to
crank the thing out in a couple of weeks."

Juanita laughed again. "Sister, you just crank away. If
anything besides link sausage comes out, I want to be the
first to know."

Pricked by Juanita and Trout's flagrant lack of confidence,
I got right to work. I picked Hattie—or, rather, Cassie—up
in pucker interruptus and tried to get Manx to make his
move. Only now a clock was ticking in my head, counting
off the impotent moments. And then it went silent. The
next thing I was aware of was that an hour had passed and
all I had accomplished was the mental cataloging of every
crease in the Kiwi's lips. Since Cassie wasn't showing the
slightest hint of razor burn, I gave up and penciled in a
notation, *First kiss, five pages* and jumped back on the barreling
freight train of the narrative.

After that first postponed kiss that I would fill in later, a
wall of mistrust springs up between Cassie and Manx. Cassie is about to flounce off the set and out of Manx's life
forever. She'll be damned if she'll let the blackmailing editor
of *Celebrity* run her life.

At the last moment the movie's still photographer is sum-
marily dismissed for leaking rumors of dissension on the set
to the media and the producer, Shel Goldstein. . . . Oops,
ethnic. I crossed out the name and typed in "John Whiteman." John Whiteman pleads with her to take the position.
Cassie still wants to flounce, but she'll be damned if she'll
let the gallingly imperious Manx Donnelly run her life and
deprive her of this once-in-a-lifetime opportunity.

On direct orders from John Whiteman, Manx is forced to
take Cassie with him to his mountain hideaway for a photo
session. Secure in his piney sanctuary, Manx finally slips his
wary shell and shows himself to be the radiant, vulnerable
man he is. Cassie sees it's no good fighting her attraction

any longer and there, amid the Seven Grey Hills Navajo blankets and the black San Ildefonso pottery, she weakens.

Clearly it was time for knees to turn to jelly and a narcotizing languor to steal over my heroine. And that was precisely where I stalled out again. The meter was running, and once more I clutched. I could not get my young breeders to work up the tiniest goose bump of shivering delight. I don't know what was wrong. I'd breezed through that original scene in the trailer when Cassie was still Hattie and she first met Manx. The brief, lusty encounter had been no trouble. But now, freighted down with the burden of Cassie's dreams and Manx's vulnerabilities and millions of readers' gauzy expectations, I stumbled beneath the load.

It isn't easy admitting that you're a washout with sex scenes. I had expected them to be a delicious high point, to enjoy the whoopie pitching in the earthy Wife of Bath way that Juanita did. But no. What came easily to me were plot and characterization, the window dressing of the romance novel. When I came up against the sine qua non of the genre, I balked. Like a child at a movie, I shrank from the gushy parts.

Around three that morning, I gave up. With far less confidence this time that I'd ever get back on the track, I took the coward's way out again and wrote, *Neck nuzzling, breast cupping, forays up the thigh, six pages.* At this rate there would be no "cranking out" a book. That meant only one thing: I would have to crawl back on my belly to Trout.

The very next morning, before Trout could get another chump to take my place, I slunk back to the *Grackle.*

"What happened?" Trout gloated. "Snafu with the *subsidiary rights?* Distribution foul-ups? Didn't like the crowd at Elaine's?"

I made no answer to Trout's childish taunts, merely put on my black plastic apron and took up my duties once again.

I swished prints automatically through the developing

baths while I tried to figure out how I was going to get
Cassie and Manx together. Three sudsy Mexican children in
a cast-iron tub grinned up at me through the yellow solution. Someone must have gone to the border and come back
with a photo essay. Sure enough, shots of a mean-eyed *vato*
slouching against a graffitied wall, a fly-bothered haunch of
beef hanging in the *mercado,* and a shy señorita in an Amalie
Oil T-shirt smiling behind her hand like a geisha followed.
Beneath the warbly yellow waves, the *vato* transmuted into
Ray and then into the Kiwi stranger. I splashed my tongs
through the solution to banish his image. If he wasn't going
to call, why should I think about him? The answer was, I
shouldn't. I needed to concentrate on Cassie and Manx's
carnal future.

I dumped the prints in the wash and called Juanita,
stretching out the cord to pull the receiver into the darkroom with me.

"Did you try getting in the mood?" she asked when I
explained my particular block.

"The mood?"

"You know. Slip into something sheer and slinky. Light a
few sticks of frangipani incense. Rub some bath oil behind
your knees. Dim the lights. Pour a little Johnny Mathis on
the stereo. Eat breath mints."

I told her I'd neglected to do all those things. "But I don't
think they would help me much. I mean, let's face it, first
kisses aren't usually all that great in real life." I thought of
my own first kisses. How they leaned heavily toward excess
slobber, teeth cracking together, and guy wires of spit looping from mouth to mouth. Toward discovery of saliva tacky
as rubber cement and breath worse than an old dog's. Except for the other night. Of course, that had only been half
of a first kiss—my half. Still, it had done more for me than
any whole first smooch.

"There's your problem. You're not surrendering to the
fantasy. Forget real life, especially yours. Real life is not

why women buy romances. If they want real life, they can turn on the news. Which is just what they'll do if you don't deliver the goods. Get with it, girl, put the meat on the table," she ordered.

"I just don't know if I can."

"Good night, nurse, G.G., live it up a little. Most women would kill to get paid for lolling around dreaming about hanky-panky."

I thanked Juanita and went back to my prints. I imagined Cassie and Manx, ripe, waiting. Try as I might, though, I couldn't whirl up the tiniest vortex of desire. I left *mis amigos* again to call Lizzie and ask her how she handled these mandatory scenes.

"Implication," she answered brightly. "I make it into a writing exercise and see how much I can do through subliminal imagery. You know, the mead heavy and intoxicating on her lips, spreading through her veins like liquid fire, turning her soft and pliant. His handling of his battle steed, masterful, coaxing the charging destrier into grateful surrender."

"I don't know about all this pliant surrender and stuff."

"There's your problem. You can't write what you don't believe in."

"You do? How can you?"

"Any woman who's been well and truly in love does. You've never really been in love."

Lizzie could be awfully dogmatic when she put her fuzzy head to it. "Hey, I fall in love regularly once a week whether I need to or not."

"You've never *really* been in love," Lizzie repeated, stubborn and abstract at the same time, like a physics wizard defending his new theory about quarks or some such thing. "If you'd ever really been in love, you'd know that by the time you get around to whether you should or not, you've already surrendered."

"Mmmm. Thanks for the illumination."

"Oh, you're welcome." The way humans can't hear high-pitched noises that drive dogs wild, Lizzie couldn't hear sarcasm that wilts most people.

I didn't know what else to say. It seemed that, at the deepest level, Lizzie believed in what she wrote.

I finished up the trip to the border and went home for the day. I sat down at the typewriter and faced my last words: *Neck nuzzling, breast cupping, forays up the thigh, six pages,* and I knew what it was to be a gynecologist. The basics of reproduction could not have held less of an erotic charge for me. I lighted a few scented candles to stir up memories that now seemed more distant than braiding gimp into lanyards at Girl Scout Camp. After an hour I was nauseated from the smell of frangipani and hadn't typed one spicy word. I decided to try a bit of Lizzie's implication.

The second day at Manx's ranch, I had my couple go horseback riding. There is an idyllic interlude in a high meadow dense with the scent of clover. The sun is a warm weight on their bodies as they lie in the grass. Manx slips the pale stalk of a tender blade into Cassie's mouth and invites her to taste the sweetness.

Hot-cha! Again it was time for some action, and again I balked. I wrote, *Everything but, seven pages,* and carried on.

Manx is the one who stops the torrid meadow scene I'd left blank. They'll never see each other again after this picture, he says, choking on the bitter words. That's the way it always is. Location shoots are dreams, quickly forgotten when cast and crew take up their waking lives again. It would be too cruel to know her in the way he so desperately aches to know her and then to have her slip away. Manx saddles up and rides off.

Cassie, as it turns out, can resist anything except resistance. Manx has finally proved his worthiness by rejecting her. Cassie follows him. It was not a motif entirely unfamiliar to me. Still, that night, when my heroine reaches the ranch and creeps, trembling, uncertain, but ready, yes, definitely ready, into Manx's bedroom, I can do nothing but short-sheet her with the notation, *Cassie succumbs, ten pages.*

This was as frustrating to me as it had to be for Cassie. Worse, I'd never sell a romance novel with all the aching chasms left unfilled. I lay down and watched the fan overhead. The same thing that had been happening to me for the last couple of days every time I wasn't keeping my mind strenuously occupied happened to me again: I thought about him. Or was it even thinking? My reflections on this leather-clad ladykiller seemed almost cellular. They waited like a virus in the blood, ready to jump into my brain at the first opening.

That was it. That was exactly it. This guy had my libido in a hammerlock. He was tying up my direct line to Venus, Goddess of Love. I had no choice. I had to see him again and chase this little fantasy out of my mind so I could get back to work, finish my book, and quit the darkroom job. I had to find him. For the book. I had to. There was no other way.

16

"You're in love with some-
one and you don't even know his name?" Lizzie was beyond incredulous. She'd stopped by for a surprise morning
visit.

"I didn't say 'love.' Who said anything about love?" My
voice got unaccountably shrill. I started over in a tone of
reasoned calm. "I'm intrigued. I think it would be good for
the book."

Lizzie looked skeptical. I kept trying.

"I think he'd be an interesting character study. That's
all."

Lizzie warned Annabelle to stay away from my gas space
heater. "You remember what I told you about hemoglobin?"

I wondered if her reminder might not be a bit advanced
for a child whose entire spoken vocabulary still consisted of
"un-kow." Lizzie put her finger to her lip and studied me.

I decided I'd have to risk opening up a little. "Lizzie,
nothing quite like this has ever happened to me before."

"Never? This mysterious stranger sounds suspiciously

similar to that faithless Truman person. Gretchen, you've
got to start considering your time as a resource."

This was the danger in allowing someone to feed you;
they started treating you like an underdeveloped nation. I
lapsed into a cringing imitation of the Dominican Republic.
"I know you're right, but I'm weak. I don't have your control."

"Annabelle, get away from that wall socket!"

Annabelle, down on all fours, was trying to plug in her
tongue. She turned around, like a fawn startled at the water
hole.

"Annabelle, sweetie, if you stick your tongue in there you
will complete a circuit and electricity with a frequency of
sixty cycles per second will flow through you. A lethal dose
of electricity will paralyze your respiratory organs and damage your central nervous system. But the really bad thing
would be if the action of your heart were interrupted. We
don't want that to happen, do we?" Lizzie shook her head
no. Annabelle solemnly shook hers in return and moved
away from the socket.

"Well, at least the danger is contained." Lizzie turned
back to me. "Holy Virgin be praised, you don't know this
miscreant's name."

"You know," I began casually, trying to pretend that I
hadn't spent the last few hours dwelling on that very problem and finally coming up with a solution that only Lizzie
could expedite, "I was thinking about that very issue." I
outlined my proposal.

"You want Mitchell to break into INS's computer system?" Lizzie acted as if I'd suggested an evening of window
peeping at the Willowhaven Rest Home.

"It would be a cinch for him."

She snorted. "I suppose it would be for anyone who could
shut down the University of Texas's entire system using an
Atari Gamester."

"See?"

"He was but a whelp then," Lizzie protested. "He didn't have a family. Security wasn't as tight. They didn't have the laws they do now. Hackers can go to jail."

She was right. What was I asking? And why? I slumped against a worn cushion. "You're right."

Lizzie sighed with maternal exasperation. "What would knowing his name accomplish? I mean, if he's hiding from Immigration, it's not too likely you'll be able to get his address from the phone book."

"I just wanted to know his name."

That was a slight understatement. What, in fact, I wanted was to wade barefoot in fountains with him as day dawned across a piazza. To press my nose into a bunch of violets he'd bought for me from an old woman in a shawl who would beam benevolently on our perfect love. To walk back to our pensione together nestling under his arm, him with his dinner jacket hooked on one finger, slung over his shoulder, me with a pair of slingbacks dangling from my free hand. Okay, I had to admit it, at least to myself: I wanted to live perfume commercials with him. But I also wanted to take tastes from his plate and feed him from mine. To watch clouds with my head on his stomach and listen to it gurgle. I wanted it all, but a name, a name, *his* name was a start.

I came up with a wistful little sigh that tugged even at my own heart. It should have, for it signaled the end of my initial, token resistance. Once I'd dramatized this transcendental attraction to Lizzie, I couldn't keep it tamped down any longer.

Lizzie tried but she could endure my downcast desolation for only a few minutes. "Oh, for the love of the Holy Rood! I must be as want-witted as you. It will probably cause us both to be outlawed, but, yes, all right, I'll ask Mitchell."

My head jerked up like a daisy tracking the sun.

"I'll *ask,*" she repeated. "But that's all. I make no promises. If there's the slightest danger, the deed will not be done."

"Oh, Lizzie, Lizzie, Lizzie, I love you!"

Once she'd peeled me from her body, Lizzie and Annabelle left. I waved and threw kisses until they were out of sight, then danced back into my house. Morning light streamed in through the abundant windows. It was a wonderful house. How could I have ever thought otherwise? I felt as if I could dive into the golden beams and sail on them like the millions of dust motes sparkling around me. Out in his backyard Mr. Cleeb was cross-hatching his lawn with his intricate mowing system. How could I have failed to appreciate the exquisite symmetry of his ingenious plan? And the miraculous gift that was the beauty of his yard? I planned on purchasing an oscillating sprinkler just like the ones he owned so that my yard too could be a thing of beauty, a shy gift to all who looked upon it.

And that luscious fuchsia crape myrtle he was carefully mowing around. Crape myrtle, what a delightful name. . . .

The rest of the day continued with me in a state that went far beyond New Boyfriend Euphoria. I knew this high was of a different order entirely because something happened to me that I'd hitherto only experienced the day after Blue Margarita night at the Ennui: I had no interest in food. In the few logical moments I experienced that day, I told myself that this was all some crazed hormone jamboree. I was out of my mind the way new mothers are, pumped up with whatever endorphin or other natural opiate it takes to keep one person from murdering the tiny visitor who won't let her sleep for months at a time. I didn't care. I rode the euphoria, and though I still didn't even have a name for him, I bonded, heart and soul, with my dream baby.

♥   ♥

"Amateurish. Laughably amateurish," Mitchell announced two nights later as the words IMMIGRATION AND NATURALIZATION SERVICE, ZONE 5 flickered across the screen.

Indeed, it had seemed remarkably easy to break into the INS computer system. As I understood it, all Mitchell had done was connect his computer to the phone through a modem, then direct his computer to keep dialing combinations until it came up with the secret code. Even given my imperfect grasp of probabilities, though, it seemed that the machine came up with the right combination awfully quickly.

"It's a matter of sector sampling," Mitchell explained. "Sort of like when you go shopping for a blouse. If you know generally that you're looking for a red blouse, you don't have to look at every color in the store before you find the one you want. Do you follow?"

I confessed that I wasn't sure, but that an example using either nail polishes or bathroom cleansers would really clinch it for me. But Mitchell had already turned his attention back to the screen, where, after punching several keys, the title EYES ONLY: AT-LARGE ALIENS TARGETED FOR IMMEDIATE DEPORTATION appeared, followed by a long list of countries.

"How fortuitous," Lizzie observed, scooting a chair in next to mine, "that the felons are listed by nationality." Though she was helping, Lizzie still made her disapproval clear.

I leaned in closer to Mitchell, who was punching the cursor down the list. NAMIBIA, NEPAL, NETHERLANDS scrolled past.

"You said he's from where? New Zealand?" Mitchell asked.

"Yes, yes, New Zealand."

He hit a few keys, and the long list of countries was swept away and a new file, NEW ZEALAND, tumbled onto the screen. "Bingo, if he's from New Zealand, he's in here somewhere." The first name to come up was Allbright, Geoffrey.

"No, too old," I said, reading the DOB: 5-12-18. Mitchell flipped Geoffrey off the screen.

Antill, Ian, 3-31-29.

"No."

Buvelot, Chauncey. 8-3-55.

"Wait," I said before Mitchell could scroll past him. "What's his file say?"

"Chauncey?" Mitchell sneered. "You fell in love with someone named Chauncey?"

"I don't know. All I know is that the age is about right." As if Chauncey was so much worse than Mitchell Potts. Chauncey. I could grow to like that name. "Oh, no, that's not him," I blurted out even as I was warming to his name. His record featured public intoxication, shoplifting, and child molestation.

"How do you know it's not him?" Lizzie wanted to know.

"It's just not possible. He's bad but not evil. Keep going, Mitchell."

Lizzie sighed and got up. "I'd better go check on Annabelle."

Mitchell tapped us through the list. Dozens of names whirred past. I eliminated all of them; too old, too young, too female.

O'Dowd, Miles. DOB 9-12-68.

"Too young."

Redpath, Norma.

"Female."

St. John, Ryemaura.

"Canonized," I droned. Mitchell flipped the entry away before I had a chance to come to. "No. Wait. Bring St. John back."

Mitchell turned to me. "Head on a platter?" He was slightly too pleased with his little joke, but he did call the file back up. I checked the DOB.

"Early thirties, that'd work."

Lizzie walked back in with Annabelle on her hip, sucking

apple juice from a bottle. Though she'd been drinking out
of a cup for over a year, she still occasionally insisted on a
bottle. And she still wasn't talking. I could understand her
position. If my mother had been as diligent about alerting
me to impaired hemoglobin and interrupted heart action, I'd
probably have chosen not to grow up either.

Back on the screen, the first notation in the file said that
Ryemaura St. John traveled under the nickname Rye.

"Rye St. John, don't you love it, Lizzie?"

Lizzie peered at the screen. "I wouldn't use it in a novel.
Too obvious. Even for romance."

All right, maybe Rye St. John was not the name of a man
who would ever buy a station wagon. Maybe he'd even
invented it himself. But it fit. And I loved it. No man with
lashes and shoulders like his should ever be called Larry.
Ryemaura St. John. I wanted to whisper it out loud. His first
name was probably Maori. I'd accumulated the odd fact
about New Zealand after spending the last two days reading
every book the library had about the country.

"Oh, my God, he graduated from Oxford!" I read aloud
from the screen. *"The* Oxford," I clarified. "Trinity College,
English literature."

"Do you really believe the INS verifies all this information?" Lizzie asked.

"Even if they do, what's it mean?" Mitchell wondered
acidly. "That they're tracking this guy down because he's
dangerously refined? Lethally overeducated?"

I ignored them both and went on to the physical statistics.
They were thrilling: six foot two, 170 pounds, brown hair,
blue eyes, birthmark upper right thigh.

"That's him!" I exulted.

"What is he wanted for?" Lizzie was not going to abandon her opposition.

"Looks like he entered on a tourist visa," Mitchell supplied, "which ran out about a year ago. There are worse
crimes."

"He's wanted for deportation," Lizzie pointed out.

"Look at this." I read from the file. " 'Author of *Renegade Tourist* guidebook series.' He writes guidebooks!"

Mitchell flicked a switch and the screen cleared. "Now what?"

"Now I know his name. Where he went to school. What he does for a living—"

"How much he weighs." Lizzie was still mocking my quest.

"Come on, Lizzie." I was in an emotionally friable state. "Okay, you're right. I want more. I want to find him. You must have characters searching for one another all the time in your books. How do they do it?"

"Gretchen, wouldn't you be in a stronger position if you let him seek you out?" Lizzie wondered.

I'd thought about that already. "Look, he—Rye—sustained serious injuries. He might still have been in a state of shock when he left. He probably has only the foggiest recollection of what happened. Besides, he left this." I pulled his penknife out of my pocket. "I need to return it to him. It's the right thing to do."

"And don't we always do the right thing when it suits our purposes," said Lizzie tartly.

"Aw, be a sport, Liz," Mitchell urged. "You've got desperate couples trailing each other all the time in your books."

Lizzie could not resist the challenge. "Well, all right." She swung Annabelle off her hip and onto the couch, where she sat down beside her. "Whenever I have a tracking sequence, I always use habits or identifying physical characteristics. In *Fever in the Blood,* Alex was a hemophiliac and Curry traced him through the blood bank. Anything like that to work with?"

"No, he seemed to be clotting pretty well."

"Hm-m-m. Uh, okay. Does he smoke Casbah tobacco, a rare Turkish blend favored by Lord Montford in *Ashes of*

Love? It can only be ordered through Cavendish's Smoke Shop in London."

"Rye's not a smoker." I hoped.

"The Oxford Alumnus Club?"

"I really doubt that fugitives from the law get involved much with booster clubs." Lizzie's suggestions were as unrealistic as everything else that came from romance novels.

"When Baron de Foucault was looking for Samantha in *Collision with Passion,* he took the rein guide that had fallen from her carriage before she disappeared around to all the shops until he found the one where it had been made. Then he distracted the owner long enough to copy her address from the accounts ledger."

Since I'd halfway stopped listening to Lizzie, it took a few seconds for her last motif to sink in. "That's it! His bike. We'll just go around to all the shops until we find the one where he's getting his bike repaired."

"We?" Lizzie asked.

♥   ♥

The shops didn't turn out to be nearly as bad as I thought they would be. Hardly anyone called us "mama." I did speak to an inordinately large number of men wearing ponytails, but none of them were particularly menacing.

Except for the owner of the last shop we visited, Howie's Hog Heaven. A mural ran across the front windows of the shop depicting a man sprawled over what looked like the bastard offspring of a motorcycle and a lawn lounger. I couldn't take my eyes off it even after we were inside the shop. Trails of wicked red flame poured from the machine. The rider was equally overdrawn. A sort of biker's fertility symbol, he was built like an ox with a weight problem, all shoulders and beer gut. Riding that body was a mean, piggy face. Piggy eyes pressed like raisins into the doughy flesh above his snout and pitted cheeks. His weedy triangle of goatee had an unsettlingly pubic look to it. The drawing captured all the worst of the biker stereotype so well I almost believed I could smell it, a high-octane rankness that only the fattest and meanest of humans are capable of producing.

"You ladies lost? The Moped-o-phile place is over on Koenig Lane."

I turned and faced a wall of blubber with that mean, piggy face on top. Howie. The artist had flattered him. Annabelle reached out a chubby baby fist for his goatee. He curled his lip back in a smile that displayed three teeth outlined in gold and two rotted away into stalactite shapes. Annabelle buried her face in her mother's neck and Lizzie stepped spryly away.

"Uh, actually, we're looking for someone who might have had his motorcycle repaired here."

Tub o' Guts's eyes narrowed warily from raisin to currant size. He tilted his great basketball of a head to the side, inspected me, and came to some conclusion that caused him to flash his wolfish grin again. "All right, mama!" He winked conspiratorially. "Tracking a dude. I can dig it."

"Well, yes. He had an accident. His ankle is sprained. Maybe broken."

"Yeah, okay, I know him. Fucked-up ankle. Rides a beautiful bike, one of those classic old Turnip Bonnie's."

"A Turnip Bonnie?" I repeated what I thought he'd said in a soft, nonthreatening voice. He still managed to become somewhat exercised at my slowness.

"A classic . . . nineteen seventy-one . . . Triumph . . . bonneville," he elaborated with exaggerated patience. "Still knocking the dings outta it. So the Bonnie lights your pilot, huh? Listen, I ride a Vincent Shadow, what's that do for you?" He brought his personal stench zone a bit closer to me. Too close.

"Oh, fab bike. But listen, if you could just give me the address—"

He froze and the neck veins started puffing up again. I

saw that Howie existed on a thin edge delicately poised between rut and a massive coronary.

"You want me to rat out a brother, is that what you're asking?" He turned around and pounded a pile of yellow carbons sitting on the grimy counter behind him. "You really think I'd just whip around here and leaf through these work orders and just lay the Bonnie's address on you? Hey, *mamacita,* you got a lot to learn. Don't matter how tight she's wound up, how good she smells coming in the shop prissing around, waving her cute butt around in them short, short hot pants that scoot way all up in her—"

"Fine! Fine. That's okay." Howie was throttling toward a full psychotic break by the time I interrupted him. I didn't think it wise to point out that I was wearing baggy khaki shorts that had a good two feet to scoot before they got anywhere. I turned around and grabbed the first item within my reach. "I'll just buy this and we'll be going." My only concern now was to get us out of Hog Heaven before Howie started in again on scooting hot pants. Lizzie, who hadn't been much help at all, was already edging toward the door while Howie accompanied me to the register.

Twelve ninety-five was a lot to fork over for a Flexcore Universal Air Filter, but at least the purchase got Howie to stop throbbing in my direction. The real loss was the only link I had to Rye. I had no clue how I would find him now. I was subtly trying to eradicate all traces of my address and phone number from my check when Lizzie, standing in front of the window, called out, "By all that's blessed, I don't see how that woman manages to stay inside that tube top. . . . God's eyes, she's not! By the Rood, she's bursting forth!"

It was astonishing to see a person as large as Howie lumber as swiftly as he did, but he was at the window before you could say "indecent exposure."

I rifled the work orders. Written on one in what appeared to be charcoal briquette were the words TURNIP BONNIE. I had just enough time to look at the address, 12 Cedar Switch, before Howie returned, yelling at Lizzie as he lumbered.

"A tube top's a tube, man. A *tube.*" He turned back to Lizzie and chopped himself across the chest a few times to indicate tube borderlines. He flailed an arm in the direction of the street outside. "That was a damned halter top, man. *Halter.* Straps. Them things never fall off." He shook his head in angry disappointment. "Chicks. Jeez."

Back home, I found 12 Cedar Switch on a map. It was right next to the lake. The lake. That too was perfect. For the next twenty-four hours I Ping-Ponged between finding his house on the map, getting my car keys, putting my car keys down, and trying to pretend I wasn't waiting for the phone to ring.

Unannounced visits on men who are like unto a fever in your blood aren't the easiest of calls to pull off with a casually insouciant flair. It's particularly difficult to pretend you were just in the neighborhood after you've faced down the killer whale of the Bandidos and committed major felonies with a computer to find out where he lives. If Rye would just call, that would make everything so much easier. That thought volleyed me back into the opposite court, where I demanded indignantly to know where it is carved in stone that I had to wait like Sleeping Beauty for the ring of the phone to jolt me back to consciousness.

That was the point at which the Home Spa Weekend mechanism kicked in and I found myself with my face over a boiling pot of water with some herbs thrown in, steaming my pores open. I depilated every hair south of my widow's peak and north of my shoelaces, then dermabraded the scalped skin with kosher salt in a stocking.

My skin tingling and smoother than the inside of a fat man's thighs, I grabbed for my keys, was halfway out the door, then stopped cold. Maybe there was no shock, no amnesia. Maybe—the crippling suspicion wormed its way in—he simply didn't want to see me again. Me? Not want to

see *me?* How could such thermonuclear chemistry not have
been mutual?

Still, the keys slid from my grip as I came up with nearly
a dozen solid reasons. My nose is too pointy. I didn't have
mascara on that night, meaning I looked like a radiation
experiment gone wrong. I have eyebrows like a beagle pup-
py's. My nails are brown from developer. I'm pale as a bean
sprout. My thighs jiggle. I stopped for him, which means
I'm cheap. I didn't stop soon enough, which means I'm a
haughty bitch. My breasts have a curious banana conforma-
tion.

For an hour or so I rode this runaway train of self-deni-
gration. About the time I decided that I'd be lucky to get
Howie to look at me in a *transparent* tube top, I got myself
under control. I called Lizzie, and she responded on cue by
telling me I was galaxies too good for this Wheat person.

"His name is Rye."

"Like the whiskey." She pointed to further proof of his
dissoluteness. As usual she advised me to pretend that Rye
was the Periodic Table and forget him.

I called Juanita, counting on the old renegade to spur me
on.

"Gretch, you shouldn't go and you know you shouldn't
go. If there's one thing I've learned about hombres it's this,
if they're regular and repeated heart stompers, they're going
to want to save you from themselves. So sometime in the
first five minutes they'll tip their hand. Takes many different forms. Maybe a few too many comments about their
bitch-goddess ex-wife. Or mother. Maybe it's just the fifteen empty highball glasses on the bar in front of them.

"Now we're not even getting *that* subtle with this character. What do we have in the first ten *seconds?* We've got a
thug in black leather trolling for new friends on the inter-
state. *Black leather,* Gretchen. Lover Boy didn't just tip his
hand to you, honeybunch, he's sitting over there with five

aces showing. Listen to an old campaigner, kid. Put your car keys in your back pocket and sit on 'em."

♥   ♥

I'm terrible at taking advice, particularly if it's well-meant and intelligent. Besides, Rye hadn't been wearing black leather. It was brown. And just a jacket. Seconds after I hung up, I was out the door and rolling down RR 2222 toward the lake. I opened all the windows and cranked my radio up until it boomed and crackled. I needed big blasts of airwave courage.

I love Ranch Road 2222. Even if most of the ranches are now dim and subdivided memories in developer's minds, 2222 still slithers around through some great slices of countryside wedged in between the half-a-mil-and-up houses. Of course, the real reason for driving 2222 is the slithers, not the countryside. Before DWI fell onto such hard times, it was Austin's favorite weekend sport to get tanked and test your tread on quad deuces. Pumped up as I was on nervous ecstasy, I depressed pedal toward metal and got into a pretty fair Grand Prix fantasy—or as much of one as is possible while driving a land barge with the suspension of a fertilizer spreader.

I was feeling so expansive I didn't even peeve out when two teenage couples drinking St. Pauli Girl beer passed me in a white Rolls-Royce convertible. Still, I did give some thought to what would be a truly worthwhile movement: punishment for DWO—driving while overprivileged. Punishment should be especially severe in the new Austin.

Around the time I shot past the Loop 360 cutoff, my antic zestfulness flattened out a bit and I was left worrying again about how this Kiwi demigod was going to react to an unannounced visit from a mortal with beagle brows and banana breasts.

As I approached Cedar Switch, my foot started to ricochet between the brake and accelerator. I was doing about three mph when I crawled toward the turnoff. This mission was coming to seem the doomed and stupid sort my mother would have grounded me for in eighth grade. Besides, this guy could really be dangerous. Who did I have for a character reference? Howie of Howie's Hog Heaven. Was ownership of a "beautiful bike" enough? I pulled off onto the shoulder. I would simply turn around, go home, and pretend I had never been seized by this flashback to boy-craziness.

As I waited for a stream of Formula One 2222 drivers to Andretti past, I glanced down Cedar Switch. It was a green haven dappled with sunlight that curved around a charming corner and out of sight. It really was just the most enchanting, most inviting little country lane imaginable. Why shouldn't I investigate it after driving all the way out there? I mean, is it against the law for a person just to meander briefly down a little country lane simply because a person the meanderer has met once lives on said lane? I was an American woman of the eighties with options to exercise and a ticket to ride. I turned onto Cedar Switch.

The thickets of cedar along either side of the narrow road baffled sound so completely that, once I'd made the first turn, 2222 was only a remote hum. The dense stands of cedar looked like herds of long-haired beasts in their shaggy coats of russet bark. Their little Lane-hope-chest smell filled the car. I breathed it in, and my mouth filled with the coppery taste of desire. The smell of cedar would never again remind me of graduation day. After that realization it was hard to pretend that my deep love of natural beauty had caused me to turn down Cedar Switch.

Admitting that I was there to cruise a guy's house really made me feel like twanging the rubber bands on my braces. Still, I pressed on to view the place where Rye lived, probably driven by the same vain hope of gaining a shred of control over one's world that compels primitives to collect their enemies' fingernails. The few houses along the lane were ecologically integrated into the landscape, which meant they were buried behind cedar and it was hell picking out a street number. Finally I spotted a big 4. I figured it was far enough from 12 that I didn't have to worry about Rye spotting me.

I must have missed a few tastefully camouflaged houses, however, because suddenly I found myself at the end of Cedar Switch staring at a small wrought-iron sign with the numbers 1 and 2 twisted into it. Rye's house defined rustic in native limestone with weathered beams. I stared lovingly at it for a couple of seconds before panic set in. It was broad daylight. I slid down in the seat as far as a low-rider, only my eyes clearing the window. The road widened at its end enough for most cars to circle around and head out. But, given that the 88 had the turning radius of the Queen Elizabeth, I was forced to attempt the dreaded K-turn.

K-turns when your visibility is limited to the tops of tall trees is a challenge. I put the 88 in reverse and rocketed straight off the side of the road into a deep gully. I shifted into first and stepped on the gas. My front wheels pawed the air like a rearing stallion. I laid on a bit more fuel, and the 88's mighty engine roared as if she wanted to be unleashed at Daytona. The only thing now standing between me and total humiliation was the choking cloud of exhaust spewing from the tailpipe. At least it would cut Rye's visibility if he was, even at that moment, watching from his window.

Feeling his eyes on me, amused, mildly contemptuous, I tromped down harder on the gas. A frightening high whine ripped from the 88 as her back wheels strained against the slick red caliche of the gully. Then, with the whine crescendoing into the screeching wail of one thousand Berber widows, she pulled free.

I plowed forward, straight and true, directly into the wrought-iron sign. Somehow it impaled itself in the 88 so that clouds of vapor poured out from under the hood. I didn't even want to contemplate what lethal blow I'd dealt my auto. All I cared about was escape. I slammed her into reverse again and hit the gas. An Old Faithful geysered up, accompanied by a gruesome scything sound. The car didn't move. Even if it had to be the last mile on the 88's odometer, I was determined she'd carry me away from this disaster. I squashed down on the accelerator again. And again the engine squealed out in some unimaginable mechanical torture.

"You'll clap out the doovelacky if you keep that up."

The voice was quiet, but it cut right through the car torture screams. I lifted my foot off the gas pedal. The vapor blew away and there he was, standing beside me at the window.

"Rye."

"You know my name. I don't remember that. Telling you my name. But then I was pretty well plonked that night. Come out to visit me, have you?"

Light sliced around behind him, making it hard to see his face.

"Not really. Just out driving. Do you live here?"

He touched the hood. "How about something cold to drink while we let her cool down a bit; then I'll have a peek under the bonnet." He opened my door. I didn't budge. My mind and body were paralyzed by the effort of getting my attitude and story together.

"Is that a cast?" I asked. His ankle, mummy-wrapped in a an Ace bandage, was encased in a clear plastic bubble.

"M-m-m-m."

"Did you go to the emergency room that morning? From my house?"

"M-m-m-m."

"Why did you leave? Without saying anything?" I hadn't planned on asking, but the question came out of its own volition.

He straightened up, and the sun fell across his face. I

thought I might have hallucinated how handsome he was. I hadn't. My heart bumped. He shrugged and everything shifted. For one second, I stopped caring about the shape of my eyebrows and breasts. When he spoke, even his voice seemed different. "Can't say as I can answer that." Kin't sayz I kin insur thet. His accent was like warm breath on my ear.

For an instant we looked at each other, just long enough so that we both knew the glance was significant. I turned away first. What did he mean he didn't know if he could answer my question? Two words picked up the accelerated rhythm of my pulse and beat through my mind: gay/married . . . gay/married . . . gay/married . . . gay/married.

"I don't know about you, but"—he hopped onto his good foot and turned away from me—"I've got to get out of this murderous sun." Muuh-drous. He hobbled away, bouncing his weight lightly off his injured leg. Odd, we were dressed almost identically in baggy khaki shorts and black T-shirts.

Halfway up the front walk, he stopped, balanced himself, and looked over his shoulder. "Come on, then." He smiled and continued. I watched until he reached the front of the house and was lost in the deep shadows cast by a couple of tall pecans.

I hesitated a moment. Had he just shown me his hand? Again? I got out of the car slowly and stood there for a moment. A hot breeze felt momentarily cool against my sweaty back. Planted in the front yard was a roadrunner whirligig that someone had obviously made with a home workshop jigsaw. The bird's legs were spinning crazily in the breeze. Juanita and Lizzie might know a lot, but I was sure ax murderers would not allow a roadrunner whirligig in their front yard. I went in.

Rye had left the front door open, and I braced myself for a musky masculine lair. I walked in expecting massive exposed cedar beams, deer heads galore, knotty pine paneling,

gun rack, guns, Jim Beam collector bottles shaped like hunting dogs, all the essential lake house accoutrements.

At first, all I was aware of was the damp, cavelike coolness exhaled by the thick limestone walls. Next I noticed a
total absence of any of the objects I'd expected. The interior
walls were covered with Nile green paneling. The ceiling
was textured into a relief map of the Andes complete with
sparkles rarely seen outside of adult motels. One wall was
dominated by a huge yellow Lucite fish blowing huge blue
Lucite bubbles. It must have been a mama fish, because
three Lucite babies trailed her across the wall. A pair of Ben
Shahn clowns in long, narrow frames capered at either end
of the school of fish. The furniture was spindly relics of the
Rocket Age. A pair of bronze lamps blasted off from
launch-pad end tables flanking a chartreuse couch. Various
other shades of green—a moss armchair, olive carpet, pea-
green drapes—clashed throughout the living room in that
especially awful way in which only green can.

"Fairly gruesome, isn't it?" Rye asked.

"Oh, I don't know, I kind of like it."

"It was the only place the rental agent had on the lake
that was furnished. I took it sight unseen."

"Oh, well," I chirped, "green's supposed to be a restful
color. Healing or something. That's why hospitals are all
painted green." I was babbling but couldn't stop myself.

"Actually, you can thank British surgeons for that color
scheme," Rye corrected me. "They found that, after staring
into a bloody wound for long enough, when they looked up
they saw splotches of red on the white walls. Green being
red's opposite made the splotches disappear."

"I didn't know that." I was so taken again by his accent,
the way he made "actually" into "ickchoolly" and "red"
into "rid," that it took me a moment to process what he'd
ickchoolly sid. "So if a sudden overwhelming desire to perform major surgery overtakes you, you're set."

"Too early for a beer?" He headed out to the kitchen

before I answered and opened a refrigerator with rounded corners and spoke into it. "This Shiner bock's far and away the best beer I've had in Texas." I recovered from how he said "Tik-sus" just in time to nod my head to the two bottles he held up in one hand. He twisted the caps off and passed me one.

Maybe it was the heat or the way my adrenal system had been in overdrive for the past few days; whichever, that Shiner was the best thing I'd ever swallowed. Once I started drinking, I couldn't stop. Rye opened the refrigerator again, pulled out two more bocks, popped the caps, and handed me another.

"You hungry?" he asked, the refrigerator door still open. He handed me a mango and took one himself. Smacking and slurping, he dived into the fruit.

Didn't he think he was overdoing this natural-man-awash-in-juice routine just a bit? Maybe he needed to go back and study his D. H. Lawrence to refine it some. I mean, I'd done this same thing with Cassie and Manx, having Manx nibble at the plump white shafts of sweet blades of grass while Cassie slowly came undone. I could imagine Cassie sitting here at this chrome dinette watching Rye's mouth sucking at the fruit, noticing how his lips were expert at getting what they wanted. I remembered our comatose kiss. My kiss. His mouth. He really was overdoing this.

Irritated, I peeled and bit into my mango. The flesh of the fruit slithered against my tongue. I could imagine Cassie imagining that Rye's lips were just this sweet. Being the impressionable romance heroine that she was, she'd probably even feel odd stirrings at Rye's uninhibited sensual pleasure. At the way his tongue lapped lovingly around the juicy folds between skin and fruit. The potent suggestiveness would overwhelm some silly twit like Cassie, I thought, wondering when it had gotten so warm in the kitchen and how I'd come to have mango juice dripping off my eyebrows. Cassie might fall for this, but it was all pretty obvious to me. My only question was, If he is gay/married, why is he going through this elaborate charade to woo me subliminally?

"You know the one thing I hate about mangoes?" Rye asked, juice running from his chin, his hands. He grinned before I could answer. His white teeth were packed with bristly fibers. "It's like gnawing on a baby's nana, what with all these nasty little apricot-colored hairs." He puckered up his lips and proceeded to suck noisily, wrapping his tongue across the front of his befibered teeth to increase suction. I tried to make out the subliminal sexual implications, but before I could he hopped up. "Only one thing to do after eating a mango," he announced.

I knew what was coming. First a little slurpy tropical fruit foreplay to soften resistance and set the subconscious stage, then *wham!* on with the show. I didn't know how they operated in New Zealand, but here in America one trip to the produce department does not a seduction make.

Before I could apprise him of that fact, he was heading out the back door. "The owner left swim togs. Some of them are women's if I'm not mistaken. Grab what fits and come for a swim. Or don't grab anything and come for a swim." He peeled off his T-shirt and shorts as he went. I looked away, then looked back. He was in a small black nylon racer's suit. Does anything look better than faded black against a tan? Particularly when both happen to appear on a body that could belong to a high school swimming star?

Mango juice dried and turned sticky on my hands and face as I contemplated these questions and watched Rye cross the back lawn to a small pier from which he dove effortlessly into the water. It closed over him, erasing his existence. I stood and went to the back door to watch him pop back out. But he didn't. I moved to the patio, then onto the grass, pulled along by an apprehension that grew with each second. A vision of him, pale green beneath the water, strangled in duckweed, flashed into my mind.

"Rye? Rye. *Rye!* RYE!"

The only answer was the distant hum of a powerboat motor. I tried to remember exactly where he'd gone in. I searched for signs of him thrashing, trapped beneath the water. But the lake, flat and unrippled as a bowl of Jell-O, gave no clues. I could no longer estimate how long he'd been under. Minutes. Many minutes. Too many minutes. Already there would be brain damage. I kicked off my shoes. I tried to remember my water safety course, but the Fireman's Carry was the only thing that came to mind.

Then I was running. A memory came back to me as my foot hit the splintery wooden pier: the Red Cross Lifesaving Jump. I was still trying to recall its particulars as I hurtled off the end of the pier. Somehow I got caught between a racing dive and the clearly remembered imperative to keep your head up and the victim in sight. The product of this union was a belly flop that created an effect not unlike being hit in the stomach with a two-by-four. Total paralysis of all thought and breathing processes resulted.

Spastically, I trod just enough water to keep barely afloat while my inoperative mouth was frozen into a silent recreation of Munch's "The Howl." My diaphragm felt as rigid and unmovable as an iron skillet in the middle of my chest. This was it. I was never going to breathe again. My corpse would probably float down and come to rest somewhere near Rye's, both of us tangled in duckweed. I wondered if anyone would conclude that we'd formed a suicide pact on our first date. Well, not really even a date if—

"Guh-haw!" Air exploded from my lungs. Rye had me from the back, administering a Heimlich maneuver that felt as if he'd practiced up by crushing garbage cans with his forearms. His fists remained neatly embedded in my sternum, where they'd just jolted my diaphragm back into ac-

tion. "You're squishing me!" I squeaked. He loosened his
grip but continued holding me.

"You're breathing, then?" he asked.

"Well, sort of," I answered in a small, sniffly voice. A
flash of brilliance had revealed to me that as long as I appeared puny and still vulnerable, he might continue holding
me, a state I found immeasurably cozy. He shifted his arms,
crossing one over my chest so that his hand caught in my
armpit. With his free hand, he pulled scoops of water toward himself while his legs rose up against my bottom and
scissored together, then apart. Together. Apart. We surged
forward. He was executing a perfect Cross the Chest Lifesaving Carry. I allowed him to pull me onto the bank, where
I tried to appear properly shaken.

He moved close and put a hand on my shoulder the way
you would a high-strung horse. Something about the gesture was profoundly human. It was just a hand on my
shoulder, concern in those quick eyes, but that was all it
took to completely realign my heart. Until that moment I'd
skipped around pulling petals off a daisy in my mind, trill-
ing "I love him, I love him a lot," while mostly imagining
kisses that trailed liquid fire and opened chasms of aching
need. Exactly the kind of stuff I was having such problems
getting Cassie and Manx to participate in. With the touch of
his hand, however, the lust elements shifted all around.
They were still there, make no mistake, but now they were
doing something dangerous; they were attaching to a de-
monstrably decent man. I'd never allowed this to happen
before.

The wrenching hug that had started my breath again
seemed also to have brought to life feelings that now fluttered mindlessly beneath my rib cage. They frightened and
left me defenseless. I looked away, afraid that too much was
already on my face.

"I thought you were drowning." It was an incoherent explanation for why I'd jumped in with my clothes on, but Rye seemed to understand.

"Thank you. That makes twice you've come to my rescue."

"And once that you saved me."

"I'm lagging."

"Hang around, you'll probably get another shot. I'm chronically on the verge of going under." Even as I spoke, I couldn't believe I was actually engaging in one of those multilayered conversations that are Cameo staples. But I took to them with as little effort as having my first period had required. Though Rye had given no hint of having any interest in me, on some instinctual level I was certain that each and every clue I tossed out about myself would fascinate him.

As if to affirm that primitive hunch, he edged closer to me. His hair, dark and sleek as a baby seal's, was slicked down on his head. It parted over his ears and flipped up at the ends where it lay on his forehead. The lake turned to a perfect platter of mercury behind him, broken only by a tiny island. His brown shoulder jutted into the silver. He was close enough that I could again smell the fragrance of cedar coming from him as the sun dried his body. Breathing difficulties alarmed me once more.

"How'd you find me?" he asked.

Thinking we were still playing Freighted Dialogue and he was speaking of the incredible odds we'd beaten to come together from opposite sides of the earth, I answered, "Destiny," with what I hoped was a maddeningly enigmatic smile.

"Well, yes. That."

I noticed that the tiny island in the perfect platter of mercury behind him was actually an old discarded playpen heavily encrusted with duckweed.

"But how did you know where I was staying, Gretchen?" he persisted.

I shriveled up with embarrassment at the image of myself
pressing Mitchell to break and enter confidential government files. That did not convey the casual posture I wanted
to adopt here. "How do *you* know my name?" I had him
there.

"It was on a magazine at your house. Gretchen Griner."

"Oh." For the first time within my memory, I liked my
name. At least I liked the way Rye said it, Gritchun Grynuh.

"So how did you find me?" he persisted.

I stared at the duckweed playpen.

"Look, the only reason I want to know is that if you can
find me, the INS can't be far behind."

I couldn't bring myself to reveal my whole scheme, the
fact that I'd pored over his file. How could there be any
"getting to know you, getting to know all about you" when
one party has studied the other's classified government dos-
sier? It would have thrown the entire rhythm off. So I told
him that on a mad whim I'd dropped in on *one* bike shop and
asked if any gimpy New Zealanders had been in lately.

"That was enterprising." Rye rewarded me with a grin
that tempted me to tell him about the full extent of my
felonious cleverness. "I'm surprised, though, that Howie
would rip my daks like that. Still, Immigration isn't quite so
clever. They'd never go to all that trouble in the first place.
Why did you?"

What did he expect me to say? Because you're a repellent
human being and I enjoy inflicting the company of loath-
some curs upon myself? Because I thought we might splash
through fountains barefooted together some day? "Uh, because I wanted to return this." Just in time I remembered
the knife I'd relieved him of and pulled it out of my sodden
pocket.

"Oh, thanks. I wondered what had become of it."

"You could have come back to find out."

"Yes, I suppose I could have."

The gay/married, gay/married tempo quickened with the

addition of a third alternative: doesn't-like-me. For a few seconds I looked into his eyes as if they were the spinning wheels on a slot machine and—instead of fruit, bells, and bars—some combination of gay/married/doesn't-like-me was going to appear there. But it didn't.

"You know, in Bali, only the insane and the saintly will stare into another person's eyes." He stared back into mine. "This is supposed to be how one goes about stealing another's soul." As he continued staring, an odd exhilaration swelled within me caused by the certain knowledge he was somehow communicating that I could eliminate the last choice. I was sure that he didn't not like me. "They might have something, those Balinese." Abruptly he broke the gaze, got up, reached down, grabbed my hand, and pulled me up. "Come on, let's find you some proper swimming togs before you finish up with black breasts."

That was when I noticed inky rivulets pouring down my arms. I was sitting in a black puddle. Apparently the frugal Pakistanis who'd made my T-shirt had used newspaper ink for dye.

Rummaging through the owner's drawers and chests in search of a swimsuit, I finally found what must have passed for a bathing suit thirty years ago.

"Crikey!" Rye laughed, making the aqua creation trimmed in white dance upside down. Stays, ribbing, and padding lifted the suit into the air, where it held its shape as if a phantom were filling it out. "This thing is better engineered than a 727."

I adjourned to the bathroom and tried it on. The suit was strangely flattering, possibly because it was a couple of sizes too large, which lent a playing-dress-up quality that was almost winsome. Winsome being something I don't do normally, I enjoyed the novelty.

Rye and I turned out to have this in common: we both seemed constitutionally incapable of being anything other than happy while immersed in water. We cavorted like a couple of otters, my aqua suit billowing around me as Rye grabbed an ankle to pull me underwater or I paddled madly after him in a game of tag. Of course, all this manic frivolity was driven by the runaway engine of carnality. At least on my part.

In the midst of a game of tag, he slipped away and the lake went deadly silent again for what seemed like minutes. The sun was lowering, and when he exploded out of the water, the long, slanting rays caught the droplets and it looked as if he were being showered in gold doubloons. I swam up to him. He squirted water through his hand, lightly pelting my face, but I didn't squeal and swat him. I didn't want to play tag anymore. I moved toward him, certain of what I was doing and wanted and simultaneously terrified. I stood still in front of him yet the water between us trembled, encircling us both in ripples that edged outward until they lapped together. We stood like that for a long moment. Then he skidded the flat of his hand across the intersecting ripples.

"Your car must be cool enough to work on by now." He struck out, pulling himself through the water with his hands and up onto the bank. And there I was, left once again to trail after him. I was finding the role of native tracker increasingly unattractive. He hobbled across the lawn in a way that seemed unduly self-conscious, unduly aware of itself.

Gay, I decided.

17

Okay, he was gay, I could live with that. I had gay friends; he'd be another one. What bothered me was the fact that he spent his off hours roaring around on the old Turnip Bonnie, stirring up lonely straights.

I flicked away a water strider. The day was moving rapidly toward silhouette time, when all the trees meld together into a solid dark mass. I brooded for a bit longer about the ethics of Rye's raising false expectations. But in the end, who could really blame him? Don't we all need an occasional ego boost? At least he had enough scruples to have been embarrassed and sneaked away that morning after recuperating at my house. I heaved a sigh. It had been a nice fantasy while it lasted, cheaper even than Dollar Day at the movies. I hauled myself out of the lake and went inside to change back into my still sodden clothes.

Out in front of the house, a nimbus of light cast by the bare bulb at the end of a long orange extension cord that Rye had hooked to the Delta's raised hood made a bright, shimmery circle around my car. Rye was hunched over, cranking a wrench around a bolt. He'd thrown on a crumpled Hawaiian shirt, and it hung unbuttoned over the skimpy suit. Bugs batted against the light. He straightened up, took a long swallow of the Shiner he had propped behind the front bumper, then stretched back into the car's open mouth. I mourned the loss from my fantasy life of those broad shoulders, those incomparably springy buns, the decent man they were appended to. A pebble crunched beneath my foot as I stepped onto the driveway.

"Gritchun? You there?"

"Hi." I moved into the circle of light. "Is she going to make it?"

"Just barely. The immediate complaint is that you've severed a fan belt. Fortunately, the owners have enough parts lying about to stock a garage."

"You're remarkably handy." I bit my tongue as soon as the words were out. Talk about stereotyping. As if it were a miracle that a gay man was mechanically inclined enough to set an alarm clock, much less repair a car. "I mean, it's just so unusual that . . . I just don't know many men—or women, for that matter, persons in general—who can fix things."

"Sort of a national characteristic, I reckon." He wrenched off a bolt and set it carefully onto a rag on the fender that held three other bolts. "Shipping and import duties are so high back home, we have to keep the old bombs running forever." Fuh-ivvah.

I rested my elbows on the fender, bending down so that I could peek under the hood. Without the danger of sex sharpening the atmosphere, everything became much cozier. I stopped worrying about such things as whether he was noticing that my breasts were banana-shaped beneath my damp T-shirt and just asked him normal questions like what he did for a living.

"I've written the odd guidebook," he answered with endearing modesty. I made some lame comment about how fascinating his life must be.

"Now that would depend on how fascinating you found the relentless accumulation of arcane and useless bits of information to be. For ex-"—he clenched his teeth and bore down on a frozen nut—"-am-*pul!*" He exploded, jerking the nut free with a grunt. He wiggled the wrench at me as if it were a pointer. "Did you know that there are meat-eating bees in Panama? That racehorses in Hong Kong wear rubber slippers? That Chinese citrus growers rig tiny bamboo ladders in their trees for pest-eating ants to climb? That Bangkok has five and a half million people and no sewer system? That the McDonald's in New Delhi serves lambburgers? That there's a mosque in Pakistan that can hold all the people in Montana? That light bulbs in New York City subways have left-handed threads to thwart thieves? That, in the middle of the ocean between Brazil and Africa, there is a tiny island inhabited by small brown moths that eat nothing but feathers?"

"You've seen all those things, haven't you?" I knew he had.

He shrugged. "I must have missed a step in my development. Things aren't entirely real for me until I've seen, heard, smelled, touched, and tasted them."

Of course, he was a crazed sensualist. Of course. Sigh. "That's astounding."

" 'Women like audacity. When one astounds them, one is sure to please them.' Théophile Gautier," he quoted.

Oh, Théophile, I had been astounded that Rye was gay but far from pleased.

"And what of yourself?" He looked up, the shadows shifting down across his face as it filled with light from the bare bulb.

For some reason, it took an inordinate amount of energy to tell him about my lab job at the *Grackle*. "The editor owes me for months' worth of stories, but he won't pay me anything unless I agree to be his slave mole in the darkroom." I chose not to mention that "the editor" and I had once dramatized blues lyrics together.

"Hm-m-m."

"It sounds more dismal than it is."

He pulled some assemblage off the radiator, put it down, and asked, "Suppose I were to hand you a million dollars. Two million. Ten million. Never mind the sum, let's just say that your money worries were over. What would you do with your life?"

That's what was different about gay friends, they cared. Straight men never asked these kinds of questions.

"Gosh." Though the question of what to do with my life had occupied an exorbitant number of my conscious hours for the past three years, I had yet to come up with a good answer. Being broke and scrambling for whatever was available to keep the Cup-a-Whatever coming in was actually a pretty good smoke screen for avoiding the issue altogether. I snorted a self-deprecating laugh. "It's terrible, really. Here I am, an American woman at the close of the twentieth century. Historically, despite a few setbacks lately, I've got the best shot at charting my own destiny that a woman has almost ever had. With the right drive, determination, direction, I could do anything I wanted. The only thing that's stopping me is I don't know what I want."

"You've lost interest in photography?"

"I don't know. The interest is dwindling." My answer surprised me. "My big dream in life was to be some globe-trotting photojournalist. Another Margaret Bourke-White. But I don't know anymore. Maybe I just wanted to wear jumpsuits. I don't really enjoy sticking a camera up people's nostrils."

"I know what you mean. One can get to feeling rather intrusive at times in any area of journalism. One does wonder if one is justified. So, if not photojournalism, what?"

He was genuinely interested. "I've been doing some writing lately. Nothing significant. Nothing—" I shrugged. "Fiction, mostly." One does not reveal to one who employs the pronoun "one" that one is currently perpetrating a romance novel, though I suspected he might consider it marvelous, campy fun. Perhaps someday we could compare notes on how *he* would go about ensnaring Manx. My gay friends and I always seemed to be attracted to the same men.

"But the thing of it is," I continued, "I'm really liking it. I *like* creating a world and people to live in it. Then messing up their lives with any sort of complication I choose and having the power to fix it all up at the end."

"An appealing prospect." He pulled a belt out of an orange-and-white box and worked it onto a grooved wheel. His lips tightened when the belt resisted and he had to force it into place. Once it was attached, he focused entirely on replacing nuts and bolts. "Get in and crank her over."

I turned the key. No smoke poured out. A good sign. I put it in reverse and the 88 moved smoothly and without complaint. I switched it off, but the living dead motor idled on. Over the roar of the engine that refused to die, I called out, "It's a miracle!"

He listened to the death rattles, brow furrowing. "Hang on, that's crook." He jerked open the hood and dived in again. An instant later, the rattling shudder stopped and the night was still. "Air intake valve's a bit sticky. I cleaned up what I could, but you'd better not drive too many miles on it."

I thought New Zealanders used kilometers.

He came over to the window and leaned in. "Thanks for bringing the knife by." He was clearly signaling an end to our meeting now that he had me safely packed back into a functioning vehicle.

"Oh, sure." My hands flipped up once each from the wrist in nervous dismissal. "It was nothing. Glad you're not suffering from a concussion or anything like that."

"No." He rapped his knuckles against his forehead. "It's a pretty tough old gourd."

"Well . . . thanks." I started the engine, but he continued to lean in the window. I felt he was waiting for something from me. "Uh, look. About the other night. I understand why you left and it's okay. I mean, it's fine with me. I'd still like to be friends."

Rye stared blankly, giving me no help or even much apparent comprehension, and I dribbled off into increasing lameness.

"I just mean that I understand." As my well-meant words trailed off, I thought about the small brown moths living on that island in the ocean between Africa and Brazil trying to exist on feathers. The vision made me very sad. I felt tired. I wanted to leave then and wished Rye would get out of my window.

But he didn't. In fact, he leaned in even closer, resting his weight on his elbows until his face was next to mine. When he spoke, his voice was low and compelling. "You understand, eh? You understand then that I wanted you? I looked in at you that morning. I was going to waken you. Tell you thanks and good-bye. But when I saw you there, asleep, I knew that if I woke you I would kiss you. And if I kissed you I wouldn't stop. You understand all that?"

My mouth was open, my lips moved, but no words came forth.

He straightened up and spoke down to me from his full height. "I couldn't let that happen, Gritchun. It wouldn't be fair. You'd better go on now." He slapped the 88's roof as if it were a trusty steed, then stepped away.

I eased off the brake and circled out of the drive. I meandered listlessly back onto 2222, too stunned to do anything more than keep in the slow lane and let the speed bullets shoot past me. I was all the way to Burnet, stopped at the light, absently watching an apple-faced waitress taking burger orders at the Frisco Shop, when the shock wore off and all the pieces fell into place. The solution was obvious, so trite and so true that only the extreme surprise of Rye's confession could have even momentarily kept it from me. It could be summed up in one word, and that word was:

Married.

18

*"If I'd kissed you once, I never would have stopped. It's just that
simple."*

*Cassie glared at Manx, anger still crimsoning her cheeks, a welter of
conflicting thoughts and emotions churning within her. How could any of
this be simple? she wondered despairingly. She'd seen the letter, evidence of
his continuing devotion to the raven-tressed Felicia. But she had other
evidence. Evidence she could neither ignore nor deny. The irrefutable evidence of her own heart.*

She loved Manx.

Cassie's ordeal comforted me in much the same way that I
imagined it would comfort readers. It wasn't for real. I knew
and they knew that I could snarl things up between her and
Manx worse than Houston traffic and everything would still
come out right in the end. Like Rye's car repair.

I wondered what his wife was like. Raven tresses did suggest themselves. But no. Only in romance novels was the
other woman a haughty bitch in spike heels who trowels on
the makeup, while the heroine is the only person in three
states who doesn't know from the git go that our hero is the
sort who really prefers a simple unaffected gal in Chapstick.

Besides, *I* was the other woman. At least I'd auditioned for the part and been turned down. It was something, though, to know that Rye had been tempted. Sort of like those silly moths trying to live on feathers. But I'd gotten along on a pretty lean diet for some time now.

I didn't truly realize just how meager the fare had been until later that day when I opened the darkroom door and beheld a remarkable demonstration of the almost carnival extent of Darci Hollister's flexibility. This agility demonstration involved two black rubber chemical-resistant aprons, a pair of tongs, a gallon of wetting agent, and my never-officially-terminated boyfriend, Trout Overton Treadwell. The Third.

"Gretchen, hey," Trout called out with as much casualness as a person can muster when an aerobically perfect midget is coiled about his naked body paying close attention to zones of greatest sensitivity.

"Trout, Darci, how goes it." I closed the door calmly. I could have caught the two of them playing "Chutes and Ladders" and I would have been more excited. There is a special hell reserved for people who have affairs with co-workers. You go there after the breakup and your torture is seeing the former beloved with someone new while trapped in a setting that forbids wailing and rending of either garments or body parts. Rye saved me from my season in that hell.

To his credit, Trout burst out a moment later, tucking in his shirt, and pulled me aside to whisper urgently, "Gretchen that,"—he waved toward the darkroom—"what you saw, what you *thought* you saw, it doesn't mean anything. It's not—"

"Tr-o-o-out!" An audible pout came from the darkroom.

"Be right there, Darce." Trout grabbed my sleeve and pulled me farther away. "Gretchen, baby." He shifted his voice down low into blues register. "You caught me ridin'

that outbound train. I ain't denyin'. But I swear, I'm bringin'
my love on home to you."

When I didn't say anything, he reverted to actual English.

"Gretchen, it's only because you hammered me! Then
there was Darci. Man, she hijacked me big-time. The
woman was *on* me. So look, let's not scream or shriek
or . . ." The list of histrionic possibilities dwindled away.
"You don't look very upset," he observed.

"I'm not. I think you and Darci make a real cute couple."

"Don't bottle it up, Gretchen. Don't hold it in and try to
pretend you don't care. That just leads to home deliveries of
vodka. I know. I've seen it happen too many times."

"I'm sure you have, Trout, although with Darci it's the
ipecac syrup you'll have to keep an eye on. Oh, look, she
appears to be clothed now." Darci stood behind us, icing
Trout with a glare that would have made the Yeti shiver. I
slid past. "Could you excuse me? I've got a couple dozen
rolls of film to run."

Trout, his cock's comb of black hair drooping into his
eyes, crowded into the darkroom with me, leaving Darci
stamping her petite feet. I shrugged and proceeded about
my business, washing stray pubic hairs out of developing
trays and filling them with chemical solutions. Trout
watched for a few minutes in silence, then grabbed me from
behind. Each hand found a breast, his tongue slithered into
my ear, and he commenced scrubbing his crotch away
against my fanny. It was all about as erotic as being humped
by an overeager panda. Trout, oblivious to my lack of ardor,
rolled my nipples around as if they were little globs from
his nose that he was forming into flicking shape. He'd gotten the impression that this enflamed me. Possibly because I
used to pretend that it did.

"Whew, Trout." I shook him off like a ratty fur coat. "It's
too hot in here for that."

Trout dropped his hands, astonished that they'd failed
him. "What? What is it? I didn't call enough? Look, I'm

sorry." He moved in close again and growled in my ear, "I'm gone change my lowdown ways, baby."

I turned and faced him. He looked great in his patented, disheveled way—crumpled white shirt, bolo tie, black jeans, cockroach-killer boots with tooled silver toe plates—but I could not have cared less. I tried to remember what it was I'd found so devastatingly attractive about him. He seemed about as seductively dangerous as Pee Wee Herman, a man sliding by on a boy's simulated charm.

I'd been more or less holding myself together until I was stricken by the awful realization that Trout and Gus "Hush My Puppies" Kubiak were the kind of men I would be left with when Rye went back to his wife and country.

Trout was relieved when tears began rolling soundlessly down my cheeks. Women weeping on his emaciated frame was a familiar scenario. "Gretchen, sweet thang, my ramblin' days are done." He wrapped his arms around me. A hug felt good at that moment, no matter what the source.

"It's not you," I sniffled.

"I know," he crooned, stroking my hair with one hand and slipping the other one down to forage for tender bits of heinie. "It's that Darci. It was all her idea. But it's over, I promise. Your big dog's home."

"Oh, Trout, it really *isn't* you. I don't care if you screw Darci Hollister and everything else in panti-liners. I don't want you," I wailed, my misery growing like mildew in the warm dampness of my tears. "I love someone else."

Trout was stupefied. "Whoa. As in: someone else other than Peter 'Trout' Overton Treadwell el Tres?"

The concept was a tough one for him to absorb.

"Who is this lowdown hound snake you away from me?"

"He's a *man,* Trout, a full-grown, decent, complicated, warm, sensual . . . married man." It was hard dragging that last adjective out, and I leaked a few more salty wet ones in the process.

"Oo-wee! I didn't think you were the type goes huntin' with some other woman's hound."

"Trout, please, don't talk to me any further in blues lyrics. There wasn't any hunting done. I'm *not* the type. I've been on the wrong end of that enough times myself that I couldn't ever pretend no one would be hurt. I couldn't live with myself, betraying another woman. I couldn't. . . . Besides, he won't go for it."

"A righteous dude." Trout was being snide, but the thought of this honorable man remaining faithful to a wife on the other side of the globe caught me in the solar plexus area, and tears welled up again. I grieved for what I'd never had.

Trout patted me awkwardly, his hands not knowing what to do when the subject wasn't foreplay. "Aw, don't cry, Gretchen." When Rye said my name it had a joyous, airy sound to it like crickets chirping in a field. In Trout's mouth my name sounded like sheet metal being distressed, the way it always had sounded before and would now sound forever.

"I'd like to be alone, Trout." I said softly.

He splayed open his hands, stepped away from me, hesitated a moment, then left. I continued setting up developing chemistry, concentrating as hard as I could on the mechanical tasks. It was ridiculous that I was devastated. I'd never so much as kissed Rye. Well, I had, but he'd never kissed me. Still, it was ridiculous. I'd fixated on him just as firmly and foolishly as Gus Kubiak had on me. Probably, on Rye's scale, I *was* a Gus Kubiak. I regretted my lack of kindness to the Wisp. At least Rye had led me on a little and made me believe I could have been the one.

Well into my second hour of work, I framed up a negative in the enlarger and splashed an image over the easel of Lou Ann Barton and Angela Strehli grinning and pointing their fingers at each other. I was bent over with my eye on the scope, bringing Lou Ann's wonderfully ravaged Betty Boop face into focus, when two distant words coming from down the hall hit my heart like an armor-piercing bullet: "Gritchun Grynuh." I jerked up and clonked my head against the enlarger. I rushed for the door and swung it open, exposing all the prints I had swirling in the trays.

"Where *evuh* in the world are y'all from?" Eyelashes fluttered and magnolias bloomed in Darci's voice. The buttery Scarlett O'Hara tones were a marked change from her usual oleomargarine East Texas twang. Maybe she was getting back at Trout. More likely, it was the autonomic nerve response that caused her to flirt reflexively with every attractive man who crossed her radar.

"Would 'you all' believe New Zealand?" My hurtling departure from the darkroom was stopped cold by Rye's jokey come-on. I stood at the door and made myself take deep breaths.

"New *Zealand!*" Darci squealed. "I just can't tell y'all how long I've been *fascinated* by that country. Koalas are just the most adorable, most cuddly creatures on earth, aren't they?"

"Quite the most. Far and away the best reason for visiting Australia. 'Fraid we don't grow them in En Zed."

"Oh, that's *fascinating.* You know, I could just spend hours, days, *nights* learning all about your country. You know what would be maximally neat? Grabbing a few magnums of Piper, then scooting on out to the lake for a sail on my boat," she purred.

"That does sound enticing," Rye answered.

My heart sank.

"But I'm afraid I'll have to pass. Now, where did you say I might find Gritchun?"

I slipped back inside, pressed the door shut, ripped off my black apron, fluffed up my hair, and slouched against the sink. A moment later, I put the apron back on and pretended to be sloshing prints through the developer. I was occupied thusly when the rap came at the door. A forceful, authoritative rap.

"Ye-es," I trilled, the soul of cheerfulness, a warm and welcoming person who delighted in interruptions. The kind of person you want to spend vast amounts of time with— your entire life, if possible. I packed a lot into that "yes."

"Gritchun, it's me, Rye."

"Rye?" I didn't think the tiniest scintilla of hesitation would hurt. Besides, it gave me time to swab off my armpits with a wad of brown paper towels and to finish crunching down the rest of the pack of Certs I had in my mouth. "Oh, Rye, yes, come in."

A wall of light sliced into the room, and Ryemaura St. John stepped into it, favoring his good leg and swinging his hurt ankle after him. He closed the door. The dim orange of the safe light suddenly seemed as intimate as a bed of embers glowing beyond a bearskin rug.

"Hullo."

"What a surprise!" I tried to sound peppy and friendly in an automatic way. I mean, let us not forget, he *was* married. Already his smell was filing the tiny room. I wanted to bury my face in his chest. My hands shook. I couldn't face him. I turned my back to him and started swishing around the prints I'd left in the developer. "Gosh, sorry I can't talk right now. I have to rush these out." I felt him step toward me and I gripped the lip of the tray, jiggling it until the solution inside sloshed wildly. He took another step. My tray jiggling became a palsied frenzy. There was very little developer left in the tray when his hand closed over mine and quieted its manic activity.

"They're black."

I felt the rumble of his voice all along my spine but could make no sense of what he'd said until I looked into the tray. All the door flapping had let in enough light to completely blacken the prints I was supposedly developing.

"Oh."

Rye pulled my hand away from the tray. "Gritchun, look at me."

I turned to face him. He was backlit like a rock star by the safe light behind his head. An amber halo shimmered around his head and stray licks of orange light glanced off his cheeks, nose, chin, eyelashes. He spoke.

"What do you want to do about all of this?"

"Oh, I can reprint, no problem."

"Us, Gritchun, you and me. What do you want?"

"I don't know." I did know, but I wasn't about to tell him that what I wanted was to peel him out of his clothes and make him break his wedding vows. About eleven times in rapid succession.

"The right, the fair thing," he said, "would be to not see you again. I know that, but I can't do it. I had to come."

Instant euphoria. I busily realigned my stiff-necked position on adultery.

"I'm trying to work all this out," Rye went on. He sounded like a man on the rack renouncing his faith. Contemptible as it was, his depth of feeling made me want him all the more. "I can't not see you, yet anything more is out of the question, unthinkable. Could we see each other? *Just* see each other?"

"Yes! *See* each other. Just look, don't touch. No one has to be hurt. She doesn't even ever have to know."

"She?" Rye echoed.

"She. Your wife."

"My wife? Gritchun, what ever gave you the idea I was married?"

"You're not? You're not married? So you *are* gay."

"A poofter?" He squinted one eye at me and asked again with amused incredulity, "A bum jumper?"

"Well, if you're not gay and you're not married, who exactly are we so worried about being fair to?"

"Us, Gritchun, you and me. Probably me more than you. I can't stay. I should have left days ago. I'm going to have to go walkabout soon as my ankle's right enough to kick-start my bike. Would it be fair for us to have it off, knowing I was bound to ride away?"

I hardly knew what to make of such ethics, not after years of men whose first requirement for involvement was that there would be no involvement.

"Oh, Rye, I can't think about fairness."

"I wouldn't want to hurt you, Gritchun."

"You won't." Not too much more than I could live with. Brain waves undulated around my head, saying, Kiss me . . . kiss me . . . kiss me. They were zeroing in, taking control of his brain, when someone knocked at the door. I immediately recognized Trout's signature pound.

"Griner," Trout bellowed. "Front and center. Bring the Barton prints. ASAP."

"Who is that currish bugger?" Rye asked, annoyed.

"My boss. He'll be in here in half a minute if I don't go see what he wants."

"Oh, bugger the sod. Come with me."

I tried to think of a reason not to. Trout would fire me? Demote me? Find me unreliable? I took off my apron.

Outside, Rye unlocked his bike. Howie had been right, it was a beautiful piece of machinery. It didn't have the cruel Darth Vader look of modern motorcycles. The black finish had dulled over the years to an organic matte gray, and here and there metal flared into lovely nonfunctional curves.

"Ever kick-start one of these brutes?" Rye asked.

"Me? A motorcycle?"

"Right, then. Today you learn. A neighbor helped me this morning, and if a seventy-year-old pensioner with bunions can kick her over, I'd surely hope a strapping lass like yourself could do as well."

" 'Strapping lass'? *Strapping?*"

"I suppose you'd rather be a pink dwarf like that individual I met inside?" He meant Darci. The "pink dwarf" part pleased, and I hopped onto his bike. I only missed the starter twice, jumping down like an enraged troll onto the pavement, before I had the Triumph roaring. Rye plunked a helmet onto my head and slid onto the bike in front of me.

We were off before I had a chance to question where we were going. All I thought about was that the last time I'd ridden on the back of a motorcycle, I'd been clinging to Ray Gutierrez. And he married someone else a week later.

19

"**S**o d'ja do it?" Juanita asked over the phone the next morning. I'd called to tell her of the exquisiteness that had been my first date with Ryemaura St. John. She'd grown impatient with the preliminaries and tried to fast-forward me to her favorite part.

" 'It'?"

"The dirty deed. Hide the sausage. Make the two-backed beast. Ride the trouser snake. Rip off a chunk of the old—"

"I get the picture, Juanita. Would Johni Lewis ever talk like that?"

"Aw, Johni's a fuddy-duddy. How was he?"

"He was funny, warm, insightful, caring—"

"Enough already." Juanita cut in again. "Save it for the eulogy. How was he in the sack?"

"Juanita!" I pretended to be offended. Actually, the whole conversation seemed distantly amusing, a radio program playing in another room.

"No action, huh? Okay, you've determined he's not gay or married. Or so he says, anyhows. What's the problem then? Herpes? AIDS? The clap?"

"For a romance writer, you sure don't believe much in your own product."

"My product is wet dreams for dry dames."

"Let's not be"—I searched for words and found one I'd never thought I'd actually utter—"coarse."

"Coarse?" Juanita squawked. "I am talking about the most sublime experience one human can share with another member of the species. Or a species not too distantly related. I mean, let's at least try to stay within the warm-blooded group."

"Oh, Juanita." My laughter tinkled.

"You're not going to spill the beans, are you, kid?" Juanita said, heaving a disappointed sigh.

The fact of the matter was that there were no beans to spill. I bade her a serene good-bye, hung up the phone, and pulled back the curtain to look out onto a day where the sun shone, not more brightly but with a richness I'd never noticed before. It poured out of the sky, making sheets smell good, backlighting chubby children grasping dandelions, and stimulating the rods and cones in Rye's fathomless blue eyes so that he too could see what a glorious day it was.

I hugged my knees. Nothing and everything had happened last night. After many Pacifico beers at the Dry Creek Café, Rye had delivered me back to my car. We'd sat in the 88 trying to say good night for seven hours and told each other everything that crossed our minds. Come to think about it, *I* was the one who'd told *him* everything that crossed *my* mind. I'd started off by surrendering to the most inexplicable desire to tell him about every guy who'd ever been mean to me, right back to Ray Gutierrez, as though he could banish all the old pain. I moved on from there to my mother's relentless redecorating.

"It never stopped," I told him. "Never. She'd just get through paneling the living room when she'd see an article that extolled the wonders of the French country house.

Next week she'd be hanging fleur-de-lis wallpaper right over the brand-new paneling. Or rather, my father would be. A couple weeks later she'd decide that the fleurs were 'too busy'; then it'd be time to haul out the paint chips again and she'd be asking my poor beleaguered father to choose between Ecru Ice and Northern Light. Then he'd paint. There are so many layers on our walls back home that, year to year, I could see the rooms shrinking. I imagine the wallpapered, paneled, fabric-covered, painted, and re-painted walls closing in on my mother until she's living in a series of long narrow tunnels and running around like a rat, redecorating her maze."

I traced my finger over a silvery lump of scar tissue on the back of his hand. "How did you get this?" I asked. He rubbed the scar too as if the memory had healed into his flesh. More than the story, I wanted the excuse to touch him.

"Oh, that. Gouged myself good and proper once on a coral outcropping when I was skin-diving for terakihi off Stewart Island."

I imagined Rye, knife between his teeth, hair dripping wet, emerging from the surf. It was nearly dawn before Rye laughed and said he'd kept me long enough. I tromped on his motorcycle to start it for him, until its roars cannonaded around the deserted street. He kissed me and rode off.

I was still awake when Juanita called that morning. A jaunty tune played in the distance. I was singing before I recognized it.

> *There once lived an Indian maid,*
> *A shy little prairie maid,*
> *Who loved a warrior bold,*
> *This shy little maid of old.*
>
> *Then brave and gay*
> *He rode one day*
> *To battle far away.*

And now the moon shines tonight on pretty Red Wing,
Something, something . . .

I went on mindlessly humming this delightful little ditty until the scratchy music had followed the ice-cream truck far down the street. Terakihi. I was possessed by a desire to go out and tell someone that I was daffy, cuckoo, in love in a way I hadn't believed possible. My insides started leaping like a trained porpoise before I'd even consciously identified the sound of the Turnip Bonnie's low, rumbling approach. I had my teeth brushed, my face washed, and eyeliner, blusher, lipstick, and deodorant applied, all before Rye had come to a complete stop.

"Hey, Gritchun," he yelled through the screen door, not letting the motor die, "I'm doing research in your neighborhood. Want to come for a ride?"

"Sure." I bounced through the door into a stoked boiler room of a day. "Great day for it."

"Couldn't be better."

"My motto is, if it's a hundred degrees in October, get outside and do something that requires you to wear a helmet and spend a lot of time on asphalt."

"That's the spirit."

I fitted myself onto the back of the bike behind him. He pushed the roaring machine backward with the tips of his toes until he had it backed up and pointed out the alley. He opened the throttle, and gravel spumed up around us. I grabbed onto him and rode clutching his back like a baby baboon hanging onto its mother.

We meandered, seemingly aimlessly, until we passed Violet Crown Heights Baptist Church, and Rye cut a sharp return path. He throttled down in front of the marquee that towered over the street.

"The Only Place Where Success Comes Before Work," I read, "Is in the Dictionary!"

Rye laughed and pulled a notebook out of the back

pocket of his jeans. He jotted down the saying, and I remembered that he was a guidebook writer.

We arced over to the east side and ended up at Austin's Largest Flea Market off 290. We parked and Rye rummaged through the saddlebags until he came up with a range finder Rollei, one of the 35-mm ones with the great optics.

"You want to know a people," Rye said as we slogged through the gravel parking lot, "have a squint at their trash."

The flea market was like a gigantic covered Mexican market. Complete with a road company of natives. Illegal aliens aren't hard to spot. They radiate a kind of stunned innocence that is as distinctive as their Indian features and straw cowboy hats with a single dingleberry bobbing on the back.

A popular item was a T-shirt that read, *No soy mojado, soy turista!*

"I'm not a what?" Rye asked.

"Mo-hado. Wetback."

Rye laughed. "I must have one." Rye pulled on the shirt, threw his arm around the man in a comradely embrace, and had me snap a picture. Rye's fancy was next taken by a T-shirt that depicted a Rubenesque señorita hand in hand with her scrawny amor. He read the caption: *Mucho jamon pa' dos huevos.*

"A lot of ham for two eggs?" I puzzled.

The owner laughed, showing white teeth that stair-stepped up and down in his mouth. He was a compact, athletic man whose relatives probably jogged up and down the Andes with bushels of coca leaves strapped to their heads. He grinned at me and grabbed his crotch for the visual aid so helpful in simultaneous translation. *"Huevos,"* he clarified. He was making grasping motions in the direction of my butt to clarify the concept of *mucho jamon* when Rye stuffed some bills and the Rollei into his hand. He put the *mucho jamon* T-shirt on me, and we stood back while the owner took our picture.

We wandered away, walking down the cement floor slick with pulped watermelon discarded by sticky children. Flies buzzed over the rinds. The smell of cantaloupe rose from a stand next to a vendor selling cardboard suitcases and rugs with dogs playing poker on them. Something caught Rye's eye and he stopped suddenly, then came up with a pair of sunglasses with lenses shaped like big red laughing lips with dark glass mouths. He put them on me, and everyone I passed smiled at us.

He wanted to try everything, so we ate sno-cones until our mouths turned blue from the syrup, and cotton candy until they turned purple from the combination of blue and red. Then he got a short, round woman in plastic sandals with a plastic daisy between her brown toes to take a picture of us showing our purple gums to the camera.

I took him to a few of my haunts: Half-Price Books where I tried to complete my hardcover Jacqueline Susann collection; Sandy's Custard for root beer floats; the Southwood Theater for a dollar's worth of air conditioning and a Sylvester Stallone triple-header. We left when we'd cooled off sufficiently and before the body count hit four figures. "I really prefer a film with some action," I commented on the way out.

Late that night, we went to the Capitol and yelled into the aqua-blue rotunda to hear our echoes. He laid the Rollei down on the seal of the Confederacy, set the self-timer, and the camera snapped us with the rotunda a boundless blue over our heads.

We rode the bike everywhere. It was the only time I could touch him, a thing I wanted to do fairly frequently. Like until all the skin on my palms wore off. I hung onto him as tight as if he were Evel Knievel and we were about to jump the Snake River. Pressing my face against his back and breathing in the smell of Rye's sweat was more fulfilling than nine tenths of my recent liaisons.

Sex was no longer an issue for me, it was the very atmosphere encircling me like an oxygen tent. The charge between us could have melted asphalt. At the exact same time, it all seemed impossibly remote. With Rye, I often had the sense that he knew all about me and I knew nothing about him and one of the things he knew was that we would never make love. It was both unsettling and wondrously consoling. At times like that I thought I could be happily platonic with him for the rest of my life.

Then there was the rest of the time when I wanted to strip off his clothes, stake him with wet rawhide strips to my bed, and write the Gettysburg Address with an eyeliner brush all over his naked body.

For the next couple of days, he brought me home, hot, dusty, and sunburned, at the end of the day and we parted without ever turning off the motorcycle. The second Sunday in October, however, I broke the conventions we'd established and asked him in. I'd worn my thinnest cotton top in anticipation of this evening. One quarter teaspoon of sweat and it was soaked and clinging to me, revealing what I had to reveal. Which wasn't exceptional, but adequate at the semiotic level I hoped to be working at that evening.

I had some Bluebell Vanilla Bean in the freezer, and we ate big bowls with Kahlúa poured over it and watched television in a haze that was half exhaustion, half a slumbrous state of frustrated lust. After the news, I turned down the sound and switched on the radio. Watching *Solid Gold* while listening to *Critic's Choice* was one of the high points of my week. I liked the contrast of Dionne Warwick flashing that dental arch you could sell hamburgers underneath and all the dancers in gold lamé diapers with INXS, UB40, and the Fab Butthole Surfers playing in the background.

Rye was particularly fascinated by a racially interesting woman with hair down to her knees that she appeared to be using to mop the floor. He watched her with an intentness I had failed to inspire. Okay, that was it, the secret of what was clearly a one-sided attraction: Rye liked exotics. He talked about not wanting to hurt anyone, but, I figured, the hurting would have commenced weeks ago if he'd been riding around with a double-jointed exotic. Instead he'd had beagle brows and banana breasts. Who could blame Rye for passing? I looked over, and his eyelashes made me want to cry. The Bluebell melted in his bowl as he laser-scrutinized the long-haired dancer doing things with her pelvis that get citizens of Georgia put in prison.

The number ended. "How in the world does that woman keep from strangling herself?" he wondered. My relief lasted only as long as it took Rye to hobble to his feet and ask if I would start his bike for him.

Gravel pattered onto my feet as he pulled out of the driveway. It was nearly midnight and I'd been out most of the day in the sun; still I was as keyed up as a talk show guest. I wanted to run after him and beg him to reconsider our look-but-don't-touch pact. However, I was certain that he'd have been the first to break any treaty he didn't feel like upholding. The temptation clearly wasn't there for him.

I went into the house feeling like my skin had suddenly become too small to hold my body. The whole internal plant was putting in overtime and stoking my furnace until I felt as if I'd just finished off half a jar of Lipton Instant. For the first time I understood the full meaning of the expression "pent up." I was afraid I would explode if I didn't press my sweat glands against another human's. But that human had to be Rye. Had to be.

I found my keys, locked the door behind me, got into the 88, and drove into the night.

20

I t was not easy finding Cedar Switch in the dark. I was forced to rely upon pheromone-assisted navigation. Even then, I missed the turn three times. Nerves. I finally cut off onto the isolated lane. I flipped off my headlights long before I reached number 12. I wanted surprise. Even more, I wanted to be able to back out at a moment's notice. A dazzling jolt of moonlight streamed into the car. It was bright enough outside that the trees cast shadows. I coasted the last bit before Rye's house, got out, and quietly pressed the door shut.

The Triumph was in front of the house. Its engine was still warm, but there wasn't a light on inside anywhere. I tiptoed around, peeking in windows, looking for his bedroom. I wasn't sure what I'd do if I found it. The screens I pressed my nose against smelled like dust and sunshine. It was dark as a cave inside. Finally a stripe of moonlight flowed into a room and across a bed with Rye's mojado T-shirt flung onto it. I huddled in the shadows, shielded my eyes with my hands, and tried to peer into the dark corners of the room. Was that Rye beneath the rumpled covers?

"Move and you're a dead man." The voice was menacing and American. "I've got a gun."

The gun pressed against my back. It felt huge. Phrases like "blow your head off" became real for me. I guessed he was one of the transients who hung around the lake. Had he murdered Rye? Would I be next? Rye and I had waited too long. Me and my manuscript would die unfulfilled. A hand grabbed my shoulder when I tried to turn around and held me in the shadows, the gun cutting into my spine.

The shaft of moonlight sliced across the man's hand gripping me. A knot of scar tissue shone silver. "Rye!" I touched the skin-diving scar.

"Gritchun?" He dropped the menacing American accent and released me. He held a croquet mallet with the handle pointing toward me and was dripping wet, wearing only the black racer's suit. "God, you scared me." He dropped the mallet and pulled me to him. His heart was pounding.

Relief poured through me. I wasn't going to have my spine severed by a shot from a .357 Magnum. I hugged him, ecstatic about living. "Oh, Rye," I squeaked in a terror-tightened voice, "I love you."

It leaked out just like that, the words I'd always been so careful to guard against saying lest I disturb some fragile male's cardiac rhythms and throw him into massive heart failure. Now I'd gone and simply blurted out the taboo declaration.

"You can't," he instructed me.

"Can't love you? Too late. I do."

He looked so genuinely sad that I had a hard time getting pissed off at him for turning out to be a cluck after all. But I did manage to pump up a little vitriol thinking of him making me fall in love with him, then telling me I couldn't. If he told me he'd never forget me I would scream.

"Gritchun, my neighbor didn't start my bike today. I did."

"Oh, okay, I understand, you gotta ramble, gotta roam."

Boy, reprisals were swift when you let your guard down and stopped sneering for a couple of seconds. "You're lobo, you hunt alone. No problem. I understand. Been great knowing you. I'll never forget you. *Vaya con dios.*"

"Don't." He grabbed me by the shoulders. "Don't."

I retreated to a distant place in my mind and there I hurriedly constructed a life that would end with my triumphant tour of New Zealand, where the scarred hand of an old man holds out one of my internationally successful best-sellers for my autograph. I pretend not to recognize Rye. But we both know what he really means when he says in his quavery voice, "I can't tell you how much your work has meant to me, Miss Grynuh. It's been my life. The biggest mistake I ever made was not picking it up when I first had the chance."

I was busy figuring out the suitably annihilating response I would make to the Rye of the future when the Rye of the present kissed me.

His kiss grabbed me and jerked me back to attention. Without my permission, my heart dived right in, allemanding left and do-si-do-ing right, prancing around with high cancan kicks and waggling a fanny, doing the slumber party Pony and Twisting the night away. I had no control. When Rye's lips touched mine, time tripped over itself and everything—every touch, smell, taste, impression—hurtled at me at once.

For once in my life, I partook of a first kiss that was actually *worth* five pages. I knew I was taking a swan dive out of a fiftieth-floor window, but the instant I felt his lips against mine, I honestly could not help myself. I needed him more than air.

I was scared when I finally moved my mouth from his and collapsed onto his chest. My ear ended up in the vicinity of his throat. The skin at his neck was soft. I listened to his breathing. It was quick, shuddery, like a child trying to stop crying.

All my insulation was gone. I had no safe place to go. Not forward. Forward couldn't be safe without insulation. Never back. Back was gone now. He held my shoulders and pushed me away. I looked into his face. He started to speak, stopped, shook his head, and looked down. He was as undone as I was. In that moment love became an exponential quantity for me. It swelled by a power of ten, crowding out my breath, my thoughts. I took Rye's hand and led him inside to his bed.

I was a virgin again. There should never have been anyone other than Rye, and when he put his hand on my naked spine and pulled me to him, there wasn't. Everything I'd ever done before seemed then like mechanical drills. Like playing First Holy Communion with Necco wafers. Kind of sweet, kind of pointless. With Rye, what our bodies did made profound, joyous sense. There was no distance between us. When he came into me I felt, most of all, relief. I had a peculiar sense of having been on an infinitely long journey, but not even realizing that I was traveling until I reached a home I hadn't known existed. Not until then did I know how weary I'd been, how much I'd been keeping at bay. I couldn't begin to explain why the relief made me cry.

"Gretchen. I'm hurting you." His voice was different, changed by lovemaking, I thought.

I shook my head no. But he stayed frozen above me, taking his weight onto his elbows.

"I never, never wanted to hurt you."

I told him again that he wasn't. Quite the contrary. Still, I couldn't stop crying. It wasn't relief anymore. I'd glimpsed the endless campaign trail and could no longer bear the prospect of soldiering on alone. I tried to slip into a we'll-always-have-Paris mode, but it didn't work. I wanted Paris now and forever. I wanted Rye and I couldn't have him. I broke into honking, quadrupedal sobs.

What finally brought me under control was Rye's face. Blurred by tears, I watched something crumble in his ex-

pression. It startled me to see another human so affected by
my pain. His mask of renegade charm slipped away, leaving
behind a little boy stricken by misery. It wasn't until my
tears slacked off, though, that I saw the little boy who'd
been left behind wasn't *Rye* as a little boy, it was someone
else entirely as a little boy. If I'd had pointed animal ears
they would have pricked up, alert to a distant danger. His
next words, though, catapulted me beyond the ceaseless
pull of gravity and insecurity.

"Would you like me to stay here with you?" He was still
doing his American accent, which was weird.

"Here? In America? How? Could you? Of course. Rye,
yes. Yes. How?"

"I could become an American."

"Yes!" This variable plugged perfectly into the basic
equation I'd formulated some time ago. Now was not the
time to be coy about giving the correct answer: "We'll get
married!" I was delirious that Rye had come up with the
same solution. "A green card marriage, of course. Everyone's doing it."

"I'd have to change," Rye warned me. "A lot."

"Of course. That's natural. There's a big difference between falling in love and life after you've landed. I know
that." I was babbling. "You can squeeze your toothpaste
from the middle of the tube. Leave the lid up. Wear socks to
bed. I don't care. Heck, I wear them myself." I laughed a
giddy laugh. Rye crimped his mouth into a tight, worried
smile.

"I'd have to speak like this."

"That's great. What an incredible American accent. A
perfect, bland white-bread accent. Oh, Rye, you'll blend
right in." I was genuinely astonished at the change in his
voice, yet there was something disturbingly familiar about
it. Something I would have noticed right away if I hadn't
been so shaken.

He sat up and the sheet fell away, clumping in his lap, his

knees sticking out. Suddenly, I didn't want him to continue. I wanted to touch his shoulders and the few tight wrinkles across his stomach. I let my hand drift down his spine to the two small hollows on either side. I touched a scar like a zipper running along the outside of his knee. He put his hand, the palm still scabbed from the accident, over mine and said, "I got it playing football."

I didn't want to hear and kept tracing the silver track of the old injury.

"I shouldn't even have been playing. I was too small back then. Junior in high school. But I was quick and the coach wanted me in and I was tired of being an outsider, a science-and-math geek. I mean, gives you some idea of how pathetically bad my high school was in football that I was recruited from the track team just because I was fast. Well, I thought football would make me a hero. Hah! Snapped my knee the first game."

I withdrew my hand. "Football? You mean soccer, right? British football? Or Australian Rules football?" I'd done my homework.

He shook his head slowly, reluctantly. "Nope. 'Fraid not."

Hearing these thudding Americanisms falling flat as an Iowa cornfield from Rye's mouth had a severely disorienting effect upon me.

"No. No more." I flagged a feeble protest.

"God, Gretchen. God." He shrugged helplessly and brought his hand to his eye. With thumb and forefinger he plucked out a blue disc floppy as Saran Wrap. He let it drop onto the ground where my clothes had pooled. He switched on the light and looked at me, a Catalooma hound with one eye still renegade blue and the other mud brown. He waited for a reaction. I checked around the bed for evidence of drug usage. My own. My one, slender, remaining hope was that I'd ingested something chemically ill-advised and was hallucinating all this.

He leaned into his hand, pinched out the other lens, and sat there with it withering on his upturned palm. His fingers opened and closed a few times like a dying daddy longlegs, and his mouth moved but no words came out.

I stared at him, my mind whirring but getting nowhere. For the first time I saw the sparkle of blond roots peeking out from beneath his pirate's cap of dark curls. I struggled as hard as I could to reject the inevitable conclusion—Rye was Gus Kubiak—and its attendant corollary—I'd slept with the Wisp. I went autistic and pulled the sheet up to my chin, leaving him naked. We were strangers in the same bed. No, worse than strangers. There wasn't even a word for what we were. I shrank from him until my back pressed against the wall. Outside, a lone surviving June bug, called by the light, battered itself against the screen.

"Gretchen, listen, I . . ." He leaned over and put his hand on my shoulder. I shook it off. "I never should have. . . . I know I shouldn't have. I wouldn't have, but there was no other way."

My hands fluttered out from under the sheet, shooing him away. "Get . . ."—the hands shooed when I wasn't able to put words together—"get dressed."

He squeezed his eyes shut. "God."

Yeah, God, I thought.

"Gretchen, I never, never wanted to. . . . It was only because—"

I flippered him away again. "Clothes. Put on clothes."

As he dressed, I pulled my clothes up off the floor and tugged them on beneath the sheet. Try as I might, I was only able to concentrate coherently on the June bug scratching at the screen. He put on some jeans and stood in front of the bed, palms out, trying to speak. Out of several constellations of questions, I settled on one.

"Why?"

He dropped his hands. "I love you, Gretchen. I've loved

you from the moment you came to your screen door and threw sheets at me."

"You love me?" I couldn't even begin to put that together with what he'd done to me.

"Yes. At first sight, Gretchen. I never believed in it until it happened to me."

I flipped the sheet back. "I'm leaving now."

"Gretchen. God, it wasn't supposed to be like this. Gretchen, please, listen to me."

I stopped but did not look at him.

"For two years, I thought I was going to die. But I lived. I had a new life. I'd wasted so much of the old one being timid. Hiding behind a computer. Not taking chances. I put my social life on hold and just thought it would happen someday. But cancer happened instead. When I got another life, I swore I would live it. Then I met you, Gretchen, and I knew from the first second that you were the one I wanted to live it with. But I didn't have a chance. Not as Gus Kubiak."

"I don't want to hear your voice anymore." My own was dull, detached. "Just don't talk. Okay?"

"No, you don't understand. I can't—"

"I'm going now."

"It was wrong. I know it was wrong. But I was desperate. I had *no* hope with you at all as Gus Kubiak. As Rye, there was a tiny chance. I never expected you'd believe in him. In those things Lizzie wrote."

"Lizzie? Lizzie!" The ice around me cracked when Lizzie's ostrich face popped into my stalled brain. "*Lizzie* told you how to do this . . . this?" I waved at the sheets, unable to refer to what had transpired.

"No. No. This was never supposed to happen. I only wanted a few days with you; then I knew I'd have to disappear." He was genuinely hurting, possibly more than I was. Tears puddled in his eyes. My reaction boinged back and forth. I looked at him and there was Rye and it was all I could do to keep from folding him in my arms.

Then he said, "At first it was half a joke. I didn't really believe I'd fool you. I laid the New Zealand stuff on so thick that first night. I thought, at some point, I'd sort of jump out and yell 'Surprise!' and just pray you thought the whole thing was funny. But you believed it. Still, I planned to give the whole thing up after that first night. Ride off and let it go. Then you kissed me. . . ."

"You were awake?"

"Well, not until you kissed me. I *had* passed out. I mean, I really did screw up my ankle."

That was when I wanted to break the Third Law of Thermodynamics by destroying his matter. Either way, Rye or the Wisp, I ached to contact his flesh.

He didn't even flinch when I slugged him below the sternum, just continued looking stricken and heartsick, which only made me madder. That he would even attempt to come out of this blameless and noble enraged me. I slapped him.

He stared at me for a while longer, as if he was hoping I'd hit him some more. But I couldn't. In my mind, I heard him and Lizzie scripting this whole farce out.

Why didn't you say good-bye?

I knew that if I woke you, I would kiss you. And if I kissed you, I wouldn't stop.

Then it all clicked. "Lizzie made me fall for the handsome rogue fantasy!"

I was too mad then to touch him. I understood guns in that instant. Hurting without touching.

"Gretchen, I can understand why you're ticked off, but I . . ." His voice dwindled away. He bent down and pulled a notebook out from under the bed and waved it feebly at me. "It's my journal. I can't excuse what I did, but maybe I can explain it."

I wouldn't touch it. He trailed me to the car just like I'd trailed Rye and stood there in the moonlight, an alien who'd taken over the body of the man I loved. Right before I pulled away, he tossed the notebook in the car window. It landed on the seat beside me.

" 'Bye, Gretchen.''

By the time I hit the highway, I was more shocked than angry and more heartbroken than shocked. I got home without knowing quite how I'd done it, the time and travel simply gone.

Once I got home, I worked on being mad again. I stomped into the living room, treading so heavily that the space heater danced on its copper coil. There was so much to be mad about that I had a hard time ordering it down from homicidal to extremely irked. I went off and on being more furious first at Gus and then Lizzie. For a couple of hours, I sat in the living room and cultivated my anger. Sheetrock-melting rage is not the most pleasant of emotions to contain, but I sensed it was preferable to whatever lurked behind the anger.

When the phone rang, I counted the rings. At an even one hundred I picked the receiver up but didn't say anything.

"Gretchen, are you there?" It was Lizzie. "Gretchen, can I come over? I need to speak with you. If you'll just let me explain. . . . Gus is here. Gretchen, he's shattered. I—"

"You pimped me."

"No, Gretchen, no. You don't under—"

I hung up and went into the bedroom. The instant I flopped onto my bed the anger left me, and all I could feel was Rye's weight on me.

I made love to a phantom. I wanted it to be an amusing conceit. I wanted to be in on the joke too. To laugh about it. But I was crying before I could convince myself of how incredibly, stupidly, funny my first true romance had been.

♥   ♥

I resisted the journal most of that first night. I didn't want to know anything about Gus Kubiak. I didn't want any of his thoughts in my head. But I had to know how he could have fooled me. How could I not have recognized him? *Smelled* him if nothing else? That was what forced me out just before dawn to retrieve the damned thing from my car.

I flipped through the first couple of months. Gus had started the journal in the hospital, shortly before he was discharged, as a way of commemorating the "new life" he had pledged to create. Those first months were little other than a medications record, how many milligrams of prednisone he was taking, how the new hydrocortisone cream was working, how tired he still was. It wasn't until the end of May when I entered the picture that I began to read seriously.

MAY 15, 5:00 A.M.

For the first time since I left the hospital, I feel as if I truly have something worth recording. As if I'm finally going to get the chance to use my new personal life philosophy. I took the Turnip out at midnight and didn't get back until just a short time ago. I'm sure you've gotten as tired of hearing as I am of writing about how many milligrams of prednisone I'm taking and what my platelet count is. You know my vow that if I lived my life would be different, and up until now it's been a big disappointment that it still revolves around numbers.

But that's all changed. Last night I met Gretchen. How a person can encapsulate a whole life's philosophy onto a T-shirt saying, "Life Is Uncertain, Eat Dessert First," amazes me. I want to know everything about her. How she arrived at that statement. But I'm getting ahead of myself. Let me back up a little and tell you the whole story.

Of course, it involves the Midge. I've finally decided that Lizzie's compulsive matchmaking is because she thinks that if I'm happily attached to someone I won't be prone to doing things like going off and getting leukemia. And since Father, just before he officially retired from being a parent, brought home a husband for her in the form of his prize grad student, Mitchell Potts, she feels it's a family tradition to get me hooked up.

Plus, ever since the bone marrow transplant, she's been even more than usually maternal. I'm still working out some of the details of my personal philosophy of life, but it's going to have to address how much of your life you owe to the person who saved it. Which Lizzie most certainly did. Without her marrow, Gus Kubiak would have been a casualty of the Leuko-Siege. Anyway, the Midge burst in on her way home from this Luvboree deal and announced that she's made a date for me. The conversation went pretty much like this:

"Grab your toupee, Gus-Busters, you've got a hot date waiting." She referred to this toupee she bought me which, according to her, magically transforms me into a normal-looking human instead of one who got too near Ground Zero. In actuality all it does is make me look like a lounge singer who got too near Ground Zero. So I told her to forget it, I wasn't ready to go out yet.

"Why not?" she asked. I told her not to be obtuse. She goes, "Come on. It's been two months. Your hair is already growing back in. You're going to look great." Then she tells me the biggest fairy tale of all. "What you've been through has put character on your face, and the kind of woman I have in mind for you responds to that a lot more than to some pretty boy."

I told her to save her fiction for Viveca Lamoureaux's readership. She told me I was the last person she'd ever expected to express such condescending attitudes. (She's been extremely sensitive ever since that blowup with Harriet Nestor at the faculty brunch.) I told her I was sorry but I just didn't want to date. She says, "I know. That's your problem. You want to go directly from 'Hi, I'm Gus Kubiak,' to adjoining burial plots." Then she informs me that things don't work that way in the "real world," which is a major laugh considering that one of the few people who know even less about the "real world" than me is the Midge. I mean, if she's such a fan of the "real world" why does she spend so much of her time hiding out in the fifth through tenth centuries? Since I know the answer is the same as it is to the question, Why have I spent so much of my life hiding out in the phosphorus glow of a computer terminal, I don't ask it. I'm sure it would only lead to years of therapy and go back to the time I got elected secretary of my Medical Explorers post and Father went around for a year calling me "Vox Populi." I think his dream would have been for his family to speak in a secret language he made up full of little puns on Bernoulli's equation and the like. Mother I'm sure would have been thrilled if she could have gotten her little band to close off from the modern world and speak Kurdish. Oh, well, it's not that bad. At least Lizzie hardly ever does her "By the Holy Rood!" stuff around me.

Anyway, I was starting to feel tired and just wanted to drop the whole discussion, but Lizzie told me that my date—"Her name's Gretchen Griner"—was waiting for me. I tell her tough noogies, I never agreed to any date. Lizzie just smiled, told me the phone number and the address and to wear the toup, and sashayed out. I was determined not to go and I wouldn't have. But jeez, if you've ever been stood up, it's like a secret pact that you'll never do it to another human being. So I tried to call Gretchen (I really like unusual names) to tell her, basically, I wasn't coming and it had nothing to do with her, but I'd been sick. I wasn't sick anymore (positive imaging!) but I had been and so on. But the Midge must have screwed up on the number (unless it's the date when a Merovingian princess got married or something, she is hopeless with numbers), because there was no Gretchen Griner there.

So I thought, Fine, I tried, and started back to work on this real neat algorhythm I came up with for determining bound water of formation based on the neutron density curve and the gamma ray trace, but I kept remembering that time with Linda Heineker. How I waited for her in the Student Union cafeteria for two hours and then, when I finally called, her roommate said she had laryngitis and couldn't speak. Lame. So I went on over. Just to tell her not to wait for my call. But I didn't wear the toup.

And there she was. Gretchen. And there I was, an albino Baby Doc Duvalier.

Yeah, even though I'm down to 5 mg of prednisone, I still have the fat-face Cushingoid features. That, combined with almost zero hair, makes me a real charmer. You know, I think if she'd had any other name in the world except Gretchen, I never would have gone over. I just kept thinking that someone named Gretchen already knew that life isn't always the way we plan.

Gretchen didn't seem too horrified. She probably couldn't see me that well through the screen. We were both caught off guard. She thought I was there to pick up her cleaning, I think. From the first time I looked at her face, her wide-set hazel-green eyes, her broad German face with that little-kid chin. Freckles on pale skin. The way she just stared, so open. The way her T-shirt hung off of those bird bones around her neck, then poked out where her nipples were. Jeez, her wrists, I loved her wrists! I've never even noticed anyone's wrists and there hers were, functional, knobby, but so tiny. I wanted so bad to put my hand around them. Weird, huh? From that first time, looking at her all fuzzed out from the screen, something clicked. I can't even explain it. I just loved the way she looked. The way her voice sounded. Her T-shirt. It said, "Life Is Uncertain, Eat Dessert First." I couldn't believe it. That's my whole new philosophy of life right there on a T-shirt! I mean, I would never, never, never have dreamed the Leukos would come for me. I always lived like I had forever. I always thought that someday I'd find a person to share my life with and things would just sort of happen. Probably because that person made them happen. Wrong, Kubiak.

It's strange, I'd just been remembering on the way over exactly what had been in my mind all that time I spent in chemo, and then with the marrow transplant. I know it's what guys must think about in the trenches when they're pretty sure they're not going to make it back. It was so clear to me, lying on those goddam cold hard gurneys the life I'd have if I lived. I'd be part of things. I wouldn't be a tech-head techno-geek social retard. I'd have someone to love.

Gretchen. What a sturdy, beautiful, barbarian name.

You know what really sealed it? And this is exactly the kind of thing I always used to think was for morons. But when she started singing "Little Red Wing," it was like a sign. See? I hate people who find "signs." But it's got to mean something. How many people know "Little Red Wing"?

Meeting Gretchen has been a turning point no matter what else happens or doesn't happen. Up until that moment, it was like I'd been tiptoeing around. Not taking the bike out. Never leaving the house. Waiting for the leukocytes to jump on me again. Living exactly the way I swore I wouldn't if I lived. Dr. Michaels told me that if I was still around a hundred days after the transplant I'd probably make it. Well, it's only Day 58, but after meeting Gretchen I don't feel like waiting anymore. After I took her to B-R, I came home and got the Turnip out and went way out on 71, yelling at the top of my lungs. It was like I was putting the world on notice that Gus Kubiak is back and leuko-cytes beware!

But first I called Mitchell and told him about Gretchen. I don't know why, I just had to say her name to someone. God, I was pissed when the Midge interrupts and asks if I'd "raked her with my glance." She'd been listening on the extension again. I've about had it with her and her sure-fire romance writer techniques. I told her that real people "rake" lawns. As usual, she was totally oblivious.

God, I just feel like going out and yelling some more. This is great. I've got the sweats, I'm trembly, my bp is bouncing off the moon, and I'm not even thinking remission!

SAME DAY

Spent most of the afternoon figuring out what invitation would appeal most strongly to Gretchen Griner. (Yes, I like that name!) My original categories were live or prerecorded. I eliminated the prerecorded (movies, etc.) because of the indistinguishability fac-

tor. *Live events are more unique. The subcategories then were drama, music, spectacle (Ice Capades, etc.). The plays for this weekend are "a cabaret showcase set during one weekend at a retreat for gay priests with AIDS," "the hilarious misadventures of a county extension agent in Bovina, Texas," and "the neo-expressionistic never-never land of a Golden Anniversary where a retired couple confront the sham of their 50-year marriage." The Ice Capades aren't going to be in town. I think the drama choices are too risky.*

That left music. For the ten years I've lived here, I've heard a lot about the "Austin Music Scene" and it's true. I opened the Grackle *and there are 77 (double sevens, should be lucky!) places advertising music this weekend. I am ashamed of myself that I haven't set foot in a single one of them. But that was the old Gus Kubiak. The new improved version isn't going to spend the rest of his life on the sidelines.*

I knew I needed to enlarge my data base still further. At the library I found microfiche of the past five years of Billboard. *I charted out the ten most popular performers as shown by number of albums sold, number of singles sold, and number of records that have been in the Top Forty. The point at which these trajectories intersected with anyone who would be playing in the Austin area this weekend is Lionel Ritchie. I may be erring on the conservative side, but my thinking is, the odds for hitting a winner with Gretchen are better with Ritchie, who's sold 93.4 million records, than they would be with an unknown quantity like Lutheran Canoe Trip, though they do have an independently produced EP out, "Tumpin' Over," that was favorably reviewed in Gretchen's publication the* Grackle *by the Troutman, and I've* been *on a Lutheran canoe trip so can appreciate the humor of the name. My horizons expand exponentially.*

The next step is ticket procurement. I noticed in Gretchen's publication in the classifieds that someone was selling seats near the front for $65. Front-row seats would be memorable. Okay, I'll get the tix, then wait for redial to get through. This would be

*scary for mortal men, but it'll be a breeze for Lt. Leuko. Hah!
Wish me luck! I'll let you know how it goes.*

MAY 16

*She wasn't home. I waited until nine this morning to call. No
answer. After a few more unsuccessful tries, I programmed ten-
minute redial. At twelve fifteen, I remembered the bonfire in her
broiler and the space heater in her house. Those things should be
outlawed. I decided I'd better go over and check.*

*I was relieved and crushed when I saw her car was gone. I
guess I was driving a little slow and staring, because this teenage
girl who was lying on the lawn of the house in front of Gretch-
en's wrapped herself up in the towel she was on and ran into the
house. She thought I was scoping her out. A few seconds later her
father came out, looking mad. I floored it.*

*For the next two hours, I cruised the neighborhood. I went back
to the B-R where we had ice cream together. After that I drove
around until I found a record store that sold the* Grackle.

*The print they use for photo credit lines is too small. Why do
writers get normal-sized print and photographers get microbe-
sized print? It's really not fair. Gretchen's photos are outstand-
ing. She had this one closeup of a rattlesnake that made the fangs
look like scimitars. The snake was being held, and just from the
calluses and gouges and diamond-horseshoe pinkie ring on the
guy's hand, you could tell so much about the kind of person that
gets into this snake-handling stuff. She really is a gifted photographer. I admire accomplishment in a woman.*

*After that, I went up and down the cross streets, pausing at
the points where my sight lines to her house were clear. A bunch
of guys in a Camaro they'd taken down to the primer coat drove
up and the girl left with them. A little while later her father
came out in a uniform with brown pants and a brown striped
shirt and got in his Frito-Lay truck and drove away. That's
when I cruised on back to Gretchen's house.*

I don't know exactly why I did it. I know she wasn't there. But I wanted to see where she lived again. It's not much. A converted garage. That's another thing I admire, when people aren't overly concerned about material things. Even though I knew she wasn't there, I had my toupee on and felt like she was watching when I got out of the car. I pretended I was a friend concerned about her, maybe familiar with her history of unsafe operation of space heaters, and I peeked in the windows.

I noticed some things I missed yesterday: a rug woven with a picture of two bears eating out of a honey pot on it; a lamp made out of a ceramic pineapple; a velvet painting of Elvis praying under a blue spotlight; a bullfighting poster; a wine bottle with a candle stuck in it and wax dripped all over it. I think it's great when people don't get everything to match.

I was too engrossed in Gretchen's interior decorating though, because all of a sudden this guy walks out of what I assume is a bedroom. Totally naked. It was obvious his head hair was dyed black, because it was a lot darker than his hair anywhere else. He was barely awake (at 3:19 p.m.!) and didn't come close to noticing me.

Okay, Gus, analysis: Does this blow me out of the water? I'm not going to jump to conclusions. There's something I have to remember to factor in the whole way here—I'm really out of it. First, all I've done for the last year, basically, was the Leuko-Siege. Then before that it was four years averaging 600 lines of code a month. Then in my "carefree college days" I lived at the computer center. That really leaves a lot of time for a social life. Hah! Jeez, it's been almost ten years since I bought an album. Boston.

So this guy could be a platonic roommate. This hypothesis is supported by the fact that Gretchen was gone. Perhaps they have a split schedule use of the house arrangement. Perhaps he's a visiting relative. Or, okay, Gus—least desirable scenario—perhaps he's her boyfriend. What does that mean? We turn tail and scrap the whole thing? First, he's not the right guy for her. Second, who says they're married? Third, I don't know what third is, but in the final analysis it wouldn't matter either. Gretchen needs me. I know that this can be interpreted as a pretty convenient assessment, considering how I feel about her. But I know it's not just that I'm crazy about her. Gretchen needs me, I'm as sure of that as I am that $Q_H - W = E_2 - E_1$.

I don't know exactly why I feel this way. (About Gretchen, not the first law of thermodynamics.) I never felt such certainty before. It's funny, I look back at pictures of myself before the Leukos landed and I was an all-right-looking guy. But I never really made any effort. I was always parked behind a terminal. And now, when I look revolting, I'm ready. Ready to do what? To do whatever it takes, even though I have no idea what that might be. I don't know. I get a feeling, and it's stronger than ever now that I've scouted out her house, that Gretchen is not one of those people who care too much about appearances. I think this can work.

MAY 17

Mitchell loved the show. I thought Ritchie was fairly bland myself. I should have realized that blandness would be a flaw in building my data base from Top Forty. I imagine Gretchen's parents would have liked him. If they really were in town. I can't decide. I think I'm pretty good at reading people's voices, and my initial impression was that she really did want to go but . . . the parents. I still tend to get exhausted by about four in the afternoon, and that's when I start doubting that her parents were in town. But, hey, once you've lived through the Leuko-Siege, one date rejection doesn't slow you down.

Whichever, even if she was lying, she left the door open. So tonight I'm going to check out Lutheran Canoe Trip for future dates. I think Gretchen and I probably prefer more avant garde stuff.

MAY 18

Once again Lizzie has preempted my prerogative. She's having a dinner party tonight and Gretchen is coming. In this real sappy voice, she said I might want to "drop by." I guess this is subtle for Lizzie. Should I go? Of course I should go. Toupee or not toupee? that is the question. Hah. I think I'll go bare. She's already seen the dome and didn't scream or faint, so I guess it's too late for the rug anyway. Now for the rest of me.

I try not to succumb to my insecurities. I try to remind myself that it was clear from Gretchen's house that she isn't impressed with appearances. I should just be myself. Especially since I don't have enough time to be anyone else.

Inspiration! I'll ask Gretchen to come to Lutheran Canoe Trip with me after the dinner party. I'm skipping the prednisone altogether today, it muddles my thinking incredibly. If this is the day the Leukos mount an attack, tough titty. I want to be able to think when I see Gretchen. Jeez, I hope Mitchell doesn't get bizarre with the food.

MAY 19

It's four in the morning and I just got in. I left the dinner party as soon as I could after Gretchen took off. From the moment I walked in, the evening had disaster written all over it. First off, Gretchen had no more idea I was coming than she did that first day at her house. I don't want to think about all the ways it was hideous.

I went home and got the Turnip and rode until almost midnight. I did some pretty death-defying stuff. Rode without my lights, almost shoulder-banked a bunch of turns. I just wanted wind in my face blowing all thought from my mind.

I ended up at the Club Ennui. I'll say it was because I wanted to check out Lutheran Canoe Trip, but all my neurons were fired up expecting to see Gretchen. Damn Mitchell for his show-off cooking. If she hadn't blown her tentacles or whatever happened, she might have come with me. Or would she? My readings on her are so erratic. The truth of it is, I've lost all objectivity. I think about Gretchen constantly. I plan out great, funny things to say to her. Then, when she's actually around, all my brain puts out is static. I was such a dud this evening I can't stand to think about it.

The Club Ennui, what a strange environment. It reminded me of the Petrology Exhibit at the Natural History Museum where everything is black so that the phosphorescent rocks turn neon-looking under the black lights. I was glad for the darkness, since this was an initial foray. Also, I wanted to be sure and spot Gretchen before she saw me. If she was there.

Okay, first thing, LuCanoe was good. Not soothing like Ritchie, but I don't want to nap when I go to hear music. I doubt Gretchen does either. Once my eyes adjusted, I got a big surprise when I saw that all the band members were dressed like guys in my undergraduate double E classes. Maybe worse. Too-short pants. (We used to call them "high-waters.") Belts cinched up too tight so their pants got up into their cracks. These goofy old-man glasses like the ones Jewish men with ear curls wear. And really, really bad haircuts. Almost scalped on the sides ("white sidewalls"), with weird tufty deals sticking out on top. I guess it's a sad commentary on my psyche, but the sense of superiority I derived from knowing that at least I didn't look as bad as they did made me feel a lot less nervous to be there.

I really don't know why I've felt intimidated all these years by the "Austin music scene." As bad a dancer as I am, I'm at least as good as the guys in the band, who were jerking around like their guitars were shorting out or something. It was hard to tell about anyone else since the place was so dark. But it seems like I just barely inched off the sidelines and I was swept up into this big group dance movement. I cut loose and didn't even notice how hard I was working out until I stopped. I was suddenly so tired I could barely stand.

Once I was outside and had the toup off, I revived. I rode up and down Sixth Street for a while. I got a charge out of coming back the wrong way on a one-way. The whole time, I felt like Gretchen was watching me and thinking there might be more to this guy than meets the eye.

Cruised her house again. Only her car was there. No lights were on. I remember every word she's ever said to me. The way she looked standing in her doorway that first day. I never really paid much attention to the radio before. To me, all the sappy songs were fake, like hymns people sing at church without ever meaning the words. Now, almost every song I hear seems to relate directly to my situation.

My body is as tired now as it was after the marrow transplant, but my mind is wide awake. I am very, very discouraged. I might as well be a serf in love with the lord's daughter or something. I feel like tonight was just one giant memo to me to remind me of my "place." I'd have to completely change the way I am to get Gretchen to look twice at me. I wonder if it would make any difference if I had my hair back and wasn't swollen up like a Cabbage Patch Doll. Of course, what am I supposed to do? Send her pictures of the "real" Gus Kubiak? Maybe I could casually work the story in about how I ran into Russell, my old cubicle mate from Digicorp, a guy I sat across from for a year and a half, and how I look so different now he didn't recognize me. Even after I said hello and asked him how the AI project was going, he still didn't place me until I told him who I was.

Oh, what's the difference? All it means is that, under normal circumstances, I'm a slightly better-looking techno-geek. Intellectually, I want to get my spirit and optimism back, but tonight I just don't have the energy. All I can think about is, I wonder why I bothered with the Leuko-Siege if it's just going to end up like this, not wanting my old life and not able to start a new one.

As tired as I was, I lay awake a long time thinking about a book I read way back in high school, Bridge of San Luis Rey. *This memory has been waiting for more than a dozen years like some buried locust for this exact moment. I found the book and the passage I'd been trying to think of: "There is a land of the living and a land of the dead and the bridge is love, the only survival, the only meaning."*

I know from being sick that it's true about the two lands. And
I know now from being well that I still haven't crossed the bridge.
Signing off, very low, very tired.

MAY 20

The Midge just left. I'm sure now that my only sibling is
certifiable. I can't think of any other way to explain how someone
could poke their nose so far into other people's business even when
you've told them in no uncertain terms to butt the heck out. She
had a big flash for me: Gretchen will never be interested in Gus
Kubiak. But, she said, she could help me become someone
Gretchen would *fall in love with.*

I asked her if a trip to Haiti would be required. Jeez, it was a
joke—voodoo, pins in dolls—but, typical Lizzie, she thinks about
it for a moment, then says, "We can come up with a much better
background."

Background? She is definitely not hitting on all six. Then she
proceeds to tell me exactly what kind of a man Gretchen would go
for. Basically, a rogue. I said, What's that? A guy who goes
around flaring his nostrils and wearing a lot of epaulettes? She
said, No, it's an attitude. I said, An attitude? Like you want to
go out and trample thatched huts and crush natives in your
powerful trunk or something? You know, as in rogue elephant?
She just heaves this big sigh and says how really sad it is that a
love that could be so sublime is doomed by superficialities when
just a few minuscule changes could make all the difference.

It kills me that here she is, kind of—okay—dumpy, and the
only time she was ever asked out in her life was when Father
practically ordered Mitchell to do it, and she keeps setting herself
up as some love expert of the ages. So, great, she writes romance
novels. That makes her Cleopatra of the Nile?

After she left, I accessed the Department of Motor Vehicles. It
was kind of a kick. I haven't done any hacking since that time
with Mitchell in college. Of course, DMV wasn't as much of a

challenge. I swear, Lizzie had better security on her five-year diary back in junior high.

God, when Gretchen's file came up on the screen, it was such a rush. It was like she was there in the room with me. Reading DOB, HT, WT was so, almost, intimate.

I have moments when I can see I'm starting to get a little weird. I zone out for hours imagining these scenes where I'm lead singer for LuCanoe and Gretchen sees me and suddenly realizes how intrinsically cool I am. Or I'm cruising her house and spot these guys inside brandishing weapons and stealing her Elvis painting and I clean them out with the Ted Williams Slugger I just happen to have with me. But the most common thing I imagine is that I'm flying. I almost can't control this one. If I'm not concentrating, I'm thirty, forty, a hundred feet in the air, soaring around, and Gretchen is on the ground just dazzled. I've always had flying dreams, but this worries me a little since I'm wide awake.

See what I mean? I just looked at the clock and half an hour disappeared since I wrote that last sentence.

I wonder what kind of "minuscule changes" Lizzie is talking about.

JUNE 6

Lizzie is double-teaming me now. She showed up this morning with her romance-writing buddy, Juanita. My house reeks of True cigarettes. But here's the real news: Gretchen is writing a romance novel! Something called a contemporary, which is what Juanita is an expert at. At least Juanita works in this century and is a little bit more in touch with current reality than Lizzie. She also told me I had about as much chance with Gretchen as a Boston fern. Jeez. Another Cleopatra of the Nile.

Anyway, they both think they know Gretchen because they've been reading this book she's working on. Juanita goes, "She can call him Manx, but he's the same old Derrick, Jason, Pierce, or

Justin that I've written a hundred times." She stops for a minute
to take a giant drag, blows the smoke out of the side of her mouth
(like, yeah, that'll really keep it out of my lungs), then goes on
talking. "Now, G.G. may tell you, she may tell herself, she can
even get down on her knees and tell the good Lord that she's just
following a formula, but I'll tell you what. . . ." She does
another big long pause and sucks on her cig until you practically
beg her to go on. I just said, "What?" But not right away.
"That Manx is Gretchen Griner's idea of one sexy son of a
buck."

Then she leans back and gives me this "So there" nod, after
which they both sit there looking at me like they just put down a
big fat kernel of corn and I'm supposed to go peck at it. Under
normal circumstances, I would have leaned back and out-waited
both of them, but as I've been saying, my circumstances haven't
been normal since I met Gretchen. Her face, the way I imagine it
when I'm flying, kept coming into my mind. I really hated giving
Lizzie the satisfaction, but I had to know what kind of guy would
make her face like that. I asked what Manx was like.

It was so predictable, I'm almost a little disappointed in G.G.
Tall, dark, and handsome. Great body. They describe this Manx
character, then Juanita goes, "But numero uno is the bod.
Women love muscles."

Another hot news flash, huh? I thanked them for the info and
said I was already working out anyway (a lie). I reminded Lizzie
that I was a cross-country runner in college (true) and former
champion Frisbee freestyler (semi-true).

Then Juanita shakes her head and goes, "Ix-nay, buddy.
Build up the legs and ignore the arms and you're going to end up
looking like a cheerleader. Shoulders, hon, shoulders." Lizzie
agreed and said that male upper-body strength had an atavistic
appeal.

I embellished my lie and said I'd already incorporated free
weights into my program. Lizzie clapped her hands and said she
was just thrilled to hear all about my new regime. She asked
when I usually worked out. I told her I ran in the mornings from

six until eight, then worked out with weights for another couple of hours. Did some work on the oil-logging program for the Kuwaitis, then had an afternoon session. The more embellishments I added to my program, the happier it seemed to make Liz-bo.

The head fuzz is now a full inch and a half long. I'm almost totally tapered off the prednisone and can already see the difference. There might actually be cheekbones down there! But most importantly, the steroid fog is lifting. My mind is a bit quicker every day.

I think I may actually get out tomorrow and run a little.

JUNE 7

The Midge must be stopped! I'm so sore I can barely write. She showed up at my doorstep at six this morning. I wasn't awake and thought at first there was some emergency with Annabelle, which got my adrenaline pounding. But, no, she just came by to accompany me on my "run." Before I could ask her what in hell she was talking about, I remembered the lies from yesterday about my Rocky program. So I had to act like I'd just accidentally overslept. I couldn't find my sweats and I had to wear shorts. Chicken legs. At least, I think, even in as bad a shape as I am, I can surely outlast the Midge with her foot-and-a-half-long legs. But no. We get out and she's going to "accompany" me on her moped. So the deal is, she gets to ride for an hour and I'm supposed to run.

Ten minutes into the run and I'm dying. My veins are on fire, my legs feel like corn flakes. But there's Lizzie putting along ahead of me on her moped with her fat butt flopping over the seat and I don't care how bad I feel, I'm not going to wuss out. To get my spirit back, I flip her birds with both hands. At that exact moment, she looks back and tells me to take my shirt off. "Come on, Gus, bronze those deltoids. The only thing women like better than muscles are brown muscles." I was planning to get some sun already.

I make half an hour. Every fiber in my body is twanging like a crossbow, I'm leaving a trail of sweat on the asphalt, and I'm not hot anymore, I feel cold and clammy, the way I did when I got shocky after the transplant. But I'm still not going to give up. I don't give up, but my body does. I trip and gouge my knee. Lizzie rides me home on the back of the moped. Then she says she wants to lift for a while with me.

I want to lift all right. Lift the Midge over an elevator shaft. Thank God, I still had the set of weights Uncle Matthew gave me for Christmas five years ago. Of course, then I had to tell Lizzie that I preferred to dismantle the weights and return them to their original wrapping every time I finished using them, which was twice a day. She goes, "Complete with a bow and everything. How festive."

Typical Midge, she zeroes right in on the instruction manual and starts telling me I'm assembling them wrong. Then she critiques my position on the bench. "Back must be flat against bench to avoid injury." So she's down there wedging her hand under my buns. Then she decides to get in the act and starts doing arm curls with the dumbbells. She does ten sets of twenty reps each. I never noticed it before, but the Midge has forearms like Popeye from holding Annabelle for two years. She hands me the dumbbells like this is the big challenge of the sexes. At first, I thought, No sweat, because they were really light. But it's the reps that get to you. Thank God her alarm beeped and she had to leave. I couldn't uncurl my fingers for twenty minutes.

What is the deal with the Midge? I guess because she has insomnia, she has more time than she needs to lead her own life, so she uses the extra to lead other people's lives. Considering how detached Mother was even before she officially "retired from parenthood," the Midge certainly never had a model for this hypermaternalism. The most intimate conversations I can ever remember having with Mother all had to do with phonological variables and consonant clusters. Not that Father was much better. Anyway, the quicker I get back into shape, the quicker Lizzie will realize that I don't need her help with my love life. Sometimes, though, I almost wish that she did know some secret that would win Gretchen.

At least my fantasies about G.G. are more under control today. Seeing my fishbelly-white body and chicken legs has made me too embarrassed to even imagine her looking at me. I'm going to Barton Springs now. Hopefully, I can find a secluded corner where I won't scare small children and I can tan and get in some laps. If I can stand up.

JUNE 15

Did I say I was sore last week? I didn't know the meaning of the word. Lizzie was at my door at six again the next morning. I made thirty-five minutes, but we only covered about half the distance because I was so cramped up and sunburned. I forgot to put sunscreen on the inside of my legs, so I had to run with them spread way apart so they wouldn't rub. Really, I ran the whole way looking like Annabelle when she had a full load in her diaper. I was a little better on the weights today.

Also, Lizzie brought over the first chapter of Gretchen's novel. I told her I didn't want to read it. Gretchen hadn't asked me to and it would be an invasion of privacy. Lizzie just shrugs and goes, "Oh, well, thought you might want to know how far the shadow fell between the dream and reality." Then she leaves the pages and goes to the bathroom. For about half an hour. I admit it, I have no principles where G.G. is concerned. I peeked. I didn't read the whole thing, but it was pretty easy to see that this Manx was a Class A rogue of the nostril-flaring variety.

Right before Lizzie leaves she grabs my hand and says, "Gusters, I've created dozens of heroes that millions of women have fallen in love with. I can help you."

God, I wish I could have just hooted at her and closed the subject forever. But my mind will not close. I go back and forth.

My original idea was to get into shape, then try with G.G. again, but even at my best pre-Leuko, I was no Manx. That's when I started thinking it's hopeless. I came very close this evening to calling the Midge and asking her just what kind of help she had in mind.

Anyway, Lizzie has shown up every morning for the last week for "our" workout.

JULY 18

Sorry, I haven't written for a while, I've been too dead in the evenings. This is a good sign that I'm still awake now at—what is it? eight thirty. And the pain has moved out of the scary level and is starting to feel like normal workout pain. I ran an hour and a half today. Lizzie gave me a tape from Juanita to listen to on the Walkman, and it took my mind off running. The tape was ninety minutes of New Zealand radio. Juanita got it from another romance writer who lives in New Zealand. She needed it to write dialogue for a character. It was interesting. Kind of Australian-sounding, but softer, nicer.

I guess Lizzie had listened to the tape too because she starts yelling at me in a terrible New Zealand accent to pick up my "trotters," stay on the "sealing," and watch out for "judder bars." (I found out later from the "vocabulary" section the New Zealand woman put at the end of the tape that those expressions mean feet, pavement, and speed bumps.) Anyway, if there's one thing I'm sure I can do better than the Midge, it's accents. I mean, growing up with the Queen Mother of Linguistics, you'd better have been tuned in to the nuances of an accent. At least I was. Lizzie seemed to have a tin ear. Just to remind her that I was the accent king, I yelled the next commercial on the tape back at her, "Wouldn't a handle of DB Double Brown be ka pai right now? Available at all Dominion Breweries Public Houses."

Not great, but I sounded a lot more like the radio announcer than she had. Then, the whole time we're lifting, we're yelling

New Zealand stuff at each other. It was moderate fun. Lizzie can be bearable if she lets up on her fixations.

JULY 30

G'day mate, been mucking about with all this Kiwi rot for the past few days until I'm fairly bent.

Wow, it's true. Every day Lizzie shows up with another Kiwi tape. Actually, I like listening to them a lot. There's one announcer, Dikkie Diamond, whom I quite fancy. It's great listening to him tell what the temperature is in Christ Church and how many tries the All-Blacks scored. I imagine him there in his little control booth, a matey bloke who's a bit airy-fairy but still managed to make it on his own bat. I don't know why, but he sounds like he has muttonchops and wears one of those black Greek fisherman's caps. Mostly, he sounds happy. I wonder if G.G. would like to visit New Zealand.

Can't believe how fast I'm coming back. I'm already up to six miles a day. I can bench press 110 and curl 40. And I'm not fluorescent any more. I'm down to SPF 5. When I swim laps at Barton Springs, I see Gretchen's face in the duckweed.

I held myself back as long as I could; then I gave in and called her house. No answer. So I cruised by. It was three in the morning and her light was still on. But the Bel Air station wagon wasn't there. I think he must have been an out-of-town guest.

AUGUST 25

I was at Whole Foods Market today and ran into Russell again. He walked right past me. I said, "Russell, it's me, Gus." The look on his face made every callus, every health nog, every frayed muscle fiber I've endured for the past what, is it really almost three months?—all worthwhile. He really didn't believe it was me.

"Gus? Gus Kubiak?" he said. "Last time I saw you, you looked like. . . . your hair. . . . it was so . . . so thin. Now you're, you're—" Then he just flapped his hands at me for a while. Basically, he was agog. "I totally didn't recognize you, man." After that he wanted to know what my secret was and I told him to get so puffed up on steroids no one recognizes you, then anything you did afterward would look pretty good.

I asked if he was still seeing Jeannie, and he said they're getting married in October. Then he asks me if I'm dating, and I told him, yes, a photographer.

I think the lie grew out of all Lizzie's "create your own reality" talk. The last couple of weeks, she's been telling me about these self-help books she's been reading. Most of it's garbage, but some of it makes sense. Such as envisioning yourself in situations you want to come true. That was like permission to spend all my time imagining me and Gretchen together. It scares me sometimes, it seems so real. I'll drift off while I'm swimming laps and in my mind my whole life will shift so that she's in it. I'll actually be disappointed when I go home and her car's not there.

I had a dream last night. I was in the bottom of a set of bunk beds. Then, all of a sudden, I realize that it's Gretchen up there on the top bunk. God, I was so happy. All I had to do was stand up and she'd be there. Then I tried to get out of bed and it turned into that gurney they used to take me for treatments and I was all strapped in and had a zillion needles poking in me and tubes running out of me. I knew I'd die if I didn't stand up. I woke up when I reached up and the outside edge of the ceiling fan nicked my hand. It was very depressing when I realized Gretchen wasn't there. I couldn't go back to sleep.

After the workout, Lizzie's friend Juanita shows up and Lizzie announces to me that we're all going shopping. "Once you move much past cloaks and breeches, you're pretty much out of Lizzie's bailiwick, fashionwise," is how Juanita explained it between hacking fits. ("Just clearing the pipes.")

I'll admit, I didn't have much faith in the fashion sense of someone who shows up wearing a wraparound skirt made out of couch material and a blouse with a Bozo the Clown collar. Plus a ton of jewelry. She also had on a charm bracelet with a charm for the major agricultural export of each of the fifty states, so there were little peanuts and ears of corn and apples. I guess she knew I was checking her out, because she points her cigarette at me and goes, "You don't have to be a chicken to know a good egg." I told them I was already researching this topic and showed them the stack of GQs I'd collected.

Juanita paid no attention and took us to this store, Treks. Everything looked like it had been salvaged from shipwrecked castaways. Faded, worn out, ripped. Juanita promised that this was the look. Along the border, they'd call it Ropa Usada. Juanita and Lizzie went rifling through the racks, stopping every now and then to hold up a jacket or something; then they'd say, "Would Manx wear this?" and ponder. I'm back there going, "Just ask me," or, "No, he wouldn't wear that on a bet."

It was moderately amazing how close I came to looking like the magazines once I had this new paraphernalia on. Juanita kept throwing stuff in at me while I was in the dressing room. Once she caught me in my shorts and I pointed out that a little privacy would be appreciated. She laughs this kind of donkey laugh and goes, "Buster, if you've got any item of equipment that Juanita Lusader has not seen, let the Smithsonian Institution know. Pronto." Next time she fans the door open, she throws in some underwear. Super bun-huggers, the sperm-cooker kind, in this green-blue called teal. I don't ever plan to wear them, but I bought them anyway. I could just see having a big fight with Juanita in the middle of Treks about teal bun-huggers.

I wore the new outfit home. As soon as we got out of the store, Juanita points down to my shoes and says, "Burn those." I had already figured out that Hush Puppies weren't going to be part of the look I was putting together. Then she tries to drag me into a shoe store. That's when I put my Pups down (hah). I know exactly what kind of footwear I want—my motorcycle boots.

I was in a pretty good mood until Lizzie says, "You know, changing the wrapping on a present isn't going to accomplish *much when the recipient already knows what's inside." I asked her what she was talking about and she goes. "Nothing, I just think you might want to consider a few more substantive changes. Your Dikkie Diamond is quite good, you know."*

SEPT. 10

Crikey! I am browned off royally. The Midge strikes again. This morning she prances in and plunks down a great lot of her romance novel twaddle and informs me that if I am to ever have a fair go with Gretchen, I'd better have a squint. Passion's Fire, indeed.

It's me again. I slip into Kiwi talk now almost without realizing it. I suppose it's because Lizzie is almost the only person I talk to during the day, and we spend the whole time doing Kiwi. I pretend I'm Dikkie Diamond. It's about the only way I can handle her anymore. The more I listen to D.D., the more my image of him changes. He talked a little bit the other day about how he's part Maori. I don't see muttonchops anymore. I'd guess he's a pretty studly bloke.

I took the new Treks-ified me to the mall today. Can you believe it? I actually needed a haircut. The pale tufties disappeared and the hair that's grown in is very different from what it was. It's darker, thicker, and wirier. The woman who did it kept running her fingers through my hair, telling me what "unusual texture" it had. I wanted to tell her, "Yeah, nothing like a Leuko-Siege to get that texture." But she was really *getting in there, massaging my scalp and shit. Denso that I am, though, it didn't click until I looked in the mirror and there she—Shannon —is, with her head sort of leaning sideways, smiling at me. I finally snap to; she's coming on to me. I was about this far from nerding out, when out of nowhere this suave voice says, "Yes, I'm part Maori. My mother's people came from New Zealand."*

I didn't exactly "do" Dikkie or anything, but it was his attitude. Shannon lights up and goes, "Oh, really?" Then she asks me if I'd like for her to come by my house for a special treatment she had in mind for me. She said my hair texture, being part Maori and all, inspired her. I said sure, but then I explained to her how I'm staying here at the lake taking care of a former professor's house. She thought that was great, tells me she loves the lake and can't wait to come out.

It's funny. I'm sure if I'd come in wearing the Pups, all swollen up, she wouldn't have cared if my hair had texture like a set of Uniroyals. It was a kick walking around the mall after that. I have to hand it to the Midge, women do like muscles. I could have made five dates if I'd wanted to.

God, I'm almost getting my hopes up about Gretchen again. I mean, my confidence is coming back a little. Still, there's a world of difference between Gretchen and Shannon.

SEPT. 11

Date report: Okay, I did go ahead and leaf through the romance novels. Just to try and get some date ideas in case Shannon wanted to go out after this special hair treatment. But only the contemporaries. I didn't figure there'd be any great masked balls around I could take Shannon to. Hah.

As it turned out, I wasn't going to set foot out of the house after this treatment. Shannon came over around six and immediately starts gooshing this stuff on my hair. Then she wraps it up in Saran Wrap and says we need to let it sit for fifteen minutes and it'll give my hair some "Maori warrior bronze highlights." Not that I'd ever expressed any great desire for bronze highlights, but okay.

Then, while we're waiting for these highlights to take hold, she starts with the neck massage again and somehow she ends up standing in front of me and we're both massaging each other's neck. Now comes the confession part. There I was, massaging her shoulders and smelling her perfume and feeling her hair against my cheek and her just slightly rubbing against me, and I haven't

*been with anyone for two years and zip, nada, nothing. Then,
almost against my will, I start thinking about Gretchen and* ka-
blooie! *the marines land.*

*Then Shannon starts quizzing me about my love life. How
many people I've been with in the last eight years. Have I ever
shot drugs. I tell her I haven't been with anyone in two years and
before that I had just been with Bettina since grad school. As for
drugs, I don't want to go into my recent history, and I'm sure
that's not what she cared about anyway. I was sure that my
short romantic résumé would turn her off like a faucet, but no.*
Au contraire. *She yells, "Practically a virgin!" and* really
starts getting friendly.

*I know it was wrong and unfair to Shannon as a person
because I knew I was just using her as a substitute for Gretchen,
but I couldn't help myself. The first three or four times, I swear I
don't think it would have mattered* who *I'd been with. But after
that, I consciously turned Shannon into Gretchen. On the surface
you wouldn't have thought that Bettina Kreutzmann, National
Merit Scholar and future lab manager for Paul Chu's supercon-
ductivity research, would have much in common with Shannon
Aldrich, hair stylist, but Shannon pretty much liked the same
things Bettina did. Five, six times in a row and she still liked
them. So, Bettina, thank you.*

*Needless to say, Shannon and I both forgot about the goop on
my hair. By the time we got to it, it had set up and my hair
looked like it had been "highlighted" by an asphalting crew. I
tried not to let Shannon see how unhappy I was because it really
wasn't her fault and she was only trying to do me a favor.
Shannon felt really bad about it, but I told her I liked it, that I've
always wanted to look like Elvis, and we just went back to bed.
Hey, it's only hair.*

*The second thing she did the next morning when we woke up
was look around and go, "Why is your bedroom papered with
photos from the* Grackle?" *I couldn't hide it anymore. I told her
I was an incredible louse and that I'd done a despicable thing.
Then I told her I loved the woman who'd taken the pictures. I told*

her she could hate me and I'd understand, but that I thought she was an exceptional person and a talented beauty operator and that I'd like to remain friends.

And then she laughs and holds up her left hand, and there's this wedding ring, and she goes, "Sweetie, I wasn't expecting us to go steady. I thought that was pretty clear."

God, I felt so much better. Than I felt a lot worse. I look like an Elvis impersonator and I've slept with a married woman! I never expected either one of those things to happen to me. Next Shannon tells me that Randy, her husband's, shift is going to be over pretty soon and she'd better get home. Before she leaves, she tells me that she'd really like to do it all again, and if this person I'm in love with can dig couples scenes, to let her know. If she's one tenth as good as me, Randy'll love her. I think I'd better get tested.

It's funny, I would have thought that last night would have taken the edge off what I feel for Gretchen, but it didn't. If anything, it's worse. One good thing about my new hair, I can risk a daylight pass. I might as well tell you since you know already, I've been following her. It started off as a one-time deal. I wanted to see her when she finished working at the Grackle. Then I couldn't believe how late it was when she got off. And the Grackle is in this seedy neighborhood downtown.

After that, I decided I'd better cruise by every night just to make sure she gets in her car all right. I usually park in this alley across from her building. It's totally dark and she can't see me, especially in my leathers. Which is just the point. I could be anyone and she wouldn't be able to see me. Most nights I follow her home just for something to do. There's no risk, since I wear my helmet with the visor down.

But, anyway, I did a daylight pass of her house this morning and she was there. Sitting on her porch. She had a giant glass of something foamy and brown in her hand. All she had on was a nightie and she didn't look totally awake. Just kind of dreamy and pretty, looking off into space with her wide-set eyes. I thought that this is probably what she looked like when she was about 11 *years old. I wanted to stop so bad. But now I have to wait for my hair to grow out. The next time I approach her, I want everything to be perfect. I want to look as good as I possibly can and to feel as confident as I possibly can. It keeps getting harder and harder to wait, though. But I feel like I'm only going to have one chance. I get very nervous thinking about it. I wish I didn't care so much; that would make it a lot easier. I never thought I'd end up this way.*

SEPT. 13

When the Midge came over this morning and saw my hair, you'd have thought I sent her into Fort Knox with a bucket. She looks at me and goes, "Yes! You've decided to change the package itself! We're really going to do it now. The only things remaining are eye color and background. Oh, and stop shaving. You know, the stubbly, sexy look. Wear *that testosterone."*

The picture finally came into focus. "You don't want me to be Gus Kubiak."

I knew just from the way she looked at me what the answer was. I left the house without saying anything. I was running down the street and she putt-putts up behind me, haranguing me about how this is my only chance. I politely tell her she's out of her mind. I will not pretend to be someone else to get Gretchen. I don't tell her that I've already learned what kind of trouble you can get into by acting on false pretenses. I mean, Shannon could have been single and available and then think of how bad a deal it would have been. Just ethically I'm opposed to the whole idea. Besides, there's no way it would work. Plus, if Gretchen isn't going to be interested in me for me, what's the point?

"Who's you?" Lizzie screams at me. "The cute but gawky goof with a cot in the computer center? The scared guy with two dozen tubes coming out of him who was supposed to die and swore his life would be different if he lived? Or this version, tanned, trim, muscular? And what does it matter? As long as any of

them wear the Gus Kubiak label, Gretchen isn't going to have anything to do with him.''

Because the workings of a distorted mind interest me, I ask her who, exactly, she thinks I should be if not Gus Kubiak.

She laughs and goes, ''Oh, Juanita and I have that all worked out. Except for getting rid of the glasses, your physical transformation is almost complete. Once you absorb your background information, you're ready.''

I tell her to give Gretchen a little credit. Contact lenses aren't going to fool her. Then Lizzie tells me to take a long, hard look in the mirror. That I'm a different person. It is true that Russell didn't recognize me. I tell her she can put donkey ears and a tail on me, and Gretchen is still going to know me.

''Bet not,'' she says.

''Bet so,'' I say before I can stop myself. The Midge is the only person in the world who can make me act 9 years old.

She says there's one easy way to prove I'm right: Let Gretchen see me.

Yeah, right, I tell her, Gretchen sees me, then she thinks I'm trying to be an Elvis impersonator. That'll make a great impression.

It will, the Midge says. First of all, I'll bet you anything you want to name that she's not going to recognize you, and even if she thinks you're trying to be an Elvis impersonator, that's more fun than old Gus Kubiak in a toupee.

I tell Lizzie she is out of her tiny mind, but inside I'm halfway convinced that I can't lose by letting Gretchen have a look at the new improved me. If I can come up with a situation that doesn't look all planned out, I might do it. **Might.** Then Lizzie goes, ''Well, I'll leave you to think about it,'' and putt-putts off. She cheeses me off, as D.D. would say. She always has to take credit for everything.

When I got home from the run, there was this folder stuck in the door with some pages inside. They were titled ''Background on a Kiwi Rogue.'' It was the story Lizzie and Juanita had made up for this character they think they're going to turn me into. I

didn't just throw it away, I burned it. Now I really think I can't
lose. If Gretchen recognizes me, I'll show Lizzie how deranged she
is. If she doesn't, Lizzie doesn't ever have to know and it'll help
me figure out strategy for when I approach G.G. again. I might
do it.

I made an appointment with the optometrist. I had planned to
get contacts way before the Midge ever brought it up.

SEPT. 25

Contact lens technology has really come a long way. Can you
believe a hologram on the lenses? The dot matrix pattern blocks
the natural color and a tinted overlay supplies the new color so
that, actually, the darker your eyes the better it works. It's amazing. They change my eyes from their natural sort of sludge color
to this neon blue. I decided that, in fairness to Lizzie, I should
change my appearance as much as possible, so I went ahead and
got them. Besides, they've got a ninety-day free trial, so I plan to
bring them back after Gretchen recognizes me anyway. So, no
biggie.

I just checked myself out again in the mirror. I do look really
different. I wonder what G.G. will think of the changes. I guess
I'll find out. If I decide to go through with it.

Crikey! Love's daft.

OCTOBER 2

I can't believe this. I can't think. I can't write. I've got to feel
wind on my face. Lots of wind. I'll tell you everything as soon as
I can understand what I've done.

OCTOBER 3

I want to run, I want to hide, I want to scream, I want to . . . I can't believe myself. I did it! I guess it was the contact lenses that really made me think there was a chance she wouldn't know me. As usual, I waited for her to leave work. But instead of following, I pulled up next to her. I was ready to start laughing the instant she looked over at me and tell her the whole thing was a joke. But everything changed in that moment when she turned and looked at me. Not only did she not recognize me, she was attracted. It was so clear. Her look was totally different from the way she'd looked at me before. She had on this fake mean look because—God, I can't believe this—she was scared. Scared and attracted. If I hadn't been so nervous or cared so much, I would have just blurted out, "Don't worry, it's only me."

But everything changed. It was like suddenly discovering you have this incredible secret power. It scared me. But I liked it. God, I was screaming when I pulled away. Then, just by habit, I turned the way I usually turn when I'm following her. I was so blown away that I didn't remember she was in back of me until her headlights hit me. Then it was too much to handle all at once. I mean, she was back there, watching me. I wasn't paying attention and went into this monster slide when I hit a puddle. Even when I saw the asphalt coming up at me, I was still thinking, She's back there; Gretchen is watching! It couldn't have been more than a few seconds, but it seemed like I fought the slide for hours. The whole time I was doing Dikkie Diamond. "Steady on, mate. She'll be right." I tried to control the slide, but the Turnip finally got away from me and I went shooting into the curb.

I must have been out, but my mind kept going. The accident kept happening over and over with Dikkie Diamond narrating. Before the accident, I was dead set against Lizzie's bizarre scheme. But I opened my eyes, looked into Gretchen's face, and saw that she wanted me to be anybody in the world except Gus Kubiak. And there was Dikkie Diamond, just waiting.

I don't think I could have pulled it off if I hadn't been so shot through with adrenaline. But it was like the words ejected out of me. It was like being in front of a firing squad smoking your last cigarette, and as long as you keep smoking you could live. As long as I could keep up the accent and the attitude, I'd be a serious person to consider for Gretchen. The pain helped. My ankle hurt like a son of a bitch. It changed my voice and made me real edgy so I didn't have to fake being surly. I didn't have to fake passing out on her couch either.

But it would have ended there. I swear it would have. I would have sneaked out of her house and never seen her again, except that she kissed me. I had just started coming around and couldn't make out if I was dreaming or if it was really happening. Then I smelled her breath. It wasn't all lilacs and violets like I'd dreamed. It was a real person's breath, a woman's. A little sharp from fear, excitement. Arousal? Up until then it hadn't been real. I just couldn't believe I'd actually fooled her. But her breath didn't lie.

God, what have I done? I can't eat. I can't sleep. All I think about is the way she talked to me. The way she looked at me. The way her lips felt. Okay, it was a thrill and something I never would have dreamed I could pull off. But I have to go over and explain everything to Gretchen immediately. Or maybe I'll do it tomorrow. Maybe I should rent a steam cleaner and take it over to get that boot mark out of her couch.

I just thought about the kiss and I cannot do any of the above.

I called Lizzie and asked her if she had another copy of that biographical thing she wrote with Juanita. She immediately bursts out, "Oh, bright boy, you're going to do it!" I told her to forget the whole thing, but she rushes over with it, takes one look at me and goes, "The face of love! You did it, and it worked! I don't care about who was right and who was wrong, count upon me to do everything within my considerable power to aid you."

I told her to please keep a lid on her considerable power, but she already had that little know-it-all smile on her face. I tried to give her back her Biographical Data, but she was too quick. I've got to end this. I'm going to burn the Bio Data at the earliest opportunity.

I can't believe it! They've got sample dialogues all written out just like Spanish class. Except instead of "Ola Isabel," it's "If I'd kissed you, I'd never have stopped." Actual romance scripts. I'm not sure I like the name she came up with for my character. Rye. What's wrong with Dikkie Diamond?

OCTOBER 4

Lizzie just called to say that Gretchen is in love. With that guy! And, Lizzie said, she sealed it by playing the symbolic parent and telling her this guy, this Rye, is no good. Then she goes, "Learn your Bio Data well. Mitchell and I will be feeding it to her this evening." They're going to pretend to break into the INS system and "retrieve" all these dummy files that Lizzie's already made up. I told her no, not to do another thing, but she just goes, "The heart has a wisdom the head knows not of," and hangs up. This is turning into a four-star catastrophe. I can never face Gretchen again. Why couldn't she have just liked me the way I was?

OCTOBER 5

I am going to have to write this down because I can barely believe it happened myself. Today Lizzie and Juanita barged in again. Juanita was carrying these two aluminum cases. Without saying anything, she immediately opens one up and starts folding it out into a table. Lizzie informs me that, out of the great goodness of her heart, Juanita has agreed to conduct her sensuality workshop for me alone, even though she usually charges $250 for a two-part presentation like the one she did at the Luvboree. While I'm telling them both I am not interested, Juanita, who's holding this crumpled table like it was a sick dog, says, "Would you secure my hinges there?"

*So I'm trapped setting up her table even while I'm telling them
I don't want to hear this "sensuality workshop." But they just
ignore me and Juanita goes right on whipping open her other
case. It contains a Resusci-Annie doll like the kind we used in
Medical Explorers to learn CPR and artificial resuscitation. So
Juanita's got this doll flopped out on the table and she starts right
in.*

*"Now, mostly," she says, "at my workshops I use the first
half to talk about how to establish and heighten your sexual
tension. I'll assume here that we can move straight to heighten-
ing?"*

*At which point I tell her straight out that I appreciate her
coming by but I just don't want to hear this. So she asks, "Does
frank and open discussion of human sexuality embarrass you?"*

*I say, "No. Well, yes, but that's not the point. The point
is—"*

*But she's off and running and tells me to please hold my
questions until the end of the presentation. From there she dives
right into this canned spiel, telling me that "making love is like
building a barbecue fire. These areas here"—she opens up a
pointer and touches Annie's breasts—"and here"—the crotch—
"are your charcoal. Now, Gus, you don't want to involve these
areas until you've got a good, hot fire roaring. And how do we do
that?"*

*By this time, I'm kind of overwhelmed and just shrug, so she
goes,*

"Come on, Gus, weren't you ever a Boy Scout?"

*Lizzie chimes in to tell her about me being a Medical Ex-
plorer. I finally blurt out that we sure never did anything with
the Resusci-Annie like that! I mean, of course there was the usual
crude talk, but that's just teenage boys. But they won't be satisfied until I finally say "kindling."*

*"Kindling!" Juanita says it like I'm some kind of genius.
"All right! Kindling, we must use kindling. And here, these are
our kindling areas." She starts touching her pointer again to
various areas. "Arms, neck, fingers, instep—"*

"Instep?" I say. That was a mistake because Lizzie shoots Juanita that isn't-he-innocent? look.

Juanita goes on to name a few even more obscure areas, then says, "These are the areas where we must fan the flames first, Gus. Tell me, Gus, what happens when you try to take a short cut and use lighter fluid on your charcoal?"

"Your hamburgers end up tasting funny?" I have no idea anymore where she's headed.

"No, you'll have fire but no heat. To make a woman truly yours, you have got to get that slow burn. Let me demonstrate."

That was when it really started to get out of hand. Juanita bends down and starts frenching Resusci-Annie, pausing only to breathe and ask me, "Do you see this what I'm doing with my tongue? Observe closely." Then she straightens up, rips open a packet with an antiseptic towelette in it, wipes off Annie's lips, and says to me, "Now it's your turn. I guarantee that this technique will stoke any woman's furnace."

That did it. I started yelling. "No! Absolutely not! I want Gretchen's furnace stoked for me. I'm not going to let that Rye jerk do that to her with his tongue!" I finally got through to them. Juanita packs up her cases and huffs out, stopping at the door to say, "Not everyone is emotionally secure enough for my presentation."

Lizzie told me I was overreacting: the Japanese had their pillow books, why shouldn't we Occidentals benefit from some expert counsel? I told her that she was stepping way over the line. It was one thing to use an altered identity to try and get a second chance with Gretchen; it was an entirely different matter to use it to seduce her. I swore to her that that was one ethical boundary I'd never cross. Then, in her uniquely irritating way, she smiles her know-it-all smile and says, "Sure, Gus. Hah! Don't romance a romance writer."

OCTOBER 6

Even though I told her never to speak to Gretchen again, Lizzie just called to warn me that she is on her way out here. I cannot go through with this. As soon as she drives up I'm going to go right out and tell her the truth.

OCTOBER 7

She drove up, I looked at her, and I could not stop myself. I want to be whoever she wants to be with. And it's not Gus Kubiak. This is a doomed enterprise, I know. The most I can hope for is a few days. But, God help me, I want them. No matter how this all turns out, I'll always love Gretchen. She was the bridge that brought me back to the land of the living.

So this is the end of Gus Kubiak's journal. I'm putting him in mothballs for a while. Say hello to Rye St. John.

21

I react slowly to things. I always have. That's why I'm such a washout at assertiveness and other qualities that require quick emotional reflexes. By the time I figure out that I'm mad, for example, the rude clerk is off being snippy to someone else, the unkind boyfriend is calling my best friend, the moment is passed. I closed Gus's journal and didn't know what I felt. The last paragraph where he called me his bridge back to life and said he would always love me almost erased all the deception and humiliation that preceded it. Almost. At least until I thought of Juanita's pointer touching my breasts. Or me "talking Lizzie into" breaking into the INS computer.

If I had combed through the knot of my feelings right then and there, I could have gone to Gus and either opened my arms to him or poured acid on his motorcycle. But both options held nearly equal appeal to me, and so I was immobilized and did nothing.

The one emotion I *was* certain of was longing. Knowing that Rye was an illusion did not stop me from missing him more than anyone else who'd ever left my life. For the next week I rooted around the house like a sun-blind mole, keeping the shades pulled and watching soap operas. I couldn't stop wondering what the actors who played the male characters were really like.

Every time I plugged the phone in it was ringing. A couple of times a day Lizzie would drive up and pound on my door. Ignoring her was good training for me. I'd never before in my life been able to ignore ringing phones and pounding at the door. Once this was over I'd be set for life with the Jehovah's Witnesses. Except that it didn't particularly feel as if it would ever be over.

The second week of isolation, just to keep my mind occupied, I returned to "Gain the Earth." There really weren't too many loose narrative ends to tie up. It was slightly futile tying them up, though, finishing a romance novel that still had no romance. But it gave me some tiny modicum of satisfaction to finish running Manx and Cassie through the maze I'd constructed for them and reward them at the end with a marriage proposal. When Cassie pretended to resist, I had Manx threaten to turn her over his knee and paddle that adorable fanny of hers. Then, tears welling in her eyes, she poked up the slender ivory column of her left ring finger and he rammed the diamond home.

Cassie's tears of joy froze right up, because I stuck the manuscript back into the freezer where it had come from. It was still a romance novel without the romance, and I was now farther than ever away from that particular modality.

Sometime in late October, just as I was settling in to watch a particularly cherished episode of *The Brady Bunch,* I heard the sound of gravel crunching and peeked out between the slats of my closed blinds to see Juanita's silver Camaro nose in next to the 88. I turned off the TV and ducked into the kitchen. Juanita pounded on the door, but I didn't answer.

"Gretchen," she bellowed, "I know you're in there, so open up!"

"I'm not in the mood for company," I yelled back.

She pounded for a while more, then left. But I didn't hear her engine. I crept back into my bedroom and was peering out to see where she'd gone when my front door swung open and she marched in carrying one of Lizzie's casserole dishes.

"How'd you get in?"

"Your landlord is very understanding. I told him I was your mother and I thought I smelled gas. He agreed that a gas explosion would diminish property values considerably. Come here and get you some of this casserole."

Completely without my permission, Juanita set up on the coffee table. I could hear her bringing out plates and glasses, the spoon clinking as she stirred up my instant tea powder.

"Soup's on."

I answered her from my post in the bedroom. "Juanita, I really don't feel like eating and I don't much appreciate you bursting in."

With that, Juanita appeared at the bedroom door, carrying two plates. "I don't have much to lose, then, do I?" She shoved one of the plates at me and perched on the edge of my bed. "Not bad," she announced, chowing down on Lizzie's casserole. She held a forkful up at eye level and examined it. "What all's she got in here? Artichoke hearts. Button mushrooms. Asparagus. Come on, girl, these are some high-dollar groceries. Looks like you'd know what to do with them. What have you dropped there? Six? Eight pounds?"

I'd kind of wondered vaguely why the waists of my shorts had taken to resting on my pelvic bones. Still, I was in no mood to be cajoled and would have stood firm indefinitely if I hadn't glimpsed the abundance of shrimp curled up like fat pink baby fingers amid the expensive vegetables. Just because I ate Lizzie's crustaceans didn't mean I forgave her. We ate in silence until our plates were clean.

For several minutes I stared at the pale roses on my plate,

a plate I had purchased in an odd lot last year at an estate sale. I wondered if the china had been a long-ago wedding present.

"Why'd you do it?" I could almost understand Gus Kubiak's motivation. I'd been crazed from the first moment I met Rye. If Lizzie had told me that the one certain way to win his heart was to dress up as a cafeteria worker, I probably would have been at his doorstep in a hair net and clear plastic gloves asking for his meat order. And Lizzie. Obviously she was more mother than sister to her brother and a lot more off beam than dead center. But Juanita?

"At first I was opposed, but then, when I saw how crazy Gus Kubiak was about you and how perfect he would be for you—well, the pieces just fell into place."

"Perfect? Gus Kubiak?"

"Yes, perfect." Juanita's answer was starchy. "As Lizzie put it, you designed the prototype. All she did was meet your specs."

"You mean, Manx?"

"Dark hair, blue eyes. Out of reach. Naturally, she embellished some. But the basic romance format was there: he had to be exotic and you couldn't have him."

"Lovers torn apart by the INS." I shook my head at the hackneyed predictability of it. "God, I just don't believe this. Any of this. It *is* a romance novel. I lived a romance novel. What about the bike shop? Howie? The work order?"

"That was kind of ad lib. Gus Kubiak really did take his bike there to be fixed, and you really did fox fat Howie out of the address."

"But Gus Kubiak? That first day, on my porch, he looked like Tweetie Pie. How could someone go from looking like Tweetie Pie to . . . to . . ." I flapped my hands to indicate the divinity that had been Rye.

"He was a highly motivated boy, Gretchen. He ran. Swam. Lifted weights."

"But shoulders. He didn't have those broad . . . hard . . ." I glazed over, thinking of Rye's shoulders.

"When you first met Gus Kubiak, he was just a couple of months out of the hospital. And that boy had had it all: chemotherapy, bone marrow transplant, steroids. He was tired and didn't stand up straight. His shoulders were always pretty fair; he just didn't have enough meat on them or strength to hold them up. Once he finished with the drugs his strength came back, the swelling went away, his hair grew in, and he was a nice-looking boy. All he really had to do was get a tan, pump up the right places, and cultivate the right attitude."

"But that first night I met Rye, *I* followed him. And *he* had an accident." A widow must feel the way I did, trying to find the flaws in the argument that her husband is dead. Searching for the loophole in the logic that will make it all not true.

"Well, yes, you did follow him and he did have an accident. Gus never would have gone ahead with Rye if he hadn't had that accident. Kind of renews my faith in the stuff I write. After that, when I saw how in love, how happy, you were, I really pitched in. Helped them with contemporary dialogue. Lizzie's hopeless at contemporary dialogue."

"But it was all an illusion. I wasn't *really* happy."

"Hell's bells, of course you were. You changed from night to day. And Gus Kubiak, he was plumb over the moon. He said it himself; it was like he finally felt there was a reason he hadn't died. A reason he hadn't died. You getting all this? Shoot, I've been around the track so often I lean to the left, and I never came within shooting distance of having a man that crazy about me."

"What you did was wrong."

Juanita snorted, grabbed the plate off my lap, and piled it on top of hers. She took them to the kitchen and dumped them into the sink. "There is nothing in this sink except bowls, spoons, and glasses. You have got single dishes, G.G. Cereal, soup, and tea. The only thing that's going to change is in the winter there'll be mugs in here instead of glasses. Cocoa and hot tea. For crying in a bucket, gal, wake up and smell the coffee! Except for brief periods of time, I been doing these identical same dishes all my life."

"So what?" I snapped. "I'm supposed to be exploding with gratitude that you and Lizzie gave me the opportunity to scrub out some manly steak platters or something?" Juanita was missing the point here so badly that being flabbergasted took my mind off being miserable.

"Good night, nurse, no. Don't be so danged horsey." I heard a rustling out in the kitchen, then, "Ah-hah! Just as I suspected. Cup-a-Soup, Cup-a-Noodles, Cup-a-Stew, Cup-a-Oats—"

I jumped out of bed, bolted into the kitchen, and slammed down the lid on my garbage can to stop Juanita from quoting its contents to me. "Do you mind? Thanks to your little prank I haven't felt much like Cordon Bleu cookery."

"I give up." Juanita stumped out of the kitchen. "You are a fool, Gretchen, and I'm tired of fooling with a fool." She grabbed her purse off the couch.

"I knew something was wrong," I told her. I may indeed be a fool, but I hadn't been completely duped. I had my doubts. "I caught him saying miles instead of kilometers. They use kilometers in New Zealand. I knew he wasn't exactly what he was pretending to be."

"Yeah, you're a regular Sherlock Holmes. When you first met him you thought you might have had a serial killer on the line. Now you come to find out all you had was a decent man who turned himself inside out because he loved you and you're heartbroken. *Real* sharp, Sherlock."

"You know," I sputtered, "it's really starting to piss me off the way the roles are getting reversed here and I'm now the villain."

Juanita didn't answer. She just walked out the front door, shaking her head.

I clumped back into the bedroom. *The Brady Bunch* no longer held any appeal for me. Something jabbed the sole of my bare foot. I plucked the object off the wooden floor and held it on the tip of my finger. After a moment of staring at what looked like a transparent, scorched-blue corn flake, I realized it was one of the contact lenses that had turned Gus Kubiak's eyes blue. It must have adhered to my clothes the night he discarded them. I blew the lint off the flake of plastic, put in on my tongue, and sucked on it until it was reconstituted and I couldn't feel any hard edges poking my mouth. I slid it off the tip of my tongue onto my finger.

God, Gus Kubiak. How could that be the same person I'd eaten mangoes with? Implication. Damn Lizzie, she'd done implication on me. For five seconds I was furious; then I started thinking about Rye's tongue on the fruit, on me. I was continually disoriented. I stared at the lens until it drooped and melted down onto my finger. Without thinking, I put it back into my mouth and bit down on it. It tasted exactly like the jellyfish had. Exactly like chewy tears.

I spit the little goober out. My house suddenly seemed like nothing but a holding tank for dirty spoons and bowls. I grabbed my keys, rushed outside, and almost tripped over DeWitt Cleeb, who was down on his hands and knees in my driveway. He pretended to snip at a pebble, but I knew he was checking to see if his mother-in-law addition was going to blow up. I did something with my mouth meant to resemble a smile and bobbed my head in DeWitt's direction. Unless the maniacal Mrs. Cleeb prodded him, a head bob was usually more human interaction than DeWitt cared for. Not today.

"You have a good visit with your mother?" This was the first time my landlord had ever brought up a subject other than grass or chips with me.

I nodded.

He stood stiffly. "I guess I can use the gas edger now." He came very close to looking directly at me. "I didn't want to wake you. Now. You know. You need your rest." His tone was shyly solicitous.

Had Juanita told him the whole story? A truncated country and western version? Though I sizzled with embarrassment, tears leaped into my eyes at DeWitt's cowboy bashful concern. I mumbled, "Thanks." But Mr. Cleeb was not through.

He looked at me with an expression so baleful that, had he been a sheep, I would have suspected anthrax. His hands, large and rough as two catcher's mitts, jerked up, reaching out toward me. "If there's ever anything Estelle or I can do, you just let us know, you hear?"

I lowered my head to hide the tears that popped into my eyes, nodded vigorously at my shoes, and jumped into the car. DeWitt stood in the drive, waving his hands to the left and right to guide me as I backed blindly out the drive.

I didn't have a destination, I just needed to get some air. I almost believed that until I found myself puttering down 2222. The BMWs and turbocharged Saabs streaked past me in watery blurs as I wiped my nose on my sleeve—or what would have been a sleeve if I hadn't been wearing a sleeveless turtleneck. I would about get myself under control, then I would remember DeWitt's forlorn and pitying expression. Or Juanita's critique of my Cup O' Life existence. Or anything, anything at all, having to do with Rye, particularly the fact that he had never existed, and I would commence leaking again.

At the Cedar Switch turnoff, stage fright overcame dripping melancholia and I pulled myself together. I crept down the twisty country lane as if it were mined. What on earth was I doing there? I had no coherent explanation until I reached number 12, the last house on the lane, and my nose filled with the smell of cedar and my mouth with the cop-

pery taste of desire. What did this mean? Was the hormone
system truly so unwired to the brain that it had missed the
big news flash that it had been duped by a phantom? Or did
I now have the hots for the tiny man operating the levers
for the magnificent Oz?

I switched off the ignition and the 88 died before the key
clicked all the way over. I should have known that a certi-
fied rogue wouldn't have been able to actually fix a car.
Truly swoony guys can never do anything useful. I sat and
waited, remembering the first time I'd come.

I peered into the deep shade that darkened the front door.
Where was Gus Kubiak? If I could hear the buzz of a hum-
mingbird's wings as it hovercrafted into the gaudy red
blooms on an althea bush twenty yards away, surely he'd
heard the Bargemobile drive up. Though October was half
over, the temperature was still in the mid-nineties, and in
spite of the fact that the 88 was heating up like a pizza oven,
my hands were icy. Nerves. The rest of me was swampy
with desire. It was very confusing to be going soggy for the
fictional creation of an ostrich in swoopy-templed glasses.

I creaked the car door open and a breeze blew through,
carrying away the smell of poached polyvinyls. I watched
the house, waiting for the front door to open and for Gus
Kubiak to come reluctantly forward. Maybe he was swimming. I had no idea what I'd say to him. Conversation could
be his burden. He'd earned it. I was the one owed some
explanations. The curtain cracked open a few inches. He
was in the house. My pulse did a heavy-metal solo. I
wished I'd at least put on some mascara. The curtain flopped
back into place, but the door didn't open. Great, a standoff.
I peeled myself off the seat and got out of the car. Enough
was enough. We had things to talk about.

I went to the window where I'd seen the curtain flip back.
"Uh, hi." I addressed the curtain. "Can I come in?"

The door didn't open, the curtain didn't even flutter. That
was annoying. I was standing out there dropping trou emo-

tionally, and he didn't even have the *cojones* to open the door.

"Look, you're the one who opened my fantasies up like a can of sardines and poked around inside. I'm the rightfully aggrieved party here." There was no answer. The way Lizzie and Gus had somehow recast this production to make me the heavy was starting to seriously annoy me.

"Goddammit, open up, we might as well get to know each other, we've already slept together," I boomed out. That got some action. I heard feet scuffling. I went to the door as it opened.

"Why were you hi—"

A tall, beetle-browed, stoop-shouldered old gentleman poked his head out. "You must be a friend of Gus's."

One wretched word seared my mind: Father. But no, I was spared the ultimate humiliation and had to settle for slightly less than atomic embarrassment. I'd just screamed out my intimate involvement with Gus Kubiak to his beloved mentor, Professor Emeritus Thaddeus Hartwell. Dr. Hartwell explained that Gus had been house-sitting while he was away on sabbatical. "But Gus is gone now. Left a couple of weeks back to train the Kuwaitis on his oil-logging program." Dr. Hartwell politely inquired if I'd like him to pass on any message.

"Uh, no, no thanks." I backed away from the door, then paused. "How is he doing, healthwise? No, like, relapse or anything?"

"No, thank God. He made it past the critical stage. I think we'll get to keep our boy for a while longer. Good day." The door slammed shut.

Kuwait, I thought on the drive home. He sure didn't waste any time getting to the other side of the earth. How much could he have seriously, sincerely cared for me if he was that ready to bolt? More than likely Gus Kubiak had been dying to slip into a gaudier persona when I met him, and I was nothing more than a handy excuse to enlist Lizzie's aid. That left me with: Gus Kubiak didn't really care, Rye didn't exist, and a severe case of the mopes.

♥   ♥

When it comes time to check out with that big cashier in the sky, I plan on asking for a complete refund on one unused month; I hardly touched October at all. I unplugged the phone, laid in a fallout-shelter supply of Cup-a's, barricaded myself into my house, and resurrected Rye St. John. It was a vivid, exciting time. I closed my eyes, and my head filled with the most succulent erotic fantasies imaginable.

It wasn't intentional. At first I resisted, banishing each thought of Rye by invoking the name of Gus Kubiak. Gradually, imperceptibly, however, it all became like a movie whose ending I hadn't liked. I simply dropped out the last reel and replayed my favorite parts endlessly. At any rate, I started off by just replaying—Rye and me in the moonlight on the Shackleford mansion lawn. Then I took to embellishing—Rye running his fingers along my arm in the moonlight on the Shackleford mansion lawn. From there it was a short skip into total fabrication—Rye pressing me to him in a powerful embrace that sang of a love beyond carnality, beyond spirituality, beyond, yes, even dishes.

The moments with Rye expanded in my memory, becoming a web that made thin air into a home, a source of sustenance. I lived there, trapping the juicy morsels that buzzed in at me. After a couple of days it occurred to me that I could make obsession pay. Sitting in my freezer was a moribund manuscript, and what I had steaming up the windowpanes of my mind was better than cryogenics. From that realization on, I simply took to transcribing my fantasies and changing the names from Gretchen and Rye to Cassie and Manx.

I would dream that Rye had kissed me while our lips dripped mango juice, *et voilà!* Cassie had a first kiss that *burned up* five pages. I dug the bones of my manuscript out of the freezer and flipped through the frosty pages until I came to *First kiss, five pages,* and filled in:

> *Manx's lips crushing down on hers were a benediction. She tasted a ferocious urgency there and knew it as her own as well. This moment's inevitability had been postponed too long; she could stay it no longer. With that decision, love and desire fused within her into an alloy of incalculable strength. Neither one nor the other could have been half so powerful alone.*

And so with Manx sucking honey from her mouth and Cassie dizzying beneath the press of his, they proceeded. I flipped on to *Breast-Cupping Etc., Seven Pages* and wrote:

> *Manx was a madman, fueled by insatiable need. He had been held back for far too long. He wanted only to feel: the silken thrust of his tongue plunging into her mouth. To smell: her delicate scent becoming dense, sexual. To hear: the strangled sounds of desire slip from her throat.*

I made quick, inspired work of that passage and ran to third base, *Everything but.*

> *"I wouldn't have believed it possible,"* he breathed, marveling as the bolt of sun lapped across her. *"You're even more beautiful in sunshine than you are in firelight. I remember the first time I saw you, driving to my place at sunset. I was dying then"*—he leaned forward, and the sheet, strikingly pale against the brown of his muscled torso, slipped down to his waist—*"to lick away"*—he leaned forward a bit more and the sheet fell away completely, to reveal the devastating extent of his arousal—*"all that buttery sunlight."* Even as he spoke, his tongue was busily fulfilling that denied desire.
>
> His hands roamed like uncaged creatures across her back, her thighs, her breasts. She fitted perfectly into the hard hollows of his body. Then his hands were gently tumbling her over onto the bed beside him where he could search out the passion-beaded tips of her breasts, stroking and fondling until he again heard the tiny gasps that signaled Cassie's pleasure. Guided only by that aim, he ventured further down the silken curve of her stomach, and further still.

The days disappeared as I roamed the kingdom of the senses. My protagonists' gluttonous passion grew fat as I filled in those blanks with my own longings. I stopped balking at romance boilerplate, and Cassie *trembled with, quaked with, quivered with, quavered with, shimmered with, shivered with, shone with, shuddered with, was transubstantiated by* lust. Manx *blazed with, burned with, flamed with, flared with, flickered with, scorched with, scalded with, smoldered with,* and *was immolated by* desire. When all that cooing and trembling met with the cremating fires of love, it was a dove roast of the first order.

Since I knew I could never describe what I'd felt with Rye, I happily plugged in the accepted lexicon. I thought of myself as an ethnomusicologists transcribing the songs of a primitive tribe that chants notes only they can make. But I was no detached scholar making my field notes. I was into a dangerously participatory mode.

I sat at my typewriter awash in a veritable bog of love juice. At a point I can't identify, I lost control and melded with the typewriter, becoming part of a machine that oiled itself. Manx's lips blazed a trail of liquid fire down the alabaster column of Cassie's neck, and I shivered with desire. Manx thumbed the rosebud center of Cassie's breasts, and my nipples pebbled up. Manx found the melting core of Cassie's secret female desire, and I went to the drugstore to buy diaphragm jelly.

Was this process therapeutic? Was it hopelessly perverse? Given that I was powerless to stop the briny flow of fantasy such questions were immaterial, so I continued casting my net and pulling in the day's catch. Whatever the effect on my mental health, it was great for the book. I had only to touch a sheet of paper and it went limp with knee-buckling ardor or turgid with metal-piercing readiness. I surrendered totally. I found every blank I'd left in the manuscript and crammed each one full of amorous delicacies.

At the end of a month I realized I could not shoehorn in another *frisson;* "Gain the Earth" was as tumescent as a saguaro at sunset. Besides, Cassie found out that Manx had always loved her, would always love her. Once the hero had been attained the story was over.

That was the law in category romance.

22

It took me one entire day in the middle of November to physically prepare my manuscript to ship off to Andrea. When I'd mailed my original proposal to her, I'd merely stuffed it in an old Safeway bag. Somehow that wouldn't do this time. I went to five stationery stores, but none of them had precisely the box I was searching for. So I battled traffic for a visit to the University Co-op to buy a couple of sheets of Crescent board in Nassau blue, a roll of gray tape, and a new tube of X-Acto knife blades. All the students were still wearing baggy shorts that showed off tanned legs. On the way home a radio announcer warned listeners that a norther would be moving in later that day. That was fine with me. It was long past time for summer to end.

Back at 4310 Rear, I assembled all my equipment around me on the floor and set to work. I fitted a new blade into the knife handle and cut along the lines I'd measured out, the knife blade pressed against a steel ruler to make the cuts perfectly straight. The prototype box I constructed had gaps and a few slanting angles, so I started over again with a new sheet of Nassau blue and a new blade. This time I pieced the blue rectangles together tight as a tiny coffin. In the end, all the joints crisply taped in gray, the box looked better than manufactured. I laid the manuscript, all those fantasies fueled by illusion, to rest in it and sealed it shut.

When the box was wrapped in brown paper, I wrote the address in Magic Marker. As I was writing the zip code, I heard the ice-cream truck. I hadn't heard it for weeks. But there it was: "Little Red Wing." As clear as if I were still sitting on cool linoleum at camp, I remembered Red Wing's story, what happened after the warrior bold rode one day to battle far away.

> *She watched for him night and day*
> *And kept all the campfires bright.*
> *Each night she would lie in under the sky*
> *And dream of his coming bye and bye.*
> *When all the braves returned*
> *The heart of Red Wing yearned*
> *For, far away, her warrior gay*
> *Fell bravely in the fray.*
>
> *Now the moon shines tonight on pretty Red Wing,*
> *The breezes sighing, the night birds crying,*
> *So far beneath the stars her brave is sleeping,*
> *While Red Wing's weeping her heart away.*

I couldn't believe they'd let young girls learn a song like that. I remembered how sad it had made me that Red Wing, an Indian maid about my own age, had lost her boyfriend. It wasn't fair. I started crying just as I finished writing the address on the package. I dragged myself off the floor a long time later, washed my face, and dashed out with the boxed manuscript to the 88. The sky had clouded over and the warm air was streaked with cold.

I started up the engine, clicked it off, and ran back into the house. Strange impulses jerked me one way, then the other, like a hooked trout. I found my Hammond's *Atlas of the World.* There, on the 30th parallel, was Kuwait, like a chunk of something caught at the back of the throat of the Persian Gulf. The capital was Al Kuwayt. I took out an index card and wrote: *Gus Kubiak, Oil Ministry, Al Kuwayt, Kuwait.* I taped the card onto the boxed manuscript over Andrea's address and then rushed back out as if it contained a time bomb I had to ditch before it exploded.

There was a crowd like the week before Christmas at the post office on Speedway, foreign students in tight synthetics, frat rats in baggy jeans and gimme caps, professors in runover Clark desert boots. The sky outside got darker. A black clerk took a long time explaining to a Taiwanese student that he couldn't accept parcels tied in string. He pushed the bundle away several times. Each time, the student would simply smile, push his package back at the clerk, and say, "Go Taiwan, please."

By the time my turn came, a serious wind was rattling the doors of the stuffy post office and the sides of my package were fuzzy with sweat. The black clerk spun the package around until the address faced him.

"Koo-*wait.*" He opened up a book of international rates and ran a bamboo-jointed finger down a long list of countries. I suddenly didn't want him to find Kuwait. I felt dizzy, as if he were searching for my name on a death squad list. His nail stopped beneath the rates for Kuwait.

"No!" I spoke too loudly. The clerk jerked his head up. He had tiny capillaries spiraling in the whites of his eyes, some fresh red, some a mottled brown. "That's the wrong address." I ripped the Kuwait card off. "It's supposed to go to New York. I just remembered." Behind me a coed tittered.

The clerk blinked, impassive as a dairy cow. "Whatever you say." He slammed the book shut and slid the package onto the metal tray of his scale. It was eleven dollars and twenty-eight cents first class. I only had a ten in my wallet. I wrote a check hurriedly, aware of the line of people behind me who'd all heard me shout. I ripped the check out, shoved it toward the clerk, grabbed my wallet in one hand, my purse in the other, and darted toward the door.

"Ma'am. Ma'am."

I pressed forward, imagining the bomb going off and showering everyone in musky odors and salty bodily fluids.

"Ma'am! Gretcher Griren!" My rs and ns tend to look alike. I turned around. The clerk was reading off my package. "With a package to Cam—" He squinted at my writing and I rushed back, but didn't reach him before he'd boomed out, "Cameo Books!" He looked up at me, stuck in the crush, and held up my check. "You wanna sign this so the Postmaster can get his money outta this deal?"

After signing the check and seeing my package tossed into a canvas hamper, I retreated to the 88. I was winded and leaned my head against the steering wheel. "Low blood sugar." I whispered the diagnosis, trying to reassure myself. The Baskin-Robbins was right around the corner. I drove slowly.

It was deserted. High season at the B-R was over—probably forever, with the ascendancy of the trendier outlets. The assaultive pink and orange motif made me feel even more fragile. I went to the counter and peered into tubs containing flavors running from ice creams nearly black with chocolate to Pez pastel sherbets, but nothing appealed to me. The girl behind the counter held her scoop at attention, waiting for my choice. Her blond hair was pulled back into a ponytail that squirted out of the back of a brown billed cap.

My concentration was frayed. I kept looking behind me, feeling someone watching. But there was nothing there except a row of desks, the desks Gus Kubiak and I had sat in when he'd quizzed me about myself. Funny, why hadn't I thought of that time when Rye had asked me about myself and I couldn't remember a straight male ever having shown such interest?

I turned around and started all over again back at the first tub. I went slowly this time, knowing what I wanted. But it wasn't there. I went back to the beginning a third time but still couldn't find it. This upset me far more than it should have.

"Where's the Died and Gone to Heaven"—I whirled my hands frantically at the girl for the rest of the name—"you know."

"Mocha Fudge Almond Ripple," she chirped. "That was May's Flavor of the Month. It's been gone for . . ."—she held up fingers and ticked off the months—"June. July. August. September. October. Half of November. Five and a half months." Almost as long as it had been since Gus had first stood on my porch and talked "Little Red Wing" to me.

"You mean it's gone?" The panicked feeling that had clutched at me in the post office came over me again. "Just like that? It's gone forever?"

The girl maintained cheerfulness in the face of my strained outburst. "We rotate Flavors of the Month. Just the favorites stay all the time."

"But what if it's the *end* of the month and someone comes in and tries a flavor and it *becomes* their favorite? Or what if they try one and don't decide till the end of the month that they like it after all? What if it's the *last* day of the month? It's just *gone* then? It's too *late?* They can't *ever* have that flavor again?"

"Sometimes a flavor will come back." The girl looked around uncertainly, as if she hoped someone would appear, but there was no one else in the store. "Tin Roof Sundae is really basically the same. Except for peanuts instead of almonds." She scooped up some on a tiny pink plastic spoon and handed it to me.

I tasted it and shook my head with angry betrayal. "No, that's different. It's an entirely different flavor."

The girl's shoulders beneath her pink and brown uniform slumped with disappointment.

God, what was happening to me? I was browbeating a Baskin-Robbins counter girl. Here she was, having to wear that atrocious cap and silly uniform, probably working her way through college, studying Special Education so she could teach disabled children, and I was yelling at her about some stupid ice-cream flavor.

"Actually, it's close enough. It really is. Give me a scoop. Two scoops."

I stuffed my ten-dollar bill into her hand and hurried out. I hoped desperately she wouldn't call me back for my change.

I went outside and the hot wind grabbed at me, lashing my hair forward into the ice cream. I flicked the cold, sticky strands back behind my ears and bit the ice cream. I never bit. I always licked. It took two bites for me to remember that I'd never tasted Died and Gone to Heaven. That Gus had suggested the flavor and I had rejected it. I tossed the cone up into a high dumpster. Looking into the gray sky made me dizzy. I felt achy now and very tired. When I saw the counter girl in the brown cap peeking warily at me, I got into the 88 and pulled away.

I drove aimlessly, meandering through the restored turn-of-the-century houses of Hyde Park until I hit Guadalupe and found myself facing the entrance of the Austin State Hospital. A group of mental patients, their gaits slowed by drugs, shuffled over the grounds, bending to pick up the fallen pecans they stepped on. They didn't speak or look at one another. I drove on down the street past one of the new ice-cream boutiques. A line of students snaked outside dressed in cotton clothes that my mother would have used for dusting rags.

I kept thinking of astronauts floating through black space. I imagined them in their puffy space outfits tumbling into infinity like chubby children in snowsuits. I had no reason to go home. My book was finished. I was beyond the gravity of any relationship that might pull me anywhere. The only thing that tugged at me were memories. But even those were confused. I could summon up Rye's face and, for a moment or two, was anchored again. Then, like two slides jamming together in a projector, Gus Kubiak's moon-faced features would superimpose themselves over Rye's and I was adrift once more.

I wished I could build a fence around my time with Rye. I wanted to segregate those days. Have them exactly as they had been, without later revelations. I was so absorbed in thoughts of time ranching that I barreled right through the red light at 38th. A horn blared, and a flatbed truck with a load of sod on the back bore down on me. I turned off Guadalupe and pulled into a Kwik-Wash parking lot and got out.

I bent over and tried to breathe slowly, deeply, but I couldn't force more than a few teaspoons of air into my lungs in quick inhalations. I stood up and a rain of black confetti fell through my vision. My hands and feet tingled with cold numbness. What was wrong with me? This was beyond low blood sugar. The longer I waited, the worse it got. The numbness crept up between my legs and into my armpits. Breathing was reduced to gulps that I had to force in. I wondered if I'd been bitten by something, a brown recluse spider perhaps. Was its deadly toxin even at this moment paralyzing my respiratory system? Deadening my mind? It felt like a distinct possibility.

Calm down. Think rationally. Maybe this was simply the postpartum depression writers talked about. Although de-pression was never such an energetic episode for me, it was a possibility. I had, after all, spent much of the day on the floor weeping for Little Red Wing. Before I even had a chance to wonder who I should consult, Lizzie's face framed by a corona of frizzy hair jumped into my thoughts.

Lizzie. Not only had she sent off innumerable manu-scripts, she was well versed in all manner of disasters. I could count on her to know the symptoms of brown recluse poisoning. Suddenly I needed urgently to hear her jittery voice.

The laundromat's air conditioning wasn't working and it was warm and steamy. A pay phone was mounted onto the wall beside a bulletin board that advertised UNO CAR REPAIR: U NO HAPPY, U NO PAY and *Bridal gown. Size 7 Petit. Never Worn.* Behind me a bum slept, balanced across three scooped-out plastic chairs. On the other side of the row of washers, a middle-aged attendant with the look of someone freshly across the river from Mexico about her pushed a damp rag over the tops of the washers.

A young man sat reading a shoppers' guide, the *Greensheet,* while his girlfriend stuffed their laundry into a machine. She had a great, tightly wound little body amply displayed in a lace-front camisole and a black denim skirt that might have come down almost to her palms if she'd put her hands at her sides. She finished filling the washer, poured in a tiny box of Tide, slammed in the quarters, and turned around, the machine churning behind her. She had dozens of bracelets on either wrist. They all clattered and slinked down to her elbow when she raised her hand to fluff up her lioness-teased hair. She leaned her bottom against the churning machine and rested her hands on its top. Her boyfriend's feet were crossed at the ankles. She kicked him on the sole. Without glancing up, he shifted his feet away.

I wasted three quarters scrambling Lizzie's number before I got it right. I knew it was Lizzie's house because the sound of moist, snuffly breathing greeted me. Nothing else.

"Annabelle, hello."

I could hear her drooling into the phone.

"Listen, Piglet, sweetheart, is your mommy there?" Soft nuzzling sounds indicated that she was now chewing on the receiver. The impossibility of communicating my emergency through a catatonic toddler pushed the numbness back up through my body like a cold tide rising. I breathed back at Annabelle, a furious panting I could barely control.

"Annabelle, *please.*" My chin quivered and the cold tide pushed tears into my eyes. "Please, let me speak to your mommy."

The snuffling stopped and a "clonk" that momentarily shorted my ear out announced she'd dropped the phone. She'd lost interest. My heart sank. But clear as a draft notice she cried out, "Ma-ma. Tell-phone for you."

Relief pushed back the chilly panic. I almost sobbed when Lizzie came on the line.

"Gretchen, calm down, I can barely understand you," she said after I hiccuped out my symptoms. "Now, put down the phone for a second, cup your hands over your mouth and nose, and take ten deep breaths."

I did what Lizzie told me to. Only the girl with the bracelets seemed to notice me with my hands over my face and the phone receiver in my lap, and she wasn't particularly interested. Around breath seven, I started inhaling normally again.

"It's the carbon dioxide," Lizzie explained when I picked up the receiver. "The diaphragm tightens in response to anxiety and you start taking shallower and shallower breaths, expelling carbon dioxide quicker and quicker. But the diaphragm needs a buildup of carbon dioxide to signal the fast-twitch muscle fibers to relax. So that's what you just did, trapping the CO_2 you were breathing out."

"Oh. Well, it worked."

"The human body is a beaker. Put the right chemicals in and the reactions are inevitable. As for the brown recluse hypothesis, you wouldn't be experiencing the generalized symptoms you described. There would be intense, localized pain at the bite site, followed by nerve damage from the neurotoxic venom and ultimately a necrofication of the flesh. In serious cases, victims have been known to lose limbs. But that doesn't sound like your problem. Have you examined yourself for bite marks?"

"No, I think you're right, it's probably not a brown re-

cluse." I took a deep shuddery breath that ended in a gulping yawn. "Do you ever feel . . . strange when you send in
a manuscript?"

"Strange? No. A little sad, maybe. Mostly because I know
they're going to cut out all my favorite parts. But not panic-
stricken. How are you feeling now?"

"Better." And I was. I took a deep breath and stood up
straight. I wiggled my toes and felt them squirm around in
my shoes. I rubbed my thighs together. All my parts seemed
to have regained feeling. "A lot better. Hey, Annabelle is
talking!"

"Chattering like a magpie. She started at dinner three
weeks ago. I was cutting up her ground turkey burger and
she just looked up at me and said, 'I don't like hamburger'—
I always call it hamburger—'I like pears.' The first words
out of her little mouth, two complete sentences. Mitchell
interviews her every day. He's saving her baby perceptions
on tape."

"I'm sorry I missed it. I'm sorry I haven't been around for
the past couple of months. I'm sorry . . . I'm sorry about
everything."

"So am I, Gretchen. We've missed you."

"We? We who?"

"Why me. And Annabelle. Juanita. Mitchell. Who did
you think?"

"No one. Just you guys."

She grunted.

"Hear anything from . . ."—I paused as if trying to recall
the name—"from, uh, Gus? Probably nothing. Mail from
Kuwait's probably impossible."

"Actually I haven't personally heard anything. Before he
left, Gus told me I meddle too much."

"Well, you do. You do meddle too much." My anger was
a memory of anger.

"My intentions were good."

The memory sharpened as my blood pressure shot up.

"Lizzie, you betrayed me! You humiliated me. You made me a pawn in some warped game. You plotted against me. These are good intentions?"

"I plotted *for* you. Big difference. Surely you can forgive a minor error in judgment."

" 'Minor error'? Lizzie, all you wanted was to prove your point. To show that you could make me fall for the handsome rogue fantasy. Well, you proved your point. I'm not immune. And, no, I can't forgive you."

"Well, join the club. Gus told me the same thing."

"He did?"

"In no uncertain terms. He told me to butt out of his life and to keep my big nose out of all future incarnations. He hasn't even called, and he's been back since last Monday."

"He's back?"

"So I hear from Mitchell. They're working on their Frisbee freestyle routine again. They want to come back as the grand old men of the flying disc circuit. In fact, that's what they're doing right now. Practicing. At that schoolyard across from the Shackleford mansion."

"The Shackleford mansion." I smelled cedar and felt fat drops of water flung by a sprinkler wet my skin. My breathing went haywire again.

"That's where they've always practiced."

My mind jumped the tracks for an instant as I watched the couple across from me. The girlfriend continued arranging and rearranging herself to best advantage against the harvest-gold porcelain. And the boyfriend continued reading the *Greensheet* as if it were a list of organ donors and he had a failing liver. Did she have Home Spa Weekends where she scrubbed herself with kosher salt dampened with almond oil? I wondered.

I thought again about that article I'd read when I was— what—twelve? that long ago?—in *Seventeen* magazine about how to get boys to talk to you. The secrets were to be interested in what they were interested in. To never ask questions that could be answered with "yes" or "no." Ask questions that started off with "How do you feel—" About turbo injection? Sudden death playoffs? Judas Priest's new lead guitar? Sixteen years. For sixteen years I'd been asking "How" questions.

The strange numbness jumped back into me. "Did he ask about me or anything?"

"I'd be the last to know."

"Oh."

"Gretchen, it's too late now, you do know that."

I didn't say anything.

"So," she said, heaving a big sigh. "You hate me."

"In the abstract, yes. But you're a hard person to hate in the flesh."

"Oh, good. Mitchell is doing a big Thai bouf next week. Stop by. No surprise visitors. And no jellyfish."

I said I would think about it.

"Splendid. Splendid. Splendid," Lizzie chirped. "Now, if you will pardon me, I have to go vomit. I'm pregnant again." She hung up.

The same wave of exhaustion that had rolled over me when I'd finished wrapping my manuscript slapped me down again. I wished I'd asked Lizzie what flus were going around. I sank into an empty chair next to the sleeping bum's feet. The laundromat was a perfect sickroom, with moist vaporizer air smelling of fabric softener instead of Vicks. The *chunk-slosh, chunk-slosh* of the washers joggling socks, jockey shorts, jeans, T-shirts, sheets, washcloths, and bath mats through sudsy gray water was immensely comforting.

The girlfriend finally got tired of slouching against the washer and sat down. She dug through a purse large as a mail sack and pulled out a bottle of nail polish. I heard the ball bearing at the bottom of the tube rattle when she shook it. She tucked her legs up onto the chair, rested her free hand on her knee, and began applying the polish in careful stripes. Her concentration drew me in. I stared, mesmerized, as she coated each nail. The bum snuffled in his sleep. The attendant went into a back room. Untended dryers spun, rivets tapping around the metal drum.

The smell of the nail polish brought back a memory of preparing for dates with Ray. I learned to play pool for him, so I had to take extra care with my hands since they were on display all the time. Twelve years ago, and the smell of nail polish still made me think about Ray Gutierrez.

The girlfriend had the bottle of polish gripped between her thighs and was working on her middle nail when the alarm shrieked. She jumped up, and an arc of iridescent pink splashed onto the linoleum tile. I looked about frantically for signs of fire, burglary, prison break. The boyfriend roused.

"The fuck's that?" He looked angrily at the girlfriend, who was standing with her half-painted nails splayed out toward the spilled polish, as if the noise were her fault. The bum raised his head and looked around.

"Someone breaking in?" he asked me. I stood, charging with adrenaline as the shrieking continued. The attendant scuttled in from the back, went to the couple's machine, and pulled back the top. The shrieking stopped.

"Jur . . ."—she waved her hand over the washer—"es no balance."

"What's she saying?" the girlfriend asked her boyfriend.

"Your load," I intervened, relieved to know exactly what the woman meant. "Your load is unbalanced."

"Oh." The girlfriend walked through the forgotten nail polish spilled on the floor and peeled a mauve bedspread off one side of the washtub. She put the lid back down, and the washer hummed evenly into a satisfying spin cycle.

"Thanks," the girlfriend said to me and the Mexican woman.

We both smiled in return and walked away.

Once I was on my feet, I discovered that the alarm had

shocked the tiredness right out of me. I pushed the glass door open against the wind straining against it from the other side. Outside, the coming norther was being preceded by an early gray twilight. A green plastic garbage can rolled down the street, pushed like a tumbleweed by the wind.

♥   ♥

The sprinklers clicked no more in front of the Shackleford mansion.

I parked at the far edge of the sloping schoolyard across the street, rolled down the window, and watched two men sling a Frisbee at each other. They were below me, down on the field at the bottom of a hill covered with grass that had been exhausted by the long heat to a tired tan. Even though the wind now came from the north, it still had ten months of heat to blow away, so they were sweating in shorts and T-shirts.

Stocky Mitchell looked like a Shetland pony capering across the dry grass, using the spring in his bulky legs to leap higher than you would have thought possible. From the back, the other man was Rye, a lean, stretched-out Arabian horse to Mitchell's Shetland. I saw the broad shoulders and remembered how I'd kissed them, as Rye, his long, muscled legs between mine, had pressed into me. Of course, though, it wasn't Rye down there on the field anymore than it had ever been Rye. Still, without seeing a face, I couldn't stop the name from attaching itself to him anymore than I could stop every molecule in my body from doing handsprings every time he moved.

Mitchell underhanded one to Rye, who plucked the hurtling yellow plastic saucer from the air with the tip of his finger as delicately as he'd pinched the contact lens from his eye. The disc buzzed atop his finger like a plate spinning on a stick in a circus as he bent backward and passed it between his legs from one hand to the other. Still pretzeled around like that, he hurled the disc from beneath his leg.

Mitchell jumped up with a grunt, and when he had both feet off the ground he tucked his knees up and reached behind and between them to grab the platter just before it smashed into his crotch. He landed and got tangled up trying to spin the disc out from beneath his butt. He failed and teetered back onto the ground.

"Oh, a burn session, huh?" Mitchell yelled. "You want a burn session." He jumped up and unleashed a sidearm shot.

Rye galloped to meet it. Still running, he launched himself into a sprawling cartwheel. With both legs in the air, he snagged the disc with a finger, popped off the ground with one hand, and landed on his feet, the Frisbee still whirling on his forefinger. Careful as a Chinese acrobat, he tipped the whirling disc over onto his thigh, where it rolled like a wheel down his leg. It spun down to the tip of Rye's outstretched foot, where it whirred for a moment like a car wheel in sand before Rye kicked it back to Mitchell.

I was astonished by this sprawling, lunatic ballet.

Mitchell barely managed to grab the disc and heave it back.

Rye raced after it, leaping into a cloud of leaves raised by the cold wind to hook the disc on a fingernail. For a split second the wind caught and seemed to freeze him in midair, the disc still turning on his fingernail. In the next instant, when the leaves blew past and I saw his face, something inside of me gave way. He wasn't Rye. He wasn't the Wisp. He was a man who was supposed to die and had lived. Someone who wanted love in his life. How had I missed so much?

For the first time I thought about what had been in the back of my mind all along. I thought about Gus dying of leukemia. Of how hard it is to love anyone, much less someone who might die. Rogues never died. A rogue might hurt you, break your heart, but—well, that was what rogues did. They didn't die. Chad, Dru, Linc, Trey—they would never get leukemia.

Mitchell jumped as the Frisbee Gus tossed back arced down toward him. He caught it between his Shetland pony thighs. Mitchell grabbed the disc in his right hand, cocked it back, and, holding out his free hand like a javelin thrower sighting in on a target, took two running steps and hurled the Frisbee back with all the force he could get out of his bunched muscles.

The disc shot downward; humming along, it mowed down tall shoots of dry grass. Gus bent down to retrieve the throw, but suddenly it rose, skimming over his head. Gus laughed at the trick shot and turned to chase it. It rose and came up the hill toward the 88. I slunk down in the seat, reached out a hand, and turned the keys over in the ignition. All I could see from my crouched-down position was a patch of gray sky and then a yellow plastic button floating into it. I pumped the gas pedal until the engine turned over. I was letting off the emergency brake when his face appeared at the window just as it had that day at the lake.

"Gretchen."

I switched off the engine, straightened up, and said the first thing that popped into my head. "Hi. I forgot what great legs you have."

He didn't answer. Instead he leaned in the window, sweat running down his face, his stomach bellowsing air in and out his mouth as he looked at me without speaking. I noticed for the first time how pale his body hair was. How good it looked, white against his tan.

Behind him Mitchell yelled, "Hey, bud, we're losing the light here!"

Gus turned to yell over his shoulder, "We're through for the day!" He turned back to me. His eyes were a stranger's. A stranger who was not happy to see me.

Mitchell crested the rise, saw my car, opened his mouth in an exaggerated O of understanding, flagged a wave to Gus, and walked back to his car.

Gus straightened up and moved away from the car, his

hands on his hips, still breathing heavily. He buried his face
in the crook of his arm and squeegeed off the sweat. I got
out of the car and went over to him. As I walked, the first
threads of cold from the north, silvery cold as Christmas
tree tinsel, wound around my legs.

"Hey, I mailed off my romance novel today."

"Good. I hope you make a lot of money." He finally
looked at me. "You have something you want to talk to me
about?"

A puff of warm humid air hurried past my head, chased
by a brisk draught.

"Why are *you* so mad? I'm the one who was tricked." I
had to make myself sound mad. Talking to him was like
running into someone from the office at a VD clinic. We
knew each other, knew something intimate about each
other, but were still strangers.

"Great, so we don't have anything to talk about, then." A
chilly breeze ruffled his sweat-slicked hair, and he unknot-
ted the jacket at his waist and put it on before he started to
walk down the hill toward Mitchell, waiting in his car. The
coolness slithered down my backbone. As usual, my reactions jammed into each other. None prevailed except the
clear need to stop Gus from leaving. To make it not be too
late.

"Gus!" I cried out. My voice warbled on a wind that was
genuinely cold for the first time in ten long months. "Wait!"

He stopped, dropped his head, stared at the ground for
several seconds, and finally turned slowly back to me.

"What happened?" The wind gusted each time I spoke,
forcing me to yell louder. "The last big bulletin I got, you
loved me."

He looked from side to side like a cowboy checking both
ends of the bar. "Maybe I had second thoughts about someone who would fall in love with a pile of cowhide and a
two-day stubble." Without yelling, his voice was loud over
the wind. He checked both ends of the bar again. There was

so much about him that was Rye, that was the Wisp, so much more that seemed to be a hybrid spawned of the mating between the two that I didn't recognize at all. "Maybe that's not what I want after all."

I threw my arms open, seeing a happy accord. "That's not what I want either. The stubble. The cowhide."

The wind was now carrying wonderful smells from the far north. All around me the air went crisp with scents of pine and apples, bonfires and cedar. Especially cedar.

"So what is it you want, Gretchen? To make up another list for me to conform to? Hold up more hoops I can jump through?"

"That's not fair! I never asked you to do anything!" Hadn't I? Hadn't I told him with my coolness, my lack of interest, that he needed many Home Spa Weekends? The only difference with him was that they had actually worked.

"Right. We don't have anything to talk about." Gus turned away and started down the hill again. This time I went after him.

"Come on, hey, can't we even talk about this?" I had to ask him again before he stopped walking. "Gus? Jesus, Gus, we've slept together already, the least we can do now is get to know each other."

"You didn't sleep with me, Gretchen."

"Well, maybe not 'you' per se, but your body was involved. Intricately involved. Don't you remember?"

He stopped walking. "Yes."

If this were going to go anywhere, it was his turn now to say something. He took his time.

"What am I supposed to do now?" he asked. "Throw my arms open to you in a 'cathartic embrace that sweeps away all remaining wisps of the clouds of doubt that had so long shadowed their love'?"

The line was embarrassingly familiar. "Don't quote my

book to me. It still pisses me off that Lizzie used my fantasies for set direction."

"Well, it pisses *me* off that that's what it took for you to
give me a second glance."

I saw an endless loop developing here. "Look, Gus, I don't
know what's supposed to happen now. If Lizzie or Juanita
was writing this, there'd be a simple resolution. I'd find out
that the 'other woman' I'd been suspecting for two hundred
and eighty pages is really your disinherited sister, or you'd
discover that I wasn't really just using you to get a feature
story. Then the scales would fall from our eyes. A gentle
rain of love would fall from heaven. We'd fall into each
other's arms and there would be an end to world hunger
and allergies. But we're sort of on our own. So I don't know
what's supposed to happen. I'd like to find out, though.
Don't you even want to find out?"

Gus studied my question. From the branches of a pecan
tree high over our heads, a squirrel, his frond of a tail
twitching, looked down and chittered frantically at us for
invading his territory. Gus didn't appear to hear the little
creature.

When it also started to appear that he hadn't heard me, I
said, "Look, I'm not asking for a lifetime commitment or
anything. Let's just go get a cup of coffee." It was chilly
enough to drink coffee.

I think the cold made him smile. The cold as a dividing
line we could step over into a new season. When he smiled,
it was like meeting him at my door all over again. His smile
had that essential Wisp sweetness about it, an innocence
that verged on otherworldly. Even if I never sell "Gain the
Earth," I will always be grateful to the romance novel for
pulling me into a universe of such hope, such trust, that I
could look at a smile like that and see what lay behind it. It
takes a romantic to see the strength behind sweetness. I
waited for Gus's answer, seeing that he had the right to take
as long as he cared to. I also saw that I would go on waiting

for just as long as it took. That I might take up certain hobbies while I waited. That they might include Frisbee freestyling. Computer programming. Vintage motorcycles. I was even considering the purchase of a pair of Hush Puppies. But I had to know one thing while I waited.

"All those things?" I asked him. "About the light bulbs in the New York subway, and the meat-eating bees, and the tiny ant ladders, and the mosque big enough to hold everyone in Montana, and the lambburgers in New Delhi, and the island where the brown moths live on feathers? All that stuff. Is it all true?"

"Every bit of it. It all came from L. M. Boyd."

"The trivia columnist?"

"Trivia to some. Small pieces of something significant to others. Let me tell Mitchell I'm going with you. Then I've got about"—he glanced at his watch—"about an hour and half before my dinner date." He loped down the hill, an easy, steady stride that "gobbled up the earth." Something that romance heroes' strides tended to do.

Dinner date, I thought as I climbed the hill back to my car. As I got into the 88, I caught a flash of forest green turning the corner at the end of the street. I squinted, trying to see through the twilight. Was it a Volvo station wagon? Was that Lizzie's curly head behind the wheel? Was she still stage-managing my love life? Had she coached Gus? Told him to be aloof, a man with previous bookings? Instructed him to make me the pursuer, himself the prize once more?

The questions buzzed angrier and angrier. Was I being set up again? Gus slid into the car. "Was that—?" I opened my mouth to bark out the accusation, and my head filled with a scent that was part apricots, part baking bread, and part cedar shavings. For a second, the air was warm and heavy again as August.

Gus flung his arm out across the top of the seat and settled back into a sprawling, seigneural posture just like he owned the place. When he was completely comfortable and at his ease in my car, he quirked an eyebrow at me. "Was that what?"

Whether it was a man pretending to be a romance hero or a man making fun of a romance hero. I could not tell, and suddenly I only cared that it was a man making the effort.

A dust devil of leaves swirled by the winter wind we'd waited so long for danced up the long hill from the playing field. It splashed across the windshield, pattering leaves against the glass in a way that reminded me of how the fat drops from the Shackleford sprinklers had rained over it. A tickle of cool air made me laugh, then it made Gus laugh with me. The instant of our laughter joining in this, the start of what had to be a happier season, joggled loose a memory I'd been tracking down for months. The name of Sleeping Beauty's third fairy godmother: Merriweather. Merry Weather. It made me laugh again.

ABOUT THE AUTHOR

In addition to her well-received first novel, *Alamo House: Women Without Men, Men Without Brains,* Sarah Bird is a contributor to *Mademoiselle, Cosmopolitan, Savvy,* and several shoestring biweeklies. She lives in Austin, Texas, with her husband and her attack peek-a-poo.